CHOCOLATE BEACH

Chocolate Beach

JULIE CAROBINI

BETHANY HOUSE PUBLISHERS

Minneapolis, Minnesota

Published by Bethany House Publishers
11400 Hampshire Avenue South
Bloomington, Minnesota 55438

Bethany House Publishers is a division of
Baker Publishing Group, Grand Rapids, Michigan.

Printed in the United States of America

ISBN-13: 978-0-7642-0261-2
ISBN-10: 0-7642-0261-8

Library of Congress Cataloging-in-Publication Data

Carobini, Julie
    Chocolate beach / Julie Carobini
        p.   cm.
    ISBN-13:   978-0-7642-0261-2 (pbk.)
    ISBN-10:   0-7642-0261-8 (pbk.)
1. Marriage—Fiction. 2. Domestic fiction. I. Title.

    PS3603.A7657C48   2007
    813'.6—dc22

                                                        2006037023

Dedication

For my husband, Dan, *of course*.

 *Prologue*

Douglas knew what he was getting into when he married me. At least I think he did. Morning after foggy morning, he'd order the same two shots of Colombian roast coffee, room for cream, no sugar. He'd smile and thank me, always putting his change and then-some into the obnoxious tip jar on the counter, the one with the dancing dollar sign on one side and a *Free Tibet* sticker on the other.

He never flinched when I called his order.

"Dougie-poo, you're up!"

Nada. Zilch. Not a smidgen of faze on his face. No matter what I said or did, Douglas remained consistently unflustered. You might even say that Douglas was routinely predictable. Here was a meticulously well-dressed man who, red sky or blue, stepped through those squeaky-clean glass doors at precisely 6:35 A.M. every morning.

Every morning!

If it weren't for my tiresome need for sustenance, not to mention my secret delight over being known as a "barista" and the generous tips from the likes of one Douglas M. Stone, I would likely have been staring at the back of my eyelids at that hour.

My best friend at the coffeehouse, Gaby, likened those mornings to a zany unfolding play, like *Tony n' Tina's Wedding*. Only we were on the West Coast, far across the country from Broadway. We had two choices in those days. Either we were actors in some farce playing head games with the suits ordering a dime's worth of coffee for $2.50, or just poor college students who'd rather be on the beach. We chose the former. Kind of like having our own reality series, *Extreme Farce*.

Something about dreamy, much-older Douglas, though, made me want to push the proverbial envelope right to the edge of the counter.

"Doug-man, your iced caramel mocha double-whip is up!" I'd shout across the shop. Or "Your toffee-nut cream with a shot of vanilla syrup has legs on it!"

One particular morning, one seemingly like the others, will forever stick out in my mind like biscotti in a short cappuccino.

The rain was coming down in big California-king-sized sheets. As was my customary attire both then and now, I wore jeans, a cami, and flip-flops. Who cared that it was a little wet outside? I lived at the beach, where tees and tanks were the norm four seasons out of every year. Not so Douglas. He dressed with an air of precision, like he studied the weather report the night before and laid out just the right suit to match the color of the sky. So you can imagine my surprise when Douglas, quite out of character, had forgotten his umbrella on that gray day.

There he stood, his cinnamon-colored hair saturated by the sky's release, his London Fog overcoat several shades of granite darker from the drenching. *Muy simpático*, as Gaby would say.

My eyebrows did a little dance. "The usual, Dougie?"

He hesitated, as if considering whether to finally report me to someone higher up on the food chain, someone who could and would actually command me to stop taking liberties with his very proper given name. Instead, he winked, nodded, and turned to scan the headlines in the *Ventura County Star*.

"Dougers, your double espresso macchiato is up!"

I'd barely set the cup of plain coffee on the counter when I felt a large warm hand enveloping my own. Electricity shot through my fingers. I felt as if I should pull away but couldn't. His touch seared me and rendered my nineteen-year-old self speechless.

In my head, I heard Randy Travis crooning, "I'm gonna love you, forever and ever, forever and ever, Amen." (Three exclamation points on that final amen!)

Some people don't believe in love at first sight. Who knows? I do know that at the instant Douglas's strong hand held my own, I was hopelessly, wildly, madly in love. For the first morning in all those mornings, I had run out of pithy comments and cutesy names. My devil-may-care attitude, the one I'd so glibly unleashed on poor Douglas each morning, had vaporized with the first brush of his fingertips. In that instant, I barely had breath to breathe.

We married fourteen years ago, and I've been breathless ever since.

As for Douglas? I'm not so sure. . . .

Chapter one

It's ten past five, and the house smells of twice-nuked Stouffer's lasagna. Some serious bubbling is going on inside that microwave, and I have to wonder, *Just how much noodle elasticity is too much?* Antsy, I dial up Douglas's office and it takes him three rings to answer.

"Douglas Stone."

"Where are you?"

"Brianna?"

Who else would be calling his back line at dinnertime? "You missed our date."

I hear him flip the pages of his calendar. "It's my Bunko night," I remind him. "And Nathan's doing a night run with the team on the beach. We were going to have dinner together." *Finally.*

"Oh. Yes. Sorry, Bri."

I sigh, overexaggerating. Most of my friends and family call me Bri, but not Douglas. Not usually, anyway. Not unless he's trying to soften me up. Douglas is a seventeen-year trial attorney with a never-ending case list, and I'm on to him.

"It's okay." I peek at the time. "I've got to get going anyway."

He groans into the phone. "I guess I just lost track of the time."

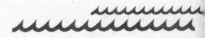

Douglas usually cuts out early at least a couple nights a week. He's always said he didn't want to be one of those wrinkled old-boy attorneys, married to his work. Lately, though, his sexy presence around here has been downright scarce.

"I'll just put dinner in the oven on warm, then." I glance at the oven, hoping I remember the trick to programming it. "The team's doing an off-season run all the way to Surfer's Point. Nathan'll probably watch the waves awhile before getting a ride home from Troy's mom. I guess you two'll just be bachelors tonight."

"That's fine."

"So . . ."

"Yes?"

"So I'll be picking up Gaby on the way. I'll probably be kinda late. You know how much she likes to talk."

"Take your time. Enjoy yourself."

I expect him to say that, and his usual line has a calming effect. "Love you," I say.

"I love you too."

Gaby's met her dream guy for the gazillionth time, and she's ready to dish. If I don't hurry, it'll have to wait until we're seated together during Bunko, and the tasty morsels will be served up in bits, like those nickel-sized quiche appetizers that always leave you so hungry. I want the whole meal, every yummy course, served up during a long conversation with my best friend. But it's Bunko night and I'm running late and she's been so gushy over this new guy that she'll probably spill it to everyone, so I'll have to just be one of the gals tonight. *Drats*.

It's not like I haven't been there before with Gaby. Oh no. Finding her a decent, handsome, God-loving man has been one of my missions in life, and I'm wearing out. I'm hoping that this one—even though I had absolutely nothing to do with their matchup—is Mr. So Right. *The* Mr. So Right.

I'm fairly blinded by the glow emitting from my friend's face when I pull up alongside the curb. Gaby climbs in, and her pretty French manicure causes me to curl my less-than-attractive fingers into a ball. I wonder if I can drive like this.

"Hey, Bri-Bri!" Gaby leans over and gives me a hug. Her perfume makes me sneeze, even though it's wild lavender, one of my favorites. I want to tell her that a little goes a long, long way, but instead I just sniff and hug her back.

"You are positively radiant, my friend," I tell her between sniffles. "In 'like'?"

Gaby tips her head toward the heavens, smiling. "What can I say?" She giggles like a teenager, and I love her for that. Gabrielle Maria Flores and I have been friends *forever*. Well, at least since our coffee-pouring days.

While some friendships cut back when one of them gets married, ours has flourished like the morning glory planted by the side of our garage. It keeps on sprouting and spreading . . . after Nathan's birth, through college, even in the midst of our dual careers—hers as a florist, mine as a coastal tour-bus host.

"So," says Gaby, turning her attention to me, "how's the 'beach-babe with a mic'?"

I always tell her that tour-bus hosting isn't as glamorous as it seems, but will she listen? Sure, there's the fabulous seafood and the glimmering ocean and the travelers paying rapt attention to my every joke. *So I've heard them nine hundred times—they haven't!* On the downside are all the elderly men with comb-overs who sit at the back of the bus and insist that I talk louder. *Hey,* I want to say, *get a hearing aid or move on up!* Instead, I strain my voice and smile, praying that a dolphin will appear from the abyss to distract them, thereby giving my larynx a break.

My secret wish? That Gaby would give up the flowers and get a

Class B license. She could be my driver, and we could really put on a show.

I study my ever-glowing friend. Always the artist, she's wearing her favorite cottony, gypsy-style blouse along with a long, tiered skirt. The kind of outfit that, if hung on my shorter frame, would dust the ground with each step. "I'm fabulous," I tell her, "but it's *your* mystery man I want to know about. What's his name again?"

"Franklin!"

I push away the mental image of that nasally turtle my son used to watch on public television. "Alrighty," I say. "Tell me everything."

"Well—Oh . . . my!" Gaby's rummaging around in my glove compartment now. She pulls out a CD, holding it up in the air as if I'm her daughter and she's found a naughty magazine in my dresser drawer. "This is contraband, missy!"

I snatch the Dixie Chicks CD from her hand and toss it back in the glove box. "That's a pre-controversy album, I'll have you know. Now, getting back to Fred?"

"It's Franklin!"

"Okay, then, getting back to Franklin."

"Oh! He is so cute. A little short, but I don't mind that. Besides, he's educated and smart. He's an architect for Swaffer and Swaffer. You know them; they're in the Victorian house over near California Street. Anyway, he's been an architect for about five years—well, not exactly an architect. He's had his degree in architecture for eight years, but he hasn't had a chance to take all the tests to become official. I think he's considered a draftsman, but you should see all the beautiful drawings he's made!"

"When do I meet him?"

"Oh, you will. It's a little tricky since he usually takes care of his mother on the weekend. She lives with him. . . ."

I keep my eyes on the road in front of me. *Did anyone else see that red flag fall from the sky?*

". . . he's so sweet. He takes his mother shopping at the farmer's market and then to Costco. . . ."

We're in front of Suzy's house now, our host for the night's Bunko game, and I think I'm sweating. Gaby is one of the most intelligent women I know. She's warmly endearing and a forever friend. But like Cher in the movie *Moonstruck*, I want to slap both of her cheeks and command her to "Snap out of it!"

A thirty-something guy with a low-paying job living with his mother. I know that judging someone you haven't even met is not nice. Okay, judging anybody is not nice, but Gaby needs a stable Christian man. A man like my Douglas. This . . . this *Franklin* sounds . . . ugh, like a commitment-phobe.

"You're not jealous, are you?" asks Gaby.

"Jealous?"

"You're always so good at playing matchup." Gaby wrinkles her forehead and gives me that little pout of hers. "I just don't want you to feel bad that Franklin might be the one, and you weren't our matchmaker."

"Stop it. You know I just want you happy."

"Okay. Just don't go around thinking you're not needed or anything. I know how much you like mothering all your single pals."

I wince. "Mother you? I don't think so. Beat you in a brownie-eating contest, maybe. Mother you, no way."

Gaby charges up the hedge-lined path to Suzy's front door. I lock up my VW and trail in behind her, watching as she flings herself into the open arms of Livi and Rachel, ready to tell tales of Franklin. The rest of the group swarm around them while I hover just outside their tight circle, my eyes drawn to Suzy's French floral wall clock. Douglas should be capping his pen and closing a manila case file just about now. Soon he'll be switching off his desk lamp and heading for home.

I glance again at the group just as Suzy steps toward the kitchen, and the circle closes up faster than a tulip in the shade. Suzy's in charge of the hospitality committee at our church, and I'm a member of the team. This means that I regularly drop off meals for new moms and the infirm. Pretty crazy since I don't cook. *Thank God for bagged salad and Meridians' pizza.* But really, this gig fits me well. Who could understand the value of a meal freely given better than me?

Speaking of dinner, the boys will be leaning against the kitchen island soon, eating rubberized lasagna on paper plates. They'll probably switch on a Dodger game and yell at the screen for a while before Douglas shoos Nathan up to homework and bed. Then Douglas'll stretch out on the couch and I'll have to roust him from deep slumber when I return. *Any chance of a real conversation, I guess, will have to wait another day.*

Kate, one of the craftsiest of the bunch, cuts into my thoughts as she breaks away from the group and marches up to the fireplace. "Would you look at that garland," she says. With all the fascination over Gaby's new beau, no one, until now, had noticed Suzy's redecorated mantel, the one she changes every season. "And all those pink lights."

"Actually, they're *salmon,*" Suzy calls from the kitchen.

A collective "Oh" fills the room. Only Suzy could pull off swagging the fireplace with acacia and eucalyptus. If I tried it, there'd be sap running down my wall. *And probably a raging fire in the living room.*

"Gold lamé? You used real lamé for your bows?" Kate leans up close to the garland and runs one of the branch bows between her fingers. Suzy's smile looks forced as she enters the living room again, both hands carrying a bowl of wedding mints and a pristine golden bell. "Lamé is so hard on my machine," Kate continues. "I've been looking for an alternative. Have you tried polyester?"

Suzy sets down the bowls. "Never."

"But it's supposed to be so easy to work with. You probably couldn't even tell the difference."

Suzy's expression begs to differ, and I can't help but think, *This is so* Trading Spaces. She doesn't answer but instead turns to the group of women chatting and mulling about. "Okay, ladies. Find yourself a seat." She rings the Bunko bell for emphasis.

Three tables with four chairs each sit around the room. Suzy has placed croissants with some kind of gourmet currant butter at each table, along with crystal bowls of fancy mixed nuts and Godiva chocolates. *Very ooh-la-la.* Rachel, Kate, Livi, and I share a table during Round One.

Kate pushes a pad of paper and a golf pencil past me. "You're smart, Rachel," she says. "You keep score."

I don't like keeping score anyway. Besides, Rachel's cool. She's someone I think I would've avoided if I hadn't been forced to play Bunko with her. Seriously. She's nearly perfect, but I don't think she knows it, and *that* makes her utterly charming. Tonight she's wearing her white-blond hair pulled back into a tight knot. Her makeup is to die for, and she's wearing a scarf loosely at her throat.

Ah, the windswept scarf. Think Deborah Kerr! Ginger Rogers! Isadora Duncan! Um, scratch that last one. Who wants to be compared to a dancer who met a tragic end?

Once again, Kate interrupts my muse. "What're Douglas and Nathan up to tonight, Brianna?" she asks, tossing out the first roll.

"Nathan's running, and Douglas is at the office."

Kate picks up the dice, ready for her second roll. She leans sideways toward me. "Working late again? I can't imagine Tom doing that."

It's Kate's presence that always makes me pray so hard before Bunko. I knew a girl like her in high school. Heather knew something about everything and never failed to share it, her abundant knowledge going down like unsweetened medicine. Thankfully, she never shared the Gospel with me. "Can't complain, Kate," I say with a shrug. "His case load pays the mortgage every month."

"So Nathan's coming home to an empty house tonight?" Kate's

still holding the dice in her hand. "See, Tom wouldn't allow that."

Taking the whole submission thing a little far, aren't we? "I guess they're not called 'banker's hours' for nothing." Tom is, after all, the vice-president of San Buenaventura Savings.

Kate rattles the dice in her right hand and stares at me.

Livi leans forward and clears her throat. "The dice," she whispers.

Kate holds me with a stare as she rolls the dice.

Livi's up next, so I turn to my refined friend Rachel. "And how's your Mr. Wonderful, Rach?" One perfectly sculptured eyebrow rises. How *does* she do that?

"He's heaven." An uncharacteristic gush of emotion spills forth. "Last Saturday we toured the Getty Museum together, and later we ate dinner in Malibu. Just fabulous." She's up now and gives the dice a sophisticated little toss. "He took me to Geoffrey's Restaurant and we sat outside and listened to the waves crash while dining on wasabi caviar and lobster bruschetta. Truly wonderful."

"I'm so glad you've found your Romeo," I say as she passes the dice my way.

Rachel touches my shoulder. "No, *you* found him! Thank you so much for introducing us, Bri."

I throw out the dice and smile, trying not to look like the pelican that just scooped up a school of minnows.

It's Kate's turn again with the dice. She drops them onto the table, and one bounces down to the floor. She doesn't pick it up. Instead, she looks over at Rachel and mutters something that no one gets.

Rachel raises that same eyebrow again. "What did you say, Kate?"

"Next thing you know, Brianna will be disparaging your boy-friend's occupation," Kate says with an edge in her voice.

While the rest of the room plays on in oblivion, our table stops cold. Livi leans down and picks up the wayward die.

"Kate, I've never disparaged Tom. He's a great guy."

Her eyes do a sort of loop-the-loop. "Right. That crack about 'banker's hours'? What about that?"

"That was—"

She cuts me off. "You think that just because Tom doesn't work late into the night like some people that he's unmotivated."

I let out a deep Napoleon Dynamite–style sigh. "I never said that—did I say that?" I look around for support. "I just meant that Douglas has more cases than time. Kate, I'm glad that Tom's job doesn't take him away from you as much."

She snorts a laugh, and her shoulders bounce. "Must be tough to have such a difficult life, Brianna . . . rich husband, kid in private school, a big old beach house."

Okay—ouch. "What's up, Kate?"

She turns to me and her face looks sad, like she feels sorry for me. *So not necessary.* "Oh, Brianna," she says. "*Everybody* knows Douglas is married to his job and that you're bored with it all. You two are exact opposites," she continues. "How can you stand that?"

Twelve women in the room and yet, except for the sizzle and sigh of Suzy's twelve-cup Mr. Coffee, all falls silent.

"*Pfsst!*" Gaby blows a raspberry, slicing into the silence. *Thank you, God, for Gaby.*

I keep my eyebrows even. "So *everybody* knows? Huh."

Livi shifts in her seat at the table. Rachel's delicate mouth forms a small *O*, and she looks disapprovingly at Kate.

"Well, how about that. I thought I'd been able to cover up my boredom. You know, that zombie-like glaze in my eyes, but no biggie." I laugh tightly.

"Bri's *anything* but bored, Kate," Gaby hollers from across the living room.

This is not good. Gaby's temperament matches her flair for the dramatic, and I'm mentally ducking for cover. "I *wish* she'd get a little bored so we could hang out more," she continues, her words moving faster with each breath. "Between driving that cute kid of hers around and hosting all those bus tours and playing matchmaker to some of us, she hasn't the *time* to get bored. Quit acting so loopy."

It seems Kate has recovered. She's staring at the table, as if reading from an imaginary script. "I do know you care, Gabrielle," she finally says, her face still lowered, "but married people recognize things that others just can't."

Livi's wringing her hands now, no doubt aware of how our Gaby will take such a scolding. "Gaby, I think Kate just means that she's concerned for Bri." She looks quickly at me and pats my hand. "Not that there's anything to worry about."

Gaby straightens in her chair, and I can tell by the expression in her brown-black eyes that she's got more to say. "You think that just because you've nabbed a man, that you know more than us single gals? Well, Kate, *estás loca* . . ."

Ack! She's going to rail in Spanish.

"Ladies!" Suzy stands, her pale skin unusually pink. "We're here to converse, not attack each other. I'm appalled." She cups the Bunko bell in her hand and deliberately locks eyes with each woman. Livi stifles a hiccup. "Let's start again, shall we?"

Oh yeah, I want to go through that again.

Mid-eighties hairstyle aside, Suzy is right on. Despite my temptation to enter into a catfight, Jesus said, "Blessed are the peacemakers . . ." and I am in no position to argue with the Savior of the world.

So I don't. Yet something tells me this isn't over yet.

Chapter two

They say that love is blind . . . just who are *they* anyway?

When I first noticed Douglas way back when, he dressed like a debonair hero of the silver screen, a formal thespian in black-and-white celluloid. Even under all that wool and starched cotton, though, who could miss that physique? He was lean and strong, kind of like a younger Tim McGraw—only without the Stetson and goatee. If that's being blind, then get me my shades!

Mr. Incredibly Handsome asked me out that very first day fifteen years ago when our hands met around a coffee cup. Only he waited until the end of my shift. Just after noon he walked through the finger-smudged store doors and stepped over to the side of the counter where I was pulling off my apron. "Would you join me for lunch, Brianna?" he asked.

I'd join you for life. "That depends. Are you planning to wear that tie?"

He fingered the narrow strip of silk. "This old thing?"

So to-die-for. "You like burgers?" I asked.

"I do."

"Pizza?"

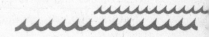

"Certainly."

"Sweet and sour chicken."

"I draw the line at Chinese."

"Hmm. This could be a problem."

He crossed his arms, his expression serious. *He must wow them in court.* "Perhaps we can work through this."

Whatever it takes . . . "Yes," I mustered. "Over lunch?"

My son's hormone-infused voice snaps me back to the present. "Uh, Mom?"

"Huh?"

"We havin' company tonight?"

I'm leaning against the kitchen sink, my latex-gloved hands caked with cleanser, my mind far away. I swing my gaze toward my one and only son. "Huh?"

"The bleach. Uh, the smell of it is kind of obnoxious."

I blow a puff of air upward, intending to dislodge several thick strands of hair stuck on my right eyelashes. It works for maybe half a second. "Your point, son?"

Nathan continues to lean against the doorjamb, looking at me. He shrugs. "Dunno. Just not used to seeing you use so much cleanser." He shifts from one unbelievably large foot to the other. "My nose is starting to hurt."

I stare at him a second longer before turning back to the sink. "I'm almost done," I say, getting back to the scrubbing. "Go change out of those stinky clothes and I'll make you a sandwich."

"Stinky? *I'm* stinky? Oh, Mama . . . let me give you a hug." Nathan grins widely and stretches out his arms to wrap me in an embrace.

"Don't you dare, mister!" Hopping away from the sink, I hold out my weapon, a sponge coated in pale blue powder. "Come near me with those pits and your mama's going to give you a cleanser bath!"

Nathan feigns disappointment, his mouth drooping into a frown.

"Just wanted to give my dear mother a kiss." His arms drop to his sides, and he tiptoes by me before abruptly spinning on his heels. Swiftly, Nathan plants a kiss on my cheek, and I hear his laughter as he bounces up the stairs and across the wood floors above my head.

I bite back a smile. Looking down at the soapy sponge, I move to scour the sink again. Only with a little less panache than when I first began, before Nathan came in from his Saturday morning run. When's the last time I scrubbed the kitchen on a Saturday morning? Weekends were for walking with Douglas or kayaking or maybe a little gardening; almost never for housework.

I hear the water running above my head, thankful that my thirteen-year-old still listens to his mother. *Lord, let it last.* I was just twenty when Nathan was born, a newbie at the whole parenting thing. And Douglas may have been a whopping nine years my senior, but he knew as much as I did: basically nothing. The one who managed to continuously remind me of this was my mother-in-law. I stifle a laugh, recalling her reaction to learning that I often took Nathan along on tours.

"A mangy bus is no place for a child, Brianna!" she always said.

Her warnings almost made me want to buy him a cap and plop him into the driver's seat. *Shame on me.*

In the other room a bell dings, letting me know email has arrived. I squeeze out the sponge, remove my gloves, and then drop them all onto the counter before twisting on the faucet, letting cool water run through my fingers. With eyes shut, I breathe in deeply and allow the steady stream of water to refresh me. "'Bored' my foot, Kate," I mutter into the air.

"I've been called a lot of things, but Kate isn't one of them."

I turn around to face the love of my life. "Douglas, you're home!"

He cups my hips, leans over, and kisses me on the nose. "For the moment. I just came back for a file I left behind this morning."

"How about playing hooky today? It's gorgeous outside. Maybe we could drag the kayaks out and paddle over to the harbor for lunch?"

"Sorry, can't. I've promised a client I'd call them by noon." He flicks his wrist over to check the time. "It's nearly that now."

Douglas's brief glance at his watch unexpectedly throws me back to a distant, unsettling memory. The emotion of that time surprises me with its power. *What's up with that?* No doubt Kate's outburst last night helped draw out this old wound. I bury my hands in my pockets and avoid meeting my husband's eyes with my own.

He hesitates before speaking. "Are you feeling all right?"

I shrug.

A spring wind bumps up against thinning windowpanes. Douglas hesitates in the near-silence before letting out a low sigh. I know what he's about to say even before he says it. "Brianna, once I'm finished with this upcoming trial . . ."

I stop him with one raised hand. "I know: 'Duty calls.'"

He gives my shoulders a slow squeeze before heading into his study to retrieve the wayward file. I hear his car roar off as I shake away my lingering disappointment, irritated with myself for letting Kate's thoughtlessness get to me. Douglas is right. The trial will pass. When it does, I'm sure we'll both make a better effort to reclaim and protect some time together.

Hands dried, I plop down into my desk chair and settle in front of the computer to check email. *Who changed my home page, as if I didn't know?* Ugh. Imagine the revolution if mothers of teenagers across America stood together and shouted, "We're mad as a flag-waving Toby Keith and we're not going to take it anymore!" Why Nathan thinks I prefer to have my home page set to CNN.com, I don't know. Maybe he thinks I'm too self-absorbed, that I should carry a deeper hunger for world events. I've a hard enough time getting the laundry done.

The first couple emails are spam. No, I don't care to buy Botox injections or padded bras via the Internet, thank you very much.

And, oh my, there's a fairly recent one from Douglas's mother, Mona. I straighten up, perplexed. Then I realize Nathan, bless his little teenager heart, has not changed my home page. At least not this time. Douglas must have been online this morning before heading to the office. He forgot to log off.

For a man who's all about details, this surprises me. Well, maybe not totally. It's not like a bit of slovenliness is out of character with the universe's male population.

There's the standard toilet-seat issue, and no, up is not the preferred position, and the occasional skivvy dropped onto the floor at the foot of the bed. And just last week I had to schlep down to Circuit City to buy another TV remote after fishing our other one out of the washing machine. He'd left it in the back pocket of his jeans.

I look back at the lone message waiting to be read. It says, "For Douglas Only" in the subject line—of all the nerve. *Dare I?*

Dearest Douglas,

My office has just secured a listing for a fabulous home with views from every corner. You really must take a look. I know how your wife prefers the beach, but really, Douglas, the home my client is offering is truly you. This property is far more commensurate with your station in life.

Consider it, won't you, dearest? My office can fax you the specifications at your request.

Best,
Mother

Oh brother. Wasn't it Mark Twain who called Adam the luckiest man for never having a mother-in-law? *Ditto for Eve.*

Mona Stone, my mother-in-law and "real estate broker extraordinaire," a label she coined herself, moves about in life like royalty. She's the queen bee amidst the worker bees of life, the ruler of the hive. Woe be unto the drone bees that fail to provide her with sweet nectar. Double woe unto the daughter-in-law who doesn't share her hunger for diamonds and caviar!

So go ahead and dislike me, but leave the hive alone, won't ya? *Grrr*. It's not the first time Mona has meddled in our marriage. It actually started before we said, "I do." And even though her long-ago attempt to derail our relationship failed, Mona still manages to slip in her quarter's worth of advice whenever possible.

It's disturbing.

And frankly, it's also surprising to a beach lover like myself. I know that Mona's a heels-and-pearls kind of gal. She made that clear the day we met. Yet seriously, who wouldn't appreciate boldly colored walls and sea stars and flip-flops on the porch? Who wouldn't just *die* to have a home that is kicky fun, and all within a shell's toss of the wide-open beach? Like a sandy slice of heaven on earth, I tell you!

I discover that I'm holding my breath, so I let it out slowly. That's it, breathe, breathe, nice. I give my head a little shake, as if to dislodge the irritating fragments of my mother-in-law's email.

In the end, her sentiments roll down my back and into the rag throw rug beneath my feet. Douglas has never shown any interest in "moving up," in trading our homey sand castle for something more highbrow. I can't imagine that he ever will.

I hear the water from the upstairs shower finally turn off, and I shake off Mona's meddling like a dog after a bath. I can hear my kid shoving drawers in and out, and the effect is startling. Wasn't it just yesterday that I had to bribe Nathan to wash off his sandy skin at least every other day? Suddenly, it seems he's spending more time in front of a steamy bathroom mirror than all his elementary years added together.

I sigh and realize that my kid's becoming a nice young surfer kid. Not like I haven't worked, no, *slaved* for this moment. Years of dragging him to Cotillion—even though it meant I had to traipse around wearing stockings with my one pair of dated flats—proves my commitment to raising a gentleman. I even learned to tie a necktie, much to Mona's glee.

It's just going so fast. That's what moms of grown kids everywhere always say. But it's true, and I'm not ready.

"Mom?"

I lean back in my chair and look toward the top of the stairway. My kid's wet head and face stare back at me. "Got any clean underwear?"

"In the basket on my bed."

He bounds back up the stairs, almost knocking over the sailboat model on the wall shelf that he and Douglas took weeks to build. *So much for independence.*

"Hey, kiddo," I call up the stairs, an idea popping into my head. "Want to go for a ride?"

I know he's up there—I can hear the floors creak. He's still pulling a shirt on over his wet hair as he clunks down the stairs. "Sorry, Mom. I'm meeting Troy and Gibson to work on our science project."

I wrinkle my nose. Science was never my thing, but hey, at least he won't be sitting slack-jawed in front of a video game in his buddy's garage.

"Bye." He kisses my cheek and heads toward the door.

"And you'll be where?" I say in my most motherly tone.

"At Gibson's. His dad's gonna take us to In-N-Out for burgers, so don't worry about me eating. Uh, and I'm takin' my board for later."

I stare at Nathan's back as he bounds out the door. Jilted for a cheap hamburger and a root beer. When the phone rings, I reluctantly pick it up.

"Did you get my email?" It's Gaby, and the fire in her voice is unmistakable.

"Hey. No, haven't gotten to it yet."

"Kate made me so mad! That know-it-all attitude, it's . . . it's *demasiado*—too much, don't ya think? She's so smug. . . . She gives you married people a bad name!"

Poor Gaby. Her impatience with wedding prep is showing. Her lament? *Always the florist, never the bride.*

"I don't think she can help herself. She's like Felix Unger trapped in a homeschooling mom's body. All that perfection sounds like too much pressure for me."

Gaby scoffs. "You are far too charitable, *chica.*"

I hold my tongue, as I'm feeling far from charitable at the moment. It doesn't help that my home is eerily quiet for a Saturday. It's just not right. "You want to get out of here?" I say. "Want to go over to the pier or something? If I stay here a second more I'm afraid I'll do something drastic like clean out a closet."

"Ew. One of those days, huh? Okay, I'll meet you there—but don't expect me to stay quiet about Kate."

"Deal."

I log Douglas off the computer with gusto, taking one last look at Mona's email. *". . . I'll fax the snobbish mansion's specifications at your request . . ."* Yeah, like we want to raise our kid that way.

I only wish I could see the zinger Douglas will surely send back to his mother.

Chapter three

The sun warms my face. We've escaped to a restaurant patio
on the Ventura pier, one of our fave spots to watch the tourist parade.
The boardwalk buzzes with cyclists and joggers. Farther down,
cherub-cheeked kids chase sea gulls, their mothers following close
behind. And men wearing placid grins wander aimlessly, lost in the
fresh monotony of the beach atmosphere.

With one elbow on the table, Gaby leans her chin into the crook
of her hand. Her fingernails look as fresh as the night before. "Okay,
tell me one more time *everything* that Mona said in the email."

By relaying my mother-in-law's latest stunt, I'd hoped to avoid the
subject of Kate. It worked. Only now Gaby wants me to keep repeating
this story. Like Nathan as a toddler. *"Read it 'gain, Mommy. . . ."*

I throw down the last sip of Coke. Chunks of ice slide down the
inside of the glass and onto my upper lip. I spit the freezing cubes back
into the glass. "I just keep reminding myself that she's Nathan's grandmother. Although she is the least 'grandmotherly' woman I know."

"No kidding," says Gaby. "I never knew my grandma, but Mother
always talked about her like she was some kind of ghost, haunting
our house."

I suck down another piece of ice and raise my eyebrows at this.

"She'd always say things like, 'Your grandmother wouldn't approve of you sliding on the grass like a boy, *mi hijita*' or 'Your grandmother's watching, so we'd best make those enchiladas with peppers that are hot, hot, hot!'" Gaby slaps the table at the memory. "Having an uppity grandmother like Mona has got to be better than one who's invisible, yet *knows all*." She draws out the last two words, her voice creepy.

"At least yours couldn't type."

Gaby flips long strands of hair behind her shoulder and laughs.

"Can we just forget about Mona for a while? Sheesh. You always get such a kick out of her. I don't know why I tell you anything."

Gaby's giving me a fake pout, then adds the batting eyelashes for effect. Emoting may work on the gentlemen, but on me? Not so much.

"More Coke?" asks our sun-browned waitress. She smiles and her teeth are blindingly white. Come to think of it, the tan looks fake too. Okay, that was catty. *Meow.*

"Keep it coming," I say, thrusting my glass onto her tray. She sashays back into the restaurant.

Gaby screws up her face. Her eyes are focused on something behind me. "Isn't that . . . ?"

"Hullo, ladies." It's the unmistakable gravel of my tour bus driver, Ned. He's standing just outside the waist-high fence separating restaurant patrons from the pier population. At least for the moment.

Gaby covers her mouth with her hand. "He's not going to . . ."

Ned flops one pasty white leg over the fence railing until his toes graze the ground. Then the other leg. With all the grace of a hippo on monkey bars, he scooches his fanny across the rail and hops down onto the patio.

Gaby and I exchange *the look*. Ned's wearing an undersized T-shirt with the words, *Is the Hokey-Pokey really what it's all about?* blazened across the front. He pulls a chair over from a neighboring table, startling a couple of lovebirds cooing over a shrimp cocktail, and plops down beside me.

"Whoo-ey." He leans back and grabs the extra cloth napkin from that same table. Like he'd just finished a marathon, Ned's panting and slowly wiping the sweat from his cheeks and forehead.

The lovebird-guy glares at me, as if I am somehow responsible for this little kink in his public display. *I'm not the one playing kissy-face on the pier, bub.*

Gaby's going to burst. I just know it. Her face is a sort of mottled red, her shoulders are actually trembling. It's like we're a couple of high-schoolers and the class dweeb has just set his bologna sandwich and milk on our table.

I focus back on my trusted driver. "What's shakin', Ned?" I ask, knowing full well that any second, Gaby's going to have to make a run for it.

He's wheezing through his nose, a sound I've become used to during our two-hour tours. "Just out for my walk," he says. "And to get a little eye candy." He winks at me and throws a nod toward a couple of emaciated blondes in bikinis and flip-flops.

Gaby slaps the table. She grabs her cinched, daisy-patterned bag and darts for the ladies' room.

The bronzed waitress comes back with my drink. I throw down a swig before giving my attention to Ned. *Bring on the oddball humor, my friend.*

Ned's sitting up and looking down his nose at me now. "Didn't I see your Douglas driving a little convert-ee-ble this mornin'?" he asks.

"That would be him. He's driving a black Z car these days, one of the newer ones. It's sweet."

"That's what I thought." He purses his lips the way he often does when the tour bus crowd turns noisy and there are still many more miles left to travel. The more agitated he becomes, the more those lips bounce up and down. Rita, the owner of Coastal Tours, says he looks like a hungry baby suckling his bottle. *Scary*.

"Was he speeding or something?"

"Nope, nope. Just lookin' a might too single, that's all."

"And how does one look *too single*, Mr. Ned?"

He shrugs, holding back this secret information. "Just does. And whyd'ja let him go and get a sports car, anyway?"

"Uh, let me see. . . . Because he wanted one?"

Ned leans in closer. "A-ha! Because he wanted one! There's your problem, Bri. Your man wants a sports car and you agree to lettin' him have one. Now he's out there drivin' around town, and all the pretty ladies are watchin' him." He shakes his head. "Sounds like trouble to me."

He's doing it again, that fathering thing. Since Ned became my driver about a year ago, he's taken it upon himself to give me unsolicited, in-your-face fatherly advice—like I'm Gloria to his Archie Bunker.

My dad died when I was twelve, God love him. I barely remember him, but I cling to the belief that his fathering instincts—had he followed them more—would have fallen more in line with TV dad Mike Brady as opposed to, well, Ned.

Crusty as he seems, though, Ned dislikes it when people take him wrong. Take the time he stepped off the bus at a rest stop up the coast. He spat on the ground, making a preschooler scream. At the sound of her cries, her two older brothers grabbed on to her and ran like mad. But which gruff-looking, softhearted bus driver bought those three kiddos ice cream bars from the vending machine? *Hmm?*

Under that cranky exterior lives a Mr. Brady wannabe. I'm pretty sure of this. So in my most Marcia Brady tone, I ask, "Are you saying that I'm incapable of holding on to Douglas?"

I'm thinking that this will have him begging for mercy, that he'll apologize and say, "Of course not, honey. That is not what I meant at all!"

Ned gulps the air and then blows a high-pitched wheeze from his nose.

I think I've got him now.

"Ain't your fault, Bri," he finally says, stoic. "Men just can't help themselves. They reach a certain age and they get a little restless. Next thing you know, they're 'working late'"—he makes quote marks in the air with his fingers—"when they're actually out ridin' round in a little sports car that their unsuspecting missus gave them the okay to buy."

"Incredible!" I say.

He's shaking his head—*tsk, tsk*—like he thinks I'm agreeing with him. "It's true."

Gaby's back now, composed as a librarian. "What's true?" she asks.

I fill her in on some Ned-psychology, and she gasps. "There is no way! Douglas is devoted to our Bri. Hey, I should know. I was at their wedding!"

"You were *in* my wedding."

Gaby's voice goes from outrage to wistful, fast as a blink. "Yes, I was." She gives me a very sisterly gaze now. "And you were such a doll in that gown. That empire waist! That sweeping train!" She breathes a heavy sigh. "The only thing that could've been improved were the flowers." She whips a look at me while an edge creeps back into her voice. "Have I mentioned *that*?"

Will she ever forgive me for this perceived slight? "Ugh. You weren't even a florist yet, Gabrielle. You must let this go," I say, counselor to her Jekyll-and-Hyde gig. Her pouty face refuses to budge. "Okay, okay. I should've asked you to do my flowers! But don't forget—I did let you arrange flowers for my baby shower." As if ordering a house full of flowers for a baby shower is the most natural thing in the world.

"Blue iris and yellow Asiatic lilies." She's breathless again now.

I pat Gaby's hand. "Yes, and Nathan loved them. I pressed a couple into his baby book."

Ned's staring at us, speechless. Frankly, I've never seen my driver's face with such a blank expression.

"Denial," he finally says. "Yep, seen it many times myself. You just don't want to admit that your man's got midlife troubles." Ned's squinting at me and nodding, and my euphoria fades like the afternoon sun.

"Because he bought a silly Japanese sports car? You think he's having a crisis because of a used car that he bought at a bargain price on eBay?" The more I talk, the louder I get. It feels great, kind of empowering. Our too-tanned waitress drops the bill on our table and keeps on going. The lovebirds at the next table scowl at us before abruptly leaving. I am woman! Hear me roar!

"Ah now, Bri, doncha go gettin' all weepy on me. All I said was that you should be on the watch. Douglas'll come around."

I slap my forehead before burying my face in my hands. Why me?

"Yep, that's what I told myself when I saw old Douglas drivin' down toward Channel Islands Harbor this mornin'."

I'm still holding my face in my hands, yet my ears perk. The Channel Islands Harbor is the next harbor over from ours, in the town south of Ventura. "You saw Douglas where?"

"I said, yep that's what I told . . ."

I'm cranking my index finger in a circular motion now. "Not that. Where did you see Douglas?"

"He was on the road to the Channel Islands Harbor this mornin', just like I said."

Strange. He went to the office today, in the other direction. I wrinkle my brow. Try as I do, I can't figure out what sent Douglas into Oxnard this morning. I'm momentarily without words. And my appetite's suddenly gone too.

Gaby shakes her head, that familiar fire playing out in her eyes. First Kate, then Mona, now Ned drops an innuendo that maybe all is not well in the family Stone. It's just too much for a best friend to take. She's drumming her fingernails on the table. "Ned," she says, *"estás muy loco!"*

He looks at me, like I speak Spanish. Me, a white-bread beach girl. Okay, he's not entirely off base. Unlike Ned, I am from California, one of the great Spanglish capitals of the world. I suppose I could give the poor guy a hint. So I lean my head to one side and tell him, "She says you're crazy, Ned." Oops, that came out a little too easily. I kind of want to say it again.

Gaby pulls her cell phone from her bag. She checks the time and then flips the phone shut. "It's getting late, and I've promised to meet Franklin at four. Sorry to have to leave you, Bri-Bri, but I've got to stop at the shop and run some errands before then."

"What's happening at four?" I ask, tensing.

She's rummaging around in her bag now, fishing out change from somewhere deep within. She places two quarters and a penny on the table. "Dinner. We're having an early dinner so that he can get home to spend time with his mother."

I'm trying to control the rise in my eyebrows. Really, I am.

Gaby stops fiddling with her purse and glances up. "What? He always has dinner with his mother at six o'clock."

"So he's having *two* dinners?" I'm picturing his mother slowly rocking in her chair, waiting for his return. *Creak, creak, creak.*

She pulls a crisp ten from her wallet and lays it on the bill tray. "I guess," she answers slowly.

As my defender, Gaby stood up to Kate, commiserated with me about Mona, and then let Ned have it. The girl's obviously whip smart yet utterly clueless when it comes to the men she dates. Doesn't she think it strange that Franklin has to squeeze in time with her between visits with Mother?

Ned runs a ragged hand across his whiskers. "There's nothin' wrong with a man who loves his mother." He points a big fat finger at Gaby. "You hold on to that one, and he'll treat you like a queen."

Gaby throws me a withering look, then flashes Ned a girlish smile. *Has the world gone mad?*

I throw up my hands and sputter. Gaby's eyes stay fixed on Ned, like he's Billy Graham and she's hearing the Word for the very first time.

I consider slipping away quietly, leaving them alone to discuss the merits of Gaby's elusive new guy, when we're invaded. Three fat white-and-gray birds have pounced onto the abandoned table next to us, their pointy jaws tearing at the remnants of shrimp tails. The rapid flap of wings causes Gaby to leap from her chair. Ned and I jump up, too, and watch the spectacle. If Nathan were here, he'd dart over and shoo away those squawking birds, just like he used to whenever gulls landed on our beach blanket in search of crumbs. The memory warms me like a wool blanket during a grunion run.

Rather than interrupt the bird fight, I just stand there, watching the scuffle, glad for any distraction. Ever since Ned mentioned seeing Douglas this morning, I've felt the beginnings of a headache, a tiny pinprick near my temple. Honestly, though, the pressure in my head began even earlier, when my mind had retrieved a long-buried memory.

Ned wads up the cloth napkin that had once graced that table and pitches it at the trespassing birds. The impact scatters them, and we hear their cries let loose in the sky above. *Okay, party's over.* With a brief nod Ned says so-long to Gaby, and then he turns to me. "Remember what I told you, Bri," he says.

You mean that I'm too ignorant to see that my forty-two-year-old husband may be having some sort of crisis?

With a captain's salute, he adds, "And I'll be seeing you at the bus on Tuesday, fog or sun."

I toss him a wave and then look upward, focusing on the blue sky hovering above the sea. Having a pair of wings sounds pretty good right about now.

Chapter four

So we're studying the first book of Corinthians at church on Sunday, and Pastor Jake delivers this little nugget from chapter seven: "But those who marry will face many troubles in this life. . . ." Huh. Right there in black-and-white. The apostle Paul seems pretty intent on putting the kibosh on anyone who thinks otherwise.

I sidle up closer to Douglas and see him glance down at me, a faint smile forming at the corner of his mouth. *No trouble here*. Kate may see a woman bored with her life, but she's daft. Ned may see a man heading for some sort of midlife crisis, but not me. Long work hours or not, Douglas exudes strength. Not only in body—and oh yeah, his is *nice*—but in mind too. The man knows what he wants.

I learned this in small ways in the early days of our relationship. Once he called me from Los Angeles, saying he'd be back in town in an hour and, "Would you like to have dinner?"

Well, a girl's gotta eat. . . .

He held the door for me at the curb when he arrived. "Where would you like to go?" he asked through my open window. His cologne gave off a heady scent.

"How about Sizzler," I answered. We had already decided we

weren't that hungry, that a salad would be perfect.

He made a face. "Not a coffee shop. I'm taking you to Windemere."

Think cloth napkins, white tablecloths, highly polished silver, and oh-so-underdressed me. "And you asked me for my choice *why?*" I said, playfully annoyed.

This exchange was the first of so many that it became our inside joke. Like all those times we met at church and chivalrous Douglas would ask me out for Sunday breakfast. He'd open the car door, wait for me to get in, and then ask, "Where would you like to go?"

I'd tell him and, I kid you not, he nearly always said, "Hmm. No, let's go to Franky's." Or to Allison's or to Hill St. Café. Pretty much anywhere except the *dive* I'd suggested.

We continued this little ongoing tête-à-tête until Nathan came along and eating at restaurants took on a whole new meaning; i.e., *let's not.* Instead of gazing into each other's wanting eyes over a three-egg avocado and tomato omelet, we'd spend the entire mealtime trying to keep our baby's pudgy hands out of the home-style potatoes. And our hands off each other . . .

So take that, naysayers. For as long as I've known him, Douglas has never shied away from honesty. If he wanted something, he'd let me know. I'm sure of it.

Sigh. It's still early morning and I'm plopped onto our camp-cottage bed, reliving moments from the past and avoiding the day ahead. I sink further into my pillow, captivated by the sounds of morning. Just outside, palm branches rustle in a mellow breeze.

I wish we had a dog. They listen and don't judge (unlike cats). They're happy to see you, even when you're the grumpiest tour-bus host on the West Coast. And they don't offer their unique take on *your* world. They just cuddle up next to you on the couch, like a fur-covered dough ball.

Who needs friends when you could have a furry "yes" dog instead?

It occurs to me now that Gaby could be sitting on her floral couch at this very moment, thinking the same thing.

Can't remember the last time Gaby and I were on the "outs." When I *hinted* last Saturday at Franklin's possible instability, she acted peeved. Since then, we've played the game of volley-call for two days, where we speak to each other's voicemail systems but never actually to each other. Not like Gaby has had much to say. Her messages have been short, terse, and clipped—like Darla, Douglas's melodramatic secretary, on a harried day. Come to think of it, this means every day.

Why doesn't Gaby get that what I said had nothing to do with her and everything to do with her barely-there boyfriend?

Ugh. "Bad friend," I say aloud to myself. "Bad, bad friend." I reach for the phone, intending to apologize, but it rings first and then stops before I can grab it. This is what it's like to have a teenager in the house. When you have a toddler, the phone might be for you but you can rarely talk. When they hit teendom, the phone might never be for you, but you are available to talk.

"Mom?"

"Ye-es?" I sing out.

"Phone's for you." Or, as in this case, the phone just might be for you, but you will never be quick enough to beat out the teenager who believes that every call is for him.

I put the cordless to my ear and hear lots of sniffling. "Gaby?" I ask tentatively.

"It's me!" She's wailing now, an open, full-on, let-it-all-hang-out cry.

I try to get a word in. "I'm so sorry, Gaby. I didn't mean to—"

"Frank . . . lin . . . broke . . . up . . . with . . . meeeeee!"

"Oh, honey."

"He . . . said . . . I . . . was . . . too . . . too . . . need-d-d-dy!"

Because you hoped to see him even after the blue-plate-special hour ended? Creep!

"I . . . want . . . chocolate!"

It didn't take long this time. Those three little words have become our mainstay, our mantra, if you will. It's what we *do*. "Get your little self over here, then." By now I've jogged down the stairs and headed into the kitchen. "I'm breaking out the chocolate squares as we speak."

I've always got a stash of Baker's Semi-Sweet Baking Chocolate Squares in the pantry. Nathan and his buddies got into them once and, well, pandemonium broke loose when Gaby showed up after a relationship-gone-wrong and we had no more brownie-making supplies. Douglas once offered to encase said ingredients in glass with a sign reading, *Break only in a male-bashing emergency*. After the Nathan and friends experience, I nearly took him up on that.

Gaby blows her nose into the phone. "I have to do some . . . some arranging at the . . . the shop," she sniffs. "I'll be there as fast as I . . . I can."

I hang up just as I hear the honk of Gibson's dad's truck. "Nathan, off to school. Your ride's here."

He grabs his backpack and Civil War–project poster and tries to rush through the doorway. Only he trips over his Igloo lunchbox and falls against the screen.

"Here." I grab up his lunch in one hand and guide him safely out the door and to the truck with the other. *He's so lost without me.*

I'm off work so it's a perfect day to throw my friend a pity party. Back in the kitchen, I switch on the radio before piling supplies onto the counters. Then I rummage around in the fridge, searching for my secret stash of butter. *If that kid and his buddies took . . . oh, there it is.* With the addition of butter, my kitchen counter could pass for a well-stocked bakery. Sugar, eggs, flour, chocolate, vanilla, salt—yup, it's all there. Wacky Aunt Dot would be so proud.

I'm using Aunt Dot's recipe. I *always* use her recipe. It's the one fairly normal thing I ever knew about her. Because my parents were always flitting around the world, they often left me with Auntie. Like them, she was a bit of a wanderer. Only, her mind wandered—not so much her bod. Like living with an older version of Phoebe from *Friends*.

Auntie always ate gobs of protein in the morning and made me eat it too. *Blech.* Meatloaf for breakfast. Double *blech.* Said it would give me stamina for the day. It usually just gave me the runs. To this day I'll have a yogurt and an apple in the morning, and I'm good to go. No pun intended.

I get antsy waiting for Gaby, and so I putter. Not that the house doesn't need some serious puttering. Just the sand from the entryway alone would attract most of the neighborhood cats. On the radio I hear Rascal Flatts with "Bless the Broken Road," and I'm suddenly lost in it like a backup singer with her sights on lead vocals. I grab the broom, then think better of it. I mean, really, how cliché would that be? To sweep and sing while passing the time away. Sheesh. Might as well be a character in a romance novel. . . .

Instead, I flop onto the lone rug in our living room and gaze up at my knotty-pine ceiling. Rascal Flatts continues to belt it out and I find myself praying, "Oh, Jesus, bless our Gaby's broken road!"

Time flies when warbling, you know? The fluorescent clock on the wall tells me it's getting late. I'm thinking that by the time the brownies are mixed and baked, and after we settle into the sand with a basketful, Nathan will be home from school—he's on half days this week. Wish I could be here when he steps through those doors to find freshly baked brownies waiting for him. Even better if he's brought a friend. They'll think I'm a regular Martha Stewart, sans a scandal. At least I hope.

"Bri-Bri?" The door slams shut behind Gaby.

Finally!

I give my friend a strong hug. She smells of sweet roses. Her red-tinged eyes give away her sadness, and I'm dying to make her laugh. But sometimes you just gotta wallow.

So we start melting butter and pouring vanilla and singing songs about cheatin' men. We sound like country rocker Gretchen Wilson with a bad attitude.

With the oven timer set, Gaby's holding up a spoonful of rich chocolate batter. Her eyes are less red and she wears a look of new perspective on her face. "You know what, Bri?" She's twirling the spoon in the air now. "I should just march over to that fool's house and smear a pot of this goo all over his lame PT Cruiser."

"Sounds mature." Although I just bet his PT has wood paneling.

"Oh-oh, wait! Maybe I should flick some through his open window on a hot day."

"Yeah, and then when the officer hauls you down to the station, you can claim sugar-induced insanity."

"I'll just say that you were my accomplice. Douglas'll work it all out for us." She's waving the spoon at me now.

I lunge for it but Gaby pulls back. The soft batter lands on her face *and* on my lime green kitchen wall behind her—like an overzealous spit wad. "Hey," I compliment, "nice shot."

She recovers and then scrapes the spoon along the sides of the nearly empty mixing bowl, managing to fill it up. "Here," she says, shoving the spoon back at me, "you try some." Reflexively, my hands try to deflect her offer, but no dice. Now I've got brownie batter on my chin, nose, and maybe my cheek. The only place I want it is in my mouth, at the beach.

"Want more?" she asks, laughing and flicking me again. It lands, not on me, but on the dishwasher door behind me.

Nice. *Real nice.*

"Here, let me get that." Gaby grabs a towel from the counter, the one I'd been using to wipe batter from my hands. She takes a swipe at the smudge on the dishwasher and creates a fat brown smear across the surface.

She stands back and scrutinizes it, like she's Picasso. "Reminds me of him," she says with a shrug.

Later we recline at the beach like a couple of beauty queens with nothing but time on our hands. Only without the beauty and time part. I've ingested three brownies already and the waistband on my shorts is starting to dig into my skin.

"Bri?"

"Hmm?"

"How come finding Mr. Perfect is so like trying to find Atlantis?"

Her nod to a country music song by Jamie O'Neal is not lost on me. "You're too funny," I say.

A low-flying plane buzzes overhead. "Seriously, then. How did you *know* Douglas was the one?"

Her question hits me like a sudden splash of cool seawater, and I think about this for a few seconds. "He was everything I thought I didn't need," I finally say.

Gaby sits up, pulls off her shades and stares at me. "That is the weirdest thing I think you've ever said."

I shrug. "I think that's how God does it sometimes. At least, that's how He did it with me. I don't know. I just remember that back then I was just, you know, having fun. Not looking for love. Then Douglas walked into the shop and, wham!—I was drawn to him like cream to coffee."

"And the God part?"

"He knew what I needed. I think He even made me want it. Or He at least showed me that I wanted it."

"Wanted what? Douglas?"

The lapping of water to shore has lulled me. I'm lying there, eyes shut, seeing Douglas walk up to the coffee counter, his stride confident. "No," I say to Gaby. "Stability." *And eyes that rev my heart.*

"Stability?" She sounds incredulous. "How romantic."

"You asked. And actually, it was. It is." Especially when you've lived as a vagabond much of your life. I glance her way. "I get surprised sometimes when I wake up and he's still there."

Gaby puts her sunglasses back on and lies down again. "Guess if you put it that way." She settles into her lounge chair. "You were right about Franklin."

I'm keeping my mouth shut. For the moment.

"He used a coupon for dinner the other night—*and* he asked me to order from the special early-bird menu."

"Oh brother. Did you have to share a bowl of ice cream for dessert too?"

Gaby shakes her head. "What dessert?"

I cough out a laugh. "Oh! I am so sorry, Gab."

"Why? You tried to warn me, but . . ."

"But you were a girl 'in like.' And that's okay."

"I guess. Bri?" she asks. "I've never really given God's opinion much thought. Like you did." She's raking the sand with her hand, making all kinds of swirly loop-the-loops in it. "Maybe I should pray more about the man-thing." She sighs. "That makes it sound like I actually prayed in the first place—which I did not."

I slide my shades onto my head and look over at Gaby. "You won't hear any condemnation from me. I forget to pray all the time. I'm like that dumb bumper sticker with the open Bible on it that says, 'When all else fails, read the instructions.' I should rewrite that puppy to say, '*Before* all else fails . . .'"

Gaby gives a wry laugh as she stares at the sand. "No kidding."

Barefoot and exhausted, we wander back to the house. A sugar high lasts only so long before fatigue takes its place. Gaby's weathered another breakup, our friendship has endured, and me? I'm just glad for the smell of salt air and the sea breeze on my skin. And for the nap I'm about to take.

Gaby's looking toward the house. "You expecting company?" she asks.

I follow her gaze and see the platinum Jag parked in the drive. *Mona's car.*

Chapter five

Being at odds with one's mother-in-law is *so* overdone. This is what comes to mind when I step into my home—this *is* my home, right?—and find Mona and her chunky dressed-to-the-nines friend stretching a tape measure along the length of my living room floor.

Nathan and Gibson peer down from the second-story landing. With hunks of brownie in their hands, the two lean over the railing, completely engrossed in the spectacle. Even at thirteen they recognize a ludicrous situation when they see one.

Mona looks toward Gaby and me, standing windblown and sandy in the doorway. "Well, hello, Brianna. Are you done playing at the beach?"

"Mona?" *Is that you or has the cast of* Designing Women *descended on my living room?*

She guides her flashy friend by the elbow toward us. "Brianna, I'd like you to meet my very dear friend Patrice. Patrice, this is my son's wife."

I brush off my hand on my shorts before offering it. "Brianna."

Patrice's eyes start at my face, roll down to my gritty feet and

then back up again. She holds out a pudgy, finely manicured hand. "A pleasure, *darling*."

I'm sure. "And Patrice, this is *my* dear friend Gaby." I slide a look at my mother-in-law. "Mona, you remember Gaby."

Mona scrunches her lips and looks off into space, as if pondering the very breadth of my question. She taps the corner of her mouth with one pointy finger and then, suddenly, snaps out of it. "Why, yes, I do remember. It is Gabrielle, is it not?"

Not.

"Just Gaby, Mrs. Stone. It's nice to see you again."

Liar, liar, pants on fire.

Enough already with the formalities. "So what's up, Mona?" I ask, eyeing the tape measure. I'm not about to mention the infamous email, the one "For Douglas Only." *C'mon, Mona, spill it.*

"Patrice is a *fabulous* designer, Brianna. She has done absolute wonders for *many* of my associates." Mona gazes appreciatively at Patrice.

"Really, Patrice?" I notice her finely tailored linen suit, her narrow-heeled pumps, her pricey jewelry. And that hair! It's fireball red. Even I'm envious. "So what's your specialty?" I ask. "Landscapes?"

"Interiors, Brianna. *Really*." Mona frowns at me, a deep crease in her forehead. "Patrice is the top interior designer in all of Ventura!"

Patrice laughs lightly. "Oh, Mona. I should hire you to be my spokesperson."

Yeah. Keep her busy.

"So what's up with the tape measure, Mona? Buying us new furniture?"

Mona eyes my denim couch and wicker chairs. "Well, you certainly could use some. But that's not all I have in mind. If you and Douglas are going to get top dollar for this house, then you will need to make some . . ." She grimaces at the blue longboard propped up against a wall the color of freshly mowed grass. "Alterations to your décor."

I start to laugh, but then Mona turns around and marches to the kitchen. *Okay, she's serious.* I'm knitting my brow and following after her when Gaby touches my arm.

"We left it a mess," she whispers.

I bite my lip and give her a mea culpa shrug. If only she'd called first . . .

"Oh my word!" Mona's standing in the center of my tropical-themed kitchen, surveying the accents of fudge Gaby and I made earlier. Both ladies appear awed by our handiwork. Patrice gasps and places one hand over her heart. *You should see my bathrooms!*

Mona turns to me. "How can you live like this, Brianna?" She sweeps one open arm across the kitchen's width. "There's cookie dough everywhere!"

From behind me, Gaby leans over my shoulder. "Actually, it's brownie batter, Mrs. Stone."

"It's on the walls. On the dishwasher." She's jabbing her fists into her sides and looking all around my kitchen now. "There's even chocolate on the cabinets, Brianna."

I run my finger across one white cabinet door to wipe away some batter. The urge to lick my finger takes over, and as I do I hear my mother-in-law scoff. I throw a look of feigned guilt to Patrice. "Sorry you had to see that," I say.

Mona lets out a sigh and slumps her shoulders with added drama. She then rubs her forehead with her hand, over and over. "Well. I will just have to call my cleaning service to come over here immediately."

Enough already. "Mona, Patrice?" I corral the ladies and usher them back into the living room. "Forget about the kitchen." I can hear the boys eavesdropping behind us. "Nathan and Gibson will be scrubbing it from top to bottom in just a bit." I glance over my shoulder and see the boys spin and slide away. "Seriously, Mona, what gave you the idea that we were in the market to sell?" *Other than your deep need to see Douglas living in a more elite zip code, say, 90210?*

"You're not selling?" Mona's mouth is stuck open, like she's momentarily aghast. "Well," she says, regaining her composure. "I suppose you could rent the house out." She takes another quick look around the room. "Yes, it would probably make a suitable rental."

"But we are not selling, and we're not renting. Mona, we have no intention of leaving our home. We all love it here."

Mona looks from me to Patrice and back again. "I . . . I don't understand."

My eyes catch Gaby's. "Don't look at me," she says, holding up her palms.

Mona blinks hard, as if a light bulb has gone off somewhere in her brain. Her face turns a deep purplish red. *Blushing? Mona blushes?* She abruptly backs up and grabs her briefcase and says to Patrice, "I'm so sorry, dear, to have wasted your precious time. It seems I was mistaken about my son's plans. Let me take you for a nice dinner as an apology."

They scuttle to the front door and with obvious effort Mona looks to me, a sunny smile pasted on. "Well. So nice to see you, dear." She gives a quick nod toward the hallway. "Kiss my grandson good-bye for me, won't you?"

As they make their quick retreat, Patrice thrusts her business card at me. "You have a truly great space here. Call me."

I stand against the closed front door, silent and, frankly, more than a little perturbed. Gaby just shakes her head, but her expression begs, *What in the world?*

I'm still frozen against the door when I hear the floorboards above us shudder. I glance up to see my son's teenage bum sliding toward me down the banister. Nathan lands on his feet with a thud.

"Dude!" Gibson's still on the landing, his sun-streaked surf locks bobbing in appreciation. "That was awesome!"

I ask you, would anyone in their right mind believe that I haven't warned my kid about the perils of slip-sliding down a wooden banister? *Only about once a day.*

Gaby's expression has moved from curious to dark. "Bri-Bri? Tell me you've talked to Douglas about the email. . . ."

A horn honks twice just outside our door as Gibson twists onto the banister and slides on down. Like my son, he lands with a terrible thud. "Dude," says Gibson, cocking his head toward Nathan. "Your mom's so rad." He flashes me a too-cute grin.

Of all of Nathan's friends, Gibson has absolutely stolen my heart. Forget that he never combs his hair or that he usually smells of salt water—this kid can empty my fridge any day. He lost his mom to cancer five years ago, yet he's probably the most joyful—if not grubby—kid I've ever known. If the good Lord had seen to it to give me more than one great kid, I'd want a Gibson.

"Hey, Gib," Nathan calls out. "Don't forget your stick. You left it yesterday."

Gibson's hands are in his pockets and he's standing there, all casual, just nodding his head and grinning ear to ear. "R—i—gh—t."

The doorbell's ringing now, and we all stand there staring at each other. *They're b-a-a-ck!*

Thankfully, when I open the door it's Gibson's dad, Max. At least I think it's Max. Somewhere beneath the grime of—and I'm guessing here—engine grease, two friendly eyes peek out. He's wiping his hands with a stained rag, like he's just checked the oil under the hood of my VW.

Max smiles at me. "Hello, Bri. That boy of mine here?"

Gibson calls out, "Yo, Pop. Gotta get my board outta the garage." He's got his hands in his pockets and he's still grinning as he passes by. "See ya, Mrs. Stone, Mizz Flores."

Gaby likes Gibson too. I can tell. Her expression says, *What a sweet kid.* Most important, she's momentarily distracted from questioning me about the notorious email. So I haven't talked to Douglas about it—so what? My man's in trial and we've hardly seen him. Anyway, I'm sure he hit the Delete button the minute he read his mother's note. After he gave her the "what for," that is.

Gaby's got her mouth open to say something, but I turn to my kid and practice my dutiful parenting skills. "What's your homework like tonight?" I ask.

He grimaces. "Like nails on a chalkboard."

I place my hands on his shoulders and gently nudge him back to the stairs. "Well, go ahead and get out your chalk, mister. And get your work done."

He groans.

I shoo him away. "Go on."

Nathan heads upstairs and stops. He screws up his face, like he's trying to remember something. "Oh yeah. Rita wants you to call her about an announcement or something."

"Got it." I walk toward the phone to call my boss, but Gaby's not letting this go.

"The email?" she chimes in. "What about the email?"

I throw my head back and let out a dramatic sigh. "No, I haven't talked to Douglas about this yet. We're like two ships lately and how would that be? He's sailing by and I say, 'Uh, honey, by the way, I read your private email . . . you know, the one that said "For Douglas Only" in the subject line. And by the way, your mom's a loon.'"

Gaby's got her arms crossed.

I continue. "I'll talk to him. But wasn't Mona's face a *scream* when she realized that I must not know anything about her proposal to Douglas?"

Gaby's eyes light up. "And then she had to apologize to Patrice! I felt like grabbing a brownie and taking a front-row seat. Hey, what a great idea for reality TV—*Designer Drop-ins*."

"More like *Barge-ins*."

Nathan calls to me from upstairs. "Mom! I need help with my homework!"

Gaby takes her purse from the couch. "You go on ahead. I've got to get back to the shop." She gives me a brief hug. "Thanks, chica. I'm sure I'll still be whimpering tonight, but once again you and your brownies came to my rescue." She looks down at her hips and sighs before heading out. "God bless your dear aunt Dot."

I click the door shut behind Gaby. *Now if I could only rescue myself.* Life is good. I've got no complaints. It's just . . . well, it's just that I'm beginning to wonder if I'm living in some sort of perpetual state of immaturity. At thirty-three, *should* I be longing for business suits and pointy-toed shoes? Does choosing marble over wood, chenille over denim, really matter?

I ponder this while jogging up the stairs. Nathan's got the radio tuned to 98.3 KDAR and he's listening to Salvador singing "Hallelu-jah." In my soul I'm singing too—singin' away the blues. *Hallelujah to the Lamb . . .*

I slip through the door and find Nathan sprawled on the floor—and don't even get me started about the piles of clothing everywhere. He's tapping his pencil to the beat and reading from a book about John Newton and "Amazing Grace" for Bible class.

He speaks without looking up. "Mom?"

"Hmm?"

"What's a wretch?"

Considering the past hour, could he ask me a more loaded ques-tion? Times like these put my Christian witness to the test. We're called to consider the weakest among us—say, our kids—and so I put aside my decidedly *un-*Christian feelings toward Mona. "Well, I think it means someone who's unhappy, sour, mean. Someone like that," I answer.

"Kinda like us before knowing Jesus?"

He twists the knife, ever so slightly . . . "Yes, I would agree with that."

He writes an answer in his comp book laid open beside him. "Did you need help with something else?" I ask.

He shakes his head to Salvador's salsa beat.

I take that as a no and step out to the hall. Much earlier I had planned on a nap. Between hosting two tours, sulking from a tiff with Gaby, and parenting virtually alone for days, I'm beat. Mona's unannounced visit only made things worse. My eyes feel dizzyingly heavy, like they'll fall shut whether I lie down or not. Oh, the hazards of aging.

I peel off my sandy shorts and top and drop them into the hamper. I yank open my T-shirt drawer, but it sits empty. Ugh. My one and only complaint about my treasured beach house is its lack of a laundry room. Instead of a cozy June Cleaver–style room to clean and fold our clothes—like much of *progressive* California—we have a washer and dryer working overtime in the garage.

Rather than scandalize my teenager by darting downstairs in search of cotton, I pull open Douglas' T-shirt drawer. I finger the entire stack of folded shirts, searching for the most worn-in, the most supple tee in the bunch. After slipping it over my head and snuggling into its softness, I push the drawer closed but it catches on a slip of paper. The paper hangs down from Douglas' top drawer—his infamous *junk* drawer. Even a hyper-focused attorney like Douglas, I learned soon after marriage, needs a place to toss stuff like loose keys, stray candies, and yesterday's mail.

With care I close his T-shirt drawer and open the one right above it. I reach in toward the back and pull out a two-page fax. My eyes scan the cover page.

Dearest Son,

You have made a wise choice. Attached please find the specifications for the truly fabulous property my office is representing.

Yours,
Mother

I lower myself to the carpet and·read it again. *Tell me I'm halluci-nating*. Douglas can't be considering a move. Not without talking to me first. Annoyingly, Kate's words from the other night blink in my mind like a Times Square ad: *"You two are exact opposites. How can you stand that?"*

Not only can I stand it, I love it. Until now, though, it had not seriously occurred to me that Douglas just might feel otherwise.

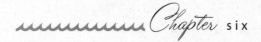

Chapter SIX

I should have known trouble would slither its way into our lives someday. From the get-go, Mona and I were at odds, rivals for the affections of the only man we both loved.

Quite frankly, my very first meeting with both of Douglas's parents gave me a pretty good idea of what a victim of *The Jamie Kennedy Experiment* must feel like. Only this was no practical joke. *If only*.

We met for dinner just up the coast at the very posh Santa Barbara Biltmore, where the green olive in a dry martini costs more than one pair of Reef flip-flops. Douglas and I arrived to find Douglas, Sr.—aka DM Stone—appearing spastic as he barked into his humongous cell phone while simultaneously jostling for better reception. His ex-wife and Douglas's mother, Mona, sat with her back to him, fiddling with her beeper.

Douglas bent and kissed his mother on the cheek. "Hi, Mother." He thrust his hand out to shake his father's hand. "Dad."

DM waved Douglas away, like he'd just been presented with a weak cocktail. With the phone still suctioned to his ear, he motioned for us to sit.

Douglas pulled out my chair and waited for me to be seated. His

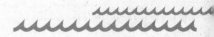

mother set down her beeper and looked at me. "Well," she said.

Do I respond? Is this how the rich say hello?

Douglas leaned over and put one arm around me. "Mother, this is Brianna." The full-mouthed smile that lit up his face after my name passed his lips gave me goose bumps. I shivered.

His mother shook my hand—or rather, she shook my fingertips. For someone with the reputation of a cutthroat, Mona's handshake lacked finality. Maybe the weight of her diamond-studded tennis bracelet weighed her arm down.

"Hi, Mrs. Stone," I said. "I've heard a lot about you." *Okay, maybe not from Douglas, but there's the mega-billboard with your picture, all those For Sale signs around town, and the ads in the paper with you holding all those wooden plaques. . . .*

"*Really,*" she said, her highly painted eyebrows raised. "How lovely."

DM shouted into his cell, his free hand gesturing with the energy of an Italian pizza maker. "Drummond! You're passing up the best offer you will ever hear from my office!" Apparently *the* deal of the '90s had just gone the way of pet rocks.

The waiter asked for my drink order. *Uh, make it something strong with a twist.* "Coke, please," I answered.

Douglas ordered his usual mineral water with the German-sounding name. His hand moved from my shoulders to my hair. I sat in a swanky restaurant with my boyfriend's so-very-wealthy-and-uptight parents, and their son was raking his fingers through my split ends. It was just too *Pretty in Pink*. I was Molly Ringwald to his Andrew McCarthy.

"Mother, Brianna and I have some news." Douglas's eyes caressed my face. He seemed to have blocked out his father, who continued to growl into his cell phone.

"News? What kind of news?" Mona looked alarmed. "Oh, Douglas. Don't tell me . . ."

Tell her what? Tell her what? I sneaked a look at Douglas and saw his eyes narrowing. He reached for my hand and cradled it in his own. "Mother, Brianna and I are engaged."

Mona's face registered a big, giant . . . nothing. No reaction at all. Maybe above the din she hadn't heard him. So I gave Douglas a little nudge. But he just stared at his mother, his expression sad.

Then, like someone had yanked hard on a pull cord trailing down her back, Mona sprang to life. "B-but how can this be? You've only just met! Surely you aren't going to rush into things, Douglas."

So much to absorb—live piano music, bustling wait staff, my future father-in-law trying to close the deal during our big announcement—but what I remember most from that anticipated moment is the plain disapproval on my fiancé's mother's face. Like her well-bred son had just brought Daisy Duke home to meet the parents.

Our waiter set down our drinks and winked at me. Not a hey-babe kind of wink, but an it'll-soon-be-over kind of look. I almost laughed.

Douglas eyed me. "You seem okay," he whispered. "Are you okay?"

With you? Always. I nodded.

"Oh, for heaven's sake, DM! Put down that phone." Mona glared at her ex. "Our son's getting married!"

DM dropped his cell phone onto the table. He raised two fingers and whipped his head back and forth like a mental patient hearing voices. "Waiter! Champagne—over here." My shoulders tensed, and I could feel my own retreat. *Please don't snap your fingers, oh, pretty please.* He snapped them. Not once, but twice. *Oh, here we go.*

The waiter—my compadre—rushed over with an ice bucket and a frothy bottle. Another waiter set four glasses on the table in front of us. DM whisked the bottle from its bucket. "Time for some bub-blay," he said, drawing out the word, his mood abruptly changed from the recent phone call. He stood and popped the cork, then slid a look around the room, reminding me of a magician who'd just performed a sleight-of-hand gag.

When he started to pour, Douglas covered my glass with his hand. "Dad. Brianna's . . ." He stopped and gave me the *cutest* wicked grin. Ooh, I could've kissed him right there. ". . . too young." He pulled both of our glasses away from the bottle's spout.

Mona gasped. And the drama could've won her an Academy Award. She put three fingers to her forehead and closed her eyes.

DM stood there, champagne bottle in hand. His grin stretched nearly across the room. "That's my boy!" he shouted. He tossed the champagne back into the bucket. "You old cradle robber!" he said, repeatedly slapping Douglas's shoulder.

In another award-winning performance, Mona wilted like old spinach.

Of all the eligible women in Ventura, I obviously didn't make Mona's cut for her son. Sigh. *Que sera, sera*. Frankly, of all the potential in-laws, neither one of these two would be my first choice either. Mona was a frigid life form, and DM? Just plain scary. Earlier, I had watched him milk the guy on the other line—ack! During the entire call he worked over a slice of French bread with his fingers until it had been reduced to a gluey dough. Can't *wait* to meet the rest of the family.

DM emptied his first flute of champagne. "So. When's the big day?"

Douglas stroked my fingers with his thumb. "Soon. We haven't chosen the actual date yet, but," he looked at me with those tempting eyes, "it'll be soon."

Mona continued to hold one hand to her brow, except now she looked resigned. "Not too soon, I hope. Short engagements are suspect, you know."

Actually, no, I don't know.

"And of course we will need plenty of time to book an appropriate

ballroom for the reception," she continued. "Where will you be holding the ceremony, Douglas? Not that little church you attend, I
hope."

"That seems the most appropriate." He looked to me. "Wouldn't
you agree?"

"I really do want Pastor Jake to do our wedding, Douglas.
But . . ." I stopped. How could I tell these people what my dream
wedding looked like? They'd freak! And Douglas . . . Would he think
he'd blown it when he picked me? Maybe he was right. Our church
would be a sweet place to have our wedding. It was probably the right
place.

"Hey," DM chimed in. "How about I talk to ol' Vince about the
annex up on Foothill?"

"*Please,* DM." Mona looked exasperated. "That ramshackle place
isn't fit for mice to get married in. Now, the Presbyterian church on
the hill—*that* is marvelous. It would be simply perfect for an elegant
wedding. I'll put a call in to a member I know."

Douglas looked from his father to his mother before settling back
on me. "Tell me your ideas, Brianna."

I shook my head.

He laughed. "Come on. I really want to know."

I looked at our hands intertwined in my lap and bit my lip. Barely
raising my chin, I blurted it out. "The beach. I've always wanted to
get married on the sand."

My love's grin was the widest it had been all night. He squeezed
my hand, and then reached up with the other to brush some strands
of hair from my eyes. "Done," he said, his gaze moving from my forehead, down the side of my face, and settling on my eyes.

Mona sputtered. The shrimp she'd just bitten into had apparently
lodged somewhere in her throat. She grabbed for her water but
knocked it over, drenching the tablecloth and scattering ice onto her
china plate. Douglas flew to her side and tried to help her up, but she

slapped his wrist. Our trusty waiter hovered behind them, a mixture
of concern and hilarity in his expression.

"St-st-op!" Mona coughed the word out. She sucked in a hard
breath. "I am ju . . . just fine!" Her eyes widened. "What is the matter
with you?"

Douglas took his seat and half hid a grin. "Sorry, Mother. I
thought you were choking."

"Not you!" She pointed a bejeweled finger at me. "You! You can't
possibly want to get married on the sand—it's positively *filthy*. I won't
have it!"

*And all those beach real estate ads? Whatever happened to your slogan:
"Live the good life—by the sea"?*

———

I'm sitting on our bed, wearing Douglas's undershirt, remembering that day like it happened last week instead of more than fourteen
years ago. The first straw became the final one for Mona, I think.
After Douglas agreed to our beach wedding, she just seemed to toler-
ate me—but barely. Guess she ought to get credit for that, at least.

When Nathan came around less than a year later, she softened a
bit, offering me tons of (unwanted) advice and plenty of bucks for his
college fund. Sigh. Mona just could not believe that we hadn't named
our son after Douglas. But we thought of Nathan as our little gift
from heaven, our blessing from God himself. So that's why we gave
him a name meaning *gift from God*. Apparently Mona didn't know
how to argue with that.

As for the beach life, it suits us. Besides, ever since his parents'
divorce, Douglas has eschewed the brass-and-marble life. Said that
kind of living cost too much. *It cost his parents too much.* When I found
this faded blue beach house, with its shingled siding and New
England feel, I ran to his office. He's always said that the minute he

saw my face, he knew we were homeowners. *If only I knew for sure that this was his dream too. . . .*

I slide down into our shabby chic sheets and pull up the covers. I want to snuggle into Douglas's scent. There's just no way he'd want to leave our home. Is there?

When I awake, there's drool on my pillow. Further evidence of my bone-weary state. Haven't slept this hard in the afternoon since Nathan's toddler years, when an eight-hour day felt more like sixteen.

I stretch and groan, willing myself back to dreamland. Can't remember all the details, but Douglas and I were building a sand-castle somewhere on a Mexican beach.

Ugh. It occurs to me that my fatigue has less to do with my non-stop schedule and more to do with wayward worries about my marriage. There. I've said it. I am worried about Douglas and me.

Not the oh-no-it's-over kind of worry. I'm not Dolly Parton singing that dreadful song about D-I-V-O-R-C-E. But like *Madeline*'s Miss Clavel always said, "*Something* is not right."

I lie awake and stare at the knotty-pine ceiling above me, creating little worlds in all its imperfections. Maybe I dreamed the whole day. Maybe Mona never showed up here in her croc-textured footwear. And fax? What fax? That *had* to be some sort of weird aberration, right?

Except that I hear it crumple when I stretch and bump it with my knee. *Grrr*.

The phone's ringing, and I ignore the impulse to run the fax through the shredder. Instead, I get up and put it back in Douglas's drawer.

My bedroom door slowly opens, and Nathan sticks his head inside the room. "Mom?" he whispers. "Phone's for you. It's Rita."

Sigh. My boss. I adore Rita, actually. Just not right now—I rarely enjoy anyone when I'm still shaking the sleep from my eyes. " 'kay," I answer before reaching for the receiver.

"Brianna, I've got some news to discuss with you." Rita rarely dallies in small talk. She's a cool-headed, through-and-through business-woman with newsprint ink coursing through her veins. Evidenced by the fact that she named her dogs Dow and Jones.

"Good news, I hope."

She hesitates. "Well, yes, I believe it is good news. I'd like to tell you about it in person, though. Can you meet me at Marie's tonight for dinner?"

Dinnertime used to be sacred around here. But with Douglas trying a court case, and Nathan still running a couple of nights each week, well? Breakfast time has now become our holy hour. Or holy minute, depending how late we roll out of bed.

"Sure. It'll have to be early so I can pick up Nathan after practice. Five-fifteen, okay?"

"I'll see you promptly at five-fifteen, Brianna."

What Rita lacks in the warm-fuzzies department, she makes up for with a kind spirit and tons of generosity. If you ask me, she's generous to a fault. Take my last driver, who wrecked two buses. She had to let him go, but she did so with a substantial severance package—and a gift certificate for Laugh-Makers Driving School.

I grab a shower, wondering what's up with Rita. *Tell me she hasn't booked the Red Hat Society for another tour!* If she has, we might as well set aside our agenda for the day, because the Queen and her court always have other ideas. Last time the ladies rode with us, our *coastal* tour bus spent most of the time navigating the windy hilltop roads of the city, in search of the perfect spot for tea. True, we could see the ocean from some of the streets, but, really, with so many ladies in big, loud hats, who could enjoy the view? *Note to self: Give it up and buy myself a pink "lady in waiting" hat.*

Right on time, I drop off Nathan at the gym for a pre-run spin class. The beauty of cross-country running is that you actually *go somewhere*, as opposed to a mouse-on-a-treadmill track course. Yet Nathan's coach says that a vigorous spin class, where riders travel nowhere at all, properly preps the kids for running hills and such. *So* not my thing, but whatever.

With Nathan safely on a bike to oblivion, I head out to meet Rita. Before I get there, though, my voicemail beeps. Must have missed a call while in the gym with Nathan.

I punch in my pin number. It's a message from Douglas. "Bri? Looks like I'm going to be tied up here all night." *So what else is new?* "I'll be meeting my client for dinner somewhere in Oxnard. Sorry, hon." Warmth creeps through my face. He was probably just meeting his client Saturday morning to discuss a case over breakfast. Ugh. I'm such a dolt for giving in to Ned-induced doubt.

Douglas continues, "When this trial's over, I'll make it up to you and Nathan. I promise. Bye."

Rita's waiting for grumpy me when I arrive at the restaurant, still annoyed with myself for doubting my husband. Of course there was a good explanation for his trip away from the office yesterday. *Probably just as good a one regarding the fax from Mona too.* I take a breath and force a smile.

It's not hard to do. Rita's wearing a jungle-print sleeveless pantsuit with strappy shoes. Her normally pale skin looks as warm as a South American vacation, and her wavy blond hair is freshly styled. *At sixtysomething I should look so good.*

She gives me a brisk hug. "Good to see you, Brianna."

The hostess seats us in the back of the restaurant, and I'm guessing that Rita requested this. Not that it'll help much with privacy. Marie's has become the one-stop meal and meeting place for local churches. Can't remember a time when I've eaten here and *not* run into a church friend.

"So what's the big announcement, Rita?" I ask, aware of her ability to talk and Nathan's need for a ride home.

She sets her menu aside. "The coast is in my blood, Bri. You, of all people, recognize that. Don't you?"

I nod.

"And even though I love the California coast, I'm getting tired. I want to explore some before I'm no longer able to do so. Do you know where I'm headed, Bri?"

"Florida?" I say, kidding.

"I'm stepping down, Brianna."

I'm sipping water as she speaks and nearly gag on a piece of ice. Rita Holland *is* Coastal Tours. She started the company with her first husband, and after he died, continued on with her second. She's known citywide as a generous supporter of the arts, of Christian schools, and of the local chapter of Habitat for Humanity. Ventura needs Rita. It needs our tour company. And I need my perch at the head of the bus!

"No, Rita." I slap down my menu and throw back my head. "Don't tell me this!"

"Now, don't be like that. I'm not closing the company or selling it."

"You're not?"

"I just couldn't. In fact, this is the main reason I called you here."

I perk up. *Yippee—my coastal standup gig is safe.* Yet my heart sinks over losing Rita.

She leans forward and opens her mouth to tell me more, but we're interrupted. "Good evening, ladies!" I glance up and see Pastor Jake from my church. He's holding a slim version of the New Testament in his hands and rocking back and forth on his heels. His smile just *gleams*. What did I say about this place and church folk?

"Hello, Pastor," I say as cheerily as possible. Love Pastor Jake, but time is tight tonight and Rita was just about to spill part two of her plans.

"Yes, hello, Jacob," says Rita. "You are looking quite pleased this evening. What brings you out tonight?"

"My men's group is meeting here and, Lord willing, several newcomers will be joining us. I'm calling tonight's gathering 'Connecting the Unconnected.'"

This does not surprise me. Some preachers use acrostics ad nauseam. Ours? Catchy phrases. They're Pastor Jake's shtick, so to speak. Guess he figures these linguistic gems will help everyone remember all the church has to offer. At *Christ the Lamb* there's the ministry to the sick, aka "Enfolding the Infirm," and we offer aid to the homeless, affectionately known as "Delivering the Downtrodden." And my personal favorite, "Engaging the Unengaged"—the oh-so-transparent name for our church's singles group.

Right now, though, I'd like to carry on with my conversation. Sigh. My patience is thin as flip-flops worn all year on asphalt—but I'm not proud of the fact. Guess I'm still smarting from the mother-in-law intrusion of earlier in the day. I shake away the memory. It's just so wrong to dislike someone this much. I shield my eyes from Pastor Jake, thoroughly convinced that one pastoral glance my way and he'll *know* how much I need to join the "Loving the Unlovable" group.

Instead of chastising me for my wickedness, though, he bows slightly. "Enjoy your dinner, ladies," he says as he starts to turn away. Behind him, work-weary men carrying Bibles straggle in. "Brianna, I will see you and your family on Sunday."

Yeah, if we're not busy packing. . . .

Rita has put on her reading glasses and is looking at the menu.

"So?" I'm not in the least bit hungry. The brownies I consumed earlier in the day have already formed little home groups on my thighs.

Rita's eyes peek out over the rim of her glasses. She folds her menu and sets it neatly in front of her. "My son, Tyler, will be taking over the running of Coastal Tours," she says firmly. "He starts tomorrow."

My eyebrows dart up.

"Ty has the business acumen to take my little tour company to new heights. He's already been able to secure foreign tours for us, from as far away as Japan." She removes her reading glasses and lowers her voice. "Brianna, you are the best host we have. Promise me that you'll stay on. Ty needs you."

Like I'd welcome change in my life right now? "Sure, Rita, I'll stay." I sigh. "But I'm going to miss you so much."

"Not to worry. I'll be checking in periodically."

We both order a side salad and water. Guess she's not hungry, either. "Tell me a little bit about my new boss," I say, trying not to sound too depressed.

"My Ty is a wonderful boy. A man, really." She laughs lightly, her maternal instinct showing. "I think you and he will hit it off well, Bri."

"What did he do before this? Before Coastal Tours?"

Rita's smile fades. "Well, you know, Brianna, he's always worked in retail and such. It's truly the same thing, only now he'll be selling a service instead of a product."

Okay, that was clear as fog. But I think I get the picture. *You're bringing in your highly schooled son, who worked summers at Wal-Mart, to run the company.*

"And Luann and the drivers . . . Will they all be staying on?"

"Yes, Luann will continue on as Ty's secretary, and I haven't notified the drivers, but I can't imagine any of them leaving just because

I'm stepping down." Her smile has returned.

The waiter brings our salads and hurries over to the men's-group table, that, if you ask me, is starting to sound a bit raucous. Must be a lot of connecting going on over there.

We take too many bites in silence, like we're a sad, old married couple noshing on the early-bird special. *So* not the way to give Rita a proper send-off. The woman's been nothing but great to me; the least I can do is try to sound happy for her, to convince her that having her bratty son for a boss will be just peachy.

I put down my fork. "I'm happy for you, Rita. Really, I am. And I want you to know that I'll do what I can to help Ty feel part of the Coastal Tours fam. Hey, maybe I'll even put a welcome announcement in the newspaper."

"No!—I mean . . . you don't have to do that, Brianna." She's adamant. "It's just that Ty is very private. I . . . I'm just not sure he'd feel comfortable with that."

"Oh. Well. Just an idea—but if it's not a good one . . ."

Rita reaches across the table and touches the back of my hand. "It was such a nice thought, though." She's composed as usual. "I just think that a low-key transition leads to a smooth transition. You understand, don't you?"

"Sure, Rita. I understand." Only I don't. Not really.

Chapter eight

Brianna,
    Had to leave early this morning and didn't want to interrupt your slumber. (You're beautiful when you snore.)
                        Douglas

I pull the note from the fridge, vaguely remembering Douglas climbing into bed at some crazy hour the night before. Or maybe it was this morning. *Is this such a good thing to not remember?* We're like married strangers these days. I try to recall our last complete, in-depth conversation, and can't. Does anyone else hear Brooks & Dunn singing that remake of the '80s song "Missing You"?

Through the kitchen window I see a damp spot on the fence where Nathan keeps his wet suit. Apparently my son woke early to the call of killer swells just down the road. Well. They'd better be *gentle* swells. He knows better than to surf alone too. Chances are he and Gibson met up early and hit the beach.

I peek around the corner to the foyer. *Bingo.* The boys' backpacks lean up against the front door. A glance at the clock tells me they should be finishing up soon. So I do what any totally rad mother

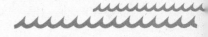

would do. I grab a couple of brownies for breakfast, slip on my flip-flops, and head to the sand.

The smallish waves break evenly, and I know the boys made a wise decision. I see my kid almost immediately, paddling away from the shore, his bare feet poking into the air. A balm of relief warms me.

Sinking my own feet into the sand, I breathe deeply. There is *nothing* on earth like the ocean breeze first thing in the morning. Add a little sea spray into the mix and you've got a rejuvenating personal day spa. *And just saved beaucoup bucks.*

With eyes closed, I drink in my surroundings. How ironic that even calm waves sound like Niagara Falls when they break. In a way, that sudden crash of water onto shore reminds me of the tumble of raw emotions within me, vying to surface. Budding resentment and fear have rushed through me like a waterfall over the past week, and I'm not sure I like the effect. I'd rather stick to sarcasm. Now, *that's* an emotion I can handle.

Gibson charges toward me, flicking sand and water everywhere. "Hey, Mrs. S," he calls out. "Did you catch my boglius ride?"

His question throws me back. Gaby and I dated a couple of surfers years ago. We met them just up the coast on the Rincon one summer after they'd parked in our self-designated spot and we'd protested. We hit it off, and they called us their groupies.

One morning we got up before most humans and joined them on the beach. Shivering beneath down sleeping bags, Gaby and I spent that dusky morning talking mainly about important stuff, like how frigid sand can get before sunup and how surfers in the fog look like giant Tootsie Rolls bobbing on the water.

After a while, between the lapping of waves and the occasional soft cry of sea gulls overhead, we nodded off to dreamland.

I felt cold water droplets hit my arm.

"Dudettes! Wake up!"

Gaby still snored.

"Didn't you see me take that gnarly wave?" one of the surf dudes demanded, incredulous.

Opening one eye, I thought, *He's got to be kidding.* The other eye refused to budge. "Nope. Must've missed it," I said, stifling both a yawn and my irritation at having been awakened from a delicious dream.

Apparently this did not go over well. He threw his board down in a heavy display of disgust and spat out a "Later!" The board's thunk tossed sand all over us, and he stalked away, shaking the water and muck from his sun-streaked locks.

That was then and this is today. I look up at Gibson's expectant face. *Forgive me, God, but I so want to lie right now.* "Mmm. Great ride." Not exactly a lie.

"Man, I iced it! O-lympic quality."

"I'm glad for you, Gibson!" We both look toward the water and watch Nathan bail on a wave.

"Bummer!" we both shout.

I pull myself up, my visit to the beach sweet but brief. "Well, I'm carpool today," I say. "You boys come on back and get cleaned up. I'll be waiting for you." No use avoiding my day any longer. I've got a midmorning tour to host, not to mention a new boss to meet. *Can't wait.*

Later, from my convertible Bug I watch the boys dawdle on their school's front lawn. Funny that my kid attends the type of school that always made me gag. Private schools just seemed so snobbish. I always imagined that most students there had names like Bunny and Edgerton and arrived to campus in a Rolls Royce.

Who knew that someday I'd be chauffeuring my surf kid in a VW to a similar school? I see another boy sidle up to Nathan and Gibson, and soon they're kicking a Hacky Sack around. I catch Nathan glancing back at me and shoo them inside with my hand. Reluctantly they turn and begin walking through the campus. With a punch of a button, I tune the radio to 100.7 KHAY and pull out of the lot.

Jon and Charlye are on the air, asking the age-old question: Why do women who absolutely should not wear belly shirts, wear them anyway? Instinctively, I touch my tummy and second-guess my decision to eat brownies for breakfast.

Back home, I dash inside. Just an hour left to get ready for work. The machine's blinking, so I hit the button and hear Gaby's voice. "Hey, Bri-Bri. It's me." I love that she can say that and I know who *me* is. "Have you heard any more from Kate? I ran into Rachel yesterday and she told me that she saw her leaving a thrift store downtown. I think it was the one by the Mission. Anyway, Rachel was driving down Main Street and called out, but Kate acted like she didn't hear. I guess she had a scowl on her face too. She's such a crabby patty these days, thought you might have talked with her. Not that you *should* talk with her after she—"

The machine cuts Gaby off. I've kicked off my flip-flops and plunked onto the floor. The second message starts while I'm pulling on my socks, an unfortunate necessity for frequent bus rides.

"—dissed you at Bunko." Gaby's an expert at picking up where she left off. "So, I've got tons of orders to fill today. And you're probably running a tour. Call me when you can. Dying to talk more about your *muy rara* mother-in-law." Funny how she lapses into Spanish like that, especially when being critical. I think she just called Mona an oddball. "Okay, well, love ya. Bye. Oh, and Bri? I'm feeling better today . . . about Franklin and all. And I'm open to your suggestions, you know, about finding the right someone—you're so good at that. Well. Bye."

With all that's happened in the past twenty-four hours, I nearly forgot about Franklin the weasel. Ugh. I'm such a bad friend sometimes. The answering machine beeps and a robotic voice tells me there are no more messages. *Mental note: Give best friend a call today.*

It occurs to me then that I haven't yet told Gaby, nor Douglas even, about Rita's sudden departure from the company. *Life's such a blur sometimes.* I make another mental note, this one reminding me to fill them both in on the sudden changes at Coastal Tours. It'll be more fun after getting a load of my boyish new boss anyway.

The sun's hiding just behind the mist when I reach the tour office at the harbor. I sit in my Bug, trying to get my bearings, feeling more like a child pouting in the dentist's office than a mature wife and mother. I so don't wanna go in there today. Maybe I'll just stow away on someone's yacht. *Oh yeah, that's the ticket.*

I squint into the sparkling fog and spot a thirty-foot-plus sloop, its tall, proud mast aiming for the heavens. *Makes me think about Kenny Chesney singing "Soul of a Sailor."* I imagine hopping aboard, throwing down the rigging, and setting off into the misty day. *Ahoy, matey!* Just last month I read in the newspaper about a local couple who did set sail for an entire year. Only they brought along two kids, a dog, and three iguanas—*iguanas!* I'd hate to find out what they'll do if they should ever run out of food. . . .

Enough of this frivolity! Ready or not, time to face the day. I take my whistle—the one I use in my "bit" to entertain the tourists—and lock the car door. Before ducking inside the tour office, I take one more look at the calm seawater and let loose a heavy sigh.

Once inside I see Luann standing behind the reception desk. She looks like she's just been handed a four-pack to Disneyland. Actually, her face is more flushed than that. It's like she's just ridden the Matterhorn—twice.

"What's up, Lu?" I ask.

She's wide-eyed, and her voice hisses in a good way. Sort of. "He's here."

Super. "Who's here?" I ask, innocent as a beach bunny.

"You know—*him*—the one from out of town." She's talking out of the corner of her mouth, voice low, like she's hiding morning breath.

"Get out! ET's here? Quick, hand him the phone."

She slaps the counter with a stack of files. "No. Mrs. Holland's son. Tyler M. Holland. Our new boss, remember?"

And I could forget . . . how? "He's here already, huh?"

"Oh yes. He seems very punctual . . . among other things." She's doing that whispering thing again and winking her right eye at me like she's got a speck in it. "Hubba, hubba, if you know what I mean."

I scrunch up my nose and nod. Great. Inexperienced and hot. A real poser—what Nathan and his buddies call a would-be surfer—someone who just looks the part. Better get out my resumé tonight, 'cuz this place is goin' down.

I hear the clicking of Rita's high-heeled sandals approach from the hall. "Brianna, you *are* here. Wonderful." Rita's all smiles as she escorts a tallish, blond-haired man toward me. She gives him a per-functory shove in my direction. "Ty, I'd like you to meet Brianna Stone, my friend and an absolutely top-notch tour host."

This is the kid? Ty M. Holland? Hmm. Taller, more handsome, and frankly, smarter looking than I'd imagined.

He extends his hand to me. "It's a pleasure, Brianna."

I shake his hand. "Welcome to Coastal Tours, Ty. Happy to meet you." I almost flinch in an attempt to avoid that incoming bolt of lightning.

Ty stands nearly as tall as Douglas, although my hubby would never wear his hair so long. Rita's first husband must have been a big man, because she's so petite and Ty is so *not*. No wonder Luann's face flushed deeper than a tomato. If I'm not mistaken, Ty could double as a swashbuckler on the cover of a dime store novel. One like that dog-eared copy Luann's hiding behind the reception desk.

"I'd like to meet with you soon, Brianna, to discuss a new market-ing strategy." The cover art speaks! "Perhaps we can work up some collaborative solutions to better compete in Ventura's burgeoning travel marketplace."

Alrighty then. "Sure, Ty. I'm not sure how I can help with outside sales, but I'd do just about anything to keep Coastal Tours number one in our area." I smile at Rita. "Your mother has done such a great job all these years. I'm going to miss her."

He surprises me then by reaching out and drawing his mother in for a hug. "Yes, she has," he says with affection. What did my driver Ned say about men who love their mother? "She deserves this new phase in her life. I'm pleased that I can be here to help facilitate that for her."

I slide a glance at our ever-efficient Luann, who's leaning on her elbow and paying rapt attention to Ty's *Fabio-meets-Dilbert* impression. *Is that saliva pooling in the corner of her mouth?*

The whole display *is* kind of charming. Bummer. I really had not planned on liking this guy. I'm already grieving the loss of all the lousy-boss jokes I'd thought up. Still, it's better to swallow that old bitter pill of pride and admit when I'm wrong. And apparently I was wrong about Ty. What did Jesus say about the meek? That they'd inherit the earth? I'm tasting a heaping scoop of topsoil right about now.

There's a lesson in here somewhere. Scripture says to train a child in the way he should go, and when he is old he'll come home and run the family business. Or something like that. Ugh. How could I believe that Rita's son would be anything but a stellar example of humanity? I really should be ashamed. Or at least a bit sheepish.

"Time to get ready for my tour," I say, almost tripping over the tail between my legs as I back up. "Rita, I hope we'll have another chance to talk when I get back. Ty, again, good to meet you."

His smile's a winner. "And you as well, Brianna. I look forward to dialoguing with you over lunch." He gives his mother's shoulders a squeeze before leaning casually against the counter. "Are you available tomorrow?"

"Um. Tomorrow." I look to Luann. "I might have a tour then. Do I?"

The receptionist gives the schedule book a cursory glance. She shakes her head, indicating that I'm free as a seagull. Her cheeks still hold a tinge of pink. "You could meet at Opa!"

"Excellent," says Ty, dropping a fist onto the counter. "Meet me there at eleven-thirty and be ready to discuss ways to future-proof Coastal Tours."

"Sure," I answer back, trying not to let my reluctance show. I'll be sure to bring along a dictionary too.

Chapter nine

Don't look now, but my folly's showing. I'm thinking this as I listen to the pluck of a lyre and watch Ty dip hot pita wedges into some creamy hummus. We're seated at Opa!, and I'm caught between considering the depth of my own wickedness and questioning the management's placement of a disco ball over the nearby dance floor.

This place is so *My Big Fat Greek Wedding*. I'm overwhelmed by the mingling aromas of gyros and baklava, and the sheer voluptuousness of the stuffed grape leaves on our table. Wouldn't surprise me in the least to see Michael Constantine stroll by carrying a bottle of Windex. Maybe a shot of that would cure my bout of foolishness.

I barely had time to read the Bible this morning—okay, I slept in, thereby sealing the outcome of my devotion time—but I did manage to read through some Proverbs. It wasn't pretty. In particular I was struck by a verse in chapter thirteen that said, essentially, that the prudent act out of knowledge and the rest are fools.

So hand me my dunce cap and a piece of chalk. I've got a hundred lines to write on the blackboard.

Ty pops a kalamata olive into his mouth. "Aren't you hungry?" he

asks, obviously aware that he alone has nearly emptied both appetizer plates.

"I'll just wait for lunch," I say, not mentioning that the smell of garlic (and chalk dust) is getting to me.

"Very good. What do you suggest here?"

Anything in a to-go container. "I've heard the lamb is popular. And the meatballs."

"I prefer a more healthful constitution. I'll have the moussaka and a salad with feta. Have you decided?"

I scan the menu quickly, hoping to find something with a familiar ring to it. "A cheeseburger," I answer.

"Is that all?" he asks, expressionless.

"With fries and a Coke."

Ty catches the eye of our waiter, who scurries over to us and takes our orders. Menus gone, Ty crosses his arms and leans onto the table.

"I understand, Brianna, that you have a keen understanding of the average tourist's mind."

I stifle a laugh. "Beach tourists just want to get away from their problems. They want to leave their worries at home, Ty. No big mystery there. Most of them just want to smell the salt in the air, eat a great meal, and get the inside scoop."

"Scoop about what?"

"You know, like who serves the freshest fish or which celebrities have boats docked nearby. And where, of course."

"And you know all that?"

I cock my head to one side. "It's my job to know. Besides, I love this city. It's my home. I guess I want to know this stuff too."

He stares at me and leans in like he's about to say something. But a commotion around the corner interrupts us.

I sneak a peek and am surprised to see Livi and Kate at another table, playing tug-of-war with the lunch check. *Have they been there all this time?* Kate's staring down Livi, who appears to be winning.

Ty frowns at the interruption. "Friends of yours?"

"Actually, yes. Will you excuse me?" I slide out of our booth, barely waiting for his response, and head over.

Livi looks up as I approach. "Bri, hey," she says, the check now fully in her possession. "Saw you over there but didn't want to interrupt. How are you?"

She's chipper as always. If I hadn't heard Kate's heated voice a minute ago, I'd never have known of the scuffle. "Can't complain. What's going on with you two?"

Kate sits back in a huff. "Nothing. Just two good pals enjoying lunch."

I purse my lips and look to Livi. She gives a light laugh. "Oh, you know how it is. Kate and I are arguing over whose turn it is to pick up the check." Livi puts the bill into her lap and focuses on Kate. "This one is mine, friend. You get the next one."

Kate's eyes avoid mine. "Sure. Whatever."

Livi's sights are set on Ty now. "So where'd you find him, Bri? He looks like one of those Greek gods come to life!"

"Ya think? Which one?"

We both giggle and I relax a little. "That's my new boss. Rita's hitting the road. She's decided to travel the world, so her son, Ty, has taken over," I say with a quick jerk of my head. "That's him."

"Married?"

I wrinkle my forehead. How could I not know this? "Guess not."

"Hmm. If I were in the market . . ."

I let out a laugh. "And you're *not* 'in the market'? Why not?"

Livi shrugs. "You know, been there, done that." She peeks at Ty again. "He is a looker, though. Love the hair. He reminds me of Travis Tritt."

Her observation switches on a light bulb in my mind. He does have that sort of bad-boy-of-Country-music thing going on. The hair, the gritty voice . . . who knows? Maybe there's even a rebel hiding underneath all that business-speak.

Kate's tapping her fingers on the table. "Isn't that your food being served?"

I catch Ty smirking at my cheese-slathered burger and fries. "Yeah. Okay. Guess I should get back. See you at the next Bunko?"

Kate exhales but doesn't say a word.

Livi's her regular smiley self. "I'll be there, and hey," she says with a nod in Ty's direction. "Why not bring him along . . . for Gaby. I'm sure you've thought of that already, huh?"

Um, actually, no. "Natch," I answer back, the big liar that I am. "But he'll have to meet her another time—away from prying eyes, girlfriend."

With a renewed sense of purpose before me, I practically skip back to the table. Gaby calls it my *mothering* instinct, and at the moment, I'm feeling quite maternal toward her. Ty gives me a wink, and I imagine my friend being on the other end of his attentions.

Then the euphoria over this moment dulls slightly after I slide into the booth, wondering where my mind has been. Why hadn't I immediately considered Ty as perfect-man material for Gaby? Maybe because I've been so myopic lately, so engrossed with questions about my own life. *How pathetic.* Or maybe because I hadn't yet shaken away my initial impression of Ty as a spoiled brat. *Shame.*

Well. It's not too late. It's *never* too late! I slip a glance at his ring finger, just to make sure it's absolutely metal-free, and dig in to my fries.

Ty sets down his fork. "Let's get back to discussing ways to facilitate a larger draw for Coastal Tours, Brianna." He leans in toward me and lowers his voice. "I want us to put our heads together and come up with a solid go-to-market sales strategy. What thoughts do you have?"

Thoughts? Hm. Well, for one, I'm wondering if the son you and Gaby cre-

ate together someday will have hair like a wild stallion . . .

He continues to stare at me, when I suddenly blurt out, "What does your middle initial M stand for?"

A flash of something crosses his face. Confusion maybe? Then he shrugs. "Just a fancy way of saying *minion*."

"Minion?"

"I'm not like other bosses, Brianna. I get in the trenches, just like everyone else."

So he's witty. "Okay, too personal. Sorry." Do I need to be so obvious? I'm an embarrassment to matchmakers everywhere. If I had a license for this sort of side job, it would be revoked and burned. He probably thinks I'm a nut, which at least offers me the consolation of never being asked to a power-lunch again.

"Brianna," he says, even after I've butted in to his personal space, "you are everything my mother said you were."

In my best squeaky-girl voice, had I actually asked, "What's the M in your name stand for?" Sheesh. "Yeah, well, I'm sure there's plenty she hasn't told you."

"Really? Give me an example."

"Hm. Well . . ." *Just how did the subject turn to me?* My mind's racing, searching for a new topic, when a half-naked woman invades our oxygen. She's wrapped in scarves and doing a curvy tableside dance, her finger cymbals smacking away. I'd forgotten about the authentic live entertainment at Opa! *Personally I'd rather watch a frog dissection while eating my lunch, but that's just me.*

I'm trying to read Ty's poker face. Maybe he, too, is squeamish inside and hiding it. Or what if he's amused, like belly dancing is commonplace in his world? *I so don't want to go there.* Actually, I so don't want to be here either. The dancer's eyes are on Ty alone (thank God for small favors), and she's swinging her mane of shiny red hair like it's a cape in front of a bull.

So help me if he pulls a dollar from his wallet . . .

He does reach for his wallet but pulls out a Visa instead. He holds his hand up in the air and signals the waiter with the credit card clamped between two fingers. The waiter has to dodge under and around the ample-hipped dancer just to grab Ty's company card. I'm relieved that this lunch has nearly ended.

Yet I couldn't have asked for a better test of Ty's character. What better way to judge a man's worthiness to date your best friend than to see firsthand his *non*-reaction to the belly dancer from *Desperate Housewives*.

With a flourish, Ty signs the bill, and I feel my shoulders relax. The fog's lifting, and a calming prayer-walk at low tide beckons me. I always head to the sand when I need to clear away my thoughts and talk to God, and there's much for us to discuss. Right now I want His take on the weird nigglings I've had about Douglas lately. I'm also ready to explode with the prospect of Ty dating Gaby. So what if I've just met the man? He's Rita's son, and that ought to count for something. It ought to count for a lot.

My heart's heady with anticipation of ending this corporate pow-wow, and swooshing my toes into wet sand. I'm glad that Ty cares so much about his mother's business that he's asked for my input. I'm flattered really. But business buzzwords are *so* not me. Besides, my mind's already creating little prayers by the sea. I hear God best there. And personally, I think He rather likes those times too. Something about the beach environment makes my Lord downright chatty.

Bill paid, we leave our booth. We're walking toward the restaurant's exit, past the bust of Zeus, when Ty suddenly turns to me. "I'd like your opinion on some new meeting space I'm considering, Brianna. It won't take long."

I follow him but hesitate to answer. "Okay," I finally say, "I've got a minute. What would you like to know?"

"Since you're available now, let's drive over." He leads me into the parking lot, to a stealth-gray Hummer parked diagonally across two spaces. "Hop in."

I gulp. *Hop in? Hey, how about finding me a step stool?* "Don't you need a special license to drive that thing?"

He laughs at this. "I like you. You're all right."

So what's not to like? Still, I bite my lip, seeing my beach walk fading away. I take another look at the behemoth machine in front of me and wonder if I should be wearing Army fatigues.

"C'mon," he says, holding open the passenger-side door. "It's a short drive to Marinawalk."

Marinawalk Resort sits waterside, with views of the main channel. Coastal Tours used to run groups through there, but then they took on a massive remodeling project and we drifted to other properties around town. I *have* been meaning to stop in and have a look around. . . .

So I relent and use Ty's outstretched arm to steady myself and climb aboard the *truck with testosterone*. Sinking into the cavernous seat, I peek at my cell phone's clock and hope I'll still have time to walk the sand before Nathan gets home. My kiddo's hanging with Gibson for the afternoon, then it'll be study, din-din, and cross-country.

On our way, Ty gives me the rundown of his plans to use Marinawalk's dockside meeting room for a special hors d'oeuvres hour for hotel guests and others interested in touring with us. Unfortunately, he misses the sharp left onto the hotel's drive and we're stuck at a stop light. *Can't wait to see this thing pull a U-y.*

I'm nearly lulled by the *click-click* of the Hummer's blinker when my eyes catch sight of a familiar black convertible traveling south. At first it's hard to tell, but then I know it's Douglas, and my heart does a little flip at the sight of him.

I raise my hand to wave—as if he'd really notice me way up here in this street tank—and stop in midair. An icy chill flows through my skin in sheets, from scalp to fingers, when I see Douglas and Kendall Beck—his firm's newest associate and a willowy blonde to boot— drive by without so much as a glance in my direction.

I flex my hands twice in response. Ty clears his throat, and slowly I come back to my right mind. Truth is, court must be dark today. That's when the judge takes a break from trial, giving all parties the day off. Douglas hadn't mentioned this. Then again, why would he? It's not like he needs to give me a play-by-play of his workday. He and Kendall must have had some big snooze of a meeting to attend. I'm sure of it. Just some real *yawner* of a meeting in downtown Oxnard.

I swallow and turn my face back to the road in front of us, feeling the slightest burn in my cheeks. Out of the corner of my eyes I can tell that Ty's staring at me. I don't look at him. The signal changes to a green arrow, but Ty's still watching me.

"The light," I say, pointing.

"Forget about the light," he says. "Why the sad look on that pretty face?"

Oh, ugh. "But you're going to miss your turn!" *Go, already!*

A driver leans on his horn somewhere behind us. Not that we could see him if we tried. Ty's *auto with an attitude* would've made a great shield during all those hide-and-seek games I played as a kid. A second horn blasts with more intensity. Or maybe it's the same driver as before, only angrier. Hard to tell.

Ty relents. He steps on the gas and manages to make the 180-degree turn in one try. We pull into the hotel parking lot and I'm suddenly wishing I had not agreed to this last stop. Seeing my husband with another woman, even though there are a million legitimate explanations for such a sight, has caused my stomach to churn. I reach into my purse and touch my cell phone. Calling him now would pique Ty's curiosity, but big deal.

Ty switches off the massive engine and turns to me. "It didn't appear that Greek food did much for you, Brianna. I've heard of this little Mexican place—"

I cut him off, glad that he seems to have forgotten about my momentary shock back at the light. I shove my phone deeper into my bag. My personal life is none of my new boss's business. "Ty!" I say with a new burst of urgency. "Want to meet a great gal?"

He blinks a couple of times, and a slow smile spreads across his face.

"I hope this isn't too personal."

"Go on."

"I'd like for you to meet my best friend. *She* loves Mexican food, she's even half Mexican. But she's more than that. She's pretty and fun and smart. I think you two would like each other." *So what if Ty's not my type, Gaby'll be crazy for him.*

He leans against the driver-side window, his eyes on me. "Sure. Just leave her number with Luann and I will contact her."

I nod, yet bliss eludes me. I know I should feel downright elated that I finally may have found Gaby's Mr. *So* Right. After all, he's my beloved Rita's son, and now the top dog at Coastal Tours. But I can't get my own Mister out of my mind. Even as Ty and I stroll along the boat-lined path to the hotel's fireside meeting area, with the summer sun attempting to burst through the clouds, I just can't shake away the fog rolling through my own head.

Chapter ten

"We are like eggs at present. And you cannot go on indefinitely being just an ordinary, decent egg. We must be hatched or go bad."

C. S. Lewis said that. Haven't the foggiest what he meant or why he said it, but I read it on the back of a paper bag from the Christian bookstore, so it must have meant something to somebody.

I've never been wild about change. Maybe that's because I spent so many of my teen years rifling through a duffle bag in search of a clean pair of undies or the like. When I finally rented a room of my own with my coffeehouse earnings, I reveled in the luxury of actually having a drawer to place my things. A place where I could *always* find what I needed. So what if that place turned out to be a file cabinet doubling for a dresser? At least it was reliable.

Back then I decided to put down roots. My mother said that was nutty—putting down roots in the sand. Both my parents, God bless their souls, were wanderers, chasing every whim of fancy, every hint of adventure anywhere but in the States. Which, *hello,* happened to be where we all were born. Except for my light russet locks and longish nose—and my sometimes flippant tongue—I might have wondered if

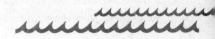

they were really my parents at all. I was nothing like them.

Which I guess made things easier when they'd fly off somewhere, leaving me with Aunt Dot. They took me along when I was little. Or so I've heard. But later, when the choice was given, I'd choose to stay near my beloved Pacific Ocean, where I could crunch sand beneath my feet and while doing so not have to fend off flying insects the size of my big toe.

The thought of my fairly unattractive, most base extremity makes me laugh, and the sensation feels good. It's dark out now and I'm curled up in a papasan chair on my back deck, remembering the first time Douglas's toes wiggled next to mine in the sand. The memory causes my heart to do a little tumble. Up until that day, about a month after we began dating, I'd seen him wearing only the finest suits and accessories. Very Hugh Grant in *Sense and Sensibility*—only without all that awkwardness.

Frankly, it's his own fault that the sight of so much of his skin caused my cheeks to burn. What was he thinking? I'd never even seen him in Dockers, let alone board shorts and a worn-out tank that had seen too many pick-up games of basketball. It both amazed and thrilled me that he owned casual wear at all.

We sat low in chairs on the beach, watching the rolling surf. My favorite kind of day. Heavy winds blew waves into a curl, then nearly dissipated at the shoreline, leaving behind a balmy breeze for sunbathers. The ocean laid itself out as a playground for surfers and bodyboarders of all ages and types.

Douglas dug his foot sideways into the sand until it bumped against mine. The move pushed cool, mushy sand onto my ankle, giving me goose bumps. "I could get used to this," he whispered.

Get used to what? To lounging on the beach, or being mine forever?
"Really?" I answered, momentarily tongue-tied.

He reached two strong arms toward the sky, clasped his hands and stretched. Mmm, could he have been any more sexy? "We never did this when I was a kid, Brianna." He relaxed those handsome arms and folded them behind his head, using his open hands to rest his neck. In the distance, a pelican circled over the water, intent on lunch. "My parents preferred the country-club lifestyle up in the mountains to the beach crowd. My mother rarely let my father forget her disenchantment with living so far away from city life. Ojai was Dad's attempt at offering her something more upscale than a beach town could offer at the time. Still, it was never luxurious enough, but we stayed in Ojai anyway, mostly on our own property. I'll tell you something we didn't do: We never sat on the sand, soakin' up rays."

Douglas uttered that last phrase with an almost right-on surfer voice. I'm not sure what tripped me out more. His attempt at surfer humor or the fact that he'd been raised so close to the beach yet never tossed a Frisbee on it. *How weird is that?* I figured he must be joking, and so I laughed.

He answered with a hearty laugh of his own. It seemed to growl right from his heart. And yet when I looked into his chiseled features, his skin beginning to pink from the sun's embrace, I saw the truth in his news flash. A heart-catching smile shaped his mouth, but the thinly veiled sadness in his eyes revealed that he wasn't kidding.

I drew closer to him, nearly tipping sideways out of my cheap aluminum beach chair. "So," I said, hoping he hadn't noticed my klutziness, "how about dolphins? You must've come down to watch them play sometimes, right? South of the Rincon?" That's a cool strip of surf beach at the northernmost coastal point in Ventura.

He searched my face before reaching over and gently touching that place beneath my chin. "Your face lights up when you talk about the beach. Did you know that?"

I felt a rosiness spreading across my skin, and it wasn't because of the shining sun. His thumb and forefinger still lightly held my chin. *Heart, be still.* I prodded him. "You've really never seen the dolphins play?"

He lowered his hand to the chair rail but kept his gaze on me. "I think I may have seen some once or twice, when we drove up the coast on the 101." He looked back at the surf and sighed quietly. "Then again, they could have been whales for all I knew. I wish I could remember."

We quietly watched as a lone pelican flew closer to shore before slowing. A second brown bird joined the hunt, and then a third. Now three ungainly birds circled, their keen eyes focused on the water below. Like synchronized swimmers, each plunged headfirst into the surf, one right after the other, and returned to the air with their pouches expanded by a brimming midday catch.

Douglas whistled. "Spectacular . . ."

I sidled up next to him. "You know what's probably coming up next, don't you?"

He raised his eyebrows and gave me a mischievous grin, causing me to again feel my face change from tan to crimson in the same flash of time. I pulled my gaze away from him and toward the surf. "Dolphins," I said, forcing my voice to be calm.

He leaned toward me, and I felt the warmth of his closeness. "You seem pretty sure of yourself."

If only you knew how wrong you are.

Douglas stood abruptly then, sending his chair flopping backwards onto the sand. He whistled once more, only this time louder and longer.

I followed his line of vision, but did I need to? Instinctively I knew what had grabbed his attention and held on to it, undivided. You can't have experienced such an event as often as I had not to at least *sense* when it might happen again. Some of the signs had been there all morning—fat waves, pelicans circling overhead, shallow waters swollen with tiny fish. Seriously, what more predictable day for dolphins to appear could there be? And appear they had, with a flourish.

Yet I was far from jaded. Not that I shouldn't have been. Back then, whenever my parents left for some far-off land, my wacky aunt Dot would wake me early and like a drill sergeant say, "Up and at 'em, kiddo!" Then we'd march the three-quarters of a mile down to the beach to watch dolphins surf the waves. I mean, I loved watching them in the morning, but at 5:30 A.M.? What ten-year-old wants to get up before the seagulls?

Still, their grace and stunning beauty gripped me each and every time they swam into view. Even as a young adult. At the first sign of their glistening bodies gliding through the surf, I became like an excited eight-year-old bouncing in line while waiting for a seat on the Ferris wheel at the county fair.

I could see that same thrill catching hold of Douglas. He continued to stand next to me, muscular arms folded across his chest, wide smile in his expression, as three dolphins danced their way up the coast. As much as I longed to watch the mesmerizing creatures, I could hardly rip my eyes from the animation playing out on his face.

He nodded his head. "You really know what you're talking about, Bri. Sorry I ever doubted you."

You doubted me?

He continued with a serious sort of appreciation in his voice. "I just can't believe how you *knew* those dolphins would be here. You're amazing."

I was unsure of how to respond, and so I said the first thing to pop into my head. "Just stick with me, Dougie."

He smiled again and shot back a simple, "I plan to."

———

I rifle my hand through my hair and groan. I'm snuggled into the thickly padded chair, listening to the endless twitter of sparrows in the night sky interrupted by the occasional goose flyover. In the background, water lofts onto shore. The sounds calm me like Aunt Dot's beloved chamomile tea always soothed her frenetic ways. That's all I want at the moment—to have my chaotic thoughts pulled from my internal, churning abyss and laid gently onto the sand. Like a mollusk shell at low tide.

I'm still wrapped inside memories of the early days with Douglas when another thought dive-bombs me from out of the night sky. She came from New York, the daughter of Mona's best friend. I remember coming undone when I'd learned, quite by accident, that Douglas had met Denise for lunch at the pier in Santa Barbara.

"The biggest mistake of my life," he had told me afterward about their lunch.

No kidding. She'd been his high school sweetheart back when her mother and Mona drank Long Island iced teas courtside on simmering Ojai afternoons. Mona had hoped to follow her best friend's family when they relocated to New York, but DM would not hear of it. That hitch in Mona's plans did little to stop her from flying Denise back to Ventura, however, in an all-out effort to stop our wedding.

It almost worked.

Nothing significant happened between Douglas and his old flame, but his willingness to secretly meet her, out of the area, nicked the tender underpinnings of our burgeoning relationship. I learned about it only after he'd left his watch with its broken band back at the restaurant. A waitress there who lived near me dropped it by the coffeehouse.

He confessed before I even had the chance to tell him that his watch was tucked into my beach bag. He dropped to his knees and swore his love for me. I forgave him and promised never to bring it up again. We were married beneath the hazy sunlight of a beach day in early spring. But some memories have roots that run deeper than burrowing sand crabs, and it can take an awfully heavy shovel to dig them up.

I hear the screen door squeak open and look over to see Nathan's freckled face, illuminated by a sliver of moonlight. He looks both thoughtful and pensive as his eyes adjust to the darkness. His expression reminds me of Douglas. "Night, Mom," he calls out softly as he sees me curled up on the chair.

"Night, punkin," I call back.

He wrinkles his nose at the nickname but doesn't say anything. Some things never change. My heart grips at the thought that they ever would. I shut my eyes. Just like when I was a young thing trying to find my one true place to call home, change is still an unwelcome thought.

Chapter eleven

Douglas was up and out of our beach pad early. The trial again. I'd waited up, half intending to unload my worries on him, but never got the chance. Despite leaving the bedroom lamp on, I fell asleep sitting up.

In a way, I'm glad. I had allowed myself a heavy dose of wallowing, and this morning my body felt as if I'd spent the night scaling and crawling across the rocky jetties of Ventura Beach. The suspicions that furrowed my brow into the night left me achy and tired, and although I long to see my husband for more than a quick moment each day, rehashing the past is not how I envision those times. Nor do I think brief interludes are the best moments to toss around accusations, especially ones rooted in old news.

It's not that I don't think I have the right to know the whereabouts of my other half when he's not with me. I didn't make up the two-becoming-one issue; that was God's idea. It's just that in my wedding vows I promised to honor Douglas, and barging into his office demanding to know where he was going yesterday with his too-thin, bleached-blond legal associate is just too daytime television.

So here I stand at the front of the bus, waiting for the customary

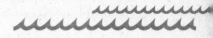

jostling to subside and for the students—my tour for the morning—to finally settle on a seat. Why the parents of a busload of junior high school students from Pittsburgh would choose faraway Ventura over the much-closer Washington, D.C., as an eighth-grade class trip is anybody's guess. I'm glad they did. There's nothing like exposing a bevy of ocean-deprived teens to a surfer's paradise to change one's mood. And mine's still needing an extreme makeover just about now.

I drag my mind away from yesterday's weirdness, lunch at Opa! included, and focus on my immediate goal of entertaining two dozen students for the next couple of hours. As I watch the fracas with a smile pasted on, I can't help wondering if my well of jokes runs deep enough to sustain this crowd today.

From my perch I can see clouds thinning over the sand dunes just across from us, and the sight wraps me like a warm blanket on a breezy day. The smell of the sea tempts me with its allure, and I'm already checking the time on the watch I wear exclusively on tour days. *Maybe later there'll be time to borrow a cheap novel from Luann and head on out to the sand. . . .*

The kids have just spent a lively morning touring the Robert J. Lagomarsino Visitor Center, where park rangers lectured them about the Channel Islands National Park, a string of federally protected islands just off the coast from here. No doubt they climbed the center's tall tower to view the majestic islands through rusty telescopes and to hang their teenage bodies over the side railings playing out scenes from *Spiderman*. Afterward they would have been asked to sit still and view the twenty-five-minute park movie, *Treasure in the Sea*. This would explain their obvious need to leap around the bus and virtually ignore me.

I finger the whistle hanging around my neck. In the back row, four women with droopy bags under their eyes chatter on into oblivion. So much for relying on the chaperones. I square my shoulders, pull in a deep breath, and open my mouth to deliver a loud and firm,

"Ladies and Gentlemen!" when Ned climbs aboard sporting a blue Dodgers baseball cap.

Funny thing, but the color of that hat alone makes me long for a Dodger dog smothered in mustard and a large soda, aka "pop" to the easterners on this bus. At just sixty miles north of LA, Venturans regularly hop on the 101 freeway to make the opening pitch at Dodger Stadium and, of course, to nosh on a foot-long dog.

From midway down the aisle, the tallest kid in the class stands and cups his mouth with his hands, suddenly yanking me from my reverie. "The Dodgers stink!"

I wince, knowing how my driver will take such an insult hurled at his beloved baseball team. *May have to ask Luann for a replacement chauffeur today.* I peek at Ned and see his lips doing that funky suckling thing. His heavy jowls have joined in. Not a good start to our tour.

Ned points at the boy. "Son," he says, "come here."

Oh my.

The kid jerks his bangs from his eyes but obediently moves forward. The entire under-sixteen population of the bus breaks out with, "Whoa-a-a," followed by a raucous, "Let's go Bucs! Let's go Bucs!"— the cheer for their own beloved Pirates baseball team.

I suppose I could step in and shoo Ned away, but I don't. I'm as curious as the next gal. So I half sit, half lean against the front dash and wait, all the while wondering how Ned's too-small hat stays on his rather large head.

Ned puts a beefy hand on the boy's shoulder. "Turn and face your peers, son."

The boy nods respectfully, albeit with a mischievous smile.

"What's your name, son?"

"Jacob."

Ned's pensive. "Ah," he finally says, "a biblical name. Although, if my age-ed mind recalls, that boy got himself in a mite of trouble, didn't he."

Jacob shrugs. "I guess."

"And you weren't wantin' to be in trouble, now were ya?"

"No, sir."

"That's what I thought. So I'm givin' you a little gift. For your faithfulness." Ned doffs his Dodgers cap and places it on Jacob's head, pulling it down snugly around the edges. I raise my eyebrows at this, but the other students on the bus reassure me with their good-natured cheers. One pretty little thing in the second row even calls out, "Blue's your color, Jakey!" This brings on another round of "Whoa-a-as" from the celebratory junior high grads.

And we're off. For the next couple of hours we mosey along coastal Ventura and points north, with Ned as our driver and Dodger boy Jake riding shotgun. I ask the kids riveting questions such as, "How much deeper would the ocean be if sponges didn't grow in it?" and "Why didn't Noah go fishing?" (Answer: he only had two worms.) The kids toss me answers from their creative young brains. It's a banner day, with plenty of dolphin and sea lion sightings to thrill them. Frankly, the sightings thrill me too. By the end of the morning, I feel a slight lift in the sullen mood that darkened my heart earlier in the day.

It's nearly lunchtime and I'm watching the kids disembark back at the harbor tour office. One by one they exit the stairway and give me their own style of thanks—a shy smile, a hoarse "Thank you, ma'am." I even received one of those cool float pens with the skyline of Pittsburgh imbedded in it.

When the stragglers have all rambled out, I get a load of Ned, waving away from the front end of the bus. I hide a smirk at the transformation. There he stands, his lips calm, his mouth smiling. A gold-and-black Pirates baseball cap—a gift from one of the chaperones—perches on his head. Proof that just maybe it's never too late for change.

I'm pondering this when my cell starts vibrating against my waist. I try to read the text message on the screen, but the sun's brilliance is just too much. We can send a man to the moon, but is it too much to ask for non-glare plastic on my cell phone?

A quick duck under a nearby building's overhang cuts the intense shine. It's Ty and he wants me to "pencil in a concept meeting" for next week. *Grrr. Here's a concept for you: No.* Okay, okay. I'm better than that. *No, please.*

I'm still scowling when I catch sight of Kate walking from the parking lot. She's moving tentatively in a straight black skirt, sandy-colored collared blouse, and strappy heels. On her face she's wearing that newly familiar frown of hers. Then again, who am I to talk? Haven't actually been my chirpy self these days.

I've got to say, though, that seeing Kate in anything other than a waistless flower-print dress has definitely tamed my touch of surliness. I'm hiding in the shadows now, like something out of a Hitchcock movie, thinking I missed my calling. Think intrigue, suspense, mys-t-e-ry. Kate stops near dock nine, bends and rubs her knee. A secret signal perhaps? Or did she just get a run in her stocking?

My cell vibrates against my hand, and I yelp. Kate spots my hideout and narrows her eyes. *Cover's blown.* I fumble with my phone with all the nonchalance of a sixteen-year-old during her first day on the job.

Kate approaches. "What are you doing, Brianna, hiding in the dark like that?" She's got this way about her, this unexplained way of bullying me. Or at least trying to.

I hold up my phone. "Just checking my messages."

"Uh-huh." She's nodding continuously. "So I suppose you just finished up one of your little tours."

I sigh dramatically. "Yeah. Had a busload of teenagers today. I'm beat."

She snorts. "If you can call riding around sunny Ventura *work*." She gives me a smug smile, like I just wouldn't understand. "Today I've already patched up two pair of jeans, mopped the entire house, mulched the back garden, and prepared turkey cutlets for our family supper tonight."

Supper? Where are we, England?

"And what are you putting in your microwave after all your work?" She draws out the word *work* like it's in need of a good scrubbing.

"Not sure," I answer, taking note of the sun overhead. "Haven't thought about it yet. Maybe I'll get take-out."

"Uh-huh." She's nodding again, like she knew I would say that.

Alrighty. Subject change. "So," I say in my most singsongy voice. "You're quite the fashion statement today, Kate. What brings you to our beautiful harbor?"

That usually purposeful gaze of hers starts flitting around. First along the boat-lined pathway, then out toward the water. She even sweeps her gaze across the parking lot. *Hmm. Being tailed perhaps? Or does she have a tick?* Then she gives a sort of vacant look. "Did you say something?" she asks, her brow wrinkled as a bulldog.

Ooh-key. "I was just wondering where you're off to . . . all dressed up."

She humphs. "Brianna," she says with drama, "just because we live at the beach doesn't mean we should dress like we're going to the beach. You know that I *always* try to look my best."

And those floral frocks say "best" how. . . ?

Kate checks the time on her locket-watch. She gives me a sorry smile. "I've got an important meeting to get to, Brianna. Take care of yourself, dear." She skitters away, then stops cold. "By the way, Brianna," Kate calls back. "You really should get home soon. It's just not a good idea to leave a teen alone as much as you do."

Ugh. Thank you, Mrs. Spock. Yet as I watch her wobble away on those spiky heels, I catch myself taking an oh-so-involuntary gander at the time showing on my watch.

I'm still standing in the shadows when I'm again startled by the phone. This time my cell's ringing and from the special tone—it's Reba singing "My Sister"—I know it's Gaby on the other end. I hesitate to pick it up because it's been days since we've talked and that's just so wrong. Did I ever return her voicemail message the other day? Uh-oh. This means, in addition to so much else, she still doesn't know that Rita's left the company, let alone that I fixed her up with my new boss. Nor that my Bunko nemesis just paid me an unwelcome visit.

"Hey," I say, bright as a best friend.

"I'm singin' the blues, sistah!"

Let's get on with the two-part harmony then. "Gaby, we've got to talk." The cell clicks in my ear. "Hang on a second . . . it's Nathan." I hit the Flash button.

"Mom, can I go fishin' on Troy's boat? His dad's off work today."

"That's it?" I say. "Not a 'Hi, Mom, how was your tour today?' Or 'Mom, I miss you so much!'"

"So it's okay if I go?"

My eyes do a little roll. "Sure. You know the rules—stay with the boat and listen to Troy's dad." And don't even think about bringing home any dead fish.

"Sweet."

"I love you, kiddo."

"Yeah, me too." He's quiet for a half second. "So, uh, Mom. How was your day?"

Quiet sigh. Do I tell him how sad I felt this morning with his dad already gone before sunrise? Or should I mention that my life at Coastal Tours has been flipped around by Rita's sudden departure?

Maybe I should let him in on my latest matchmaking score of Ty for Gaby. Then there's the craziness with Ned and the Pirates hat. Hmm. Amazing. A day's worth of doings can seem more like just a flash inside my head. Is my teenage son ready for this baptism into a woman's world?

Probably not. "Overall, I had a decent morning," I tell him. "Have a good time this afternoon, okay?"

He mumbles a "Yeah," and I hit the Flash button again. "Still there, Gaby?"

"Well, *ihola!* to you too, missy. Where've you been?"

"Sorry, Gaby. I've got so much to tell you, but wait, forget about it, what're you all blue about?"

"Ah! I had to make a delivery today because one of my regular guys, Sammy, you know the guy—skinny, pimply skin, piercings all over the place—anyway, Sammy's girlfriend is paranoid. That one's from the dark side, all right."

"You lost me."

"She thinks everyone with a driver's license wants her 1974 rusted-out Beetle, which by the way, is one of the saddest-looking Volkswagens I've ever seen. *Así feo*—so ugly!"

Can't really argue there.

"Sammy's engine block split in two or something, so he couldn't get to work. He couldn't make deliveries either."

"And he couldn't borrow the girlfriend's car? Or is it just too lame looking to allow your arrangements to be seen in it?" I tease.

"Well, that's the thing. She's so obsessed that someone might take off with her car that she actually pulls the distributor cap off and keeps it with her."

"Okay, um, that's weird. But if the cap's with her, then she must be home—it's not like she could go anywhere. You know, with the cap gone and everything." *Like I've got any idea what this really means.*

"She fell asleep on it." Gaby lets out a spectacular sigh. A real

pathetic I-can't-take-it kind of sigh. "Sammy says she works as a bar-
tender until 2:00 A.M., and then comes home dead tired. Apparently
she fell asleep on the thing and nothing he could do would wake her."

I wait for her to laugh or something. But nothing. Finally I just
have to ask. "And you believed that?"

There's a serious amount of shock in Gaby's voice when she
answers me. "C'mon, Bri-Bri. You don't think he'd actually make up
a story like *that*?"

I don't?

"Oh! There's no way I'd have been able to run this business for so
long if I was such a . . . a . . . ninny!"

"Okay, okay," I say. "*Ex-cuse* me for asking. It just sounded kinda
farfetched, but what do I know anyway? You're right, Gaby.
Shouldn't have doubted you." There's been an awful lot of that
doubting stuff going on. "Sorry that you got stuck doing deliveries. I
hope you at least stopped for a latte."

"Having to do the deliveries wasn't such a big deal. It's just that,
well, I ran into somebody."

"You mean, as in 'with your car'?"

Gaby gives a light, tinkling laugh into the phone. "Don't be *tanta*!
Silly girl." I can hear her draw in a breath. "I ran into Franklin."

"Eww. Did you say anything?" *Like "How's Mother?"*

"You'd be so proud of me, Bri-Bri. I made eye contact and, in a
very calm voice said, 'Hello, Franklin.' Then when he asked if he
could call me again, I waited a whole three seconds—three Mississ-
ippis!—before answering him."

"Good girl! And what did he say when you told him, 'Not on your
life, bub!'"

I could hear a small release of air into the phone. "Oh, Bri, I said
he could call me."

At the moment, I'm speechless. The cat has ripped out my tongue and is chewing on it by the water's edge. All I can do is sputter into the phone.

Gaby's voice is tentative. "Bri? You still there?"

I cough. "You, me, coffee," I say, my voice coming back. "Let's go north." I'm figuring that a ride up the coast will keep my love-starved friend away from the telephone and me from wringing her neck.

Chapter twelve

The Channel Islands in all their sculpted glory rise out of the deep blue sea to our left as I drive us north on the 101 freeway toward Carpinteria, or "Carp," as it's known to the locals. Yucky Franklin-slash-Kate sightings aside, we couldn't have asked for a more spectacular afternoon to escape. Exiting at Casitas Pass Road, I turn left toward coffee. Solid Grounds on Linden Avenue is always our first stop when we get into town.

We order two double espressos with nonfat milk and a shot of Belgian chocolate. Steaming cups in hand, we plop down on the plump couch in the middle of the store. A scruffy-faced guy gets up from his perch on the sofa facing us, no doubt unwilling to listen to our impending enlightened banter.

The place is mad with beach folk. I mean it—you'd think the way chubby kids in swimsuits carrying icy whipped coffee drinks traipsed in and out of the place that this was midsummer and we were on Waikiki. I look over and see Gaby, ever the free-flowing artist in her silky sundress, twirling an extra-long strand of hair and peering at the beach photography on the wall. The faint scent of her lavender perfume is in the air.

She squints at the picture of a surfer riding a tube. "I think I know him," she says.

"I think you *want* to know him," I shoot back, remembering our surfer-watching pastime of way back when. I take a sip and then chew on the slim red stirrer in my cup.

She stops in mid-twirl. "What's got you? Did you and Douglas finally have it out about Mona?"

Mona's the least of my worries at the moment. And that thought is as startling as it is true. I'm *so* not discussing this now, though.

"You know, I haven't told you everything about my new boss yet, Gabrielle," I say, a quick subject change. On the way up, I'd filled her in on Rita's speedy exit from Coastal Tours and on my new boss's mistaken assumption that I somehow hold the key to our company's bright future. But I'd stopped short of telling her to watch for his number to flash on her Caller ID. "Did I mention that he's got hair down to here," I slap my shoulder, "and that he's as tall as my Douglas?"

Gaby stops in mid-sip. "So he's . . . pleasant looking?"

Pleasant looking? Yeah—okay. "Well, you should have seen the way Luann swooned every time he walked through the reception area. Cracked—me—up!"

Gaby starts playing with her own tiny red straw, using it to mix the whipped cream into her coffee. She's still staring into her cup when she asks, "So any chance of me meeting him sometime?"

I put a hand to my heart in feigned shock. "What about *Franklin*?"

She looks at me over her cup and flashes those long eyelashes. "I said he could call me sometime, Bri-Bri. I didn't promise to answer the phone."

"Promise me you won't even *think* about seeing Franklin again, and I'll see what I can do."

She hesitates.

"You deserve better," I say. "Promise?"

She throws up her left hand, showing off her pretty nails. "Give."

"Good, because I already told Ty all about you and gave your number to Luann. He should be calling you any day." I take a nice long drag of sweet coffee.

Gaby throws an arm around my neck, and I sink deeper into the lumpy couch cushions. "You *are* the best! Rita's son . . . I can't wait to meet him. He must be . . . he must be such a great guy. Gosh, she's just the sweetest person and a Christian too! Can you just see Rita as a mother-in-law?"

A sharp pain stabs into my right shoulder. Stress, perhaps? "Sheesh, Gaby, I just gave him your number. I mean, I'm sure you'll like him." *At least, I think you will.* "But why don't you wait a bit before shopping for your veil, crazy girl."

"I know, I know. I'm just excited about a new prospect. He does sound like a winner, though. Maybe I'll finally meet my prince, like you did back at the coffeehouse, huh, Bri?"

I feel another stab of pain, only this one's centered more on my heart. The nigglings of the past week have once again grown into all-out shouts, and I'm worried that Douglas and I are growing farther apart with each passing day. I want to talk with him, but when he climbs into bed late each night, thrashed from his day in court, I can't bear to bother him with my fretting.

Of course, feeling the flame of love shrink to an ember is one thing. The suspicion of infidelity is another fire entirely, one of fatal proportions.

All of a sudden a bell starts clanging and it sounds like a jackpot hit in Vegas. The gals behind the counter shout, "Java!" and ceremoniously tear up a petite woman's coffee card, letting the tattered pieces float to the counter. Poor baby. She's dressed in a blue-green plaid skirt and white blouse, but her young face has turned scarlet. Didn't she know about the Java ritual? Whenever a frequent-buyer card is filled, the baristas make a party out of it, including but not limited to embarrassing the holder to the full extent of their power. At the moment, they're chanting "Java!" with apparently no intention of stopping soon.

I watch the young woman hurry out with her free grandiose-sized coffee. Secretly, I'm glad for the distraction. What was I thinking? That Douglas would actually cheat on me?

Puh-lease! I remember reading somewhere that forgiveness is a choice, not a feeling. I chose to forgive Douglas years ago. He had been truly sorry back then for hurting me, even though his heart never actually strayed. I just wish I could let things go and trust that, despite his current preoccupation with work, he's still the same man who's loved me so deeply for the past fourteen years. I give my head a tight little shake, and the movement catches Gaby's eye.

"I thought I lost you there, missy. What's got you so wrapped up?" She's still glowing, probably from the rush of Ty daydreams she's already having.

"Nothing," I say, unwilling to share my tumble of fears in the wake of the jovial Java ritual. "Let's make a quick stop at Robitaille's, then head back, 'kay?"

We take a piggish romp through the neighborhood candy shop, home of the famous red, white, and blue inaugural mints, and of course those yummy milk chocolate haystacks—and then hop back onto the 101 freeway. While Gaby licks chocolate from her fingers and dusts me with questions about Ty, I fret about Douglas and me. What's that verse about being anxious for nothing? My brain's trying to retrieve the actual words so I can pull the meat out of its shell and somehow apply it to my life.

The radio DJ is on the air with his daily trivia question. Today's contest winner will receive dinner for two at the Cliff House in Mussel Shoals. Quiet, romantic, and full, captivating ocean views. Sigh.

I'm thinking that Douglas and I could use a night out like that. And fast.

Or would that be like trying to cure a wart with cleanser? If the virus is still in there, no matter how hard you scrub, that puppy's gonna grow right back. I flinch at the thought.

Gaby's watching me. "Are you ever going to tell me what's got you so preoccupied?"

I send her a look of innocence. "Nothing really. Just a busy time."

"Well, you've been more preoccupied today than I ever remember." She drums her cranberry-colored fingernails on the dash. "On second thought, you were a lot like that when you first noticed Douglas. You actually became kind of a ditz after he showed up."

"I beg your pardon."

Gaby cackles. "When I think about it, you were always so confident. *Muy segura!* Girl, sometimes you acted like the customers were there to serve *you*."

"So not true. I was just a nice little beach girl pouring coffee to pay my rent. I can't help it if *some* people might have been threatened by my self-starter attitude."

She slaps the dash hard this time. "Self-starter! Good one! Ah, but then Douglas started showing up in his *power suit*." She says the phrase with a sort of lilt. "At first you laid that tough barista attitude on him. You probably figured hey, this guy's not around for the long haul. He'll be taking his coffee tips somewhere else eventually. I think the fact that he showed up practically every morning, despite your abuse, scared you to pieces."

"Oh, right. You're just making up stories now. And since when did you decide to study psychology, with me as your guinea pig, O Wise One?"

Gaby gives me a guilty little giggle now. "I got it from *Gilmore Girls*."

Her reference to our secret vice from what is now the CW

network perks up my ears. Our favorite show's humble beginnings as a family-friendly program drew us in. Gaby got me hooked with her sets of complete seasons on DVD. Oh, the brownies we consumed watching Lorelai date Max, break up with Max, date Chris, break up with Chris, and all this as single mom to sweet, intellectual daughter, Rory.

Of course, once Rory became a coquettish college co-ed with temptations galore, our once family-friendly habit became, let's just say, somewhat less praiseworthy. Too late for us, though, as we were hooked like worms for bait. Can anyone say "frog in the kettle"?

"So, gleaning wisdom from Stars Hollow, huh? Gaby, I do appreciate your resourcefulness. Such a clever girl." I'm mocking her and truly loving it. "But I have to ask, just what from our heroines' complicated lives can you apply to me?"

"That's easy. Remember when Luke first kissed Lorelai?"

Like I could *ever* forget that. Romance at its finest. Luke and Lorelai had been good buddies for years until Luke decided to go for it and plant a big smacker on the lips of unsuspecting yet very receptive Lorelai. "Uh, yea-h," I answer, incredulous.

"Well, at first she was all confident, kissing him back and all. But then, the next day, remember how she became a klutz, knocking things over in the diner like a giggly teenager? When I think back on your reaction to Douglas's very clear interest in you, I think of Lorelai and how she changed from a fast-talking gal with an attitude into a tongue-tied schoolgirl."

"Ugh. That lasted maybe one episode!"

"Yes, well, that's TV for you. In real life, chica, I really did see a big change in you with love in the air. Including times when you seemed so far away. Mentally, that is."

"Well, life's become a little more challenging than episodic television, Gaby. Just have a lot on my mind these days. I'm sorry if you think I shut you out. Didn't mean to do that."

"No worries. I guess I'd be pretty absorbed, too, if my employer suddenly left me stranded and brought in her *fabulously* handsome son to boss me around." She sniffs. "Actually, I'd kind of like that."

I shake my head at her. "Have you forgotten? You're your own boss. And in the end, you may not think he's that great looking anyway."

"Well, a girl can dream, can't she?" Gaby turns her smile toward the window and fixes her gaze on the islands. A second later she's humming the theme song to *Gilmore Girls*. Look who's lost in thought now. In my head I'm hearing the same song, "Where You Lead," by Carole King, when the first few lines of our favorite Brad Paisley tune comes on the radio.

Gaby snaps to attention and shakes her hand toward the radio. "Ooh-ooh! Turn it up, turn it up!" She doesn't wait for me, but twists the dial herself while singing, *"'I've got some big news, the bank finally came through, and I'm holdin' the keys to a brand-new Chevrolet.'"*

I glance at her and realize that she's the happiest I've seen her in a while. Either that or she's picturing Ty as a shiny new car.

"'Cause it's a good night to be out there soakin' up the moonlight . . .'" She's leaning her head out the window—why didn't I just take down the soft top earlier?—and serenading passing drivers. The effect is contagious, and despite my inner blahs, I soon find myself joining in on the chorus.

"'You got to get a little mud on the tires!'" We're really moving now, pedal to the floor, singing at full lung capacity. Gaby's loam-colored hair looks electrified, with locks flowing in all directions. Two surfer dudes riding in a Nova from another era give us an appreciative nod. It occurs to me that anyone witnessing our very public lack of restraint would have no idea that while I'm singing the blues my gal-pal is crooning to the heavens. Her own countrified version of the "Hallelujah Chorus," if you will.

This is not lost on me as I hear the sudden blare of a siren. Gaby's too busy waving both arms out the window like a tipsy party girl to notice the flashing lights bearing down on us. While my eyes rivet on the lights in the mirror and I slide deeper into the sewer of gloom, she's taking it up a notch with another run through the chorus.

Either way, there's no getting around that just inches behind my back bumper, a highway patrol siren shrieks.

Chapter thirteen

We're sitting in my VW on the edge of Pacific Coast Highway, an ocean breeze wafting from the right, and a lecture rolling in from the left. *Yes, Officer, I know that speeding is against the law. No, sir, I didn't realize that my friend's imitation of Minnie Driver in* Phantom of the Opera *was distracting to traffic. Yes, Officer, I'll slow it down the next time.*

He rips the ticket from its pad. "You have a nice day now," he says, handing it to me with a pudgy grin stretched across his mug. *Grrr.*

Gaby elbows me and points at the patrol officer. She's mouthing some sort of reply.

I grimace before saying, "Thank you, Officer."

Throwing it in gear, I head for home, too fightin' mad to speak. I can feel Gaby's eyes on me every couple of seconds and almost sense her mouth opening up to talk before snapping shut.

Just seeing Seashell Lane before us causes my blood pressure to drop ever so slightly. Once in the drive, all I want to do is run through the door, bury myself in our fluffy bed, and mope.

"Bri-Bri?" Gaby's voice is tentative as we exit my car.

I drop my head to one side and look at her without a word.

"I'm sorry about the ticket. Really. I had a good time today,

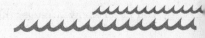

though. Come on—you did too, didn't you?"

For like a second. I sigh and squint toward the beach. After a big swallow I turn back to face my friend. "Something's got to change, Gab. This just isn't working for me anymore."

Gaby's eyes grow wide. "You're just stressed from the big changes at work, Bri. It'll work out, though, you'll see. I'm sure Rita wouldn't have left her company in Ty's hands if he wasn't the perfect one to take over. She's worked too hard all these years."

This goes way beyond the job, my friend. I inhale sea air and gently breathe it out. "Yeah, okay. We'll see." No sense going any deeper here.

Gaby steps into her Volvo, the one with the battered exterior, and I think, *Yeah, I've seen better days too*. "I'll call you later, all right?"

I nod and then face my faded old beach house, readying myself to find Nathan back from his fishing trip when I step through the front door. Hopefully, I can manage to avoid the topic of my most recent brush with the law. A few years ago, something like this wouldn't have bothered me much. You win some, you lose some, you know? But that's really just my own brand of denial. Truth is, mature people don't speed. Nor do it with the radio blaring and singing a duet with their lovelorn best friend.

Once inside I wonder if Nathan's already freshly showered from his day on the ocean. *Yeah, sure*. A mom can dream, can't she? Hmm. Gaby made a similar comment earlier in the day about dreaming. Big sigh. Hopefully I'm not steering her wrong with Ty. He seems nice enough. So he's a little geeky. Even Livi noticed his Greek godlike physique. That ought to account for something, am I right?

I drop my keys and bag on a wicker chair in the living room. I don't hear water running nor do I smell freshly caught fish. I check my cell for the time and see that I missed two calls. Guess the music was just a tad too loud in the car today. *Sheesh*.

It's nearly dinnertime now. I assume Douglas won't be home, but you never know. Stranger things have happened—like seeing Kate wearing pointy heels, for instance. I punch in the code to retrieve messages, yank open the freezer door in search of dinner, and cradle my cell on my shoulder.

You have two new messages. First message . . .

"Mom, it's Nathan. I'm at home. What're we havin' for dinner? Call me back. Bye."

Beep. Next message . . .

"Brianna, it's me. The judge dismissed all parties early today. I thought we could all have some dinner together. Anyway, I've just pulled into the drive and see you're not here. Well . . . Oh, Nathan's here. I see him on the stoop. I guess he and I will go out together then. At least you won't have to cook a huge meal tonight." Douglas laughs at his own joke. "Sorry I missed you. I'll bring Nathan home afterward and then head back to my office. Bye."

Is this some sick gag? My absentee husband spontaneously decides to carry me off to dinner and instead of being home, where I should be, I'm stuck on the coast highway being chewed out by the CHP! My hand's gripping the open freezer door. Icy white smoke surrounds me, but I'm too frozen to take another step. Ya know, maybe this whole thing, whatever it is, is not really about Douglas. Maybe it's about me. I almost throw out a warped laugh. *It's not about you, it's about me!*

Maybe—no, probably—C. S. Lewis was right. I, Brianna Dorothea Stone, am an egg. Well. Either I'm gonna get hatched or spoil and stink to the heavens!

I slam shut the freezer door and spin around like a madwoman, taking in my surroundings. A hokey hula-girl doll on the old Formica countertop shimmies from the sudden turbulence in the room. Pineapples and palm trees mock me from their stenciled spots on the walls. The old Dole-company clock screams out the time.

I take one more look around and realize it's all got to go. I want changes. Big changes. And I'm starting with everything *me*.

The phone rings, tearing me from my self-loathing.

"What!"

"Hello? Is this the Stone residence?"

Aargh! A telemarketer. "We're on the no-call list! We're not buyin'!"

"Brianna? Is that you?"

I stop. That hula chick on my counter is huddled in the corner, trembling. Okay, maybe not huddled, but she's shakin', all right. "Um, this is Bri. Can I help you?"

"Ty here. I wasn't sure if I had the correct phone number for you. Is this an inappropriate time?"

I wilt and give the phone one big eye roll. Wouldn't you just know it's the boss? "Uh, no, not at all. I was just having fun with you."

"Oh, I understand. You must have Caller ID."

"Uh, yeah, that's it." I turn up my hands to the empty room as if to say *who knew?*

"Brianna, you really are a tease, aren't you." He clears his throat. "I understand that it's late, but I wanted to make sure that you had marked your calendar for our concept meeting scheduled for first thing Monday morning."

I grab a half-chewed pencil from my kitchen junk drawer and scribble a note to myself on a paper towel. "Yes, of course, Ty. I've already noted the meeting in my official Day-Timer."

"Well, then, I'm impressed."

But of course.

"I'll see you early Monday. And Brianna?"

"Yes?"

"I'm having breakfast catered for the two of us, so bring your appetite."

Just say there'll be brownies, and I'm there. I say so-long, flip shut my phone, and immediately start making plans. Nothing throws me faster into gear than getting caught acting like a freak. With elbows rested on the counter, I'm tapping the eraser of the disfigured pencil against my chin now. Thinking, thinking. How does an ordinary egg go about being hatched, anyway?

In Nathan's preschool, eggs were kept in a wooden and chicken-wire box, along with a heat lamp. Teacher Lois, a regular farm gal, always made sure that the eggs were kept heated at 100 degrees. Kinda gives new meaning to that old adage: "If it's too hot, get out of the kitchen." Or in this case, climb out of the incubator.

Ever since Kate decided to publicly assess my marriage at Bunko, I've been feeling the heat too. Even before that night, though, I had begun to question Douglas's suffocating schedule. Instead of facing the fact that my once-attentive husband has been dizzyingly busy, I'd been going along in my beachy ways, just as I always had. While he was obviously changing, I was not.

A glance into the living room flashes me back to just a few days ago, when Mona and her interior design sidekick, Patrice, were contemplating a complete redo of our home. I feel my temper start to burn again as I take in the light wicker, the waxed longboard, the painted lighthouse collection. Guess the place could use a shot of elegance. *Note to self: Find a designer specializing in homes of distinguished lawyers.*

My eyes catch on the latest edition of *Coastside Homes* flopped open on the couch. A mature woman is walking the beach with her dogs. Other than her bare feet, there's nothing careless about her appearance. She's laid-back all right, but in an off-white flouncy pantsuit. A couple of gold bangles encircle her wrists and she's wearing small hoop earrings. Very Montecito chic.

With a peek at my side-striped track pants, white lycra workout blouse, and cheapy flip-flops on my feet, I'm guessing I could use a bit of elegance too. Douglas has never much cared about what clothes I wear. Yet does he think I just don't care? Maybe my laid-back ways have begun to bore him, or worse, turn him off.

An idea pops into my head and so I race upstairs. I charge into the closet and kneel into the thick carpeting. Before long, I'm tossing lightweight footwear over my shoulder, one shoe at a time. I'm like a dog sending dirt clods flying while searching for a buried bone. With a basketful of flip-flops ready for the Salvation Army, I jog down the stairs to the kitchen.

I rifle around beneath the sink, looking for a large trash bag and come up empty. *Nathan!* Ugh, he's been told a million times to refill the cabinet with bags when they're all used up, but *never mind*!

I'm in the garage now, the place where spare parts and busted toys go to die. Garbage detail has always been left to the men in my home, the only clause I added to the wedding vows. Not really. Actually, I only buy can liners by the 200-bag roll, narrowing my chances of having to dig around in the garage for more. Usually one of the guys takes care of this. But with Douglas so busy and Nathan's teenage "I forgot" motto . . . well, guess it's up to me.

This lovely two-hundred-fifty-foot space is all about clutter. Except for two modular Lowe's cupboards high up in the far-right corner, and a slim slot for Douglas to park his car, pretty much everything needed to run a household sits stacked up along the left-hand wall. Everything, that is, except the trash bag I need at the moment.

I wend my way around the stacks of necessities and head for the cupboards. I can't recall the last time I looked inside them. If ever. I've always thought of those hard-to-reach shelves as Douglas's special space. I got the house, and he got the cabinets. Besides, I can only reach them by tiptoe, and barely that. All Douglas has to do is stretch one muscular arm up and yank on the handle.

I'm teetering on my tiptoes when I hear Douglas's car pull into the drive. Guess he's dropping off Nathan. With a defeated sigh I realize that I'm too penned in to rush out and blow him a kiss before he turns back toward work. Just as my fingers finally reach around the cabinet-door handle and give it a good pull, I hear footsteps near the side garage door.

"Brianna?"

The sound of my husband's voice startles me. Just as I yank on that door, a plastic sack plops onto my head, its contents spilling to the ground below. The deflated grocery bag lies there atop my head like a Southerner's bonnet, and I give Douglas an embarrassed smile. He hurries toward me, and I feel like leaping into his arms. *M' lord, come fetch your damsel in distress!*

Unfortunately, Douglas doesn't appear to share my enthusiasm. "You should've asked me to help you, Brianna," he scolds while stepping over an upturned skateboard. I smell the barest hint of onion and cilantro and just know the boys have been chowing down at Evita's. When I drop to my knees to join him on the garage floor where he's begun to clean up the mess, my stomach rumbles.

Sitting on my haunches, I watch him shove a bunch of things back into the bag, his arms tanned and strong. Adrenaline seeps from me as I study him and breathe in his closeness. I wonder if this would be a good time to finally put the Kendall sighting to rest. With effort, I let loose the words I've been struggling with all day.

"Saw you with Kendall yesterday," I say.

Douglas stops mid-stuff. "What's that?"

"Yeah, you two were heading down Harbor."

He starts stuffing the bag again. "That around lunchtime?"

"A little after, I think."

"Hmm."

"Big meeting?" I prod.

"Quite. Spence was there."

"Oh? I didn't notice him."

Douglas grins at me sideways. "He had to drive on his own. The Z only has two seats, you know."

"Oh. Yeah." *How silly of me.*

Douglas finishes stuffing the bag, then twists the plastic handles into a tight knot. I sense the knot in my stomach begin to unravel as he stands and offers me a hand up. "Next time you want something from the cabinet," he says, "just wait until I get home. This place is dangerous."

I'm hanging on to his hand, hoping he'll change his mind about the office so we can reconnect, when my eye catches on the bag he's still holding. Curiously, none of the items that fell from his cabinet are familiar to me—men's sneakers, a pair of drawstring shorts, a plain soft cotton tee, a lone key, and a jet black cap. A cap! Uh, *hello,* the number of times I've seen Douglas wearing a hat of any kind falls somewhere between zero and never. While some men stow away hooch or cigars in some unreachable locked garage cabinet, apparently mine's hiding casual wear.

Douglas's eyes catch mine for a brief second before he looks away. Then with a quick flick of his wrist, he tosses the bag behind my rarely used "Perfect Glutes" machine, a bridal gift from DM's new girlfriend, and helps me up.

"Uh, hon?" I broach, looking into those heavenly eyes and hoping for the truth. "What's up with the spare clothes?"

Douglas still holds my hands in his. "Just some of Spence's things," he says, referring to one of the associates in his office. "I forgot they were up there." He takes both of my cheeks in his large, warm hands and nuzzles me. "I've missed you," he says simply, kissing me with the passion of a sailor who's been away at sea.

The week's great cloud of craziness shrinks before me, and I wonder if just maybe I'd created much out of little. I flash back on some of the fanciful stories told to me when I was young. Maybe my mother's tales of adventure and intrigue in the wild became more a part of me than I'd ever imagined, causing me to try to shake rain from just a handful of mist.

Douglas wraps his strong arms around me, pulling me close, and I melt into him like milk chocolate in the sun. For the moment, I'm choosing to ignore any lingering doubt.

Chapter fourteen

I'm still clinging to Douglas all the while thinking that onions have been given a bad rap. Oh yeah, it's best to avoid them raw, especially before boarding a plane or dining on a first date. And true, some varieties resist even the toughest hand soaps. Still, I ask you, what better way to truly know how deep your love for someone runs than by giving them a big smooch after they've noshed on Mexican food?

This, too, is why marriage *rocks*. When you're in it for life, it's good-bye to that unattainable mask of perfection and hello to the cozy, naked truth—onion breath and all. Maybe that's what Alan Jackson meant when he sang that song, "Too Much of a Good Thing (Is a Good Thing)." I'm snuggled against Douglas's chest, dissing my built-up worries and thinking about these comforts of marriage, when Nathan pokes his head through the doorway.

"Dad," he cuts in, "client's on the phone."

Douglas grumbles. He mutters into my hair, "Tell 'em to get lost."

Nathan stands at the door, the cordless phone dangling from his right hand. *Sure hope he set it on mute.* "So?" our son says, averting his eyes from our display of mush.

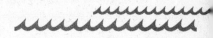

Douglas leans back and looks into my eyes. The hair at his temples seems grayer than a month ago. He gives out a let-down grunt. "Got to go. This case has turned ugly, and, well, I can't let myself get distracted right now. And you do distract me, you know." He offers me a brief smile and then drops his hands from my waist. "I'll probably be late. Don't wait up," he adds before pulling away.

I watch him back away and duck under the *derriere* exercise machine, whisking away the plastic bag hiding Spence's clothes. Bag in hand, he grabs the phone from Nathan.

Not so fast. "So why are you the keeper of Spence's beachwear, anyway?" I call out.

And for that matter, what's up with the fax from Grandma? And the afternoon drive with Kendall?

He's got the phone in his ear now and squints back at me, like he's confused. Or maybe he's overwhelmed. From across the room I can hear his client bellowing through the earpiece, and I watch Douglas becoming uncharacteristically flustered. Case must really be going south. My husband looks my way, but his eyes seem to be focused elsewhere. I can tell I'm losing him. He blows me a kiss, but it lands somewhere on the wall behind me. Metaphorically speaking, of course. *Ugh.* He didn't hear a word I said.

I stand there in the garage, my own hands on my hips now, listening as he turns on his more formal "lawyer" voice before heading back out the door.

———

**Eight symptoms of the male midlife crisis,
and my take on each one.**

1. He says life is a bore.
   Frankly, he's not been around much to inform me of this. Shoot, he's too busy to be bored!

2. He is thinking about (or already having) an affair.
   The way he just kissed me? Oh, puh-lease!

3. He is drinking too much or abusing other substances.
   Good one.

4. He is overly nostalgic and constantly reminiscing about his youth or his first love.
   Okay, this one would be me.

6. Steamy emails from women—if you're the kind to snoop.
   Yes, I am that kind. And I wouldn't consider Mona's emails "steamy."

7. A state of preoccupation.
   Bingo—he's livin' there these days. At least he hasn't had time to put up a For Sale sign on the house.

8. Often "works" late.
   Uh, yes to the "working late" thing. (But don't tell Ned; he'll think he was right.)

I slap down my copy of *Modern Gal* and groan. Why do I read this garbage, anyway? Oh, that's right—because it's *there*. Luann loaned this rag to me one afternoon when I decided to take a break and head for the beach. I took it along but got distracted by the calming of the sea, not actually opening it up until now. Well, I wasn't missing anything.

The palm-frond fan above my head whirs, making a dull, repetitive sound and chilling me with its breeze. As soon as Douglas left to go back to the office, Nathan hijacked the phone. He's been upstairs with it all evening.

I peer up the stairway and hope he's not talking to a girl. A quick glance at one of the magazine headlines, "Why He Wants You to Make the First Move," has me scared to bits. I *so* don't know what I'll do the first time a cute little thing shows up on our doorstep carrying a basket of brownies and asking for Nathan. I laugh at the thought.

Of course I know what I'd do—I'd help myself to a little taste-testing, that's what.

Still, it's a swirling world out there, with plenty of unbiblical truths masquerading as gospel. I just hope our son can spot a lie when he hears one.

"Mom?" I look up again at the stairway, where Nathan's got me in his sights. "You busy?"

I slide the magazine from the couch onto the floor, more than a little nervous that maybe Douglas *is* showing signs of some sort of crisis. "Not at all, punkin," I lie. "What's up?"

He hops down the stairs a couple at a time, carrying a copy of the *Surfers Bible.* "Check this out," he says, plopping onto the floor. His legs are sprawled haphazardly, and he's reading Psalm 93 to me. "'The ocean is roaring, Lord. The sea is pounding hard. Its mighty waves are majestic, but you are more majestic, and you rule over all. Your decisions are firm, and your temple will always be beautiful and holy.'"

He looks to me. "That's major, huh."

"Uh, yeah. I'd have to agree with you there."

"I was thinkin' that maybe I should give this to Gib. He's been kinda out there since his mom died. You think I should?"

I tousle his hair with my fingers, noticing the bits of gold sprinkled throughout. "I think that's a great gift. Why don't you keep that one, and we can pick up another for him tomorrow?"

"Okay," he says, getting up. "I just thought of him when I started reading about the ocean and everything. And about all these pros who got turned on to Jesus. Most of the time Gib just wants to rip it at the beach. Maybe if he sees that God made the ocean, then he'd start talking to Him again."

"So you think that Gibson doesn't pray anymore?"

Nathan shrugs. "Guess not. I don't know. He and his dad go to church sometimes, but he doesn't talk about his mom much." He's moving back toward the stairs again, obviously done talking. A young man of few words.

And yet that kid has a heart of gold. I slide Luann's magazine across the floor with a quick shove of my foot and think, *How nuts is this?* While I'm downstairs digging in to a reader's quiz, he's up in his room devouring Scripture. There's something so poetic (okay, lame on my part) about that.

Still, I guess I'm not that warped. Jesus did say, "Let the little children come to me," and I'd never hinder him. Besides, I'm too busy sitting here counting my faults to get in his way.

I take another peek toward the upstairs landing. Stinky room aside, my kid's changing a lot these days. Dare I say, maturing? I wiggle my toes, as I happen to be wearing a pair of Sponge Bob Square Pants slippers at the moment. Hey, didn't Jesus also say something about His kingdom being only for those who receive it like a little child? Hmm?

The phone rings and stops in a flash. Apparently the Bible's not all Nathan is hanging on to. He clomps down the stairs and sticks the cordless receiver in my face.

"Gaby. For you," he says.

I take it from him. "Hu-llo," I say, sure that she's called to wallow with me about the traffic ticket, something I'd completely forgotten about until this moment.

"Ty called! He's taking me to lunch next week. He sounds dreamy, Bri-Bri!"

Apparently she's forgotten all about her recent road act and my subsequent speeding ticket. My stomach lurches. Probably because I haven't eaten in hours.

"Lunch, huh. Where's he taking you?"

"He mentioned trying out Café Nouveau. I've heard it's fabulous. Everybody says so. I think Rachel likes to eat there a lot. And you've been there—it's good, right?"

"Impressive. Yeah, it's good." Out of the way, quiet . . . but good luck parking Ty's army tank on that skinny street.

"He sounds so formal on the phone. Is he like that in person?"

"Actually, he really is into business-geek, I mean *speak*." I stifle a laugh. "I think he just wants to make sure he doesn't mess up his mom's business. I'm not into all those 'logistical concepts' and stuff, but whatever. If that's what it takes for him to get a grip on the tour business, then full throttle to him, ya know?"

"He sounds noble. You can pick them, can't you, Bri."

"What's that mean?"

"Look at Douglas. He's the suave-urbane type." Long sigh. "Tall, handsome, imposing as all get-out, and he runs his office like a tight ship! If I had what you had, I don't know if I could keep up, but I'd be willing to die trying. Or to at least get a little sick—ha!"

Phone in hand, I take another gander at my feet and see hyper-faced Sponge Bob cackling up at me. So I've been wearing cartoon slippers since I was two. Is that so bad? Maybe so. Deep down I know Douglas hasn't strayed. He has been troubled lately, though, and I'd be lying if I said I wasn't worried that temptation might overtake him someday.

I realize that Gaby's right. Some things are worth fighting for, and at the top of that list is my marriage. Douglas is changing, Nathan's maturing, and even Gaby's willing to wear herself out to impress. So that's it. Bandwagon, here I come.

Chapter fifteen

I'm a hypocrite in action. I'm thinking this as I schlep through the Pacific View Mall, unable to grasp why entire families travel in packs around here on such a beautiful Sunday afternoon. I want to shout, "It's warm and fogless out there, people!" and shoo them toward the nearest beach. Instead I file in behind the others at The Coffee Bean & Tea Leaf and pathetically wait for a large mocha ice blended with whip. Just a little something to get me through the weekend shopping ritual that every in-the-know women's magazine out there tells me I'm supposed to adore. *Sheesh.*

Feeling several pounds heavier, I ramble past Old Navy, willing my eyes away from the beachy clothing displays in the window. Soft summer cottons, muted pastels, the season's newest line of flip-flops . . . oh, now *that's* a shopping experience I could wrap my wallet around! Alas, with sugar-induced determination, I forge ahead to Natty's, the most upscale department store in our fine seaside city. I'm on the hunt for professional attire, you know, to show off the new *moi* at my power breakfast tomorrow morning.

Not that I care what Ty or anyone else at the office thinks. *Psfft!* I'm just using the meeting to practice walking in heels taller than the

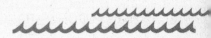

thickness of a copy of *Sunset* magazine. Can't let my distinguished husband see me wobbling around like a newborn calf, now can I?

I wander through Women's Shoes and nearly become unglued when I see that wedgies are back in style. Oh sure, they're simply called "wedge" these days. And with red, blue, or black suede, they are funkier than the old cork type worn by Aunt Dot. But *come on!* These positively scream out *wacky!*—not unlike my lovable old auntie.

I scoop up a shoe and then just as quickly place the Porsche-red wedge back onto its glass display cube.

A camel hair–suited salesman with a smile too bright for someone stuck indoors on the weekend approaches me. His name tag reads *Francois*. "Ah, those are 'Attitude' by Melanie Cane," Francois drips. "A perfect choice. Shall I fit you with a pair?"

I shake my head. "No thanks."

"Are you certain?" He takes the beribboned leather shoe from its case. "You won't find detailing like this just anywhere. Certainly not at *Cost-Less*." Francois laughs mockingly at the name of the nearby discount shoe store.

Hey! I want to say, *I happen to swoon over that store's kicky flip-flops*. Francois slides the curious throwback under my nose like it's a tray of tempting desserts, and I reconsider the overdressed pump in his open hand. The blue's kind of okay, I think. Still I just can't help myself when I ask, "Do these *wedgies* come in size six and a half?"

I detect a hint of an eye-roll just before he disappears into the stock room. I cluck. This shopping thing isn't so bad after all.

Later at home I spill out my bounty all over our comfy old bed. Instead of the outrageously garish wedge, I eventually settled on the "Flirty Girl" by Angiana Cole, a low-heeled sandal that's a step up, pun intended, from a flip-flop. Very voguish, if you ask me.

I rummage through the other spring must-haves spilled out before me: suiting jackets, tailored blazers, crinkled skirts, draped tops. I've never seen so much herringbone, tweed, and silk piled high, and in such disarray. A picture of my mom pops into my head. She's cutting a swath through the jungle, blade in hand, wearing hiking boots and thick layers of cotton. Could my life be any further away from that image at this moment? Instead of the rain forest, my bedroom looks more like the cloak room at the Saticoy Country Club after an implosion.

I pick through the clothes on my bed. For my meeting at the tour company tomorrow, I decide on a cool silk-front cardigan in aqua. This, a new ecru pant, and my new sandals, and I'm ready for some serious brainstorming.

————

The fog has again lifted this glorious Monday morning. I zip along Schooner Drive, tossing a wave to a group of surfers peeling the wet suits from their backs. There's white water within eyeshot, and no doubt this Ventura crew spent the early hours coming down on the clean breaks out there.

I pull into the harbor lot and park. Fishermen have already labored away the morning, and I can see several of their large rusty vessels heading in along the main channel. Sleek yachts captained by retirees with cash to burn rock in their wake. I get out of my VW and walk over to Coastal Tours, my heels clicking like Morse code on the concrete path beside the channel.

It's more than sunny skies and a wardrobe makeover that's lifted my heart today. I was barely lucid this morning, cuddled up in bed when Douglas's soft whisper nuzzled my ear. "Hopefully we'll have closing arguments today," he had said to me, which when read between the lines means, "I'll be around more for you soon."

So, yeah, all the way around, things are looking up. I push open the glass doors into the Coastal Tours reception area, and Luann wolf-whistles at me. *Oh brother.*

"Good morning, Luann," I say, ignoring her impression of a construction worker on lunch break.

"You rent *Working Girl* this weekend?" she asks, scrutinizing me with pinched lips and scrunched-up eyes. "You look like Melanie Griffith in that movie."

You mean except for the bleached-blond puffy hair circa–1988, right?
"Oh, Lu-lu. Can't a girl shop a little without everyone getting crazed about it? Sheesh."

She stares, her eyes traveling the length of me. "Come to think of it, the shoes could be different. If you're really serious about a makeover, I could go to the mall with you, Bri. You know, to give you some pointers." She looks down at my sandals. "For instance, those heels are far too low."

I examine the painted-red wooden beads around her neck. They match her nail polish. "Thanks a bunch," I answer noncommittally. "By the way, have you seen Ty? We're supposed to have a meeting today."

She sighs long and low and nods in the direction of the hallway. "Luck-y," she says, and in my head I'm hearing Napoleon Dynamite. "He ordered from Front Street too."

Well, yum. Front Street Deli caters events for us all the time, but usually while the tourists feast, I'm too busy giving directions or a Ventura history lesson or answering questions to have time for food.

The aromas of smoky bacon and sweet syrup waft downwind from the conference room. Thankfully, my stomach grumble is masked by the clicking of my heels along the hall floors. I push open the door and find Ty's back to me. He's sitting behind his desk, his feet up on the credenza below the window, his gaze fixed somewhere out on the harbor.

On his desktop sits a silver-domed serving tray—not unlike the kind found in sitcoms about the lives of the *nouveau riche*. Another silver-lidded plate waits on a TV tray between two nubby wing chairs. I feel like I'm on the set of *The Fresh Prince of Bel-Air*. Except I'm not.

"Morning, Ty."

He drops his feet to the floor with a thud and swivels his chair around. "Good morning, Brianna." He stands and reaches out a hand, his eyes running down the length of my new outfit. *Ugh. Again with the inspection! I didn't count on looking so obvious.* He clasps my hand in his and motions for me to sit.

My stomach lets out a growl, and Ty gives me a wink. "Please," he says, motioning to the silver dome next to me.

I resist his offer, something more pressing on my mind. "I heard you'll be seeing Gaby for lunch, Ty."

"Yes, based upon your recommendation, I set something up with her this afternoon, in fact."

Based upon my recommendation? Is that sort of like a dating "referral"? I know Gaby likes the business type, and she'll probably dig Ty, but I *so* don't get him. "So," I say, stealing a look around the room. "Won't anyone else be meeting with us this morning?"

Elbows on his desk, Ty leans into his clasped hands. He stares at me, one eyebrow slightly raised. "I've spent the weekend analyzing our company's deficiencies and have found that most of my mother's employees have a complete LOK of the tour business. Except you, that is, Brianna."

"LOK?"

"Lack of knowledge," he says, still staring.

But of course.

"You, however, are ahead of the curve in this game," he says. "This is why I've invited you alone here to assist me in mapping out a succinct strategy for productivity in the days ahead." He glances toward the untouched tray at my side. "But first let's dine together, shall we?"

From the hall behind us, I hear a familiar *click, click, click* on the tile floors. Ty's office door swings open wide. "If I'd known you were serving breakfast, son, I wouldn't have eaten such a large one today."

"Rita!" I squeal.

"Mother?"

I nearly leap into my former boss's arms, wrapping my own around her small frame. "I thought you'd be knee-deep in packing by now. It's so good to see you!"

Rita returns my smile, but her eyes look troubled. Missing the tour biz already?

"And it's wonderful to see you too." She stands back, taking my hands in hers, and looks me over. "My, what a beautiful outfit, Brianna. That color of blue is absolutely stunning on you."

I give her a playful curtsy. "Why, thank you."

Rita drops my hands and turns to her son, who's standing now. Funny, but the last time I saw them together, Ty towered over his mother. With her chin lifted toward him, Rita appears to have grown. *Either that or Ty shrank.*

"I hope I'm not too late," Rita says, her eyes riveted on her son.

Ty scoffs. "Of course not, Mother." He whips his gaze around the room. "Here," he says, leading Rita to the second wing chair. "You sit here, and you can have my breakfast." He picks up the tray from his desk. "I haven't even touched it yet."

Rita raises her eyebrow at the shiny tray but waves it away. "That's quite all right. You two get back to your meeting, and I'll just relax for a moment. We will certainly be talking later."

Sitting there on Ty's fine furniture, Rita resembles royalty. I, on the other hand, am starting to feel more like the court jester. While this mother–son team is obviously cut from the same tweed cloth, I'm longing to fling off my heels, low as they may be, and swoosh my toes in the sand at the nearby beach. Catching up with Rita is tempting, but power-noshing? Not so much.

"Rita," I say, seeing my way out of this meeting, "why don't you take my breakfast? Ty and I can talk some other time."

Rita again glances at the silver on the end table between us, her eyebrows perfectly arched. She opens her mouth to speak when Ty cuts in.

"Allow me to explain," he begins, ignoring my suggestion. "What you ladies see before you is what is known in the business world as the 'lipstick effect.'"

I crinkle my forehead.

Rita snaps her tongue. "Son, I'm well aware of the meaning of the lipstick effect." She turns to me. "The idea behind this phrase, Brianna, is that during tough economic times, people will buy smaller things—like lipstick—that make them feel good." Turning back to Ty, she continues. "However, I don't see the connection here."

Ty swivels back in his chair, smiling widely now. "Ah, but don't you see? We've got to stay a cut above the competition. So I say let us give our full-tour clientele something more than what they would find at Tiki Bob's in Oxnard. Instead of bland burgers by the bay, let's put cloth and silver on their lunch tables. If we can accomplish this in a cost-effective manner, then it will make our customers *feel* like a million bucks, while not actually costing them anything near."

I'm crossing my arms now, just shaking my head. "Wow. I'll never see lipstick in the same way again," I say, thinking about the drawer full of color in Gaby's apartment. "Seriously, though, it's a nice idea, Ty, but I'm not sure that such formality would work around here. People are pretty casual. I wouldn't want anyone to feel uncomfortable, like they're underdressed or something." In my head I'm picturing my favorite rotund bus driver bellying up to a classy banquet table, dressed in a goofy tee, walking shorts, and trail sandals.

"Nice try, son," Rita says, her voice uncharacteristically clipped, "but I tend to agree with Brianna. Perhaps you should think harder about what you should be doing here at Coastal Tours." She leans an elbow onto the armrest of her chair and rests her chin in the crook of her hand. "When you've come up with more ideas, call me. We can discuss them prior to bothering your top employee."

Uh-oh. Ty looks like he just swallowed a dry vitamin.

Rita turns to me, and her expression mellows. "You do look quite lovely, Brianna."

Great—quick subject change. "Thank you, Rita. By the way," I say, avoiding Ty's sickly gaze, "I've been thinking about making a few changes at home. Can you recommend an interior designer?"

"How lovely! There's nothing I enjoy more than making my living surroundings as comfortable and elegant as possible."

"Yes—that's what I want. Something elegant."

Rita snaps open her purse. She pulls one of her own business cards from her wallet. "I'm going to give you the name of my enormously talented cousin, Pati. Now listen," she says, waving her card at me, "she is quite busy—she's a top designer. But you tell her that I sent you, and I'm sure she will make time in her busy schedule to consult with you."

I watch Rita pull a golden ballpoint pen from her purse and write her cousin's number on the card. She presses it into my hand.

Grateful for an excuse to leave the office, which has become downright chilly, I stand and frown at my untouched breakfast. "Nice thought, Ty." One look at him and I'm thinking that it's a good thing he's having lunch with Gaby. She'll cheer him.

I can't think of anything else to say, so I look to Rita. "And thank you so much for the referral. I'm excited to meet your cousin! If she's anything like you, I'm sure I'll love her."

The sun continues to shine as I head for home, nearly sweltering in my new linen pants. Yet all in all, I feel newly refined, dare I say professional, in my business attire. Too bad for Ty that the meeting spiraled downward so quickly, though. Apparently Rita's less willing to abandon Coastal Tours than I'd thought.

Not a problem for me, though. I'm zipping along Harbor Boulevard toward home, and all I can think about is step two of my personal makeover: redesigning our beach pad into a castle fit for my king. With my beloved Rita's cousin there to help, what could possibly go wrong?

Chapter sixteen

I'm leafing through the latest issue of *Dwell*, picked up on my way home, and considering just how far we live from the new modern aesthetic. Instead of glass and concrete fashioned into every imaginable geometric shape, we Stones bunk with surfboards and miniature sailboats on the walls. Asian influence? Nineteenth-century classic styling? Not even close. I glance around our living room, taking in the colors of sea and fog. Yup, sort of a beach-meets-beach inspiration all the way around.

But that's about to change. I breathe in deeply, readying myself for the challenge. My mind wanders to Bunko queen Suzy, who swags her fireplace according to the season. Tulips in February, flags on the Fourth, paper turkeys in November . . . Okay, some challenges are worth skipping. That is *so* not what I'm going for here.

I want Douglas to step inside the front door after work and feel like he's *arrived*! Like he's *all that*—and then some. Not like he's just stumbled into seaside mishmash!

Speaking of the man of my dreams, I pick up the phone and dial his office.

"Mr. Douglas Stone's office. Darla speaking." Douglas's longtime secretary always sounds so melodramatic. I'm picturing her sweetly puckered face hidden behind those monstrous eyeglasses.

"Hey, Darla. Any word on the trial?"

Darla gives a sigh-infused groan into the phone. "Yes, yes. The attorneys finished closing arguments this morning. It's in the hands of the jury now. Mr. Stone decided to stay around, just in case they come back sometime this afternoon with a verdict."

"How did he sound when he called in?"

"Oh, he sounded upbeat, as usual. Mr. Stone says he'll be glad to get this one over with." She harrumphs. "Frankly, I would like him to be done with it soon too. I've been very, very busy taking all of his many messages. He has enough on his desk to wallpaper the ladies' rest room."

Oh my.

"And you'd think the staff would get used to the fact that my boss is an extremely important man," she continues, singing Douglas's praises like a protective mother. "Every one of them keeps pestering me regarding Mr. Stone's whereabouts—the mail clerk, Spencer, Kendall . . ."

Kendall?

"By the way," she says, shifting gears but not slowing down, "did Mr. Stone bring a fax home from the *other* Mrs. Stone?"

"Um . . ."

"Oh, never mind. I'll put that on the list to talk to him about when he finally wraps up this trial. By the way, Mr. Tuzzi has been on the warpath lately. He has a very big case to handle in the South— very big—and keeps buzzing my desk, wanting to know when Mr. Stone will be back." She sighs wearily. "No, no, I don't expect to have things slow down around here any too soon!"

I open my mouth to wish her well, but she continues. *Here it comes . . .*

"The legal secretary is forever the unsung hero in the legal profession, without a doubt. I'm telling you, Brianna, that without the legal secretary, the entire court system would fall into frightful disarray. Just think of all the civil litigators who'd show up in family court, and vice versa, without their faithful legal assistant to light the way with her organizational torch. And who is it that ends up living high on the hog up on snob hill?"

"I, uh, hmm . . ."

"The mighty lawyer, that's who. He lives in his castle, far from the little people, stepping out only long enough to toss a dry crust of bread to the underlings running his mill of a firm." She takes a breath. "Of course, I'm not talking about our Mr. Stone. Never, never, never!" She lowers her voice, slightly. "I'll have you know that if it weren't for Mr. Stone, this firm would no longer have Darla Krusteez to kick around. Oh, absolutely not! Oh, if you only—"

I cut in and thank Darla for her time, telling her not to leave him a message. I'll just try to catch him on the cell later, I say. I think she sounds relieved. Or maybe that's me.

The phone's still in my hand when it begins to ring. "Hi?"

"Ms. Stone, please."

I'm thinking this is a sales call, but considering my track record, I decide to play nice. "This is Bri."

"Fabulous! This is Maybel Scott, calling from Ms. Blanc's office about your design appointment."

I straighten up.

"Ms. Blanc asked me to tell you that she received your message. You'll be so tickled to learn that she has an opening this very afternoon!"

"Really? Um, great."

"As you can imagine, this is highly unusual. However, a client just called to cancel, making Ms. Blanc available to you. She can be at your home at four-fifteen today."

I gulp, but a quick look around at my living room's overzealous surf-meets-sand motif and I agree to the last-minute appointment. "Four-fifteen will be just fine, Mabel. I'll be here."

"That's May-*bel*," she corrects. "Ms. Blanc will see you at four-fifteen *sharp*. Good-bye."

I turn off the phone and wonder what sort of designer Ms. Blanc might be. I'm hoping for someone as genteel as southern belle Laurie from *Trading Spaces*. I read somewhere that in real life she too is married to an attorney. I imagine their home sprawling and elegantly decorated—plantation-style, of course.

Yet fear hovers inside of me. Maybe Ms. Blanc will instead turn out to be more like *Trading Spaces* designer Hildi, and glue hay or feathers to my walls! Or worse, maybe she'll be like Kia and give my living room some sort of hieroglyphics-themed makeover. Ack!

I shake my head at the memory of so many reality TV designs gone wrong. Face it—plans are bound to derail when you've got absolutely no control over them. Unlike me. I plan to tell Ms. Blanc—er, Pati—exactly what I want. Just as soon as I figure it out.

Nathan throws open the front door and storms in. His backpack hits the floor and slides across the sandy entryway like a rogue bowling ball.

I stretch my eyebrows upward but keep my mouth closed. He stomps around the corner and into the kitchen, and I can hear the unmistakable creak of the fridge door being yanked open. "Mom! Do we have any Coke?"

"You don't have to shout, punkin," I tell him, having crept over to the kitchen island. "I'm right behind you."

He slams the door. "Quit callin' me *punkin*. I'm not some baby."

O-key.

He heads for the stairs.

"Nathan, wait." He stops but doesn't turn around. "For the moment, I'm putting aside the apology you owe me for that outburst," I say to his stiff back. His shoulder twitches. "Wanna talk about what's bothering you?"

Nathan swivels around, his face sullen. He slumps down the stairs. The front door still stands open, and it sways as Nathan slinks past. "Gib was a jerk today."

I place my arm around him and lead him toward the couch. "You two fighting over a girl?"

Nathan jolts away from me. "M-om!"

I give him an innocent smile. "Wha-at?"

"I gave him the Bible, okay? And he just acted like I was all bogus or something. He called me a Barney!"

"A Barney?"

"Yeah—someone who surfs like a beginner. Like a *baby*!" He's glaring back at me now.

Ooh boy. Not fun. Nothing like emptying your heart about God and having it filled back up with insults. *Been there!* If I had a seashell for every time Aunt Dot told me to fight the good fight, I'd have a beach named after me. It's so easy to preach it at Sunday school, but with friends who've been through hell? Not so much.

I pull him close. "You did the right thing, Nathan. I'm so proud of you. God is too. Somewhere in the book of Romans it says that those who bring good news have beautiful feet."

Nathan curls his lip. He peeks down at his toes and back up toward me, his expression still bumming.

I hug him. "Guess you'll be answering to 'shiny feet' from now on, eh? And not because of all that running you do."

He groans. "Mom, that's crazy. I just thought Gib would 'preciate the Bible, that's all. No big deal. He didn't have to get all rudish on me."

"You did what you could, Nathan. That's all God asks of us, to do as He leads, and to let Him take care of the rest. You and Gibson will make up, I'm sure of it."

"Yeah. 'Cept I called him a *bawler*." He grins sheepishly.

"A *what?*"

He shrugs. "Just means he's a crybaby. Like a guy who cries on the beach when he breaks his board."

"Oh, Nathan!"

"He was so mad."

A shadow hits us from the doorway. "Who was so mad?" Gaby asks, standing in our entry and looking like she just stepped out of a movie. Her dark waves are pulled away from her face, with several loose strands framing her cheeks. She's wearing a pretty off-the-shoulders number in sunflower. It hits me that my pal reminds me of Belle from *Beauty and the Beast*. Considering she just had lunch with Ty, I'm suddenly overtaken by the irony.

"Gaby!" I rush over to her and feel Nathan blow past me before tearing up the stairway. *Mental note: Pick up conversation with Nathan later*. I focus again on Gaby, whose olive skin is positively glowing at the moment. "Well?"

"He is absolutely gorgeous!"

Well, he does have that Fabio-thing going on. "So ya hit it off? Lunch was good? He was . . . nice?"

"All of the above!" She sighs. "I've just come from the most perfect first date a girl could have, Bri-Bri. He's very chivalrous—opening doors for me, pulling out my chair, even placing my order with the waiter. Quite the gentleman, that Ty."

Forgive me here, but I'm heaving a big sigh myself—of relief. I don't like admitting this, but I had second (and third!) thoughts about matching up Gaby with Ty. For one thing, the man's my *boss*. For another, he's a tad, well, geeky. Yet he's Rita's son and the head of a great company, and from what I can tell, he's all about making it even better—even if his mother's a bit hard on him.

I reach out and give Gaby a squeeze around the neck. "So this is

good news! What was it like?" I lower my voice like we're spies.
"What did you two talk about?"

"We talked about everything! Coastal Tours. How he likes living
in Ventura. You."

"Me?" *Ew.*

"He's so grateful for your expertise at the tour company, Brianna.
I'm so proud of you, missy! You've made such an impression on him."

"You're too kind. I bet you're the one who made the impression.
Your hair's a knockout, by the way. When did ya have that done?"

She giggles and swirls around in her flouncy dress. "I went over to
Salon Panache this morning. Tami squeezed me in between a perm
and a color job. Do you like?"

"I do!"

Gaby plops onto the couch while I lower myself to the floor. I sit
cross-legged, wanting to know *everything*. "You didn't warn me about
the Hummer, Bri," she says abruptly. "I'm sure watching me climb
aboard that thing in this dress provided plenty of entertainment for
the neighbors." She's giggling, like she didn't really mind. "I don't
recall you mentioning that silken hair either, nor that cute way the
corner of his mouth tilts when he smiles!"

And just like that we spiral into the world of TMI, aka *too much
information!* Suddenly, it feels like she's divulging the intimate secrets
of a family member like, say, a brother. Very yuck. I fight the urge to
leap into the kitchen and dive into the brownie mix until I realize
how inappropriate that would be. Brownies, of course, are reserved
for breakups. Not just for the moments when I'd like to make a break
for it.

". . . and he ordered the Cobb salad, Brown Derby–style. It looked
divine. Oh, and he's very funny. He does this great Carrot Top
impression."

"Shut up!"

"No, seriously." Gaby starts giggling really hard. "Someone in the restaurant got a call on their cell," she sniffs, twice, "and he acted out one of those dumb collect phone charge commercials, you know, those old ones. It was a scream!"

I'm lying on the floor, clutching my sides, trying to picture Ty funny. The more I imagine, the more I laugh. I'm barely noticing the dust bunnies hanging from the corner of the living room rafters.

Gaby's voice has turned quiet again. "I'm seeing him again," she says.

I roll over and stare up at her. She looks so happy. "Cool. When?"

"Saturday night. He's taking me to dinner at the Aloha Steakhouse. I told him all about that waiter-guy's recipe for flaming steak. What's his name again?"

"Kenny."

"Right. I told him about Kenny's famous filet, and he wants to check it out."

"And to spend more time with you," I add.

She blushes. "What can I say?"

The doorbell rings and I drag myself up off the floor. "Who could that . . . oh!" I dart a look at Gaby. "What time is it?"

"Four-fifteen. Why?"

I start brushing off my clothes and glance around the room for my flirtatious sandals. "I completely forgot that I've got an appointment." I wriggle my toes into one shoe, hopping like a freak to scooch into it. I'm still not quick enough. Before I've got both sandals on, Nathan's already sliding down the banister and heading for the door.

I file in behind him, anticipation over meeting Rita's cousin rippling through me. I'm still patting down my hair when Nathan throws open the door, sending the sand-laden breeze careening in. A familiar face stares back at me.

"Brianna, how lovely to see you again!"

Like a bad reveal at the end of *Trading Spaces,* I'm horrified to discover Mona's designer, Patrice, standing on my doorstep.

This is *so* not happening. I fight the urge to peer around the corner in search of a camera crew. I just know that at any minute, someone's going to jump into view and shout, "Psych!"

"I was positively thrilled to receive your phone call," she gushes. "I told Maybel all about your lovely space here at the beach and how much I would love to dig my hands into this project. Truly."

"I . . . I was expecting Pati. Rita's cousin," I whimper.

Patrice thrusts both of her hands, spread eagle, onto her chest. Her acrylic nails poke at her cashmere sweater. Her fiery hair, piled high atop her head, bobs when she talks. "That's me! I am Rita Holland's cousin, Patrice Blanc. Members of my family often call me Pati."

From my side, Gaby whispers, "Invite her in."

"Oh. Uh, would you like to come in?" I step back and land on Nathan's foot.

"Watch it," he mumbles. "Those are beautiful to God, you know." He tosses me a teenage grin, the kind that says, *Try getting yourself out of this one, Mom.*

I scold him with my eyes and nod toward the stairway. One look

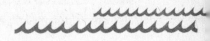

from me and the kid knows it's homework time—or else! He spins around and lunges for the stairs.

I can hear Nathan's footsteps bounding down the second-floor hall. Holding my breath, I turn to catch Patrice's ample self pacing through the living room. She's got one hand on her hip and the other stroking her chin. "As I was saying, Brianna, I was simply overjoyed to receive your call today. Nothing could have made me happier. And when I heard that you were one of Rita's employees, why, I raced to the phone and called my cousin immediately."

"You called her?" You mean there's no easy way out of this?

She turns to look at me. "And she tells me that you are an absolute treasure to her. I had no idea."

Yeah, well, right now I'd like to be buried. Buried treasure, that is. Hidden far, far away.

"Anyhoo, she tells me that you are interested in something a little more—what shall we call it?—elegant, perhaps?" She says this while resting one bauble-encrusted hand on the shade of our monkeys-under-two-palm-trees lamp.

Gaby clears her throat. Her eyes flash at me, and she mutters, "*No comprendo,* chica."

"Hadn't had a chance to tell you yet, Gaby," I say, explaining loudly while watching Patrice as she continues to give my living room the once-over, again and again, "but I've been thinking about doing some redecorating. Rita recommended her cousin Pati to help me out."

Patrice cuts in, "And the timing could not have been more superb! I have oodles of items in my studio that are just *perfect* for the home of a prominent attorney." She gives the room yet another swipe with her eyes, her head bobbing. "Oh my, yes. The things I have on hand will be utterly sublime in this space."

Startled, I hold up my copy of *Dwell*. "Well, I haven't exactly decided what I'd like to do in—"

"Oh, but darling, that's *my* job!" Patrice pulls the magazine from my hand and sets it on the coffee table. She doesn't look at it. "I'm a highly trained professional, and I simply *know* what you need just by canvassing the area and by talking with you, of course. And darling, believe me, I have just the ideas and décor for you."

That's right! I will make you an offer you can't refuse. For only $39.95 . . .

I'm standing there, dizzy with dilemmas, when Nathan calls to me from the top stoop. "Mom, Dad's on the phone."

The phone rang? When did the phone ring? I glance upward. "I'll grab it down here. Excuse me a minute, Patrice, would you?" I can feel Gaby's eyes boring into me as I step into the kitchen and grab the cordless phone. I suck in a breath before answering, "Hi, hon."

"Great news, Brianna! The jury came back with a decision for the defense."

He won! I'll never get over that whenever my smart, well-educated husband wins a case, he sounds more like a ten-year-old Little Leaguer. It's like he just hit a homer. I feel like patting him on the rump and telling him to hit the showers.

"Right on, my *brilliant* husband! Congratulations!" I say.

"This was a tough one, Brianna. Very, very tough. But it's over. The client is ecstatic and I'm glad to be moving forward."

"So you'll be home early?" I'm thinking we could hit Aloha Steakhouse or maybe even Capelletti's for a celebratory dinner.

"I'd like to do that, of course, Brianna, but my client wants to take my team out for dinner tonight." He lowers his voice. "You know I'd rather not, but—"

"No, no. You should go. Order something expensive on him."

His voice lightens. "My client's assistant was taking copious notes throughout the course of the trial. I would like to replay the decision and what led up to it. Besides, my client says that he has another case to discuss. May be another late night."

"Sounds fun," I say, hiding my disappointment. "Before you go, I've got a quick question."

"Shoot."

"I'm thinking of doing some redecorating. Okay with you?" I'm picturing Douglas standing tall and important amidst a sea of suits in the Hall of Justice lobby. He's on his cell phone, telling me about his big win, and I ask him about home improvement? Could I be any more pathetic?

"Hmm. Well . . . just a minute." His voice trails off, and I can hear muffled voices in the background. Several seconds pass before he's back on the line. "Sorry, Brianna. The judge has requested a meeting with the attorneys, so I'll have to get going. What did you ask me?"

"Uh, the redecorating. Any thoughts?"

He pauses. "No. Sure. I thought . . . no, that's fine. Whatever you want."

He's off again to save the world, and I'm back to my own version of *Designer's Challenge.*

"Oh, Brianna?" Patrice is tapping her forefinger on her chin, staring at my walls. "I'm seeing color. Lots of deep color. Burgundy, deep rum, merlot, perhaps."

Gaby's face lights up. "Ooh, ooh, and how about accents of Chardonnay braiding on your window treatments? And matching pillows?"

Am I sensing a pattern here? While we're at it, why not just stencil two large *A*s on the wall?

Now Gaby's pacing along behind Patrice, mirroring her every move, kinda like that Lucille Ball–Harpo Marx bit. My friend's initial apprehension seems to have passed, and it's time for me to face facts: *I am invisible.* I'm thinking this as I shuffle over to the door after hearing a decidedly firm knocking.

"Brianna, hello!" It's Rita on my doorstep, looking as tan and smart as always. "I certainly hope you don't mind," she says. "I stopped in to see how your consult with my Pati was going."

Join the club.

"It's always fun to see you, Rita. Hmm . . . twice in one day. C'mon in." I step back for her to enter. "I really haven't decided yet what kind of décor to go with, but—"

My words are cut off and left to dangle amidst two very high-pitched squeals. In the center of my great *space* (and don't you dare call it a *room*—that's just so *yesterday*), Rita and Pati cling to each other like sisters reunited after being separated at birth. In the years I've known Rita, I've seen her be professional, confident, and kind. I've watched her smooth over rough spots brought on by our most difficult clients. And I've witnessed her generous spirit in action.

But scream like a teen in a mosh pit? Never.

The cousins hold each other at arm's length—a good thing, too, since Rita's arms would never make it around Patrice. They survey each other. "Rita, you're such a peanut!" Patrice is saying, like she hasn't seen her in *ages*. "Oh, to be so petite *and* truly gorgeous. I'd swear you received the finest genes in this family of ours. Truly you did!"

"Stop it, stop it, my dear. You look lovely as always," Rita answers back, her softer side continuing to emerge.

The doorbell rings again and I have to marvel. Is this not the twenty-first century? It's Grand Central Station around here today! I'm as laid-back as the next gal, but c'mon. Use your cell phone, people!

I'm standing there, trapped between the kissing cousins and the front door. Gaby winks at me. "I'll get it," she mouths.

It's Max, Gibson's dad. Sigh. I'd almost forgotten about the rift the boys got into today. Hope Max isn't here to set Nathan straight. I just love his kid. Hoping I can smooth this over, I excuse myself, but neither Rita nor Patrice seems to notice. They're too busy playing "pass the compliment."

"Hey, Max," I say, reaching the door.

He smiles, and I'm struck by how much he resembles country singer Clint Black. He's got thick, brown hair, a gentle grin, and the kind of deep creases that women hate for themselves but love on a man. He and Clint probably stand at similar height too. Funny. I'd never noticed the similarities. Then again, the few times I see Max around, he's usually covered in grease. This afternoon he's squeaky clean and looking downright dapper, if you ask me.

"Hi, Bri. I was just telling Gaby that Gibson left his wet suit here." He shakes his head slightly. "Sorry about the trouble between the boys. I thought I'd just come on by and get it—to avoid any more skirmishes."

"Max, I'm sorry too. The boys'll work it out, though, I know they will." I'm wondering if I should mention the Bible, then think better of it. "I think the suit's in the garage. . . ."

Gaby touches my arm. "Go back to your meeting. I can help Max find it."

I watch as my well-dressed friend heads toward the garage with Max following closely behind. I cringe thinking of Gaby having to gingerly step over all the stacked-up junk while wearing her storybook dress.

Resigned, I turn back toward the living room, where Rita and Patrice have made themselves cozy. Patrice has pulled fabric samples from her satchel and is spreading them out on the area rug at their feet. I peek over their shoulders. Hmm. The colors seem less garish than I'd earlier imagined. Rita's pointing at a fairly okay tapestry design and nodding her red bouffant vigorously.

She glances up at me. "I'm so pleased, Brianna, that you've decided to go with Pati for your design." She stops and looks around. "These grand walls certainly lend themselves to something handsome and classic."

Like my Douglas?

She continues. "You've always been quite the free spirit, Brianna. Frankly, I was surprised by your desire to hire an interior designer." She's chuckling now. "But I guess that we all grow up and change our ways, don't we? That husband of yours has made a name for himself; you must be so proud. Now I suppose you have become very busy being a charming hostess to his wealthy clients. Just don't forget about us at Coastal Tours, all right?"

She warms me with her smile now, and although my mind cries out an SOS, I know there's no way I can *not* hire Patrice. Just how would that look? Patrice designs for the rich and famous of Ventura. As a favor to Rita, she squeezes me in to her busy schedule. I'd seem like an ingrate if I told her to take her swatches and head for the foothills.

"I don't have any plans to stop hosting tours, Rita. Not at all. But I would like to give this place an update. Maybe have a few more guests over . . ."

"Fabulous!" Patrice whips a contract from her satchel and stands. She waves the paper and a pen in my direction. "I'll just need your John Hancock at the X—it's just a formality—and then we'll be on our way."

Uh, but I have to run it past my lawyer first. . . .

"I'm sure you usually have Douglas look these things over, Brianna," Rita says. "But I can tell you, it's a standard contract. Trust me, dear. I've seen a million of them."

Patrice jumps in. "Oh, and time is of the essence, Brianna. As I said when I arrived, I've got scads of items in my studio, too many to mention, just perfect for your space. They won't last long, though, no they most certainly will not. And I must tell you, if this were an addition or a remodel, under no circumstances could we move this quickly. But, darling, I have everything on hand for a redo such as yours. Painters at the ready!"

The contract leaves the budget negotiable, and so I sign. *Besides, there's always that three-day buyer's-remorse clause. Sigh.* Last weekend, I sprung for a new wardrobe, today I committed to a living room do-over. What's next? A heart tattoo on my ankle? *Heaven forbid. Although, wouldn't Mona just love that?* And yet I'm pleased with myself. I set out to make changes, and I'm making them.

I hand back the form to Patrice. Behind me, I hear Gaby saying so-long to Max from the doorway. It must have taken them eons to find that wet suit. *Note to self: Clean out that garage!*

After Patrice takes some measurements, she and Rita slip out with an air kiss and a wave. Gaby follows me into the kitchen, joining me for a cup of coffee and confession.

"I hired Patrice," I say simply.

Gaby reaches a hand across the counter. "I was thinking, chica. Room designs can take *months*. Maybe the fact that Patrice has so much in stock . . . well, maybe that's a God-thing. Yes?"

I shrug. "I guess."

"You don't sound too excited. I mean, if I were about to have my home redone, I'd be doing the happy dance—*olé!*"

I laugh. "Okay, okay. Hey," I say, changing the subject, "sorry about the mess in the garage. Find the suit okay?"

"It's not that bad, Bri-Bri. We found Gibson's wet suit just fine."

"Good. You two were gone for a long time. I thought maybe you'd tripped and gotten buried in there."

"We were just talking. That's why it took so long."

Talking? To Max? "Yeah?" I say. "What about?"

"Well, for starters, I told Max that Gibson's such a terrific young man! Then I offered him some advice."

Uh-oh. I draw in a breath, hoping that Max wasn't offended by Gaby's meddling.

She continues. "You should have seen him, Bri. Max's face turned cherry red when I picked up that smelly wet suit." She giggles. "So I told him that in order to avoid that dreadful 'eau de neoprene,' he should have Gibson splash wet-suit shampoo on it. And I said to always have Gibson leave it either laid out flat or draped over a thick hanger. Then I talked to him about the grease between his fingers."

"Oh, you didn't!"

"He's got really beautiful hands, Bri-Bri, have you noticed?" My eyebrows stand at attention, but she continues on, oblivious. "Anyway, I just told him to rub some sweetly scented shaving cream on them and the grease should dissolve nicely."

I'm giggling now too. "Sheesh, Gaby. Let me guess. You also told him to use peanut butter to remove bubble gum from his hair, and that cream of tartar gets out ring-around-the-collar, didn't you!"

"Well, they work, chica! My mother swore by them, and her mother—may she rest in peace—did too!"

I shake my head, smiling. Maybe I ought to try some of Gaby's tips rather than just toss them aside as old wives' tales. I'm thinking this and pouring us a second cup when the phone rings. It's Douglas.

"Brianna? It's me," he says, his voice cautious. "There's been a change of plans."

Chapter eighteen

"Atlanta?!" Gaby's holding her cup in midair, her face screwed up like she's just swallowed some coffee grounds.

I smack my mug onto the Formica counter and grab for the half-empty pot. *Like I really need another shot of adrenaline.* "He says the senior partner is double-tracking out there," I mutter.

Gaby wrinkles her nose. "So?"

I stare at her. "It means he's got several sets of depositions going at the same time. He can't be everywhere at once, so he's calling on Douglas to fly out with him and handle some of them."

"But he's just finished up such a long trial. Can't he just get out of it?"

"Guess not." I blow out a long puff of air. "The client wants the best, and Douglas just won his big case, so that makes him it."

We both fall silent. Gaby cradles her mug of coffee in her hands but doesn't take a sip. I, on the other hand, am guzzling caffeine at the moment, thinking that I can't remember a weirder time in my relationship with my husband. He's like a vapor, only with a voice. One that's usually saying, "*Hasta la vista,* baby."

Gaby bolts from her stool and starts rummaging around in my

cupboards. "Well, you can forget dinner tonight, girlfriend. I'm making *brownies*." She wraps her arms around a pile of ingredients and dumps them onto the counter, spilling a spoonful of cocoa.

I give a wry laugh. "That's sacrilege, you know."

"There's more where that came from. Now go change out of those nice clothes and . . . hey! You're all dressed up. I just noticed." She cocks her head. "I *knew* something was different about you." She walks around the island, checking out my outfit. "I can't believe you went shopping without me! Why did you go shopping without me?"

Why did *I go shopping without her?* "Not on purpose! I just wanted to pick up a few new things, you know, to wear to meetings and stuff." Although, come to think of it, the romantic free-flowing look ala Gaby is *so* not me.

"Hmm." She looks like she doesn't believe me. "New clothing, redesigned living room—anything you want to tell me about? Are you having a not-quite midlife crisis or something?"

Or something. "Don't overreact. I just peeked at my feet one day and thought about that women's lacrosse team. You know, they wore flip-flops to meet the president? I figured that if I were ever invited to the White House, I'd better have some decent shoes."

Gaby laughs and swipes the spilled chocolate from the countertop with a damp cloth. "That was pretty shocking, wasn't it?" She's wiping down the entire island now, and all I can think is, *How does she keep her nails so perfect?* "I mean, those were college ladies wearing flip-flops at our nation's Capitol!"

"Oh please. I was kidding! You're beginning to sound like Mona now." Gaby gasps at me, but I continue. "Seriously, if you ask me, the whole thing was kinda blown way out of proportion. It's not like they had sand sticking to them or anything. Sheesh."

"Okay, okay. I get it. You're grumpy today, missy. I'll get these brownies started, and you can just sit there and pout if you want. Or," she says in her best mother-tone, "you can march up those stairs and change into some proper brownie-feasting clothes."

I give a half sigh, half growl. "Sor-ry, Gaby. It's just been so odd around here lately. I feel like a single parent!" Or just single. Period.

"I'm sure it's only for a season, like Pastor Jake likes to say. Douglas will get through all this busyness, though, and you'll be back to being the same old sickening lovebirds that you used to be. Only you'll be that much more stylish." She giggles at her joke. "And maybe he'll even call you from the airport, crooning 'I'm Already There.'"

My stomach sinks at her mention of the Lonestar hit about a guy who travels too much and misses his family. At the moment, I feel like I'm on the spin cycle. That's what Gib calls it when surfers get stuck in a churning wave, unable to figure out which way is up. I just wish low tide would hit. Maybe when the water pulls back, laying bare all that was stuck beneath it, I'll be able to restore order in my mind.

"So," Gaby says, "I take it Douglas won't be home for dinner tonight?"

"Uh-uh. He won't. After he relives the glory with his client at dinner, he'll come back just long enough to throw some chonies into a bag before heading for the airport."

Gaby's laugh spikes the air. "Ha—chonies! That's funny."

Like that animated paper clip with the wiggly eyebrows that appears out of nowhere in my Microsoft Word program, Nathan pops his head around the corner. "Dad's not coming for dinner again?"

I open my mouth, readying myself to defend his father's current state of busyness. I tell myself that this is only temporary and that it's up to me to explain, in a nonjudgmental way, that his dad's an important guy and that he still loves us. Before a word escapes across my lips, however, Nathan continues. "So can we get pizza tonight?"

So much for my maternal instinct. "Pizza sounds yum," I say, suddenly in no mood to cook. *Like I ever really am.* "Grab a coupon from the drawer, and go ahead and order it, 'kay?" I look over at Gaby, who's spooning more brownie batter into her mouth than into the pan. "I'll just pull on some sweats and be back to, uh, help you."

My best friend throws a smile in my direction. At the sight of chocolate smeared across her cheek, I can't help but grin.

———

I'm biting into the last slice of pineapple and ham pizza, wondering who I have to thank for this hug to the taste buds. Seriously, now. Italians? New Yorkers? Hawaiians? Mmm, mmm. Pineapple and ham. Who knew? The master chef who first threw these two opposites together has my undying respect.

Nathan leans across the kitchen island and tears off a strip of dried cheese from the pizza box. Gaby raises her eyebrows at me. We've been sitting around the island together all evening, each of us seemingly lost in thought. Presumably Nathan's thinking about his fight with Gibson, and Gaby's still glowing over Ty, while I wonder just how long Douglas's latest foray away from home will last.

"A-hem," I say to my teen, offering him my half-eaten slice of heaven. "Want it?"

He's licking his fingers and shaking his head. "Nah. I'm good." A string of cheese hangs from his mouth. "Can I have a brownie now?" he asks.

I hand him a napkin. "Let me see you eat some of those carrots first," I order, the yoke of parental responsibility bearing down on me.

"What? I had a bunch of pineapple, Mom." My teen suddenly looks and sounds like a toddler.

"Canned," I shoot back. "It's not the same thing."

"It's a fruit, at least, so it must be healthy."

There's a whole déjà vu thing going in my mind right now. Somewhere in my head I'm remembering a similar tête-à-tête with my aunt Dot. I'm not sure of the exact conversation, but somehow I remember the word *roughage* coming into play. By the look on my son's face, this topic is having a similar impact on him.

Gaby slides a plate with the biggest brownie slab I've ever seen under Nathan's nose. She leans over. "One carrot, and it's yours."

Kiss-up!

It works, and he's crunching away. "Oh yeah," he finally says in between bites. "I forgot. There's a message on the machine for you. Somebody wants you to teach Sunday school."

"*This* weekend?"

"I guess. Not sure. I dunno."

Gaby stifles a smile. I look in her direction and roll my eyes. "You're good at teaching," Gaby tells me. "You should do it more often. When's the last time you taught?"

I shrug. "A long time. Can't remember when." Back then, hanging around a tumble of rugrats got to me. Douglas and I wanted more kids, but it never happened for us. So I guess it was just easier to avoid the whole Sunday school scene rather than relive the disappointment. Bitterness, I figured, did nothing for the skin.

Gaby chuckles. "You used to say such goofy things when you were working with the kids in there."

"*Moi?*"

"Don't you remember?" Gaby's got her arm propped onto the counter, holding up a slab of chocolate like it's on display.

Nathan's already dug into his dessert but stops long enough to cut in. "I remember! You used to say, 'Turn that frown upside down!'" He shakes his head, keeping his sights on the brownie before him. "So embarrassing."

Mmm, yes. I remember it well. Growing up, I spent many weekends playing teacher alongside my auntie. Years later I felt grossly underqualified to step into her comfortable shoes, so when I was asked to teach, I borrowed a bunch of "Dot-isms" to help me get through it.

Gaby's wagging her finger and looking up at my ceiling. "What was that other thing you always said? Something about God not fighting . . .."

I snort. Another Dot-ism. "He's a lover—not a fighter!" I say in my best Mary Sunshine imitation.

She points at me. "That's it! I always loved that!"

I grab for a gooey brownie. "Give me one of those, wouldja?"

"So you gonna do it? You gonna teach on Sunday?" Nathan's got a brownie in each hand now. "I could come in and throw some of the little brats around, if you want."

Gaby gasps. "Nathan!"

He grins, and there's mushy crumbs stuck to his teeth. *Ew*.

The phone rings, and I smack my hand on his shoulder. "I'll grab it," I say, shoving my teenager back down onto his stool. I dust off my hands before picking up the receiver. "Mel's Diner," I answer.

"Oh my. I believe I must have dialed the wrong number."

Oh brother. "Hello, Patrice," I say. "You've got the right place. This is Bri."

"Of course it is. Now I recognize you, darling." She sucks in a deep breath. "I have such wonderful news for you, Brianna. It's truly like a miracle. Are you ready?" She doesn't wait for my answer. "I've already chosen the perfect color for your walls, and a paint crew can be at your lovely home tomorrow afternoon!"

I cough. *Color? Paint crew? Tomorrow?*

"Did you hear me, darling?"

"Um, ye-yes, I did. Wow. Already. You know, I'd like to take a look at the color—"

"Of course, Brianna, of course. You have final approval on simply *everything*. Not to worry, darling. Not one swipe of paint will be put onto your walls until you have given the go-ahead, no it will not."

I envision my living room becoming a haven for drop cloths in just a few short hours. Talk about no turning back. Part of me screams, "Fugeddaboutit!" but the other half remembers Gaby's words from earlier. Things do seem to be falling into place quickly and perfectly. So what if I'm as ready as a nine-year-old for the prom? Like she said, it must be a God-thing. And how could I turn my back on that?

"Well, then, Pati," I hear myself saying, "I guess we'll see you tomorrow."

"Fabulous, darling. You won't regret it, no you will not!"

It's 10:00 A.M. and while Douglas lunches with the big guns in
Atlanta, I'm about to hang with visitors from Tokyo. A few hours and
a couple thousand miles, and once again, my husband and I are living
separate lives. Just like that.

Irony hits me as I watch a luxury-liner bus carrying twenty just-
married couples from Japan pull into the harbor lot. For the next
three or so hours, I get to escort forty love-struck honeymooners in
and around our pretty city. God has such a sense of humor.

I can't help but note, though, that the group's bus-hopping has
taken them from a decked-out, no-expense-spared coach to our more
down-home, comfort bus. Kind of like comparing a limo to a nice,
solid Ford van. While their driver wears a tux, our Ned's strolling
across the pavement in his customary tee and shorts. From this distance, I can see he's chosen his personal favorite, *Redneck, and proud of
it!*, for our day's tour.

So. Who's the joke on now?

I invite our guests aboard, startlingly aware that, standing next to
these dainty women, I'm like Godzilla in business-casual. But I smile
and bow, as they do the same. Many of the ladies avoid eye contact,

as if they're nervous to approach me. This compels me to smile brighter, which is unfortunate, because the more I show my teeth, the more they seem distressed. *R-a-a-r!*

An intense young man dressed in a silky black suit rushes to the front of the line. "Hi, hi," he says, bowing and shaking my hand. "I am Hiro. Very good I meet you. I am guide. I translate." He scurries down the line of guests, displaying more energy than that adrenalized bald guy from the Six Flags commercials. I watch as he bows and speaks and gestures for the rest of the couples to move forward.

I join Hiro in welcoming everyone aboard with my Western congeniality. "Welcome, welcome," I say as the line moves along. After the last couple embarks and Hiro follows, I, too, hop up the steps. I notice that two rows of seats, just about midway down, have been left completely empty. Hiro's already at the far end of the bus, talking and pointing out the window. I glance out the window to the parking lot, looking for stray guests, but it's empty as a ball field in the rain.

I turn back to find Ned scooching his rather large self deep into the vinyl driver's seat. I'm trying not to stare here. After all, he's just making himself comfortable behind the big, wide steering wheel. "Psst," he hisses, grabbing my legitimate attention. "They're a sup'r'stitches group."

"Wha. . . ?"

"Sup'r'stitches. Like 'n bad luck 'n' all that. They won't sit in those rows down there."

I look down the aisle and do a quick calculation in my head. Rows four and nine have been left completely vacant.

Ned's watching me and nodding. "Yup. They avoid numbers four and nine altogether." He lowers his voice to that raspy whisper again. "In their language, 'four' sounds like 'death,' you know," he adds, enlightening me.

"Really. And nine? What about nine?"

"Torture. It sounds like torture."

Hmm. Torture. Yeah, I can relate.

One thing I can't get, though, is the whole "group honeymoon" concept. When I saw this tour listed on the docket, I figured Luann had just encountered a burst of creativity. Maybe the tour would actually be made up of couples celebrating a golden anniversary or the like, and that the name "honeymoon tour" would serve as a sort of wistful reminder of yesteryear. But real-live newlyweds with not a wrinkle in sight? Unbelievable!

I mean, to me, just the word *honeymoon* alone calls to mind lingering dinners . . . moonlit strolls . . . passionate nights. Not dinner reservations for forty at eight o'clock! Uh-uh. No way. When Douglas and I honeymooned along the shores of Maui, the last thing we wanted to see was people.

Sigh. I remember those bliss-filled days like they happened last week, rather than more than fourteen years ago. We stayed in a cottage by the sea (no surprise there). When we arrived, I/we were surprised by a fluted crystal vase filled with water and a lone white rose placed on the glass table top in the sitting area of our suite.

"Isn't that a kick?" I remember saying. "At these prices, they could only afford to give us one flower?"

"It seems rather nice," I recall his generous answer.

Each day for the next six, another rose was secretly added to the vase. Five more white roses, and a final red one. On that last day, the seventh day, a note appeared with the final rose. *You are more beautiful than the rest, a standout in a sea of colorless forms. I will love you forever. Yours, Doug.*

The memory gives me goose bumps. I search the throng of serene faces before me and wonder, *Would any of these porcelain beauties ever live such a fairy tale? Yeah, yeah, they've got it in the looks department, but what's up with the mass honeymoon, ladies?*

"All aboard!" Ned's brusque voice cuts into my daydream. I see Hiro still scuttering around, bowing and nodding like a butler on steroids. I want to tell him to relax, that we're on our way and all will be peachy. Just how do I say that in Japanese?

I don't have to. Rather than take a seat in infamous rows four or nine, our Hiro has scooted in next to one of the eensiest-weensiest couples in the bunch. The three of them sit side by side, shoulders touching, gazes staring straight ahead. Apparently discomfort is preferred over torture or death.

Well, alrighty then. I smile and grab my mic, welcoming them, once again, to beautiful Ventura. I might as well be telling them I've got a pinched nerve. Their expressions don't change one bit. I look to Hiro and raise my eyebrows, but he's stone-faced like the rest. *Just three hours. Three short hours . . .*

North of the harbor, we park at Emma Woods State Beach for some serene wildlife viewing. We hit the jackpot with two great blue herons wading in a shallow tide. *Be still my heart.* We watch them strut and stab at the water for their food. I tell our visitors to look for the nearly seventy-inch wingspan of these incredible creatures and to listen closely for their deep, hoarse croak.

Alarmingly, they take to the sight like a toddler to lima beans. It's not that they're not polite. Oh, if I could only bottle their manners and sell it to middle school principals across this country, then Douglas and I could retire to Hawaii *forever*. Uh-uh. Nope, my Japanese guests show a level of courtesy to be envied, to be copied even. It's just that behind the gentle smiles and constant nodding, well, they look bored.

I clear my throat. "Let's double-back to the visitor's center," I mutter to Ned, doing my best Edgar Bergen–Charlie McCarthy impression. "I have to get them out of these seats."

"You're the boss."

I usually like saving the center for last, but this group needs a little livening up. I figure a clear shot of our spectacular islands from the upstairs balcony will do the trick. It's a brief drive along the shoreline to the center's parking lot, and for once I see their faces change.

"Idoru? Idoru?" I hear some of them ask as they exit. Suddenly, excitement fills the air. . . .

I smile. I nod. I watch the men beam at the ladies, and the blushing brides glance over their shoulders at one another, covering their mouths and giggling. *Good move on the side trip.*

One couple holds back. The man points upward at the center's top balcony, where other tourists have already gathered en masse this sunny morning. He's shielding his eyes with his hand, while his new wife tugs on his sleeve.

"Idoru?" she asks him demurely.

Again with the *idoru!*

Hiro scrambles up to them, motioning quickly. "Come, come," he says. The man utters "idoru" again, and Hiro just nods and hustles them along toward the center's doors.

Inside, Ned's already dug his hands into the real, simulated tide pool exhibit. His arm's in the air and he's got his fingers wrapped around a soft, blood-red creature. "This here's your sea cucumber," he's saying, passing the dripping wet animal under the noses of two nearby brides. Seawater drips down the sides of the creature and lands with fat *plops* onto their shoes.

"Oooh!" cries one of the ladies. She hops backward and nearly stumbles over the other bride.

Ned keeps a death grip on the spiny-skinned creature, ignorant of the cries, the stares, and the all-around mess he's making. "Yup, this here's a miracle from God," he's saying, although his audience has mostly vanished. A lone man still stands at his side, but he's not even with our tour. "Didja know he spits out his guts when a predator gets too close?" Ned asks, oblivious.

I'm getting ready to corral my group and direct them to the staircase when I hear another round of the curious "idorus" bouncing through the crowd like a beach ball at Dodger Stadium. I'm thinking that maybe it's a sort of praise word, like the very French *ooh-la-la*. Or like Gaby's favorite, *¡bravo!* I pause and roll the Japanese word around in my head, but it just doesn't seem to carry the wow-factor of the others.

I turn to let Ned know I'll be taking the tour up deck and see him drying his hands on a brochure. At my stare, he folds up the high-gloss flyer and stuffs it into the pocket of his cargo shorts. We're the last ones to reach the crowded viewing area upstairs. A few vaporous clouds drift by, but otherwise, there's a clean, clear view of the Channel Islands. Perfect.

A tiny woman stands on her tiptoes and hangs on to the guardrail. She's pointing and sighing. "Oh," she cries. "Shangri-la!"

Now, there's a word I get!

A hush moves through the group of honeymoon tourists as they take in the view of our local paradise. I shut my eyes for just a moment and let the cool breeze tickle my cheeks. Being up here is like going on a mini-vacation. All of a sudden, life's big worries seem more like a hiccup, something that'll go away sooner or later. In my head I've got a picture. Douglas is home, Rita's still my boss, and I'm back to living in flip-flops. Mmm, yes, Shangri-la!

I barely notice that a small group of high school girls has made it up the steps and crowds in around us. Scratch that. I probably would not have noticed had my own group of guests not suddenly spun on their heels and stared. "Idoru?" several of them are asking.

I zip a look their way and cup Hiro's elbow as he tries to scurry past. We sidle over to the corner. "Okay, I've got to know. What *does* idoru mean?" I whisper.

He smiles, he bows, he starts to pull away. I hold fast to the sleeve of his jacket. He gives off a staccato sigh. "It's pop star."

I'm stunned. "As in Hilary Duff?" I shoot back.

"Yes."

"And they're expecting to see Hilary here?"

"Yes. No. Ah, yes."

"And *why*?"

His eyes won't meet mine. "Sorry. Sorry. The brochure said near Hollywood. Someone say there may be pop star here."

My mouth opens, yet nothing comes out. Then like a gurgling stream, I feel laughter bubbling up. "You've *got* to be kidding me!" I crack up, and Hiro's eyes dart around, probably hoping no one figures out this mistake of *Godzillian* proportions. "Well, my friend," I say, fighting the laughter, "we're fresh out of pop stars today. You'd better tell them. *Pronto.*"

"Ah, well, ah. I hope you will be telling them."

"Oh, no-no-no." I'm shaking my head. That sudden urge to mother someone has come over me, and I lay my palms on Hiro's shoulders. "*You* need to tell them."

Driblets of sweat appear on his forehead. He's nodding vigorously. "Yes, ma'am."

Annoying ma'am reference aside, I'm glad he's going to nip this now. Ugh. Can't believe these people were actually led to think that this tour included celebrity sightings, nor that one of *our* brochures said "near Hollywood." That's sixty miles of rush hour to the south, people!

But we're too late. The girls on the balcony have been surrounded. *Oh no!* I nudge Hiro toward the group, and together we wrangle our way back into the crowd. Most of the teens stand around tittering. All, that is, but one. She's wearing a green cheerleading shell with her name—*Marcy*—embroidered on the top and a skirt to match. Her blond hair's in a tight bob, she's chomping on gum, and— signing autographs! *What's up with that, girlfriend!*

This is *so* wrong—and I'm not just talking about teenage Marcy's lengthy acrylic nails. My guests are being misled! I move in to break it up, when Hiro touches my arm. I whip my chin around and throw him a questioning look with my eyes.

"Please. No," he's saying. "It's good. It's good." He's jerking his head up and down.

Correct me if I'm wrong, but telling a lie is one of the top ten sins, is it not? "It's *lying*," I tell him.

"It's good. It's good," he keeps saying, trying to shoo me away. I see my trusty sidekick Ned over by the railing, fidgeting with the coin-operated telescope. I wiggle my fingers at him, hoping to get his attention, but he's fixed on the machine's lens. I see him twist it, then check the focus, again and again. *Boys will be boys. . . .*

I turn back to Hiro. "Who in your office said there'd be pop stars?"

"No, no. Coastal Tour office say so. I'm sure."

My eyebrows arch. "Wha. . . ?"

A whistle suddenly screeches, its pierce ricocheting off the tower's cement walls. The school chaperone has arrived! The jig is up. A buxom woman in Dockers and an Izod polo shirt, all six-foot-plus of her, has appeared at the top of the stairs. At the shrill of the whistle call, most of the students slowly line up.

Some from our tour continue to stare openmouthed at our resident "pop star" and her lingering groupies, seemingly unaware that they're just teens on a field trip. Others have already wandered off into smaller cliques, chattering and examining their forgeries together. Hiro's grinning and bowing and gesturing again, moving among the group like a savior.

Yet I'm reeling. Someone tells a fib, and now forty starstruck Japanese tourists stand around treasuring an autograph from a *non*-star. This is good *how*?

Chapter twenty

While some people live on the edge of reason, I tend to hover closer to satire. Why depend on sanity when life is so much funnier than that? I'm trying to remember this about myself as I head toward the tour office, feeling the heat rise within. Normally unruffled me is about ready to explode. Go figure.

I shove open the office door to Coastal Tours just in time to catch Luann tossing a paperback novel under the counter. "Oh my goodness, you're back!" she says to me, her voice overly loud. She smoothes her permed hair with her fingers. "How was your first international tour, sweetie?"

"Hello, Luann. My first international tour. Well, let me see." I lay out a palm and tap it with my other hand. "They were bored with the sights of wildlife and the sea, they don't eat cheese—so much for taking them to Queso Jack's for lunch—oh, and for some reason they seemed to think that our little tour included pop-star gawking. Know anything about that?"

She's fanning herself with a copy of *Vogue* magazine. "Not so good, huh? Shame, shame."

I drum my fingers on the reception counter, oddly aware of just how short my fingernails are. "So you don't know anything about this?"

"I . . . I'm not sure what you mean." Luann starts shuffling and stacking the same files over and over. She has yet to meet my eyes with her own.

"I mean, do you know who told our Japanese tourists that hunting celebs was part of our package?"

"Well . . ."

I cock my head to one side and stare her down. "Luann?"

She bites her lip. "Well, I guess I might have mentioned that it was a possibility."

"Luann!"

"He—I mean, Mr. Holland—said to." She sucks in a breath and abruptly covers her mouth with a stack of files. "Oh-oh," I hear her say behind all that card stock.

I exhale and let my shoulders drop. "Thanks a bunch, Luann," I say, spinning on my thick-soled shoes and heading toward Ty's office. I burst through the door and find him with his feet propped up on the desk, leafing through *American Executive*.

Doesn't anybody have any work to do around here?

Ty looks up from his magazine. "Welcome back, Brianna. Are you all finished up for the afternoon?"

My hand's still wrapped around the doorknob. I'm tired and cranky and have no plans to shoot the breeze this afternoon. "Just got back from a nightmare, actually. Can you tell me, Ty, why we are telling customers to expect pop-star sightings during our tours?"

Ty's expression doesn't change. Unless you count the slight curl of a smile forming on his lips. "As I recall, you told me over lunch that celebrities dock their boats near here. Isn't that right?"

"Yes, but—"

"So it is possible that when visiting our fine city, one might run across a celebrity or two. True?"

"It's possible, but—"

"Good enough." Ty folds up his magazine and slides it onto his desk. He drops his feet to the floor and sits up, leaning his clasped hands on the blotter in front of him. "Did you have something else to add?"

"Ty. These people were expecting bubble-gum pop singers. You know, the teenage kind created by talent agencies, ala Britney Spears. They seem to think that finding one and getting her autograph was the sole purpose for their little jaunt up the coast."

"Ah, I see. And you felt insulted by their lack of interest in . . . you."

I spit out a sigh. "Uh, *no*. They are the ones who should feel insulted, though. They were the ones . . . misled."

Ty stands and walks toward me. I clamp down on the doorknob, refusing to release my grip. Although, I'm thinking that with free hands I would find it easier to wring his neck. Or at least give a good yank on that mane of his.

"Brianna, let me ask you something." He's Donald Trump, calm and focused during negotiations, right before he swoops in to close the deal. "Do you guarantee with every tour that guests will, with the utmost certainty, view dolphins or sea lions or other types of wildlife?"

Oh, sheesh. "Nothing's guaranteed, Ty. You know that."

"But you *do* tell people to expect to see some type of coastal animal life, correct?"

I so don't want to answer him right now. "I tell them to be on the lookout. Of course."

"Brianna, I've done some research." He turns and taps a stack of magazines on his desk. "Did you know that our local beach areas, from Oxnard to Carpinteria, boast vacation homes for some of Hollywood's brightest stars? There's a rich history of performers traveling north away from the fray of big-city Los Angeles. Ever since the filming of *The Sheik*—"

I cut in. "*The Sheik*? You mean, as in that Rudy Valentino movie filmed just south of here in the 1920s? That's reaching a bit, don't you think?"

Ty smiles, making me think he's enjoying this debate. "History, I believe, tells the future." He points at me. "Listen, Brianna, it sounds like you had a difficult tour today. That is regrettable. If our new advertising campaign . . ."

Campaign?

". . . had anything to do with that, perhaps we'll have to revise how we inform our guests of possible celebrity encounters. I concede that with our international tours, perhaps we will have to make better strides to communicate skillfully. In this case, I suspect that language may have been a barrier." He moves closer, nearly towering over me. "In the meantime, keep up the good work, Brianna. Your people skills have served our guests well. I am certain that you are completely capable of handling anything that comes your way."

Reluctantly, I think back to the last stop on today's tour at Neptune Beach in Oxnard. I'm thinking about the hilarious delight on the brides' faces as they burrowed their toes into those fine grains of sand. And Hiro with that frenetic energy of his. What a crack-up! It took more than one groom to pry him off of that old, rusty, whale-on-a-spring playground toy.

Sigh. So my guests spent the first half of their tour searching for elusive celebrities? It all came out in the wash, as my aunt Dot used to say. Not that I'm happy about what occurred this morning! Nor will I let it happen again! But, I guess, it's time to move on.

I twist the door handle, readying myself to leave, but stop and turn back. Ty's leaning against his desk now, just staring at me. *Probably congratulating himself on turning my angst around in less than thirty minutes. It's like I'm Marcia Brady.* "By the way, Ty," I say coolly, "heard you and Gaby had a fun lunch yesterday."

. Other than a slight jerk of his mouth, he's expressionless. "Yes. Yes, we did. I found her to be quite charming. Thank you for the introduction."

Okay, so he's not the emotional type. What did I expect, that he'd gush like a schoolboy? "You're welcome. See you, Ty." I toss him a wave and I'm out of there for the next couple of days.

I dash to my car and switch on my phone, noting that I've got voicemail. It's Lisa from church, asking me if I got the message that she *really* needs me to teach Sunday school this week. Oops—forgot to return her call. I text-message her that, sure, I can help. But instead of feeling the heavens open and my heart lift over serving the Lord, my tummy aches like a rock's just been dropped into it. Haven't worked with little kids in years. Not sure I remember how.

Next message . . .

"Brianna, darling! It's Patrice! My absolutely five-star painting crew arrived early, which is highly unusual, I might add. Well, darling, since they could not reach you by telephone, they dialed me instead." She blows a theatrical sigh into the phone. "I suppose I will have to step in here and make an *executive* decision—since we cannot reach you, that is. They used the key you left them—thank you for that, by the way—and have already prepped your entire living room! Now they are ready to apply the first coat of paint, darling, but you are nowhere to be found!"

Why am I getting this sinking feeling?

". . . So I have given them the go-ahead to start painting away, darling. Oh, I just know you will be so pleased. . . ."

I snap shut my phone and throw my Bug in gear. Fear has gripped me. Tell me I haven't made a huge mistake! I'm having scary thoughts here, really morbid ones. What if Patrice's snobbery is really a cover for outlandish, dark designs! Visions of black Goth walls and dripping candles fill my head, and I'm freaked that my new living room might soon be better suited to *Beetlejuice*.

Now, now, now, I'm telling myself. *Get a grip!* This is Rita's cousin, after all. She wouldn't *purposely* do anything to mar our beach house. She's a died-in-the-wool professional designer. I've seen her persnickety clothes, her pointy-toed shoes, and those expensive rings. Let me tell you, this gal knows upscale. And that's what I'm going for, right?

I'm rounding the corner to Seashell Lane, acutely overtaken by the thought that maybe I have yet to *own* the idea of change. I know it's what I must do, I've figured out how to do it, but I'm resistant to it. Like mildew to mild soap.

Once in our drive, I have to squeeze in my VW next to the painters' monster truck and then squish myself between the two like one of those stress-reliever balls. Deep breath in, I step up on my stoop and fling open the door.

"Ye-ow-w-ch!"

I peer around the half-open door and see a rotund man in sweats, rubbing his elbow. He's scowling at me. "Sorry!" I say, forcing a smile onto my face. "Guess I was just a little excited to see the paint job. You the boss?"

A paint-splattered guy calls to me from nearly the top rung of an amazingly tall ladder. "Can I help you?"

I look up. *Are these ceilings high or what!* I clear my throat. "Hi. Um, I'm the owner, Bri Stone." With a stilted gaze, I glance around. Nope, nope, no creepy swaths of dark paint here. I feel my shoulders relax. "So, couldn't wait to get started, huh?" I say to the man on the ladder.

"Patrice said you'd be fine with that. It's a nice color you chose." He points a roller toward a spot on the wall.

I tilt my head up. "Oh yeah. It's nice. I didn't pick it, but it's nice."

"It's called Buttered Rum. Has a nice ring to it."

Again with the booze reference. I'm expecting to hear Brad Paisley crooning his hit, "Alcohol," at any moment. "Yeah, well, I like the buttered part, at least." I look around, a stranger in a strange, drop cloth–covered land. It does have that sort of deep, beigy law-office thing going. So far I'm not hating it. *Not too much, anyway.*

"I'm Bud, by the way." He stays focused on the wall before him.

I hear a skateboard skid across the front patio just before Nathan and Troy appear in the doorway, eyes agog. "What the—!" Nathan's still holding his backpack, taking in our new and (hopefully) soon-to-be-improved living room.

Troy stands next to him, skateboard flipped up and leaned against his jeans. He gives the room the once-over and whistles.

I tiptoe over the sheet-covered floors. "Hey, guys!" I call out. "What's happening, Troy?" I'm welcoming Nathan's buddy, secretly wondering if his out-of-the-blue appearance has anything to do with Gibson's absence from our lives. I'm suddenly feeling a kinship with my pals who have daughters. From what I've heard, *drama* in their homes is an all-weather friend.

"Hi, Mrs. S." Troy wears glasses and his face is covered in freckles. *Just want to squeeze him.* "You got your house all torn up," he says to me. "That's cool."

Nathan crinkles his face at Troy. "Whatever." He looks my way. "They're not gonna paint my room, are they? I like it the way it is."

You mean smudgy and dirty? "We're starting with the living room, Nathan," I tell him. "Don't get in a snit. Go ahead up and you guys can start homework. Be careful around the paint cans."

"Cool, Mrs. S." Troy's nodding now and following along behind Nathan as he takes the stairs, two at a time.

Watching them go, I'm wondering if I should get involved with the whole Gibson mess. Nathan hasn't exactly asked for my advice. Then again, maybe he never will. Our kid's hovering somewhere between childhood and manhood, and I'm just trying to figure out where to stand.

Bud's voice pulls me from my thoughts. He freaks me out by

crying out, "Timber!" A roller tray careens from atop the twelve-foot ladder in the middle of my living room and lands with a *thwack* on the floor. I jump backwards, narrowly missing a full, open paint can with my nicely shod foot.

Yes, knowing where to stand is definitely the question on my mind at the moment.

Chapter twenty-one

I slept with the windows open last night, sucking in fresh air to offset the paint smell wafting up from the first floor. I'm sure the chaos and stink will be worth it eventually, but living the HGTV life is just not my thing. As long as I live in this eclectic beach town, though, I'll never get some of my neighbors. Around here, it's abnormal *not* to have some type of remodeling going on. The retired couple at the end of the block even ripped out a palm tree, paving over the spot just so their contractor would have a permanent place to park his truck.

Call me crazy, but I'd rather spend our money on an island-hopping trip.

Along with the thick smell of wet paint, the sea's waves rode fiercely onto shore all night long, keeping me awake. With every swell heaving onto land, a new thought careened into my mind. So along with clean ocean air in my lungs, my head had its fill too.

Crash . . . is Douglas busy because he has to be or because he wants to be? *Crash* . . . is Ty the upright person I'd hoped him to be, or have I done my best girlfriend wrong? *Crash* . . . will my home end up with a *Divine Design*, or will I be left *In a Fix*?

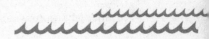

It's no wonder that I'm dragging this afternoon like a U-Haul trailer with a flat. I'm sitting outside in a meager sliver of sun, avoiding the commotion going on inside my house, trying to keep my eyes ajar. Flopped open in front of me is the Sunday school lesson I must consume and digest by this weekend.

Nathan's been quiet all afternoon. My eyes pop open as I repeat that thought. Nathan's been quiet all afternoon. *All is not right in teenager land*. I break out of my malaise and head inside to his bedroom.

I tap on the door. "Nathan. You all right?" I hear nothing so I quietly turn the knob and step in.

Nathan's got his back to me, and he's wearing earphones. On his desk sits a new bottle of glass cleaner and a wadded-up bunch of used paper towels. I watch him as he admires the mermaid decal he's just finished sticking onto his mirrored closet door.

"A-hem."

He jumps. "Whoa! Mom!" He looks cross, as my aunt Dot would say. His face is screwed up into a pout and his arms flail at his side. He pulls off the earphones and drops them onto the floor. "Why'd you do that?"

"Just checking in on you." I glance around the room. It's the neatest I've seen in months—except for the earphones sprawled on the carpet, that is. It even has that chemically induced fresh scent. "Guess the ocean's taking a rest from its big party last night. Waves flat today, huh?"

He shrugs and turns back toward his closet. "Dunno."

I take another step into his room. "Hey, how 'bout them Dodgers?" I jibe.

He tosses me another look with that scrunched-up expression. "What?"

I move toward him and give his shoulders a rub. "You're just not your chatty self, mister. What's up?"

"Nuthin'. My room was starting to stink, that's all."

"*Starting* to!"

"Mom! I just wanted to clean all this junk up." He kicks his running shoes farther under his bed. "I'm starting to hate it here," he mutters.

I plop onto his bed and sit cross-legged on his nearly smooth comforter. "Hate it as in 'love it'?" I ask him. "Like, that's *bad* when you really mean, man, that's *good*?"

He grabs a fist full of paper towels and pitches them into the trash. "Nothing's like it's supposed to be, Mom. When you tell someone you're prayin' for them, they're supposed to be happy, not tell you to forget it."

"So. That what Gib did?"

"Sorta. He just really bugs me."

I sigh. "I think Gibson's been missing his mom lately. I've heard that around. He's probably pretty angry with Jesus too, but he took it out on you. He really wasn't rejecting you, Nathan, although I'm sure it feels like that."

"Whatever." He looks away, and I'm thinking that, yeah, big boys do cry.

"I told you about Gaby, right?"

He looks around the room, like he's thinking.

"She didn't care a bit about knowing God when we were working at that coffeehouse," I say. "Whenever we worked on Sundays she'd always whisper 'Jesus-freak alert' when people would come in at noon wearing their church clothes."

"So she called you a freak too?"

I laugh. "Well, yeah, sometimes. I didn't care. For some reason she thought I was different. I just kept loving her, even when she acted like a fool."

Nathan scoffs. "I'm telling her you said that!"

"You do and you're walking everywhere for the next month! Seriously, kiddo, Gaby had it rough for a long time. She never knew her dad, and her mom married a bunch of times. She'd tell you this her-self, I'm sure. It was hard for her to trust anyone, especially a father figure like God."

"Like *God*?"

"Yeah, He's the *ultimate* Father, you know. Anyway, I felt like you sometimes—when she'd make a snide remark—but my aunt Dot helped me get that Gaby needed time. And prayer. Lots of prayer! Thankfully my auntie was better equipped than me in that vein. Or else I'm not sure Gaby would have received all the prayer she needed."

"I wish your aunt Dot was here right now."

I think back to my auntie's late-afternoon snack ritual. Black cohosh tea and wild yams. *Mmm-mmm*. Said it cured her hot flashes. Just made me gag. I glance at the alarm clock by Nathan's bed and realize that if Aunt Dot still walked among us in Ventura, she'd be sitting on her old front porch just about now, smashing yams with the back of her fork. And I'd be ducking for cover.

I touch my son's shoulder. "If Auntie were here, she'd say some-thing like, 'This is a good day for plantin' some seed, Nathan!' Then she'd grab you with her big, soft hands and get you to pray with her."

"Sounds gross."

I sock him one. "What's *wrong* with you!"

He smirks. "Okay, Mom. I'll pray with you."

———

The three of us, Gaby, Nathan and I, sit in the front pew at church on this blustery Wednesday eve. It's been months since any of us attended a midweek service, and I'm feeling a little sheepish. Mary Roselli, our church's hawkish head greeter, even made a point of our sporadic attendance. "Oh now, isn't this a surprise!" she called out when we tried to slip in through a side door. "Jocko, look who's enter-ing the heavenly-gates-on-earth tonight!"

Her big bear of a husband with a voice to match made sure we'd be anything but unnoticed. "Well, would you look who's here. Follow me, ladies and gent," head usher Jocko commanded us in that booming voice of his. Of course, he led us to the much-avoided front row. Spitting distance from Pastor Jake. Literally. "We saved you a special spot," he said to us, his grin pushing up against his apple cheeks. "Just cuz we like you so much."

We almost didn't make it at all tonight. Just before leaving the house, a crew had showed up on our doorstep. And I do mean *crew*. Something like five guys loitered about my patio and sidewalk. Before letting them in, I had stood there hopping from one foot to the other, trying to decide whether I should. A twenty-something man with a shaved head and a pencil behind one ear had scowled at me while I debated.

Apparently, Patrice had sent the guys, along with five boxes of stuff for my living room makeover. I could have sent Mr. Impatient Delivery Guy and his whole motley crew packing, but being rude on the way to church is such a snare. Gaby later told me that the box parade made it look like the Rescue Mission was actually dropping things *off*. Huh. So this would explain all the rubbernecking from the neighbors.

I'm sitting here at church thinking about the mysterious boxes of bric-a-brac stacked up in our kitchen, fidgeting with my bulletin, and waiting for my inner child to quit whining. I notice Gaby chatting it up with a couple of teenage girls in the row behind us, and she's glowing like the sky during a full moon. I glance to my left. Nathan sits between us, staring straight ahead. Hmm. *Like he's lost his best friend.*

I sneak a look at Pastor Jake making his way up front. *Somebody hand me my raincoat!* He stops by our pew. "Welcome, Nathan!" he says, giving my son's hand a vigorous shake. He turns to Gaby. "Good evening, Gaby," he says and then lowers his voice. "Don't forget that the 'Engaging the Unengaged' group will be meeting for donuts and coffee in the fellowship hall after service tonight, all right?" And finally, he turns to me. "Brianna. So nice to see you. I've heard you'll be helping in our 'Chasing the Children' ministry this weekend. Bless you for your servant's heart!"

There. The entire front row, all three of us, has been greeted. Our places have been verified. There'll be no graceful exits this night, no quick escapes should a sermon-drenching pour forth. As Pastor Jake climbs the steps of the altar, I have a flashback. I'm watching the giant killer-whale show at SeaWorld. Suddenly, I learn the meaning of the term "splash zone."

I shake away my sacrilegious thoughts. The worship band turns it up and within seconds we're rattling the roof with our praise. And it feels *good*! Who said that Christianity is for the dour-faced? My eyes are shut and I'm smiling toward the rafters, forgetting what's behind and looking ahead!

Then I open my eyes. A chill ripples through me. The church's heavy ceiling beams remind me of the ones hovering over my own living room. My gaze is simply riveted on those fat slabs of wood. Like they're about to dislodge and come crashing down, and there's nothing I can do to stop it. I flinch.

Pastor Jake's voice rips me from my fatalistic wanderings. "Are you acting like who God says you are?"

I glance around. *You looking at me?*

"Beloved, where do you place your faith?" he asks. "And where is your security?" He's pacing the altar now, eyes toward the people, speaking as if he's involved in a private conversation with each one of us. "It's time to take those mistakes of yours, your fears, even your insecurities, and drop them at the foot of the cross! Do you know . . ."

Do I know. . . ?

He takes a breath and starts again. "Do you know that you're a beloved, no, a *most* beloved child of God?"

I feel Nathan stir beside me. Gaby's beaming. I fold my hands together, aware of their distinct clamminess. Of course I *know* that I'm a child of God. I think I do. Do I? I rarely think of myself and the word *child* in the same sentence. Except for my zany aunt Dot, my childhood rather stank. But I don't dwell. I focus. On Nathan's childhood. My parents may have built orphanages miles from home, but I've been building my family right here in Ventura.

Only I'd hoped for more children. *Whatever*. Instinctively, my hand covers Nathan's and I'm at peace again.

"And so, Most Beloved," Pastor Jake concludes, "place those wicked worries . . ." *Again with the alliteration!* ". . . and He will replace them with security. The security in *knowing* that, yes, you are a most . . . beloved . . . child . . . of God."

———

After the service we stop by Elaine's Seaside Creamery for a perfectly ridiculous-sized scoop of chocolate–peanut butter ice cream. The smell in this place alone deposits fat right where I don't need any more. Yet what do I care? I'm a beloved child of God. Pastor Jake said so. With each bite of this swirling excess, there's just more of me to, uh, love.

"Wasn't Pastor Jake's message fabulous tonight?" Gaby dips into her dark chocolate–dipped cone and savors a bite. She goes on, talking loudly over the Garth Brooks song playing on the jukebox. "He's got such a way with words, don't you agree? Honestly, the way he strings words together, well, it's as if God just gave him a gift." She stops and looks at Nathan. "You were quiet tonight."

"Yeah?" He's busy gouging out some of the marshmallow mix-ins.

Gaby arches her eyebrows at me and then looks back to Nathan. "What are you thinking about?"

" 'Bout how many of these marshmallows I can fit into my

mouth." He stuffs a spoonful of them in, and it appears that he has no intention of stopping.

I grab his spoon. "I'm not in the mood to perform the Heimlich. Swallow first before answering, please."

He smiles at me, squishy whiteness poking through his teeth. *So ew.* He gulps. "I was just thinkin' that, I guess, Gib's a child of God, like Pastor says. Even though I'm kinda mad at him right now." He takes a bite of his cone. "Can't believe he called me a *Barney!*" he says with a full mouth.

Gaby smiles an I'm-not-sure-what-you're-saying kind of grin at him.

He swallows another bite of cone. "Hey, Gaby. I was just wonderin' if you pray about all your weird boyfriends."

I shoot her a wicked grin. "Yeah, what about all those odd ducks you go out with?"

Nathan's laughing now. "Most of them are creepy. Remember that guy Coon?"

Gaby giggles, Betty Rubble–style. "Yes, I remember Coon. He was a little . . . oh, a little over the edge."

Over the edge? That's how you describe a guy who wears leather all over and likes to sit in a tree, strumming a guitar by the light of a half-moon?

"Mom used to call him 'Coon the Goon.'" Nathan's lips drip with ice cream.

I take a napkin to my teenager's mouth. "Oh, I did not!" I whip Gaby a forgive-me look. "Okay, I did too. But only once. Or twice. Maybe."

"That's all right, Bri-Bri. I called him a few names too." She giggles again. "In answer to your question, Nathan, no, I haven't prayed much for the men I've dated. I probably should, shouldn't I? Especially now that I've met Ty." She says his name with a breathy sigh. "I did invite him to come with us tonight."

"And?"

She plays with her spoon. "He said maybe next time."

I glance at Nathan. "Then it'll be just you and me, kid."

"Until Douglas gets home, you mean." Gaby takes another bite.

"But of course."

Somebody fires up the jukebox again, this time with "Long Black Train." Nathan's mushing ice cream around his mouth, obviously content to ingest sugar till the cows come home. As for me, I'm just sitting here, licking a cone and letting my mind wander back to something else Pastor said tonight, right before the end of service. He had stood there, palms splayed toward us, saying, "Go forth and cast off the old and embrace the new life we have in Christ."

Well. Both my wardrobe and my home have begun the casting-off process. Guess it's time I figure out what's next.

Chapter twenty-two

The new paint on our walls smells like sour milk, but I press on toward the goal. I'm thinking this as I step away from Nathan's room after kissing him good night and get a gander of myself in the hall mirror. Tonight I wore a black blouse beaded in white. So high contrast, so très chic. Except for the shoulder pads that make me look like a quarterback for the Oakland Raiders, I may have actually appeared respectable during the evening's service.

Now there's a thought for you. Appearing respectable at church. Like that's a requirement. I'm thinking it's more like a habit than anything else. Wasn't it Nash who said a church is a hospital for sinners, not a museum for saints? I'd have to agree. Personally I wouldn't mind seeing a few more naked toes during church. But that's just me.

Anyway, this isn't about church. It's not about *image*. Okay, it sorta is. But really, I'm just trying to adjust my thinking, to catch up with my *highly regarded* husband, who has obviously become bored with the whole laid-back beach life. Basically, to show him that I care about what he thinks. Love may mean never having to say you're sorry (although I question the sanity of the believer in that

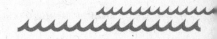

sentiment), but it does mean being willing to shod one's feet with acceptable footwear at the company dinner. And so on.

I strip off my beaded blouse, hang it neatly in the closet next to one of Douglas's barely used polos, and throw on one of his traditional undershirts. Just a plain old one-hundred-percent cotton T-shirt fresh from a Downy bath. Sigh. The phone rings just as I snuggle under our comforter.

I hear my husband's voice. "Brianna? Sorry to call so late."

There's music and noise in the background, like he's in a very public place. *At nearly 1:00* A.M. *eastern time?* "It's not too late," I tell him. "It's never too late for you. How's it out there?"

He laughs. "Crazy. Exhausting. I sat in a windowless room for more than ten hours today deposing a chain-smoker with a gutter mouth."

"Is that so? And I heard the business of law was *glamorous.*"

He grunts. "If you call stale cigarettes and ring-around-the-collar glamorous, then I suppose you're correct. Is Nathan already asleep?"

I take another peek at the clock. " 'Fraid so. School tomorrow, you know."

"Right. Would you tell him I'm sorry I didn't have the chance to talk with him today? Tell him that I love him too." Through the receiver, I can hear the din level rise. It's like the whole room breaks into laughter at the same second. Someone begins talking to Douglas. I strain to make out the voice, but can't. It's muffled and sounds oddly like that teacher's voice from *Charlie Brown.*

Douglas is back on the line. "Brianna? Sorry. I guess I'm not used to the big-city life anymore. Kendall just wanted me to know that the musicians were back for their next set."

Excuse me? "Kendall's there? With you?"

There's a roar in the phone, followed by a shudder of applause. "Bri . . . what? Sorry. Cell reception is pretty poor in here. I keep moving around, trying to catch a better signal." This would explain the scraping and jostling assault on my ears. "What did you just say?"

I'm frozen, and yet my face feels hot. "Um, so you guys are in a club somewhere?"

"In the heart of Atlanta. Just trying to unwind before another long day tomorrow. Haven't done anything like this in ages." More laughter in the background, followed by the distinct, sultry sounds of a sax. Douglas lowers his voice. "There's a guy on stage who plays his sax like it's his third arm. I'd swear he was Stan Getz reincarnated—if I believed in that kind of lunacy."

Stan Getz? He anything like Kenny G? "You sound happy," I say simply.

"As happy as I can be at the end of a ridiculously long day, I guess."

"No, I mean you sound like you're in your element there. In Atlanta." *With a bunch of lawyers, Kendall included.*

"Element?" He laughs in my ear. "It's not what I'm used to, that's for sure. After all, there aren't too many clubs in Ventura where I can unwind after an insufferable day, listening to cool jazz. It's different."

"So Kendall's with you?"

"Yes, Kendall's here. There's a whole group of us tonight."

"Miss you." *Even though I can't stand the fact that you're halfway across the country with a woman who'd be blind (and dumb and stupid) not to notice how hot you are. But I trust you, I trust you. . . .* "Your—our schedules have been nuts lately. I feel like we haven't talked in for-ever."

"I miss you too, Brianna." He sighs into the receiver, and I picture him, his eight-o'clock shadow stretching across his cheeks, the slight creases near his eyes deeper than when he first awoke. *Does he know what he does to me?*

An idea pops into my head and I can feel my heart race. "How about I plan a getaway for us?" I say. "When you get back, we could head up to Cambria for a few days. Maybe even a week, if I can get my tours covered. I bet Nathan could stay with Troy's family." (Douglas *knows* that staying with Mona is not an option. Not after that first trip when we came home to find our toddler dressed like Little Lord Fauntleroy. Where she found a velvet suit with knickers, I'll never know.) "Summer's coming soon, so I'd better call and book something now. . . ."

"You know I'd love that," he cuts in. "But I can't get away just yet. She's . . . I mean, my work load has been piling up around my ears since the trial."

"She's?"

"Slip of the tongue. Anyway, you understand, right? It's just not possible now."

Sure. I understand. You'd rather work or hang at jazz clubs with a bunch of suits. Anything than spend time rekindling with me. "Sure. Whatever," I say, hearing my voice sound like an emotional teenager, yet not caring one bit.

"That didn't sound good. Care to tell me about it?" I can tell that Douglas is getting annoyed. But so what.

"Not really. Sounds like you've got it all together. Doesn't really seem to matter what I think. Never used to be that way, but whatever."

Douglas lowers his voice again, yet I hear him clearly. It's like he's pressing his mouth against the receiver, controlling every word. "This is exactly what I've been working to avoid," he says. "There are things you just don't understand, Brianna."

"Oh please. Don't patronize me. I may not hold any advanced degrees, I may not have my *juris doctorate*, but I see what's happening." The noise level from his end of the line spikes. Apparently, the reincarnation of Stan Getz has begun a solo. What may sound cool and sultry in Atlanta comes across dirge-like over in my end of the country. Yes, the mood has definitely turned dark.

"Brianna, we've got to talk. But this just isn't the time. All flights were booked solid for Saturday, but I'll be back in Ventura sometime late Sunday. I can catch a ride back from LAX with Kend . . . with one of the others. We'd better talk when I return."

"Sounds peachy," I say and hang up the phone. Only I do it with such flourish that I knock over the glass of water I'd earlier set on my nightstand. The contents saturate a doily, a hand-me-down from Aunt Dot, and splash all over my kitschy beachcomber clock radio. *Aargh!*

I sulk for the rest of the night, dwelling on what my husband may say to me on Sunday. I try late-night channel surfing, but that bores me. Even David Letterman is *so* not funny tonight. I used to think that dropping large, heavy objects from atop tall buildings onto the streets of New York was a scream. *Not this time, mister!* Even Dave's banter with Biff Henderson puts me to sleep.

Okay, not really. The truth is that no slumber actually comes, so I walk restlessly through the house, winding up in the kitchen. It's dark and I whack my toe on a stack of boxes left by the crew that showed up unannounced this evening. After the customary whining and grousing, I find the wall switch and light up the kitchen. At the moment, I'm refusing to think about anything that matters, including my marriage.

I open the fridge and stare into it. Not one thing amidst the sea of foil and plastic wrap even remotely seems appealing. I shut the door and head for the cabinet instead, pulling out a blue tumbler. After filling it with water, I squat down to the floor to take a better look at what Impatient Delivery Guy and crew brought me today.

Wide strips of packing tape hold the contents of each box hostage. *Where are Gaby's long nails when you need 'em, huh?* After standing and grabbing a sharp knife from a drawer, I plop back down and rip away at box one. My sour mood momentarily lifts in anticipation of what lies beneath the thick padding of bubble wrap. I reach in and feel etched glass beneath my fingertips. Wrapping my hand around the short, heavy glass item, I pull it out and into the light.

A shot glass?

I blink. In my hands I'm holding a burnished-colored shot glass hailing from Miami. Huh. I reach into the box and pull out another, one with clear glass and the words *Hello From The Big Easy* painted on it. *Oo-kay.* I throw open all box flaps and dig in only to find nothing but the predictable little souvenirs from around the globe stuffed inside. I grab another. Uh, hello! A gold-rimmed Vatican shot glass. *Who knew?*

Well. When Patrice said she had a studio full of décor just perfect for a man like my Douglas, somehow cheesy glassware hadn't come to mind. I sit here on the cold wooden floor like the heap of nerves that I am. First Douglas and I snip at each other on the phone, and now this. Worse, I just put a deposit check in the mail to Patrice today. *Aargh!*

Sitting here on my rather unmopped kitchen floor, I'm contemplating how much lower I can sink. My head's starting to feel heavy, like there's an oversized L hanging from it. For years I've been going along, just moving at my own kick-back pace. Not everything's been perfect, but, hey, when is it ever? The trouble started just days ago, really, when I began to wake up to the fact that my son's growing up, my husband's losing interest, and my Bunko pals saw this coming way before I did.

From the get-go, all I've wanted is to make things right again with Douglas and me. I lift my chin toward the glossy kitchen ceiling. *I'm trying to do this casting-off thing, Lord. I really am!*

Chapter twenty-three

The trill of the phone yanks me out of a fitful sleep. That and the sheer pain from having fallen asleep on a hard floor while leaning up against rigid cardboard. I pull myself up and my knees crack in several joints. *Real nice.* I pick up the cordless from its cradle as it ripples through the quiet morning for a fourth time.

"Did you get my packages?" It's Mona, before 7:00 A.M. Lord, have mercy.

"Mona?" I say, stifling a yawn. "Um, no. I don't think so. Haven't seen any packages from you."

"Are you sure? Have you checked? What about Nathan? Maybe he took them."

I'm up and wandering around my kitchen now, stretching myself awake. "Well, Mona, I haven't checked exactly." I stifle a yawn. "Then again, I didn't know to be checking for anything. As for Nathan, I haven't heard a peep from his room. Chances are he's still in dreamland, catching that perfect wave." I reach for the coffeepot and start filling it up.

"Is that running water? Can't you slow down for just one minute and look for those packages?" My mother-in-law sounds exasperated,

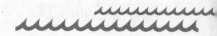

and so I turn off the faucet and plunk the coffeepot onto the island.

"Okay, Mona. I'm more awake now. Start again. What did these packages look like?"

"You should have received five square moving boxes. I specifically directed them to be delivered straight to your door. If this has been botched, then the Starving Students will never again work in this town!"

I drop my gaze to the boxes sprawled along my kitchen floor. My eyes catch on the one I opened last night. The one with the mother lode of garish souvenir barware. I hover closer and inspect the small label on the top of the box. *To: Mrs. Douglas Stone, From: Ms. Mona Stone.*

I gasp. "Mona? *You* sent me shot glasses?"

"You found them after all! You frightened me to death, Brianna. Maybe if you hired someone to help you keep things tidy . . ."

I'm squatting down next to the open box now, scouring through it and questioning whether I'm really awake. If not, then I'm having a sick dream, filled with all kinds of unhealthy thoughts. The shrill voice on the other end of the line keeps hammering in my ear, and I'm getting that, contrary to what I'd hoped, Mona's still yakking.

"Brianna. Brianna? Are you still there?"

Sigh. "Yes, Mona. I am."

"Then why don't you say something? You haven't said a thing about my shipment, other than scaring me that perhaps they'd been stolen!"

Now, there's an idea. "Sorry, Mona. Haven't had my coffee yet. Besides, your packages came late yesterday and I didn't see the label. I thought they were from Pat . . . from someone else."

"Well, of course I heard all about your little redo from my very dear friend Patrice. I have to say that I was pleased, Brianna, that you'd taken my recommendation. It takes a brave lady to admit when she is mistaken."

I roll my eyes.

"When I heard, I knew at once that you should have our souvenir collection in your possession."

"And why's that?"

Exasperated sigh here. "Because they meant so much to Douglas when he was a boy, of course. I have wanted to get them to you sooner, but quite frankly, I wasn't sure they would be appreciated. You do understand."

I try to imagine Douglas, age eight, dressed in a striped barkeep's apron, juggling shot glasses. Uh-uh. Can't do it. "You know, Mona, I was hoping to go with a slightly more formal living room design. Comfortable, yet elegant. Know what I mean?" I glance at the ravaged box of glassware. "I don't think there'll be room for your souvenirs. But thank you anyway."

"Nonsense! The house's other drawbacks aside, your living room is simply *cavernous*. I'll call Patrice and make sure that she has her builder create an ornate cabinet for Douglas's coveted collection. You simply must feature them prominently."

"Mona? I don't want to insult you." Okay, that's not exactly true. I want to insult her, but my Christian conscience simply won't let me. "But I'm doing this redesign with Douglas in mind. I really don't think he'd want these displayed in our living room . . . and there're so many of them."

"I see. Well, then, I won't bother you any longer. Close them up and I'll have a driver retrieve them as soon as possible."

"Thank you for understanding."

"Of course I understand, Brianna! I'm just sorry that you don't understand just how much the proud display of these souvenirs from Douglas's childhood would mean to him. Have you even looked at them? They're from all around the world, Brianna. When our son was a boy, we made certain that he was well-read on cultures from around this planet. It's what's made him who he is today."

Here we go. This is where she tells me that living the quiet beach life will stunt Nathan's growth, and that he's somehow suffered from his lack of globe-trotting. She thinks I'm too unrefined to see that traveling the world would expand his mind. But I do see this. My parents caught the travel bug when I was a tot, and they expanded their minds as far away from me as they could get. It's one thing to embrace other cultures but entirely another to abandon your child in the process.

Not that Mona's suggesting anything with even a *hint* of nobility attached to it. No. Her idea of introducing a son to the wonders of the world is pretty much limited to a day-long shopping spree at Harrods of Knightsbridge.

I can hear Mona drag in a long, harsh breath. "I deeply regret not having pictures from those days. Douglas was such a beautiful boy. I had an office at home then, and many mornings he would carry a box full of our souvenirs from his bedroom and set them up on my oriental rug. I remember quite clearly the way he would spend hours arranging our bounty in alphabetical or geographical order." She's waxing poetic, and for just a second I'm thinking she's human. She continues. "Oh my, and he always requested that I play an old Duke Ellington record for him. Of course, I'd have to play it very low; wouldn't want my clients to think I was calling them from a club in the Deep South, now would I?" She laughs heartily.

He liked jazz as a kid?

"Well. Listen to me. I sound like I just took a wrong turn down Memory Lane. I won't bother you any longer, Brianna," she says, her normally clipped voice back in action. "I'll send for the boxes today."

I'm drawing swirly designs on the island counter with my finger.

At the moment, I'm feeling the hot breath of guilt against my neck. *Well, nuts. I didn't mean to hurt her feelings.* I bite my lip before saying, "Why don't you hold off on having them picked up, Mona. Maybe I can fit them in somewhere."

"Well, then. All right." I can hear a smile in her voice. True, it's a bit smug, but at least I'm no longer a candidate for the meanest daughter-in-law award. *There's always tomorrow, though.* She continues to gush, "I can't *wait* to see how Patrice can use them."

Yeah, that ought to be a kick.

We say our good-byes and I quickly make the coffee and roust Nathan from teenage slumber. He sits up, his hair a stellar example of early-morning bedhead.

"*Dude.* What time is it?"

"Dude, yourself. It's late. Get your little self out of that bed and wash up. I'm driving today."

He moans like I've just told him he's heading to the dentist's chair for a root canal. "It's too early."

Tell me about it. While he holes up in his bathroom, I dash off to my room and throw on a pair of cozy surf sweats and a Rip Curl hoodie. I've got an afternoon tour, but there'll be time for showering later. There's an idea lofting around in my head, and I want to hit it after dropping Nathan at school.

Less than an hour later I'm strolling into Beachside Books, Java & More, the bold aroma of freshly roasted coffee beans hugging me as I step inside. I will myself past the coffee counter and head directly to the CD section in the back of the store. A guy with straight, in-his-eyes black hair greets me with a rather professional-sounding, "Mornin'."

"Back atcha," I say, my eyes flitting around the music section. "Where can I find jazz?"

The clerk whips his head back, tossing the bangs from his face. "What kind? Progressive? Cool? Swing? Bop?"

I chew on my lip. "Just jazzy jazz. The normal kind." I clap my hands and point at the clerk. "Duke Ellington!"

"Okay. A traditionalist. Right over here."

He leads me past several listening stations. An older woman with—I kid you not—ice-blue hair and wearing headphones is swinging her head side to side. I glance at the section title over her head: Gospel and Soul. *Well, then. Right on.*

We stop at a collection deep in the store's cavern, and he starts flipping through CDs, never looking at me. "Ellington's a good choice," he says, surprising me that there's data behind all that hair. "Man, that brothah jammed! He started it all off with hot jazz of the '20s, then *smack*, made the switch to swing in the '30s." He grabs up a CD and holds it out to me. "You gotta have this one."

I take it from him and turn it over, looking at the track list. It means nothing to me.

He combs his fingers through his bangs. "Check it out. This one's got 'It Don't Mean a Thing (If It Ain't Got That Swing),' 'Hot Feet,' 'Sophisticated Lady' . . .

"'Sophisticated Lady'?"

"Boo-ya! Ya gotta have it!"

I look up at the clerk, his eyes thoroughly hidden behind that straight hair. I feel myself suck in a breath and huff it back out. Up until our spat, Douglas sounded content last night to sit in an Atlanta night club and tap his toes to the sweet sounds of jazz. This morning Mona tells me how much he loved listening to jazz as a boy. Well. There's only one thing to do.

No more Nashville-by-the-sea for me! "I'll take it," I say to the kid with the black hair. I pay for the CD and wind my way back through the aisles of books toward the front. A flyer on a bulletin board near the exit catches my eye:

Chocolate Cooking Classes—by the Sea!

Forget chocolate bars and brownies!

Learn to dazzle your guests with
Satiny chocolate soup,
Glazed chocolaty potatoes,
Sumptuous chocolate chili
And more . . .

Hosted by Chef Kelly

I jot down the phone number listed on the sign. I can't think of a more perfect next stop on the Brianna Stone makeover train.

Chapter twenty-four

When I called the number listed on the chocolate cooking flyer, I had no idea classes started tonight. But I signed up anyway. The afternoon flew by at reckless speed. When I got home from buying Douglas that jazz CD, the painters were back, prepping for some type of final finish for our living room. I grabbed a shower then, slightly squeamish that a couple of strange men (i.e., not my husband) were downstairs at the time, possibly putting strange things on my walls.

Afterward, I dashed out the door (not stopping long enough to assess the damage, uh, *changes* to our front living "space") and headed for my afternoon tour. Ned and I led the local Seasoned Saints Seniors group on an adrenalized seaside journey to points north. Except for the unfortunate slumber of an octogenarian in row one, the tour rocked.

I then picked up Nathan from school, cracked the whip on him to finish his algebra, fed him beanie wienies, and now I sit. I'm truly waterside in the Ventura Keys, waiting with two others for more students to arrive and for the chocolate class to begin.

Talk about decadence! You can walk to "the Keys" from my home

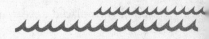

at the beach, but, *hello,* it might as well be a different world. Instead of filtered views of soft sand and white water, the houses here sit on flowing waterways. Instead of tiny beach-house backyards, Keys dwellers step out onto a deck that leads to their own private dock on the channel. From my vantage point at Chef Kelly's sleek Corian countertop, I sip water and watch as boaters sail by in the twilight. The sight is both mesmerizing and relaxing.

A thunderous clap startles me. "Ho-yeah! Welcome to paradise, ladies!" A beefy man wearing a flamingo-covered Hawaiian shirt has entered the kitchen. He rubs his hands together before sticking one out to greet me. "I'm Chef Kelly!"

Um, but you're a guy. "Oh. Okay. Nice to meet you, uh, Chef," I say. He shakes my hand like he's pumping a well.

Two other students have also arrived, a woman in her late 40s dressed more like she's attending a play, and a college-aged girl who told me her name was Toni, pronounced *Taw-ny.* Toni's sassy and sexy—it says so on her belly T-shirt. The two say their hellos to Chef Kelly, just as a chatty bunch enters the foyer.

"Well, do my eyes deceive me? Is that *my* daughter-in-law? The woman with Domino's on her speed-dial?"

Mona?

I'm mid-swallow and the unfortunate shock of seeing Mona waltzing into Chef Kelly's kitchen causes that sip of water to careen down the wrong pipe. That and her attempt at a funny. My lungs erupt into a coughing fit, with no apparent end.

"Give her some water. Would you give her some water?" Mona starts shouting orders into the air, like the room's filled with her servants. *Great.*

I drag in a deep breath and shudder. My voice sounds like a harbor seal at feeding time. I grasp for another breath. "I . . . I'm okay. Thanks, thanks." I grab for my water and accidentally knock over the second glass placed next to it. Again with the klutziness! A room full of women gasp, and two ladies hop backward to avoid the splash. *Just take me now, Lord!*

Toni's watching me with disgust, her chewed-up gum snapping with each chomp.

A couple of Good Samaritans start sopping up the water with napkins. Soon the counters and chairs and floors are dotted with soaked paper, not unlike a man's face after a too-close shave. At the moment, I'm feeling quite sheared myself.

"Ho-yeah, ladies! Show's over. Let's *get down* to some great cookin'." Chef Kelly says *get down* like a '70s disco king. I can't help but notice Mona nodding and running her eyes over him like he's John Travolta in a snug three-piece suit.

The women slip into their seats around the counter, and suddenly I'm overcome with fumes. *Perfume* fumes. I try to avoid inhaling too much of the intersecting scents, fearful that another coughing fit will erupt and move me further down the returning guest list.

Mona slips in next to me and pats my hand. Her heavy rings clack against the bones in my fingers. "How nice to see you bettering your-self, dear," she says. "Heaven knows your seventy-five dollars won't be wasted tonight." She lets out a sort of country-club laugh, and sev-eral of the other women join in.

I'm mulling over her comment when a familiar voice disrupts my thoughts.

"Brianna? What are you doing here? You don't cook." I look up. I'm startled—no, actually I'm baffled—to see Kate suddenly standing next to Chef Kelly. She's wearing a hairnet and an orange apron over her bird-of-paradise muumuu.

"Guess I could ask you the same thing, Kate," I say, curious. "Moonlighting?"

She opens her mouth wide, then snaps it shut. Chef Kelly rubs her back. "Kate's my kitchen assist—"

"The sous chef!" she cuts in. Kate slides a peek at Chef Kelly and lets out a nervous laugh. "The sous chef is pretty important, you know, Brianna," she continues. "Second in command . . . under the master chef, that is."

Chef Kelly arches one hairy eyebrow at her, then looks back to the group of eager ladies before him. He claps those two beefy hands together again and I'm the only one who jumps. "Shall we get started? Oh! Wait!" He reaches under the counter. "Before we start, how 'bout a glass of vino all around, eh? I consider myself a merlot man," he says while uncorking the bottle, "but tonight we're going to stick with a simple Muscat. Sweet. Rich. Really, ladies, it's a no-brainer."

Hmm. Chocolate and wine. Sounds more like a headache waiting to happen.

Kate places an empty goblet in front of each guest. She avoids my eyes. When the pouring starts, I opt for water. *I've caused enough commotion for one evening.* "Been doing this long, Kate?" I ask.

She shrugs. "Not too."

"I don't know how you do it, Kate," I say.

She freezes. I can see the whites of her fingers as she grips the wine bottle. "How did—"

"I mean, Martha Stewart has nothing on you. You're so creative, always making memory books for your kiddos, and you sew and decorate your house with cool stuff. Now you're assisting a chef—and you're already better than the Barefoot Contessa, in my book."

The crease across her forehead lessens. She's not smiling, but at least that perpetual frown is gone. *You can catch more flies with honey . . .*

The focus of the room shifts. Chef Kelly lifts his glass to his mouth and takes a drink. His chunky wedding band catches the light from overhead. "Ahhhh!" he groans. "Now it's time to begin. Am I right, ladies?"

"Here, here."

"Yes, Captain!"

"Yes! Yes!"

"Right you are, Chef Kelly," says Mona, her tongue on her top lip while toasting him with her half-full goblet.

My eyes widen, but I keep quiet.

Mona harrumphs, her glass still poised in the air. "Brianna, would you please relax? Chef Kelly's is more than a cooking school." She's smiling big at the chef now, not unlike Mrs. Robinson. *The* Mrs. Robinson. So *ewww*. "The man is absolutely an artist, Brianna. He will teach you to, finally, cook for your husband and son the way they *deserve*." She sweeps her hand across her chest and into the air on that last word.

Kate's busying herself in the background, but not enough that I can't see the smirk forming on her face. She's nodding in agreement too. *Sheesh. Buttering her up got me absolutely nowhere.*

"I want you to watch how I do it, ladies," Chef begins. "There are plenty of hack cooks out there, thinking they know the way to a delicious chocolate soup. Oh, but do they have the proper finesse?"

You mean like you?

He leans toward us, his teeth oversized and gleaming. "I think not," he says with showmanship-sized sarcasm. "Allow me to show you a proper, decadent, sumptuous soup that you can serve to anyone, anytime."

Well, alrighty.

He starts with heavy cream and dark chocolate pudding, pouring them simultaneously into a Le Creuset pot. Kate steps in and stirs the concoction over heat with a wooden spoon. Chef Kelly then adds more cream and some espresso flavoring. *Um, okay. I'm seein' the light!*

He grabs a bottle from a top cabinet. "And my personal favorite—now, don't go around telling my secrets, ladies." Chef winks at me and all I can do is freeze, my eyebrows stuck pointing toward the ceiling. "A wee bit of Irish crème," he finally says while pouring a long swig of the creamy liqueur into the nearly boiling pot. He puts the lid back on and tucks the bottle back into its spot in the upper cabinet. He looks at me again with that big old grin. "The truth comes out when the spirit goes in, isn't that how the sayin' goes, pretty lady?"

"So I guess you'll be setting up some sort of confessional booth after class, then?" I say.

He leans close and winks at me again. "If that's what you want, it can be arranged."

Oh brother. All eyes are on me. Not that I'm looking back at any of them. It's just that I can feel their curious stares boring into me like lasers. I clear my throat. *What? Didn't anyone else get my Holy Spirit reference?*

He chortles. "A little spitfire, are we? I like that."

Mona's gaping at me. Toni clucks her tongue. Kate's smirking in my direction. *Oh please*.

Chef calls out behind him, "Kate! Over here. Time to fill these bowls and show these ladies why I've got the *keys* to the kingdom in these parts. Heh-heh."

Kate adjusts her hairnet, wraps a hot pad around the soup pot, and scurries over to the counter with it. We *ooh*. We *ahhh*. Tasteless flirting aside, we can't get enough of Chef Kelly's chocolate soup. I'm wondering if the class fee includes carry-out, when I feel a tap on my arm.

It's Bobbie, one of the quieter of the bunch. She leans toward me and whispers, "I like your necklace."

Seeing as I rarely, almost never, wear jewelry, I put a hand to my chest. Beneath my fingers I feel the smooth, straight lines of a gold cross. Douglas gave it to me as a wedding gift. I'd forgotten that I'd put it on. "Thanks," I say. "It was a gift from my husband."

She nods. "If you don't mind my saying, you seem uncomfortable. Not a chocolate lover?"

I blurt out a laugh. Mona throws me a look of disapproval before rejoining her tête-à-tête with the chef. I glance back at Bobbie. "Um, actually? I love chocolate. My best friend and I make a wicked brownie recipe. These thighs of mine have seen more chocolate and butter than a professional fudge maker."

"Really? Sounds de-lish. I love brownies. Maybe you could give me the recipe?"

Kate's hovering nearby and puffs out a strange sound. I raise my brows at her. "What? You don't like my brownies, Kate?"

She doesn't look at me but keeps stacking dishes instead. "Break-up brownies are so gauche, Brianna. I just can't believe that you and Gabrielle still spend so much time wallowing in self-pity while eating fattening food. It's kind of immature, if you ask me."

She turns her back to me and I notice how her love handles ooze over the sides of her apron strings. "Ah well, I guess maturity has its place, Kate. Just not in my kitchen."

She stands up straight and digs one fist into her side. "What about the beach? Don't you two still eat mounds of brownies while sitting on the beach?" I'm almost sure she wants to add the word *loser* to the end of that sentence.

"But of course. What could be better than chocolate *and* the beach, my friend?"

Chef Kelly spins around and wiggles his eyebrows at me. "What *indeed.*"

What is up *with that man?*

Bobbie's laughing now. "You know, I think I may try that soon. I just walked away from a three-year relationship with the coward of Ventura County. Kept saying we were going to get married, but whenever I brought up the subject, you'd think I was asking him to shave his head and join a commune. A little chocolate, a little beach . . . mmm, sounds like a healing experience."

"Sounds like avoidance to me," says Kate, wiping down the counter. Chef Kelly clears his throat, and she scuttles away toward the kitchen's wide workstation.

For the next hour or so we learn to create dishes to satisfy every woman's inner chocoholic. Besides the soup, Chef covers glazed

chocolaty potatoes, sumptuous chocolate chili, and the pièce de rés-
istance? Chocolate Cherry Fondue. I'm chugging water, washing
down enough sugar to fill one of Aunt Dot's vintage metal canisters
and thinking that recipes like these can take avoidance to a whole
new level.

Chapter twenty-five

The message light flashes on the answering machine, and in my head I'm hearing the foreboding *Dragnet* theme song. *Duuu-du-du-du* . . . I reach to hit Play, but stop. What if Douglas is still angry? What if he wants me to call him back tonight and hash it all out? What if he wants to discuss our problems over a long-distance connection while he lounges with Kendall at an all-night supper club?

Not happening!

Besides, Nathan's asleep, and I'm beyond tired. Last night's sleeplessness followed by a day filled with more twists and turns than Disney's Matterhorn ride has me drooping like a palm frond after a windstorm. I've neither the vim nor vigor to deal tonight.

Then again, maybe he called to say *"I'm sorry, babe!"*—to confess that he's simply been overwhelmed at work and that when he gets home, our world's gonna change. No more late nights at the office! Forget the last-minute trips! And dashing around to who-knows-where in his sleek Z car? *"No more of any of it, beautiful!"*

I plop onto our bed. With a sudden lift in my heart, I tap the Play button and fall back onto the headboard.

"Hello, Brianna. This is Suzy calling."

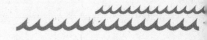

I sit up. I crinkle my nose. *Suzy?*

"I know you've already delivered several meals this month, but would you be willing to do one more? The Sanchez baby—a sweet little pink thing—was born this morning. Nearly a month early! I'm sorry to ask again, Brianna, but I'm short on helpers. If you can provide a meal for them tomorrow night, well, I would be grateful." She pauses to laugh. "I almost called Meridians for you but figured that since you're such a regular customer, they probably offer you a great discount. Anyway, Brianna, please confirm with me if you can do this. Bye."

My mouth's agape. *Not so.* I don't *always* pick up meals from Meridians for those in need. Sometimes, when I'm especially sick of Italian, I go Chinese! *Sheesh.*

I sigh and take a regretful glance at the answering machine, its red light as still as a possum in the daylight. Guess Douglas was too tired to call. Or too something else. Yet what did I expect? I could dial him up, but would that really accomplish anything? I shake my head. No, he said we'd talk on Sunday when he returned, so that'll be good enough for me. It'll have to be.

I jot myself a note to take dinner to the newly expanded Sanchez family after work tomorrow, when an idea strikes. Chef Kelly made a chocolate chili that had me licking the bowl clean. (Okay, *practically* licking the bowl . . .) I could make that! I scribble down the ingredients from memory, adding soft bread sticks and salad (bagged, of course), along with a batch of my buttery brownies to the list. There. I hold the list before me, checking it twice. I'm *so* making the Sanchezes something from my own kitchen tomorrow night.

I huff a sigh. Once again, for just a few minutes, my mind has pulled away from the clouds of worry forming over Douglas's return on Sunday. I never thought that marriage could be so *high school*. It's surreal, feeling like I can't talk to the one I've already shared so much with.

I set the list down on my nightstand and turn my thoughts back to Suzy. She's so good about keeping our little hospitality team organized. She's got that whole anal-retentive Monica of *Friends* thing going. Too bad her hair's still stuck in another era.

Speaking of Suzy's hair, I'm thinking about a new *'do* myself, maybe even a little added color. I make a mental note to call Tami at Salon Panache tomorrow, and turn off the light.

I've always considered grocery shopping to be a necessary evil: Don't want to do it; don't like to do it; have to do it. Then again, my idea of a thorough shopping has always been to grab two barbecued chickens from beneath the heat lamps in the deli department *and* a loaf of pre-buttered garlic bread. But I've turned over a new loaf, so to speak. It's *good-bye* microwave meals! *Adios* to food on the run! At the moment, I'm at our local grocer, tossing recipe ingredients in my cart like I'm Rachael Ray prepping for 30-Minute Meals.

So caught up am I in the flurry of this newfound shopping experience that I neglect to watch for Mario, the deli guy, moving in to position. From the corner of my eye, I see him leaning over the counter to greet me. My shoulders tighten as I pull up to the dairy section and suddenly realize my unfortunate misstep. Any attempt to pretend to be fully engrossed in deciding between organic or regular old toxic milk becomes lost when I sense his unwavering eyes stuck to me.

"So good to see you, Mizz Stone," he calls out. "Come over here. I got something you're gonna like."

I toss him a weak wave. "Hey, Mario. Sorry. In a hurry today," I say, not stopping my cart.

He flips his palms over sharply. "What? You don't have time for some of my home-style meatloaf? Sure you do! Come on over." He gestures to me with a wide arc of his arm.

I keep moving. Slower now. "Really," I say, tossing a pound of butter into my cart. "I'm not buying from the deli today, I . . ."

His hands jerk up, his thumbs spiking the air. "Not buying from the deli today? You're one of my best customers. Come on. See what I got here." He points to several crocks of steaming soups. "You got your Bistro Bisque, your Chunky Turkey, your Creamy Carrot, and oh, look at this one here, Jambalaya. I know how much that lawyer husband of yours likes his spicy food—huh, huh?"

I roll my cart slowly past the counter, my eyes flicking from one delicious quick-pick meal to the next. I *am* kind of busy today. Have to meet with Ty later, have my hair cut, prep for Sunday school, check in on the painters . . . maybe I should save my inaugural from-scratch meal for the next time Suzy calls. I pick up a container of ceviche and hold it in front of me, studying the label. The chilies, the lime juice, the cilantro, oh my! They all cry out to me.

Mario looks over his shoulder and shouts to his crew in the kitchen behind him, "What did I tell you people? I knew our local beach bunny couldn't resist. Eh? Eh?"

I gaze up at Mario, his grin stretched across his grizzled cheeks. "And don't forget to try my gotta-have-some egg salad. Your kid'll love it," he says, looking just a little bit too proud of himself.

With reluctance, yet determination, I set the ceviche back into the case. "Not today, Mario," I say quickly before grabbing hold of my shopping cart and dashing away from the counter. I don't look back. Even so, I can feel Mario gaping at me as I dart toward the chocolate aisle.

Back at home, my countertops and island stand covered with my store-bought bounty. And yet the term "utter disarray" couldn't be further from my reality. No, I'm thinking that the best way to crank out a top-notch meal and still have time to taxi myself and Nathan around in the afternoon is to have a plan, which is why I've laid out all non-perishables alphabetically. I've also dusted off the necessary pots, pans, trays, and bowls to cook and serve the meal in and scattered them around the empty spaces on the counters and stovetop. Hands on my hips, I survey the room. For the first time ever, I think, I'm noticing just how tight of a kitchen *space* I've had to deal with all these years.

"I can't work like this, people!" I say to the rafters, but there's no one around to respond. Even the painters, God bless 'em, have vanished. Unfortunately, they left behind a strong, lingering scent of wet, glossy paint. At least the smell will keep me from double-dipping my taste-testing spoon.

Despite the awful smell in the house, and the uncharacteristic lack of counter space in my kitchen, a spark of hope ignites within. Armed with Chef Kelly's yummy chili recipe and my own dare-to-change heart, I'm both challenged and mystified. Challenged to serve my brothers and sisters in Christ with a delicious, awe-inspiring, home-cooked meal, and mystified by where I keep my apron.

Before I have the chance to plunder the drawers, the phone rings.

"Chateau Brianna," I say with pluck.

"Well, ¡hola! Reservation for one in about an hour." It's Gaby and she's giggling on the other end.

"But of course," I say. "I must ask, my friend, why do you dine alone?"

"Oh, well, um . . . it's because I know how you cook!"

I gasp. "You're such a freak! I'll have you know that I am the proud graduate of Chef Kelly's cooking school. Anyone would be delighted to place their feet under my table!"

"Chef Kelly. That hot Irishman over in the Keys? I just love his gorgeous smile and that top-o'-the-mornin' brogue. *Qué bien!*"

"Down, girl. He's married."

She sighs. "I know. Can't you just imagine waking up to him every morning, though? He's probably lovely to look at, *and* I bet you he whips up breakfast for her too. Some women have all the luck."

"Oh, puh-lease! He's pretty obnoxious, like an Irish Emeril—

bam!" I laugh. "I was over there last night. He came on stronger than a Category Four hurricane, throwing around ingredients and sloshing his liquor. It was quite the show, my friend."

"But he's a great chef! We deliver over there all the time. Did you see the anthuriums everywhere? Those were mine, all mine! He's got great taste in tropical florals, missy."

I huff a brief sigh. "Yeah, yeah. A great chef. Hey! Did you know that Kate's his assistant? Actually, she says she's the 'sous chef.' It was all very bizarre. I just looked up and there she was all decked out in a hairnet and garish apron." I laugh. "What's up with that?"

"*No sé*—I don't know! She does seem to be popping up all over the place, though, for a homeschooling crafts maven, that is. Maybe she's tired of that life—bored with it, you know? When I think back to how she accused you of being the one who's bored, it just makes my blood boil! Maybe she was just putting her own feelings about *her* hum-drum life onto you! *Aye!*"

"Oh, quit it. Why'd you call me, anyway?" I tease.

"Huh? Oh yeah, I called *you*. Just wanted to tell you that I spoke to Ty today." She sighs a dreamy sigh. "He's so beautiful, Bri."

I scrunch my eyes together. "So he called you, hmm?" I say while starting to prep the chili.

"Well, actually, I called him. But he took my call, and we had the loveliest conversation."

I stop what I'm doing. *She* had to call *him*. I stare out my kitchen window, my eyes resting on Nathan's faded wet suit.

"We're going to Aloha tomorrow night for dinner. I told you that, right? Anyway, I suggested he wear something comfortable to walk in. He's never strolled along the promenade right outside the restaurant, so I proposed that we do that after dinner. I hope he doesn't think I'm too domineering. You don't think he'll be turned off, do you?"

Sweet Gaby. Don't try so hard. "I can't imagine any decent guy being turned off by you, Gabrielle. Maybe you should let things just play out naturally. After dinner, see if he takes the lead and asks you to walk. He'd be crazy not to, but why not just see."

"So you thought that was too pushy?"

"No! Not at all. It was a sweet idea. Listen, girlfriend, I'd love to keep yakking, but I've got some cooking to do."

"Cooking?"

"Yeah, Suzy called last night. Lori Sanchez had her baby, a girl, almost a month early! I'm bringing dinner."

"Oh, so when you say *cooking*, what you really mean is picking up the phone and dialing Meridians. You had me worried there for a minute!"

"Uh, no, I meant cooking, as in *I am Paula Deen, I am the Iron Chef, I am—*"

"The Naked Chef! I love that show! Seriously, what in the world do you mean *you're* cooking. You hate to cook." She's accusing me now.

"I don't hate to cook. Just never learned. Didn't you hear me? I just told you that I attended Chef Kelly's cooking school."

"You were serious? I thought maybe you were over there, I don't know, giving a tour or something. You actually sat in on a class. Oh, you are so lucky!"

I told her about the flyer and my last-minute decision to sign up, how Chef Kelly put our brownie-making abilities to shame with all his fancy chocolate recipes, and how I'd decided to treat the Sanchez family to a home-cooked meal rather than my usual—the stop-and-pay variety. Gaby *oohed* and *aahed* into the phone, obviously impressed.

"Well, this does my heart good! I'm proud of you, Bri. You keep surprising me. First the new wardrobe, then all the redecorating, now you're cooking avant-garde cuisine? Pretty impressive! Next thing you know, you'll be hosting fancy dinner parties for Douglas and all those rich clients of his."

A flash of darkness startles me, as if a black-light poster has suddenly appeared in a room full of Monets. My stomach drops. But then, just as quickly, the moment fades away. The afternoon sunlight streams through my kitchen window, illuminating my spotless cooktop and I think, yeah, maybe a dinner party at Chateau Brianna is my next logical step. Someday.

Chapter twenty-six

I'm feeling very French standing here in my bare feet while wearing my one and only chocolate-stained apron. Very *oo-la-la*. The French are known for their lustiness toward good food, and as I again dip my spoon into the chili concoction bubbling on the stove, I offer up a jovial "bon appetit" to the air around me.

I'd forgotten the creative bent to cooking, the *joie de vie,* as Aunt Dot always said, of melding rich foods together into one flavorsome meal. My chocolate chili simmers on the stove, its mouthwatering essence filling the air and completely obliterating any *odor de paint*. I inhale the concoction and give myself a figurative pat on the back. My decision to add a couple of extra dashes of ground chocolate to the pot has paid off in sweet, aromatic dividends.

Not without regret, I drop my spoon into the sink and begin to gather up the rest of the dinner for the Sanchez family. I switch off the burner and check the clock. No sign of the painters who were due an hour ago. I peek around the corner at my living room walls and cock my head. Those walls looked better wearing their first coat of matte paint. This second coat shines like my nose after a long day of touring around in the fog, and frankly, that ain't pretty. No time to

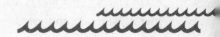

follow up, though, as it's nearly time for my twice-yearly cut and style.

Half an hour later I'm in Tami's chair, pointing at pictures of wafer-thin beauties and the chichi locks that frame their air-brushed faces. I share neither their bone structure nor their bored-with-it-all attitude, but I *so* want one of their lush hairstyles fashioned on my head.

"So you're sure about this?" Tami stands behind my chair, grimacing at me in the mirror. "Because I don't have a magic wand that'll turn back time, you know. What comes off, stays off until the good Lord lets you grow it back." She examines a wisp of my hair now, rubbing it between her fingers. "'Course, I can always try and weave your natural color back in, I suppose. If you suddenly change your mind on me." She's smiling now and shaking her head. "That's what you were counting on, wasn't it?"

"What, that you had a magic wand buried in your brush drawer?"

"That I could do whatever you, my elusive customer, want. You want color, I give you color. You don't like color, I take it away." She snaps her fingers twice in the air.

It's not like I don't like my sandy-colored hair. It's just that I've never thought that much about it. It's just hair. I wash it, brush it, and *voilà*! I'm done. About the only thing that's ever had me smiling about it at all is its color. My hair reminds me of wet sand, and to me, that's a good thing. Not real dark, not too light. If I were laying out on the beach after high tide, my locks would blend right in.

"Go for it," I say, still watching Tami through the mirror. "Give me something that'll knock Douglas's tie off."

Tami smiles warily and wraps a towel around me. She turns to Rikki, working in the station next to hers, and mumbles as if I were invisible, "Okay, but don't come cryin' to me." They both laugh and Rikki reaches over and touches my shoulder. "It's about time, girl-friend," she says and pats me on the head like I've just told them I finally got a date for the backwards dance.

I relax into the chair, vaguely aware of the scent of chocolate on my skin. The moment passes after Tami snips away and then begins glooping some pasty mixture on my hair. Ah, the road to beauty is filled with toxic chemicals! What a concept. I feel like one of those doodle dolls created solely for kids to scribble on. Yet I want blond highlights, the quintessential California-girl kind that'll make Douglas's eyes light up when I step into the room.

Unfortunately, when Tami turns my chair back around after washing and combing me out, I peer into the mirror and my mouth goes slack. I gulp. Stripes. Six of them streak down my hair from root to end like a paint spill gone wrong. I give Tami a tentative glance, hoping that like my walls at home, this isn't the final coat.

Tami plugs in her hair dryer, unfazed. "Give it some time, Bri. It'll take some getting used to. Rome wasn't built in a day, you know." She flips the switch and starts blowing out my hair.

Yeah, but Douglas will be home in two.

Later as I drive through the harbor entrance, scrunched down in my seat, I'm dreading my meeting with Ty. My dread's accentuated by the blond bands that stick out like road dividers all over my head. I only hope that Luann's nose is too buried in some bodice ripper to notice.

I dash into the Coastal Tours reception area, giving the lobby a cloak-and-dagger glance. I'm in luck! Luann has left the building! I head toward the tour company's inner sanctum, where Ty'll be waiting in his glass-enclosed office, ready to toss around buzz words like poker chips. Before Rita left, I could count with my encircled thumb and forefinger the number of meetings she held in there—zero. Sure, she was always a professional, but Rita's idea of a business meeting was brainstorming tour ideas over a grande latte at Starbucks. What I wouldn't do for a mocha frappuccino right about now. . . .

Ty spots me before I reach his office. Guess that means he's ready to deal. "Good afternoon, Brianna. Welcome," he says. I freeze. *Is he really wearing a ponytail?* He takes me by the elbow and ushers me into a seat. After he takes his own behind the massive desk, I can't help but notice that he's sitting quite high, while I, on the other hand, appear to be sinking like the *Titanic*.

"I asked you here today, Brianna, to validate you."

I slide my bangs from my eyes, noting the glint of yellow in a single strand. "Listen, Ty, if this is about my hair, I'm okay with it." *Although yours has got me a little freaked.*

He wrinkles his brow. "Your hair is lovely, as always. I've been thinking about our last conversation. You were—how do I put this delicately?—distressed over the unintentional distribution of misinformation to our Japanese guests. And I'd like to rectify that."

I blink. *Could you translate first?*

"I'm extending you an olive branch, Brianna. I am personally willing to take air cover for this situation. We both know that bad cosmetics can do great damage to a company such as ours. I would not wish for anything to come between us as we build this business." His eyes linger on mine.

Uh, whoa. I hold up a palm. "You mean as *you* build this business, right? I mean, I'm glad to be a part of it, to see Rita's company continue to thrive and all. But, Ty, I'm just a lackey." Should I be admitting this? That I'm in this for the fun of it? If Coastal Tours ceased to exist, I'd be bummed, but I'd also probably pull out my neglected surfboard, re-wax it, and give surfing the old college try.

"Brianna, you may think you're just window dressing around here," Ty says, standing up and moving around to the front of his desk. "But I know better. You're a clueful one."

"You mean clueless."

He laughs well, and I'm caught off guard. What did Gaby say about Ty and that Carrot Top impression? "No," he explains, his ponytail swishing when he shakes his head. "It means just the opposite. You know more than you think." He winks at me then, but I'm still, well, clueless as to what he's talking about. He opens his mouth to say something, then stops and abruptly moves back to his seat behind the desk.

"Before you leave, Brianna, I'd like you to take a look at some figures that I have prepared." He tosses a thick file onto the desk in front of me. "You will note that I have budgeted some perks into our tours that we in the business world like to call 'carpool couture.'"

O-key.

"Don't think I haven't noticed how stylishly you dress, Brianna."

Now, there's something I never thought I'd hear.

He continues. "To stay competitive in this marketplace, we need to appeal to everyone, including all the ladies in our community who think they have no time for some R & R, when really a romp through this beautiful town is precisely what they need." Ty comes back around the desk for the umpteenth time. He grabs up the stack of papers that I've let sit cold in their stark manila file. I'm still musing about Ty using the word *romp*. "Here, let me show you."

Luann pokes her head through the doorway. "Sorry to interrupt," she says. Ty's still looking down at the file when she catches my eye. She nods at his bum and gives me a wink along with a hubba-hubba smile. *Ew.* "Brianna," she asks, "any way you could pick up a short tour tomorrow afternoon? Cole was supposed to do it, but he's got a bad toothache."

"Um, okay. Douglas is out of town, and Nathan's got big surf plans. Why not."

Luann's eyes get big. "You did something with your hair! Let me see, let me see." She trots into the office and sniffs my hair. "Wow, and it's new too. Douglas has been gone all week. Man, while the cat's away, you, Miss Mouse, are playing."

"It's not like that."

She puckers and smiles. "Whatever you say."

"Just let me know what time to be here tomorrow. I'll grab the group's spec sheet on my way out," I say, dismissing her. She gives my hair one more once-over, then takes in my pleated pants and lacy blouse. She pumps her eyebrows up and down a few times, spins on her hot pink espadrilles and shuts the door behind her.

Ty pulls my mind back to the file. "As I was saying, let's bring in soccer moms from all over the county. Let's give them a tour they won't forget, and leverage that with you modeling designer wear all the while."

I laugh. "Good one. Gaby told me about your sense of humor."

I think he's starting to scowl, when instead a smile appears. "I am being completely up front with you, Brianna. To these bedraggled mothers, you will be the model citizen, the quintessential career mother. Talk about your son. Talk about San Buenaventura. When the tour is over, they will be refreshed and in awe of you. To absolutely capture the moment, they can then step off the bus and into our new Coastal Tours gift shop." He pulls a rendering out of the file and runs his fingers over it like it's inlaid with gold.

I'm standing just barely behind him, mouthing the words *no way*. Can't you just picture me wearing skimpy garb while smiling and waving *tootles* like one of Bob Barker's girls? I decide right then that no matter what Ty may offer me in compensation for this little addition to my touring duties, the price just ain't right.

Ty clears his throat. "By the way, Brianna, I understand that your husband is an attorney. I was going to ask him to review the proposed lease for the office connected to ours, to give it a good legal scrub, but I take it he's out of town." He gives me a regretful look. "Still?"

"Douglas'll be back over the weekend. Sure, I'll ask him to check it out. He'll probably be busy catching up when he gets back, though. How soon do you need this?"

Ty sets down the file and leans back onto his desk. He crosses his arms at his chest. "Sounds like your husband's a busy man. That must be difficult for you."

"How so?"

He shrugs. "You're a beauty, Brianna."

I wrinkle my nose. "Beauty? As in like a horse?" *Again, I'm distracted by the ponytail.*

He goes on. "It would seem to me that a man would have to do more than put a ring on the finger of a woman like you. That husband of yours ought to be staking his claim and making it known."

What is *up* with all this sudden outside interest in my marital status! "Ty," I say, barely concealing the sarcasm creeping into my voice, "this conversation's a bit out of nowhere, but here goes: You're wrong about the ring thing. Douglas staked his claim one incredible summer day when he said 'I do' out on the beach before a bunch of witnesses." *Okay, his stake actually came way before that, like when he first brought his drop-dead-gorgeous self into the coffeehouse. But I'm trying to make a point here.* "Long days are the tradeoff we have had to make," I continue. "No getting around it. But it was never a one-sided thing, my friend. Douglas and I promised forever to each other."

For the second time today, I'm thinking Ty's about to frown when he doesn't. Instead, a smile shines on his face. "Speaking of love connections," I say, a sudden spike in the pitch of my voice, "heard you and Gaby are hitting up Aloha tomorrow. You'll love the flaming steak."

Ty nods and then stands abruptly. He starts walking toward the door, and I get his thinly veiled hint. Apparently, our meeting has ended.

Chapter twenty-seven

I've never been able to get the Mrs. Kravitzes of the world, those in-your-face busybodies who think *they* have the answer to all your troubles. Blah, blah, blah, you know? That's what I'm sayin'! For the past couple of weeks I've become surrounded by the Dr. Phil posse, a swarm of advice-givers all on the *save the Stones' marriage* train.

I'm at a stoplight on the ride home from Coastal Tours, when I suck in a breath. I flick a glance in the rearview mirror, and my new blond highlights nearly blind me with their brightness. *Who do people think they are, sticking their noses into my life?*

The red light's taking forever to change to green, so I pass the time by tapping the steering wheel with my stubby fingers. I would never think of noseying around in other people's lives. Yeah, yeah, I can be a matchmaker, but that doesn't count. That's helpful. That's saying, hey, I want all your sunsets to be filled with passion, sistah!

Yeah, right. Passion. That's been an elusive quality of my marriage of late. That fact hits me in my windpipe and I find myself gasping for breath. *Will this light ever change?* Douglas has been so distant lately, so busy. I want to talk to him about it, I really do. But . . . but I

just can't get the words out, you know? He's my knight, my rescuer, and always has been. I don't want that to ever change. *Unlike this light!*

And Ty stuck his opinion in where it wasn't welcome this afternoon. He doesn't even know Douglas, he hardly even knows me, yet somehow that fact didn't keep him from offering his two cents about my marriage. When I gave him back my own nickel's worth of an answer, he cut off our conversation like it was a strand of gray hair in his otherwise blond mop. *Go ahead and keep the change then, buddy.*

Finally the light changes and I stomp on the gas. Back at home a beat-up work van and a funky Mini Cooper block my driveway. *Grrr.* I pull onto the empty lot two houses down from mine and march back to my front door. When I step inside, I nearly smack my head on a ladder standing squarely in the center of our small foyer.

"Lady, watch out!"

I tip my head to see the tattered edges of a workman's jeans. Farther up, a massive chandelier sways in his grip, and I gasp. You know those old Road Runner cartoons where Wile E. Coyote invariably ends up with an anvil denting his head? With this hulking light fixture swaggering overhead, I somehow can't get that image out of my mind.

Impending death aside, I take another gander at the electrical eyesore that at the moment has nearly become one with my ceiling. It's gold. No, actually, it drips with golden chains and beads and— whoa!—*is that a medallion dangling from above?* What is this, 1977? I half expect to see Tony Manero around the corner, shaking his booty in my living room.

Instead, I turn to see a tall, skinny gal with white blond hair stretching nearly to her Birkenstocks staring at my newly painted, high-gloss living room wall. She's wearing a stretchy beige headband, a long-sleeved flowing blouse, and jeans with bell bottoms wide enough to hide a friend. She holds a pencil poised over a notepad and doesn't turn around.

"Hello," I say to her back, stepping over a bunched-up drop cloth to move closer. I feel my burning anger dissipating into disbelief.

She swings one arm behind her and throws up a palm, the pencil still clutched between her thumb and forefinger. Instinctively I stop, one foot hovering over the floor. She continues to stare at my wall (and to ignore me). Again I step forward and offer a hello.

This time the woman hisses, "Silence!" while continuing to keep her eyes focused forward.

I cough out a sigh. "Uh, can I *help* you?" I say like I'm a clerk at Natty's on Christmas Eve and she's the last customer, trying to decide between the blue tie or the green.

She drops her sketch pad to her side and rattles her head back and forth. "Gone. The moment's gone," she says, clearly aggravated. Finally she turns around only to size me up, her eyes darting up and down my length. She puts out a hand like she's suddenly all business. "Trinka Lane, a pleasure," she says, unsmiling.

I grasp her hand and shake it back. "Brianna Stone. Likewise."

"So," she says, swishing her gaze back to my blank wall. "You're wanting something special for your wall, something that says 'I'm a powerful businessman in this community.' That right?"

"Uh, no, not exactly. Elegant, yes, but . . . wait, who sent you?" *Do you come in peace?* "I mean, are you a painter sent by Patrice, or . . ."

She throws back both shoulders and stands stiff as an ironing board. She looks me in the eyes. "I am an artist. I specialize in oils. Patrice commissioned me to create something extraordinary for your space, but the feng shui has been corrupted." She sighs and gestures toward the man on the ladder and, I think, at me. She snaps her notebook shut. "I must return another day, when the negative energy cords have dissipated. Another time, perhaps. Will you excuse me?"

I step out of her way as she moves her ethereal self past me and toward the front entrance. Just as I open my mouth to call after her, Nathan and Gibson spill in through the door, nearly ramming into the feng shui–blocking ladder in the foyer. Fortunately, I guess, the disco-era chandelier no longer hangs precariously from Mr. Electrician's grasp. I glance up. Yup, it's bolted to the ceiling as if it's now part of the family, while he tinkers with the ladder.

Both boys plant themselves in place. Hands in pockets, they fling back their heads and stare wide-eyed at the latest addition to our space.

"What the—!" Nathan's eyebrows freeze in their arched position.

Gibson's just standing there next to him, bobbing his head in that familiar way of his. *Oh, I missed that!* He just smiles and strings out the word, "Dude . . ."

"Boys! Hi. Gibson, it's good to—"

Nathan darts me a look that screams, *Don't say anything, Mom.* Then his already-widened eyes grow larger. "What did you do to your hair!" he accuses.

Gibson's still bobbing his head. He's laughing now too. "Righteous!" Forget surf lingo; I'd swear sometimes that our Gibson's living in the '60s.

Nathan scrunches up his freckly teenage face as he approaches me, while also staring at my head. I touch my new 'do with my hand. *Ugh. Forgot about the hair.* I put on a happy face, wiping away the afternoon's aggravation. "You like?" I ask.

"Nuh-uh. Dad's gonna freak." He throws a glance back toward the foyer before looking down at the floor and shaking his head. At the moment I'm not exactly sure which change he's referring to.

Not only have highlights been added to our foyer as well as my head, the living room's been nearly stripped of its beachy self, save my old couch. Patrice had told me she'd have movers store the old furniture and knickknacks in our spare bedroom, but I wasn't prepared for the breezy shell that would be left behind. Buttered Rum walls aside, the room's as cold as a foggy, wintry day on Anacapa Island. Even my conch shell clock is missing!

Realizing how late it must be, I bolt for the kitchen. It's nearly time for me to drop off the Sanchezes' meal, and I'd been too distracted to pull everything together. The boys follow me around the corner in silence and, as usual, dive into the pantry for their after-school snack. Only their idea of a snack would feed a small village in the Ukraine.

I throw on my old apron, just in case, and start dishing everything up. So involved am I that I don't immediately catch the ape-like stares from the boys standing in my kitchen, noshing on peanut butter pretzels.

"Dude, your mom's wearin' an apron," Gibson says between bites, as if I'm invisible.

"That's her brownie-cooking apron. I think she bought most of the other stuff and is just putting it in her own dishes."

I gasp. "I am so not doing that! I cooked this chili with my very own two culinary hands, Mr. Know-it-all. It's got chocolate in it," I say by way of enticement.

"Dude, I want some." Gibson grabs a spoon from our dish drainer.

Nathan pulls the spoon out of Gibson's hand and tosses it back into the sink. It makes a jarring crash. "I just saved your life, *dude*. You can thank me later."

In silence I open the silverware drawer and pull out a spoon. I give Gibson a heaping scoop of chili to taste and throw a haughty *nanner-nanner-nanner* look at my kid.

He shrugs. "It's your life," he says to Gibson, who's licking his chops. His expression changes. "Hey, who was that chick with the white hair?"

I wash off the spoon and pitch it into the dish drainer. "Some *artiste* sent by my designer. She had kind of a 'tude, though. Not sure she'll work out."

"I don't know why you need her anyway. There's nuthin' wrong with our house. What's for dinner?"

I give my head a shake. Which random thought do I answer first? Fortunately I don't have to decide. The phone rings and it's Patrice.

"Brianna! I'm so pleased that I found you home. Darling, we have a situation. Trinka tells me there's a yin-yang imbalance in your living room. She simply must rectify this if we are going to complete the design process.

"I don't mind telling you, darling, that we are so fortunate to have her on our team. She's a highly sought-after artist from the Bay Area who simply feels *called* to our Ventura Area." Patrice lowers her voice. "You know, darling, Ventura could use an infusion of the aesthetic that an artiste of Trinka's quality can offer."

Phone plastered to my ear, I stuff the Sanchezes' dinner into a cardboard box from Costco. "So what's wrong with our yip-yap again?" I ask, not really wanting to know.

"That's *yin-yang*, darling. It's very complicated, but in the simplest terms it means that the balance of light and dark energy is off. It must be adjusted in order for your family to reach complete fulfillment in your home."

I huff. My arm's flopped over the box holding the dinner and I'm staring out the window at Nathan and Gibson, who've just grabbed a couple of wet suits from the fence rail. I so want to know what's happened between those two!

"Brianna, are you there?"

I huff again. "Patrice, I'm not sure that Trinka's the right painter for me."

"Oh, she's so much more than a painter, she's an *artiste*."

Whatever. "Right, Patrice. But she didn't like me very much. Her 'tude was annoying, actually."

" 'Tude?"

"Never mind. What kind of finish was she planning for the wall anyway? The walls looked great until that second coat of high-gloss . . . it's not done yet, right?" I sense I'm being paged and glance up. Mr. Electrician gives me a salute and a wave. *Ugh. Need to talk to Patrice about that chandelier . . .*

"Don't worry about the end result, darling," Patrice says, cutting back into my thoughts. "That's my area of expertise. And please do not consider any other artist for this project—no, that will not do. She's rarely available, and I had to work like the devil to convince her to travel all the way to our lovely seaside town just for your project. Trust me, darling, won't you?"

The phone's lodged between my shoulder and my ear as I carry the dinner box out onto the patio. I lean up against the garage wall. "Um, Patrice? If Trinka's such a catch, why's she suddenly so available?"

"Hold a moment, darling, will you? I've got another call coming through."

The box I'm holding weighs down my arms. Though I'm feeling tired like a cat after a day of chasing mice, the aroma of my first-ever attempt at chocolate chili thrills me. Silly, I know. But when you've spent more time waiting for your order to be up than hovering over your own Amana range, knowing you *can* follow a recipe for something other than decadent brownies can be heady.

Patrice's voice is back on the line. "Brianna, I'm terribly sorry but I must go. The mayor's wife just phoned and she needs my services right away."

If she were an EMT or a plumber, I'd understand. But a design emergency? *C'mon.* I straighten. "Listen, Patrice—"

She cuts back in. "I am so pleased we had this chance to chat! I know how you must be feeling right now. Your living room is simply in tatters, but it will not be for long. No it will not. I will reschedule Trinka to return early next week. Ta-ta for now, darling!"

The phone clicks in my ear, and I sigh. Maybe she's right. The room's in disarray, but it'll be pulled together soon enough, I suppose. I shove myself away from the garage's outer wall, still hugging the heavy crate containing my homemade chili. In all the years I've been on the hospitality team, I've never actually done the cooking myself. But, hey, there's always a first time. I set the box onto the passenger seat of my VeeDub and zip around to the driver's side before plopping my own self down. I inhale and smile for the first time in hours. Maiden voyage, here I go. . . .

Chapter twenty-eight

I barely slept the past couple of nights. For hours I replayed those
nasty words I said to Douglas a few days ago, wondering just how
much damage my striking out had done. So now I'm paying the price.
I arrived at the four-year-old's Sunday school classroom this morning
weary as a washwoman, secretly hoping that spring fever had hit late
this year. *Maybe families will be more drawn to the great outdoors on this
crystalline beach day rather than to, uh, church.*

Sacrilegious thought, I know.

To my surprise (chagrin, actually), the classroom buzzed with
bouncy children by the time I got there. Thankfully, though, I've got
Nathan for my right-hand guy today. Right now he's playing bounce-
the-kid while crawling around like a bear with Josh on his back.

Manuel Sanchez leans his head into my raucous classroom. The
proud papa gives me a burly grin, his white teeth shining beneath his
thick black mustache. "Man, Brianna, you make a mean chili! The
kids and I scarfed it down. Hey, thanks a lot for that, huh?"

I blush. Imagine, someone actually complimenting me on my
cooking. *Who'd ever thunk it?* "*Gracias,* my friend," I say.

Manuel's third child, Zachary, clings to his father's leg. "Come on,

Mijo. Get in there." The moment throws me back to a time when Nathan's clinginess kept my church attendance as sporadic as snow in California. That kid could bellow with the best of them! Just like little Zach's doing right now.

I squat down and look into the little guy's tearful eyes. "Hey, sunshine," I say. I reach out my hand and pull him gently toward me. "How's the new big brother doing today? I bet you're taking real good care of your baby sissy, aren't you?"

He peeks out at me from behind balled-up fists. "We're gonna have the best time today," I coax. "C'mon with me, 'kay?"

Zach turns back to his dad, his young face momentarily doubtful. "Mijo, she's the lady who puts chocolate in her chili!" Manuel says. "She fed us the other night. You remember!"

Zach glances back to me and steps closer. Next thing you know he's latched on to my leg like barnacles to a skiff. And so I drag him around for the next twenty minutes, giving new meaning to the phrase "thunder thighs."

"There you are, chica!" Gaby's lilting voice sings out in the middle of my chaotic classroom. "I forgot you were on kiddie duty today. How's it going?"

Zach releases my leg and tumbles over to Nathan before climbing onto his teenage back. I rub my knee. "They haven't tied me up yet, so I guess we're doing okay."

I'm about to ask her about the big date, when her mouth falls open. "Oh wow. What did you do to your hair? It's, it's so, so . . . gorgeous!"

I push out the breath I was holding in. "Ya think? Not too striped?"

She leans her head so that her ear nearly touches her shoulder. "You'll get used to it eventually. I think it's fun."

"Thanks. Hey, tell me about your date. Did Ty just love Aloha?"

She rings her hands, and I can see a chip on one of her pearlescent nails. "Well, as usual, the food was stunning. We started with steamed artichoke topped by sautéed mushrooms. Of course I ordered the macadamia nut–encrusted halibut—delicious as always. Let's see, Ty ordered Kenny's famous steak."

"Were you worried about the hair?"

Gaby giggles. "No! Okay, a little. I tell you, Bri-Bri, I almost jumped up from my seat just so I could hold Ty's beautiful mane away from the flames." She sighs now. "I just wish we had stayed at the restaurant."

My eyebrows dart up. I lean forward to whisper, "You guys didn't, uh, cross the line, did ya?"

Her face grows pink. "Bri!" She lets out a hard breath. "We went for a walk on the Promenade. I thought that would've been the perfect end to a perfect night, but . . ." She just shrugs.

"But?"

"But . . . I don't know. He became quiet, almost brooding, you know? I keep thinking back on what we were talking about at the time, but I'm not sure what exactly did it. I mean, we were just talking about the meal and what a beautifully warm night it was. We were watching the waves crash on the beach, it was all very okay."

"So what made it not okay?"

"For one thing, he hates lawyers. Out of the blue he starts talking about how the world is run by them, how the state is overrun by them. He made some snide remark about them even owning the beaches. But I told him about Douglas and how he's just the best!" She looks at me now with an expression that I'm trying to figure out. "He thinks Douglas neglects you."

I give her a sarcastic laugh. "What?"

She's nodding, her saucer-sized eyes bobbing up and down. Her voice turns soft. "Bri-Bri, I told him that wasn't true. Douglas is a busy man because he's such a great lawyer, that's all." She sounds like she's trying to convince me.

I throw up my hands. "I don't have time for this." I spin around and clap my hands, calling together my charges. "Hey, Bucking Bronco," I call to Nathan. "Ride on over here, will you?"

Gaby follows me. She touches my shoulder. "You're not mad at me, are you?"

I shake my head. "Nope. Just have a class to run. Wanna stick around?"

"Sure. Teach me," she says. She plops onto the ground, her gypsy skirt encircling her. Doe-eyed Ali climbs atop her lap.

I brush a strand of striped hair away from my face and begin the morning's lesson. In between the children's wigglies, I manage to eke out words about being a disciple. "Anyone know what a disciple is?" I ask. Most just stare at me. Emi has an answer and dutifully raises her hand.

"Emi?"

"It's when you get a spanking."

I'm startled. "Um, why do you say that?"

"It's 'cause of dis-plin. When your mom and dad give you dis-plin, then they give you a spanking."

I press my lips together, trying to hide a smile. Nathan starts cracking up, though, and I'm thinking he could use some old-fashioned discipline himself.

"Um, okay. I guess that's one way we can look at it. Think of it like this. Discipline helps us grow up to make right choices, doesn't it?" I'm surveying the group, trying to figure out if four-year-olds can hang with me here. By their slack-jawed expressions, I'm thinking not. I glance outside and point. "Everybody see that tree out there?"

Their voices are a mix of jumbled yeses. "Good!" I say. "We're kind of like that tree. What would happen if that tree didn't get water or any sunshine? What would happen then?"

Tedi raises both hands, shouting out, "It would die!"

A couple of boys jump up and start shooting at each other and making machine-gun noises. Their fingers point at one another like pistols. "Die! Die! Die!" they shout.

I roll my eyes. "Boys! Come on back." Nathan lugs over to corral them, and I look back to Tedi. "You're right. The tree would not grow like it's supposed to. Just like that tree, all of us need good things to help us grow."

"Me! Me! I like pizza!" shouts Renee.

I brush a hand along her hair and lean in toward her. "Yeah, I like pizza too, Renee. What are other things we need, though, things other than food?"

They call out all kinds of answers: clothes, American Girl dolls, the Internet, Ipods . . .

And these are four-year-olds! I shudder to think what teens might answer. A Porsche, perhaps? I hold up a Children's Bible. "What about this?" I say above the chatter. "What's this?"

Zach bounces on his knees. "The Bible!"

"That's right! We need God's Word, don't we? It helps us grow." Tedi stands up. "Like that tree!"

"Yes, Tedi. If we read our Bibles and do what God says, we can grow up to be really, really strong, just like that tree." *After a good pruning, that is, my aunt Dot might say.*

Most of the group runs over to the window and gathers around. They're staring and pointing at a spider dangling from a web that's been knit between two branches, and I know the lesson is done. I get up and head over to the Play-Doh table, determined not to let it all dry up on my watch. Homemaking skills I may not have, but pride is another thing altogether.

I'm punching down some of the smooth yellow clay like it's a fat loaf of bread and thinking about Gaby's date with the lawyer-basher. Not that I'm exactly one to talk. My idea of a good time has never included spending time with members of the legal profession. But hey, I'm not all that judgmental. I married one, didn't I?

"Quarter for your thoughts, chica." Gaby joins me at the table, sitting herself demurely on one of the kiddie-sized chairs.

I swing my gaze in her direction. "Nothing much. Just thinking about your date from H-E-double toothpicks."

"Sshhh!"

I click my tongue and shoot a glance at the kids. "They're not listening. Besides, they can't spell yet. And let me just ask you one thing."

"Yeah?"

"Did you order the volcano souffle?"

"What do you mean?"

"You know, Aloha has that cool volcano souffle, the one that takes a bazillion minutes to bake. Did you order one? Because if you had, I can't imagine that Ty would have been anything but lovely on your moonlight stroll."

Gaby bats her eyelashes at me. "You *are* mad. You're still thinking about what Ty said about Douglas."

"*Psfft!* Yeah, right."

Gaby looks around. She leans forward. "You're going to scare the kids!"

"I don't care what Ty thinks about Douglas. Ty doesn't know him. I do care, however, that he's discussing my love life during your date. C'mon. How weird is that?"

"It didn't seem that weird, just kind of sad. Bri-Bri, I've been thinking. Ty's dad died when he was so young. And he was a lawyer, wasn't he? Maybe he has issues about his dad and all. I think I just caught him during a bad moment. If he could just meet Douglas and see how great you two are, maybe he'd come around. I doubt he remembers his parents being together at all."

I'm smirking now. Am I suddenly Ty's therapist? The man's my boss, for heaven's sake! I zip closed the last bag of Play-Doh and toss it into its cubby. Church has let out and parents have begun to stream in. I nod toward the door, letting Gaby know this conversation'll have to wait.

Zach races across the room, charging nose first into my leg. He grabs my pant leg in both of his fists and stares up at me, smiling.

"Hey, Mijo. Time to go, son!" Manuel's at the door, that familiar grin stretching across his face. "Thanks again, Bri, for that delicious chili. Hey, if you ever have a dinner party, be sure to invite us, eh?"

I peel Zach from my thigh and scoot him over to his dad. "You're such a flatterer, Manuel," I accuse with a wink. When I turn back to the class, Gaby's watching me and wearing a happy smile.

"That's it! A dinner party at your house, Bri. Please, oh please!" She's grabbing on to my arm and hopping in her sandals. *Oh brother. And I thought the kids were clingy.* "You could make something from your cooking class at Chef Kelly's! We could celebrate your living room makeover—and it would be so great for Ty to see you two in action. *Ple-a-se!*"

"You want me to invite you *and* Ty over? For dinner? Have you lost your mind?"

"Look at you. Your clothes are different, your house is getting a makeover—okay, at least your living room is, you're learning to cook fabulous things from a hottie in the Keys . . ."

I feign shock.

"My guess is that Douglas will become senior partner sometime. Right? Then you'll have to be entertaining dinner guests often, won't you? Why not give it a trial run with us?"

"Nice pun."

She swats my arm. "I'm serious, Bri-Bri," she says, batting those pretty eyelashes again. "And could you do it soon? I really like Ty, but I feel like there's something bothering him. This would help me so much. Pretty please?"

Like my kid so often does, Gaby's standing before me, wanting an answer *now*. Douglas left me a message early this morning, and for some reason, his voice pops back into my head. He sounded disoriented and depressed, like an insomniac working a twelve-hour shift. Again, I cringe at the thought of my nastiness from earlier in the week. I glimpse Gaby's expectant face and wonder if maybe a fresh start might be good for all of us.

"Why not?" I finally say.

Gaby hugs me tightly. "I can't wait! Let's do it next weekend, before the summer hits and nobody's available. I'll go call Ty."

I watch her grab her beaded purse and dance out the door. I should feel giddy, I know I should. In one swoop, I get to dazzle my husband and further my best friend's love life.

This is what I wanted, right?

Dead to the world. Aunt Dot used to say that a lot when she couldn't wake me for church. I always thought the phrase was kind of creepy, but now I get it. I couldn't be more exhausted if I'd just walked from town to town with Jesus, passing out New Testaments and wearing nothing but a tunic and hard-soled sandals. I'm too weary even to climb the stairs. Instead, I've pushed aside a canvas drop cloth and burrowed myself into the comfy softness of my denim couch, the lone piece of furniture in my living room.

"Mom, what's for lunch?" Nathan's voice, in the throes of deepening, prods me from my Sunday afternoon slumber.

"Go away," I mumble.

His breath heats my face. I open my eyes to my kid peering at me. "What'dja say?"

I wince and grab a pillow, covering my head with it. "Aargh!"

He's saying something and laughing as he scampers away, but I can't make it out. I hear him yank open the fridge door, and I wince again. Someday he's gonna rip that door clear off!

And so I roll myself off the couch and stumble into the kitchen.

"This stuff's not half bad." Nathan's eating the leftover chili

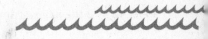

straight from the bowl. "Maybe you could put some in a bottle and sell it, like you're Martha Stewart or somethin'." He cackles.

I roll my eyes. The message light's blinking on the machine, and I give it a punch.

"Brianna, this is Rita. I was so hoping we'd have a chance to chat today, but I am afraid we may have missed each other. I will be flying to Cancun this afternoon, and cell phones are rarely allowed these days." She sighs. "Well, perhaps we can talk when I return. There's something I've been meaning to . . . discuss about—well, we'll talk later, all right?" The line appears quiet, and I think she's hung up. Then I hear her voice again. "By the way, I'm tickled that you've chosen to hire Patrice's . . . Trinka for your wall finish. How truly wonderful. It's so difficult to find someone this quickly. I'm hoping that you will be pleased. Perhaps we'll speak when I return. Good-bye."

"So not fair!" I shout at the machine.

Nathan's mouth is full, which doesn't keep him from talking. "You mad you missed her?"

"She's on her way to Cancun! Ugh! Your dad and I should be doing that." I force aside the palpable tension that currently exists in our marriage, choosing to swoon instead. I'm picturing Douglas shirtless and wearing board shorts. *And still madly in love with me.*

Apparently Nathan's picturing the same thing because he's screwed up his face. "You and Dad half naked on a beach? Sounds gross." He cracks himself up and takes another bite of chili. "Maybe you oughta stick to cookin'," he says, unconcerned that his mouth is still too full to be yakking.

I give him a haughty gaze. "I'll have you know that I intend to do just that."

He raises his eyebrows but says nothing.

"Oh, you think I'm kidding, mister, but I'm not." I place my hand on my heart and gaze at the ceiling like I've just won an award. "I am about to give the *ultimate* dinner party."

"Oh yeah? And I'm Dave Navarro." He plays air guitar with his spoon, and his laughter reaches high-soprano levels.

I straighten and stare at him. "I'm serious."

He stops in mid-pluck. "Cool. Can I come? I'll bring pizza, just in case."

I toss him a clean rag from the drawer. "Wipe your face, kiddo. Don't you know some other mom you could be harassing right now?" I turn my attention to the dirty dishes in the sink. Then, just as quickly, I turn away. Sunday's a day of rest, you know.

Nathan plunks his spoon into the sink. "Gib'll probably want to grab some waves today. I'll call him later. Gotta go wax my board first."

"You never told me what happened with Gibson. I guess you two made up, huh?"

He shrugs. "Not really." He starts drumming his fingers on the island like he's antsy and wants me to release him. But I can't. I'm holding him captive with my motherly death ray, willing him to give me answers.

"We just don't talk about it. Okay?" he finally says.

"Seriously? You had that big fight and you're friends again. Just like that?"

"That's what guys do, Mom. Hey, I think there's gonna be some rippin' surf today." He's pretending to stare past me at the window behind my back. Yeah, that's something else guys do, they change the subject. I'm thinking about Douglas and how hard it's been to get a straight answer to cross his lips lately. The realization crept up on me during the past couple of months, and then jarred me awake after that dreaded Bunko game. I realized then how little I'd seen of my husband and how guarded his conversations had become, and it was as if I were Tom, and Jerry had just hit me over the head with a frying pan.

I break eye contact with Nathan, and he's out the door. Hmm.

Kid knows when the going's good. Following behind him, I stop short. I'm standing just beneath the garish new foyer chandelier and realizing that I forgot to call Patrice to let her know that it's just not working for me. I'm picturing the fourth commandment, the one about remembering to keep the Sabbath day holy, and thinking of making an exception. It's not like I'm planning to insist she shimmy up the ladder this very day and replace the thing herself. I'm just going to leave her a message telling her that I'd like it to be replaced. That's it. I've had enough of suspicious behavior, of half-empty conversations. No one's going to accuse me of beating around the bush, of ducking the issue, of—ack!—I've run out of clichés.

I punch in Patrice's number.

"Blanc Slate Designs."

"Patrice? This is Bri Stone."

"Brianna, darling! How are you? I was just going to phone you today. Trinka's available first thing tomorrow morning. Isn't that divine?"

I glance around, glad the ladder's gone. "Yeah, that's all right. Hey, Patrice, I have to talk to you about the lighting. In the foyer."

"Isn't it *marvelous*? Oh, you do love it, don't you? Tell me you do."

I straighten. "It's just not us, Patrice. It's just too, too . . ." I'm searching for the words here. What do I say? That it's too cheesy? That it makes me feel like doing the Hustle every time I step inside the front door? I sigh. "It's too gold. Remember those fabrics you showed me? I just don't think this light will match too well." *Yeah, that's good. Tell the designer that her design's about to clash. She'll be giddy, I tell you, knowing that I've saved her from a huge designer faux pas.*

"You say it's gold? Oh, darling. Let me see. No, that is not right at all, no it is not. I'm going to call that electrician right away, oh yes I will. I told him the *crystal* chandelier, not the . . . oh, this is not for you to worry over, darling. I'll handle this right away." She pauses. "Anything else?"

I glance upward at the '70s schlock hanging from the ceiling. "Don't think so. Not unless you have a Bee Gees album I could borrow."

"Excuse me?"

"Never mind. Thanks for your help, Patrice. I'm glad you understand."

"Before you go, Brianna, I wanted to let you know that once Trinka has completed your wall finish—the piéce de rèsistance of your room design—I will have the movers set your new furniture in place." Her already high-pitched voice squeals at the word *furniture* like she just sat on a whoopee cushion. "It has arrived already, has it not?"

I swish my gaze back and forth across the room. "Uh, not."

"Are you certain?"

"Let me see. The floor's still here, and so is my old couch. Don't see any new furniture, unless of course you're counting the chandelier. Seriously, Patrice. No one has delivered any furniture."

"Well, it was picked up from my studio on Friday. You should be receiving it any day now, darling. I've instructed them to call you first. Anyhoo, darling, do not be tempted to peek. I want you to be surprised by it all. Ta-ta for now."

I'm off the phone thinking that, despite the gaudy lighting mixup and the missing furniture, Patrice proved to be a good sport. And I need her to be. May's a busy time at Coastal Tours. With June gloom heading its foggy way to Ventura, my tour docket is nearing capacity. Everybody and their sister-in-law's third cousin, or so it seems, wants to board our bus while the sun's still making an appearance. And if Cole's tooth still aches, I don't even want to think about how crazy it'll be. Anyway, I can't be bothered with the finer points of home decorating. That's why Patrice gets paid the big bucks.

"Knock, knock." Gaby charges in through my front door. "It's all set!"

"All set? And that would be. . . ?"

"The dinner party! Ty can come on Saturday. I told him to pick me up at six-thirtyish. Don't worry. I'll come over earlier and help you out. I'll go back home and freshen up before he picks me up. I'm thinking of wearing my velvet skirt—whadd'ya think?" She clasps her hands together as if in prayer and sighs. Her eyelashes flash with their characteristic flutter. "I can't wait. It'll be a night to remember, that's for sure."

Yeah, a night to remember. Me, the hostess with the mostest and head chef to boot. "Ugh. I haven't even thought that far ahead. I'm counting the minutes until Douglas's plane lands. We've got some catching up to do, you know."

Gaby blushes. "Thanks for sharing."

"And I'm literally lined up with tours this entire week."

Gaby leans her head to one side. "You changing your mind about the dinner party, Bri?"

I look at her and see her as she was when we met back at the coffeehouse. Young, skinny, and more boy hungry than a princess at an all-girl high school. "Nah, it'll be a blast. Douglas and I have this entire week to catch up." *And to have some heart-to-hearts.* "The tours are no biggie. I just need to figure out what to feed you all. I think you're right. Douglas's charm is bound to rub off on Ty."

Gaby's mouth drops open.

"Um, didn't mean it like that. Just meant that Ty'll get a chance to see an honest lawyer *and* a fabulous husband all in one night, in one guy." I'm smiling just thinking about it.

Gaby glances around the living room, her eyes landing on the groovy chandelier over the foyer. "I'd forgotten that Patrice wasn't done yet. Do you think a week's enough time?" She looks at me now, one eyebrow cocked.

"Yep. The painter will be here tomorrow to finish up, then my new furniture will be delivered. Oh, and that chandelier's on its way out too."

"Thank God!" She laughs. "I didn't want to hurt your feelings, but . . ." Again, she stares up at the ceiling.

"It's hideous, isn't it?"

Gaby nods vigorously.

"So in answer to your question, yeah, I think a week'll be enough time to pull it all together. No sweat."

She hugs me now and I'm nearly overpowered by the scent of lavender. I sneeze, and sneeze again, all the while secretly thanking God that I don't have asthma. I pull away and head for the stairs. As I do, the phone rings. "Would you get that, Gaby . . . *ah-choo!* . . . I need a tissue," I say, taking the steps two at a time.

Behind me I hear Gaby call out, "Hope you're not getting sick!"

I suppress a giggle. *A little sick of your perfume, that's all, my friend.* I grab a tissue and blow, hard, while half listening to Gaby as she answers the phone and whoops it up, her laughter breaking into the air. *What in the world?* I'm still blowing and leaning one ear toward the door, wondering who she's carrying on with downstairs when I hear her sing out, "See you!" and plunk down the phone.

"Bri-Bri, guess what!" Gaby's nearly breathless.

I stand near the top of the stairway, my nose raw, my shoulders stuck in a shrug.

"Your aunt Dot's coming to dinner next Saturday!"

Chapter thirty

"Wha . . . how. . . ?" I bound downstairs and look at the phone, then back to Gaby. "That . . . was . . . Aunt Dot?" I pick up the phone, but Gaby takes it from my hand and sets it back on its cradle.

"She was on one of those expensive plane phones, Bri-Bri. She couldn't talk long but she wanted you to know that she's coming for a visit. I tell you, I was so excited to hear that raspy voice of hers that I nearly screamed."

"Actually, you *were* screaming."

"She said she missed you and that a visit was long overdue, and that she'd be in town on Saturday afternoon. Of course I told her about the dinner party, and she sounded delighted. Maybe even a little surprised."

No, uh, surprise there.

Gaby grabs my hand. "She's coming to our little party. How fun! I just *love* your auntie and can't wait to see her!"

I plunk myself onto the hardwood floor, the one thing in the room that won't be replaced. Aunt Dot's coming to visit. *Who knew?* I haven't seen her in . . . in . . . well, since Nathan was still toddling around as a two-year-old in the nifty tiger Speedos she gave him. Ever

since, news from her has been sporadic, at best.

"You know, you haven't mentioned Dot very much lately," Gaby says. "It was almost as if she was, well, no longer with us. Know what I mean?"

Yeah, like my dad, who died in the middle of the rain forest with nothing but giant turtles to bury him. Oh, except for Mom. I swallow. "Ah, she's as hardy as an old sea salt. Even though she almost never calls, I figured she was alive and nagging somebody somewhere in the world."

Gaby's standing at the edge of the living room, peering into the odd-shaped nook around the corner that we Stones affectionately call "The Deserted Dining Room." It holds an old rustic farmhouse table that I found at a thrift shop on Main Street—much to Mona's horror. Have to give her credit, though. She fought valiantly for its demise, and lost. In the end Douglas relented and surrounded the seatless table with some modern chrome-and-black-leather chairs, castoffs from one of his dad's former offices.

Come to think of it, that only made Mona angrier.

Gaby's face is bunched in thought. "Maybe if we angle the table a little, we'd all fit better. What do you think? Will Nathan be joining us?"

Sigh. "Um, do whatever you want, Gaby. I'm open. And I doubt Nathan'll want to hang with the grown-ups. I'll have him show good manners by saying hello, then release him into the wild." The shock of hearing that my long-lost auntie will soon be sweeping into my beach pad hits me once again. I give my head a tight shake. "Anyway. I'll make sure he's here when Aunt Dot gets in."

"Bri? Can I ask? Where *has* your auntie been all these years?"

I shrug, indifferent. "All over the place, I guess." I drop my shoulders and swing my gaze to the vaulted ceilings. "Let's see. She sent a few postcards from places like Bangladesh, Mozambique, the Philippines, Romania . . . oh, and a couple of years ago she sent a note from Cambodia. Apparently she got her picture taken with Angelina Jolie."

I look over at Gaby and roll my eyes.

"Wow. She really followed in your mother's footsteps, didn't she?"

That makes one of us. I give a wry laugh. "You can say that again."

"I mean, most people who catch the travel bug take off for short jaunts on the weekends, like to San Francisco or Palm Springs, maybe. If they're some of the lucky ones, they hop a plane for a week on Kauai. *Your* family, on the other hand, has this thing about Third World countries." She shakes her thick brunette hair. "I don't get it."

Well, my family isn't "most" people. We're a regular Swiss Family Robinson, except my parents actually chose *the shipwrecked life. Ugh. What am I crying about? I got to stay here, nice and close to my beloved beach, with Aunt Dot. Until she, too, got bit and flew away. . . .*

"Do you hear something?" Gaby's looking toward the front door.

I snap out of it. Through the window I see a large truck bellowing down the narrow lane in front of our house. The truck parks, and a woman with curly strawberry blond hair and a whistle around her neck jumps out. *Our treeless neighbors probably bought another underused, unnecessary appliance. Like a leather-lined wine bar or hot dog–holder drawer for the fridge.*

She stands on the street outside my door and harangues on the whistle dangling from her neck. I wince. Two redheaded teen boys spill out of the truck and immediately throw open the latches on the truck's roll-up door.

Instead of heading across the street, the woman turns and approaches me. "Good afternoon!" She sticks out her hand to shake mine.

"Hi . . ."

She looks down at the clipboard she's carrying. "You must be Brianna Stone. Am I right?"

I nod.

"Great! I've got your new furniture for you here. My boys'll unload it. Where would you like them to place it?" She looks again at her paper work. "Oh yes, the living room." Before I can duck, she blows hard into the whistle. "This way, boys!" she calls out and points to my front door.

"Did . . . did you try to call?" I ask, not even mentioning that it's Sunday, the day of *rest*.

"Yes, ma'am, I did. Phone was busy like a freeway. You oughta think about getting Call Waiting."

Gaby must've ignored the call when she was on the phone with Aunt Dot.

I follow behind the woman and her crew like a dog that just had its snout whacked. Hey, I'm just the homeowner. What do I know, anyway? So what if it's Sunday and I've worked all weekend—cooking, touring, teaching, oh my! I can almost hear Patrice's voice saying, "Design never rests, darling!"

No kidding. The movers, the painters, and all the other subs come when they'd like, and woe be to those who'd rather be curled up on their ratty old couch, dreaming away the day. I'm like a cat and these people are dangling a ball of yarn in front of me, causing me to lunge and lurch at their every whim.

I'm standing in my drop cloth–covered living room now, watching Gaby squeal over the bubble-wrapped furniture delivery, wondering what happened to me, the bouncy beach girl, the one who didn't care what she sat on, as long as she could hit the sand at any given moment. *That* girl laughed much, loved much, cared little about what people thought of her. Suddenly, I'm twisting in the Santa Ana winds, and it's not fun, I tell you.

"So if you'll just sign right here, the boys'll finish up and we'll be on our merry way." She's dangling—uh, holding—a pen out for me to take. I grab it, sign away, and stifle a *meow*.

With the delivery crew gone, Gaby's running her finely manicured hands across the thickly wrapped furniture, a sparkle in her eyes. "Well, let's open it up!"

Patrice told me not to peek. But since when do I do what people tell me? After all, she's the hired help! (My Mona-like reaction gives me pause.) Anyway, I can do what I want. *I can, I can, I can.* I stand back, considering what to tear into first, when it hits me. I really don't care. Okay, I care. A little. But still, that doesn't mean that I don't want to be surprised.

"Patience, Gabrielle," I say, holding out my palm like a Stop sign. "I'm going to wait until the grand unveiling at the end of the week. Kinda like Paige used to make everyone do on *Trading Spaces*." I'm conveniently setting aside any recollection of those episodes that left participants weeping off-camera.

"Just a little peek. Pretty please?"

"Nope, sorry. Get your own reality show. This one's mine and I'm waiting."

She stomps her foot, although it's such a dainty act that it comes off more like a soft-shoe bit. "Oh, fine." She brightens. "Hey, isn't Douglas due home soon?"

I glance at where the clock used to be. "Uh, yep, he is." She doesn't need to know that although I'm beside myself with joy over seeing my Douglas tonight, I'm dreading "the talk" that he said we should have.

"I'd better get going then. I do have so much paper work to go over tonight before opening the shop tomorrow—ugh." She pseudo-glares at me. "Don't be giving me that holier-than-thou-it's-the-Sabbath look, missy. Some people have more to do in life than re-decorating their living room."

"Uh, ouch!"

She hugs my neck and giggles. "Just kidding. I'm a ninny. Go lay out your clothes for your tour tomorrow or something." She grabs her plush handbag—*did she really change purses from this morning already?*—and stops in the doorway. I cringe at the sight of that disco light fixture hanging over her head. "When you see Ty tomorrow," she says, "tell him I miss him."

Ew. I will not. " 'kay," I say, hoping she doesn't see my nose growing ten feet long.

I'd like to say that I, too, spent the next few hours prepping for the week. In a perfect *Mission Organization* world, I would have laid out my outfits and matching shoes (of course!) for my upcoming week of tours. I would have planned the menu for next Saturday night's dinner soiree and while at it, would have figured the seating plan as well.

But that's the stuff of dreams.

It's true that I have felt the power of change. I no longer wear flip-flops to the office, my home's going from eclectic to elegant, and let's not forget about the new glam hair. I've got more highlights than a Washington, D.C., tour. But even a headstrong beach gal has her limitations, and spending the rest of my Sunday afternoon toiling away on what's to come the following week? Not on option.

"Man, Mrs. Stone," says Gibson, his mouth half full, mustard squirting from his lips. "Your dogs are the best!"

The three of us, Gibson, Nathan and I, sit under the twilight sky, huddled around the fire pit, munching on hot dogs and chips. A late-spring breeze kicked up both wind and waves this afternoon and into the evening, and so I've brought out extra blankets to extend our time outside. There's no place I'd rather be than sitting here, swooning over the ocean's embrace, waiting for my handsome husband to return home.

Max pulls up in his old truck. He hops out and hovers near the gate. "Hate to be the Scrooge," he says, his kind eyes smiling, "but it's time to head out, Gibson." He looks at me. "Thanks for feeding my boy, Bri. I figured I should come and get him. If I waited for him to walk home, I might not get to see him before hitting the sack myself."

I wink at Max. "Gibson's welcome here anytime. Wanna hot dog for the road?"

He turns down my offer but offers me a soundless *thank you* before heading out. Nathan drags himself from his chair. "Gotta go do some homework," he tells me, and I marvel at the responsibility gene that's taken root in his teenage brain. I stay put outside, taking care of the unfinished business of my Sunday afternoon (and now evening!) nap. My eyelids loll amidst the sound of lapping waves and I snuggle into them before drifting off.

I'm awakened by the distinct sounds of a car's engine. I shiver beneath the blanket wrapped around me, its fabric damp from the dew. A car door shuts, and I yawn, momentarily stunned by sleep.

"Brianna?"

I jump from my chair. "Douglas? You're home." I rush toward him, then slow on approach. Even with only moonlight as my guide, I can see that my husband resembles a bent-over old man. His face is haggard, and mustering a smile seems to take much effort. I stop just short of throwing my anxious arms around him and holding on for dear life.

Maybe this won't be the reunion I'd been hoping for, the moment when we'd throw off the ropes of confusion and untangle what we'd been feeling for months. Maybe the time away, the long plane ride, the drive home, gave Douglas all the time he needed to think about us and what has gone wrong lately. Maybe he's got something big and terrible to tell me. I take a deep breath and hold it.

"Brianna," he says, his voice thick and hoarse, "I've got a terrible cold."

Chapter thirty-one

It's not like we didn't talk at all last night. After I helped him peel off his Dockers and navy blue sweater, and after I tucked his feverish body deep into our shabby chic linens, I think I heard Douglas groan and offer me a whisper of thanks. Then he sank like an anchor into heavy slumber and snored heavily the rest of the night.

The sunrise streaked across our bedroom this morning, waking me easily. (I slept little, thanks to the fog horn by my side.) And so with that first light, I rolled out of bed, slipped on sweats and my lone pair of flip-flops, and now here I sit, feet burrowed into soft sand and watching the waves as they call out their relentless, "Good morning, *Ventura.*"

I'm sipping espresso this morning. Not plain coffee, but the strong stuff, dark and bitter. I'm hoping that it'll work its miracle and wake me from the inside out. All it seems to be doing is making me have to use the bathroom.

I sigh and stand urgently, yet with reluctance. And then I notice her. A woman walking the beach in a cottony dress, her head dropped low, her feet bare. Not that this is an unusual sight, mind you. It's just that from where I stand, the woman trudging along, so deep in

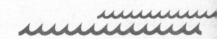

thought, looks like Kate. Seriously, I think it might be her.

Kate, the perfect homemaker, the dedicated homeschooling mom, the craftswoman extraordinaire. Granted, these are titles she's given herself, but still. *That* Kate should be home right now, living out the life of the Proverbs 31 woman and watching over the affairs of her household. She should be providing food for her family and then crowing when they arise and call her blessed! *So why's she here, strolling aimlessly on a deserted (well, almost deserted) beach?*

I take a step toward her and bite my lip. Ugh, I've really got to *go*. I manage to hold it and move closer to the shoreline. "Kate!" I call out to her and wave.

My voice pulls her out of her deep funk, and for a half second I'm thinking maybe this isn't Kate at all. Maybe it's just another slacker like myself, a woman whose day would be incomplete without a toes-in-the-sand moment to start it out. Her face registers surprise, then . . . is that *fear*? It is Kate, and I start jogging toward her. Never mind that I really have to *go*!

She turns a quick one-eighty then and bolts. For some reason, I keep jogging after her, like I'm Richard Gere and she's the Runaway Bride. She's heading for Marina Park and I'm marveling. She's got speed, she's got agility. Unfortunately, she lands on a sharp rock in her bare feet, stumbles into wet sand, and now she's got sloshy mud on her bare legs and muumuu.

I reach her, breathless and naggingly aware of my need for a rest room. "Oh my gosh, Kate. You okay?"

She sits there, dazed, and I squat down, eyes on her. I think she might be crying. "Kate? Are you hurt?" She sets her chin and rolls over onto all fours. Her hands plunge deeper into the wet sand, and she hoists herself up from the awkward position. She's a sight, with her muddy palms and knees and glaring expression.

"Brianna Stone . . ." Her face turns from anger to shock. "What did you do to your hair!"

I run a hand down my locks and start to answer her, but her face changes again.

"And don't you have anything better to do than to spend your morning harassing me?" she says accusingly.

My mouth hangs open. *Harassing* her? Yeah, right. If I'm not mistaken, that would mean that I somehow annoy her with my repeated pestering. Like the infamous Newman on *Seinfeld*. Or the lecherous JR Ewing from the old reruns of *Dallas*. I laugh. "Good one! I guess I could ask you the same thing, Kate."

"What in the world . . . ex-*cuse* me?"

"Every time I turn around, you're right there," I say, my voice lowered to a mysterious-sounding whisper. "At the harbor, at Chef Kelly's . . . now at my end of the beach."

She snorts. "It's not enough that you've got the perfect life, is it, Brianna? You have to own the whole stinkin' beach too."

My eyes switch rapidly to the left and right and back again. *Am I being X'd? Is this another new version of* Candid Camera? Did Kate really just utter a quasi–swear word? All is not right in her world, I can feel it.

"Can I ask you something, Kate?" Big blast of wisdom blowing in here. In my head I'm hearing a Dot-ism on spiritual maturity coming on—*"It's time for a forkful of solid food, my dearie!"*—and I dig in. "Have I done something to offend you?" I ask her. "Because if I have, I want to make it right."

There. I did it. I'm hoping that whatever's been bugging her, whatever she's holding against me, she'll just lay it out like a bared soul prepped for some superglue-style healing.

She blinks, and I'm thinking I see tears rolling in like thunderclouds. Then, just as quickly, she blinks again and the clouds roll out. Still, her words stumble from her mouth. "I, uh, no, no. Brianna, it's just that . . . you wouldn't understand." She turns toward Marina Park, looking ready to bolt away from me again.

I touch her shoulder. "Hey," I say, "forget it. I didn't mean to upset you. I just thought something was up, and I wanted to help fix it. But if you're not—"

She turns swiftly toward me but doesn't make eye contact. In an unusually hushed voice, she whispers, "Forgive me," and as I suspected she would, she runs in the other direction.

I'm still thinking about what I'm now referring to as the "Kate Episode" as I rush past Luann to grab my tour docket for the day. I'd wanted to hang out at the beach longer this morning, if only to stare at the waves and contemplate what's gotten into Kate, but my bladder wouldn't hear of it. So I jogged home.

The morning had been quiet. Nathan took off with Gibson and Max, and Douglas hadn't moved in more than ten hours, and so I slipped into my nubby linen pants, silk top, and comfy yet oh-so-stylish sandals and went to work.

There's a definite murmur in the Coastal Tours building as I lean against the wall in the break room and pore over the list of guests I'll be seeing today.

"There you are." Ty hurries into the room, his uptight stride reminding me of Miles Crane from *Frasier*. He whisks up to me, stopping annoyingly close. "Did your husband have a chance to look over the lease I gave you?" he asks.

I smack my head with my palm. *The paper work's still on my dresser at home. Oops!* "So sorry, Ty, but no. He came in late last night, sick as a wet dog. I haven't had much chance to talk to him at all."

He sighs and I can feel his breath on my shoulder. He's that close. I take two big steps backward, barely hiding an eye roll. Maybe Gaby can teach him some better social skills. Despite my arm's distance away from him (times two!), he reaches out and gives the top of my arm a consoling pat. "I see that you are still sticking up for him," he says.

I cough out a gasp. I'm standing there with my mouth hanging open, wondering if all of Ty's business-speak has somehow been hiding his lack of tact. He, however, is unmoved. Instead of hanging his follicly-charged head in shame, he's assessing me and looking downright cocky, if you ask me.

Luann's voice shrieks over the loudspeaker, "Call for Brianna on line two."

Wordlessly I walk toward the phone hanging on the wall and answer it. "This is Bri."

"Bri, it's me." Despite the rasp in his voice, hearing Douglas on the other end and knowing that he's less than two miles away soothes my ruffled mood.

I tuck the phone in closer and spin away from Ty. Not before giving him a dagger-infused look, however. "You're up," I say. "How're you feeling?"

"Been better. I was hoping we could talk soon. What's your schedule?"

I grunt. "Full to overflowing, unfortunately. I've got a full day of tours—almost every day this week. Plus I've got a parent-teacher-fellowship meeting after school today." *And have I mentioned the little dinner party I will be hosting on Saturday?*

He groans into the phone.

"You're feeling pretty sick still, huh." Ty's still in the break room, and I have this sudden urge to reach out and slap him with my clipboard.

"Nah, well, yeah, I'm feeling nasty." He sighs. "I just didn't want to wait any longer to discuss some things with you. We really need to talk, Bri."

He rarely calls me Bri, and it melts me when he does. Well, usually it does. Sometimes it's a buttering-up ploy, and his sudden usage of my nickname just sent my radar up. "I want to talk to you too," I say as quietly as I can.

"Oh," Douglas says suddenly. "Were you expecting someone today? I think I heard the doorbell ring, but maybe I was just dreaming. Anyway, I didn't get up to answer it."

Trinka! For the second time, I smack my forehead with my palm. *Patrice is gonna freak.* "Not a biggie," I manage to say. "I completely forgot someone was coming, but I'll take care of it. You sure you're doing okay?"

"Well . . . oh, I think I'd better stay in today." He groans. I know him so well. He rarely gets sick, but when he does, he always tries to push through, to scale Mount Workload instead of resting and healing. There's always the spiral down, though, the point where he collapses like a baby going down for his afternoon nap. That's when I step in and start the pampering. He'll need chicken soup, water, and lots of tucking in, but when I'm going to find time to do all that for him is the mystery.

"Douglas?"

"I'm okay. Just dizzy. I'll . . . just . . . try to . . . sleep it off. Check on me, okay?"

He's such a baby. Yet his childish plea makes me smile. I say I will, content that my mothering instinct just got a good stroking. I hang up to find Ty still standing in the break room.

"Do you need to discuss a tour, Ty?" I tap my clipboard. "Because I'm swamped and need to get moving."

He hesitates before answering. "It can wait. I will longline you later, Brianna, so that we can talk at leisure." He holds the door open for me. "After you."

"Thanks, Ty," I say, heading toward the parking lot.

Ty stops. "By the way, Brianna, I understand we're to have dinner together on Saturday night."

"Um . . . yes, we are." *Don't even get me started on how much I've got to do this week!* I swallow. "Glad you and Gaby can make it. Should be fun," I say, questioning my honesty here.

"I am looking forward to seeing your home and to dining at your table. Gaby says you have been taking instruction in the culinary arts."

I giggle. Me and art in the same sentence? *I don't think so.* "Oh brother. I hope our Gabrielle hasn't built me up too much. I'd hate for you to be too disappointed, boss."

He cocks an eyebrow. "I have great doubt that you could ever do that."

I'm laughing now. "A little doubt is healthy," I call back to him as I breeze through the door and head over to greet my first tour of the morning.

Ned's on the blacktop, tossing a Frisbee with a couple of preteen boys from the hot, inland city of Valencia. Unlike the resident beach folk who can't leave the house without a windbreaker, these inland kids wear nothing but shorts, tanks and flip-flops. My job? To show these landlubbers a thing or two about beach living. *Can't wait!*

"G'mornin', Bri."

"Hey, Ned. Nice socks." With his sandals, he's sporting thin blue socks with pictures of breeching whales.

"Thankie," he says. "I picked them up on my way up north a couple weeks back." He cranks a thumb toward the Coastal Tours office. "The boss says we should sell 'em in our new gift shop."

"Oh, so I guess you're our model for the day. We sellin' that shirt too?"

He throws back his shoulders, tucks in his chin, and struts around the parking lot, his arms pumping at his sides. The word *dweeb* is printed in bright orange across the back of his shirt. Some of the kids have stopped playing just to point and gawk. I'm thinking this would be a big seller.

"I heard you'd be the one modelin' outerwear, Miss Bri. The boss says you'd be a natural." Ned tries to wiggle his eyebrows at me, but it looks more like he's having some kind of attack.

"Oh please. Just get on the bus, mister, or I'll make you start coming to work in a suit and tie."

"Aye, aye," he says with a salute. He's looking past me when he salutes a second time. I turn, shade my eyes with one hand, and see Ty standing at the office's glass door entry. Catching my eye, he gives me a perfunctory nod and widemouthed grin. *Oh, ugh.* Did he just have his teeth whitened? Although I'm quite sure that Rita kept a close watch over her employees, Ty standing there like a statue behind thick glass gives me the willies. Except for the grin, he's stiff as a board, just watching, like one of those paintings where the eyes seem to follow the viewer's every move. It's unnerving.

I turn back to Ned and point toward the west. "Let's boogie, my friend."

Chapter thirty-two

To: The Love of My Very Life
Fr: The Girl of Your Dreams
Re: I Miss You

As you now know, we will be entertaining guests in our (hopefully) newly remodeled living room this Saturday night. I can't wait to see your charming self sitting at the head of the table, swapping office war stories with Gaby's new beau (and my boss!), Ty. Just to liven things up, Aunt Dot will be with us that night—have I mentioned that she called?—and I've decided to bribe, er, invite Nathan to join us, to round out the group.

So when the night is through and the dishes are cleared and the guests have gone, will you meet me in our rarely used but nicely appointed (I learned that lingo from the decorator!) backyard spa? We need to "talk."

My index finger hovers over the Enter key. It's come to this. I've written my man a memo. He's spent the past few days curled up in the fetal position, and now it's early morning and he's bailed out on

me—*poof!*—like backwash into a wave. No note, no nothing, just gone.

I guess this shouldn't surprise me. As Darla always says, *"He's a very busy man."* He's also been sick from a cold, and have I mentioned distant? We've had two or three tête-à-têtes, yes, but most of the time I've found him either asleep or with his furrowed brow buried deep within the pages of lengthy legal documents dropped off by his trusty secretary. Sometimes I think I feel his eyes burning into me while I lay beside him, but whenever I finally pull my lids open to check, he's zonked. Or staring at the pages in his hands.

My pointer finger draws circles in the air above the keyboard. He could've told me he was leaving this morning. I would've rousted early too and made him some coffee. We could've sat together on the back deck, listening to the seagulls awaken and begin their daybreak hunt for breakfast—even for a little while. I take another look at my memo to Douglas, my finger ready to hit Send.

Instead, I hit delete.

Sigh. I'm at the kitchen island, shutting down my laptop after having moved it there for the duration of the living room redo. It's Thursday, just two days before my dinner party *debut*, and Trinka has yet to finish the wall treatment. She began early in the week but has kept a swath of flowing fabric hung in front of her work, essentially hiding it from unwelcome critiques. Like I've got the time right now.

Anyway, she's here now looking like she's ready to finish up— thank you, God!—her face serene and peaceful. I guess the yip-yap or whatever it's called has been righted in our wayward home, and all is right in artiste's land. I'd hate to disrupt the flow of positive energy, so I slip on my shoes, intending to make my way to the door. Besides not wanting to block the feng shui of the moment, I've got another long day ahead.

Nothing new there. Inland temperatures have spiked to record-setting highs for late spring, bringing folks west to our sunny but much cooler coast. These newcomers, along with the regulars—school kids, birders, even another visit from the Red Hat group—has equally spiked our numbers. In between running from home, to tour office, to Nathan's school, I've been warming up Trader Joe's soup for my ailing husband, planning Saturday's meal, and pacing the living room, hoping I can soon cry out, "It's a wrap!"

Last night Douglas's face finally got back some of its warm color. I noticed this when I bent to kiss him on the forehead, just before smoothing clean sheets over his chest and turning out the light. That man just brings out the mothering instinct in me. Of course, with the return of his health, he's, uh, brought something else out too. But since he opted to drop out of sight in the wee morning hours today, I won't go there. Not now, anyway.

Nathan took off early this morning too. *Et tu, my son?* He left me a note saying he'd be catching a ride to school. I'm guessing he and Gibson are back to being true-blue buds again, and that all is right in teendom. For the moment, it seems.

I really need to catch my tour, but I'm antsy and so I dial up Douglas's office. "Darla? It's Bri," I say. "Would you connect me with Douglas, please?"

"Mr. Stone is at home, *very* sick, Brianna. Don't you know that?" Once again, Darla sounds overwrought and incredulous. *She's so odd.*

"Oh yeah, Darla, I know. I've been nursing him back to health all week. He snuck out on me this morning, though, and I just want to check on him. He's probably hiding in his office."

She harrumphs into the receiver. "I think I'd know if Mr. Stone had arrived. I'm very conscientious about things like that."

"Of course you are. Do me a favor, though, okay? Ring his office for me, just in case." I'm drumming my fingers on the island, wondering how long until she retires.

She comes back on the line. "Like I said, Mrs. Stone, Mr. Stone has not yet come in. I would be happy to take a message for him if you'd like to leave one. Or, of course, you could always try to reach him on his cellular phone." She says it like I should've thought of that in the first place. *Grrr*.

"Thanks anyway," I say, sweetly as possible, before hanging up. And I *would* have tried the cell phone, only it's still sitting on the kitchen counter where Douglas left it when he dragged himself in from the airport three days ago. *So there*.

I don't get it. The man's been shivering and whimpering beneath our lumpy comforter for most of the week. He's torn through a dozen boxes of tissue and grumped about for days. Then again, I've also heard him complain more than once that the phone rarely cooled down in between calls from the office. Too soon or not, with all that work piling up in his office (and around Darla), I guess I really can't blame him for giving up the comforts of our bed and going back to work.

Only it looks now as if he didn't go to work at all. He's gone out but apparently not to the office. At the moment, all I know for sure is that he's AWOL. Again.

Breathe, breathe, breathe. I start pacing my kitchen while sticking a stud earring into my lobe, something I've not done in I don't know how long. I'm hauling in deep breaths, trying to calm my nerves. And what is *up* with that? I remember one of Aunt Dot's pals—I can't remember her name anymore—always wringing her gnarled hands and saying she had a case of the nerves. Always seemed like some gross disease, like saying she had a case of shingles or gout.

I've got no time for this. Trinka is working her magic on my walls, and it's nearly time for my next tour. Eyebrows lifted, I peek around the corner, only to see my resident artist still in thinking mode, her gaze fixed on the gauzy fabric hanging on our wall. Sigh. Okay, so maybe she's actually just on the *brink* of magic. Time will tell. I'm just hoping that everything really does pull together in the next couple of days. Patrice has promised to send in her design team tomorrow to unveil the new furniture and put it in place. She's also got a ton of things to hang, and she insists this will all be done in plenty of time for Saturday night's party—provided that our ship's captain decides to show, that is.

I shrug off my anxiety. Isn't there a Scripture to back me up? *Be anxious for nothing* . . . The phone rings mid-thought, and I consider letting the machine get it. Instead, I grab the receiver. "Hello!"

"Brianna, it's Douglas. I just wanted to let you know that I'm in the office."

"You *are* at the office? I thought . . ."

"I stopped for a latte, a big one. It's kicking in right now."

I glance at the clock. It's nearing 9:00 A.M. That was some *big* coffee. I let out the breath that I hadn't realized I'd been holding. "Sounds so great about now. I'm glad you're . . . okay."

"I'm okay, somewhat groggy, but not too bad. I will survive." He sighs. "There's a mound of paper on my desk the size of El Capitan, though, so I'm going to have to stay with it for a while."

I feel a catch in my throat. "I want you well, my love," I say, my voice small. I'm fatigued, realizing how much anxiety I'd been holding on to.

He's quiet. Then he says, "I want to be well too."

There's dead air in the phone line. I'm looking around the kitchen, seeing nothing in particular, emotionally hovering in that place between wanting to shout out the truth of what I'm feeling and keeping it tucked safely inside my heart. I swallow hard and say, "Don't forget about the party we're having here on Saturday."

"So that's why you want me well?" he says, his voice somewhat brighter. "So I can take care of your 'honey do' list in time to host a bunch of strangers in my unrecognizable home?"

In the not-so-distant past, I might have enjoyed his lob and volleyed one back to him. I sense that he's trying to make nice, but I'm too raw to enjoy it. I feel like offering up a spike instead.

Doesn't he know how much I need to know what's going on inside that head of his? Doesn't he sense the gap that's widening between us? And what the hey, hasn't he noticed my new look or appreciated the room makeover or reveled in the fact that I'm throwing my first-ever dinner party? And what about the talk he keeps mentioning? Has he forgotten about that too?

Tears push their way to the rims of my eyes. "You don't have to do a thing," I say. *Just show up. Please show up.*

He clears his throat. "Good. Then I guess I'll see you when I get home. Will you be home early—or is this another marathon tour day?"

Does it matter?

"Only one tour today," I tell him. "Then in the afternoon I'll be driving on a field trip for Nathan's class. We're heading down to see some exhibit in Thousand Oaks. There's a chance we won't return until late afternoon."

"Ah, that's right! Nathan mentioned it to me."

I'm startled. When have they had much chance to talk? Douglas's relationship with Nathan had seemed to me to be as sketchy as our own. I've been worried about that, actually. "So you boys had a chance to talk? I'm so glad."

"Oh, uh, yes, we talked this morning," Douglas says. "I gave Nathan a ride."

My heart lifts, just a little, over this revelation. One less thing to worry about, I guess. Just wish I had seen them together. "Don't overdo it today, Douglas, okay?" I say, softening. "We'll be home by dinnertime."

We hang up, and I head for the door. I peek at Trinka, who's sitting on a rung near the top of the ladder. She's got a small can of paint in one hand, a brush in the other, and both the brush and her nose stay just inches from a point on the wall where the fabric has been pulled away. I shrug. Maybe she's a Monet protégé, and all those tiny brushstrokes she's intently making will in the end reveal some sort of big picture, a breathtaking and intricate tapestry created by thousands of miniscule droplets of paint. I step out into the sunshine, hoping with all of my heart to find just that by the time I return.

Chapter thirty-three

"Forgive me, Bri-Bri!" Gaby's caught me in between gigs. It's just after my tour and right before I leave for the school to drive Nathan and his classmates on their field trip. "I've been such a bad friend—*muy mala*! I didn't mean to desert you this week, I really didn't. Sammy didn't show up for deliveries again today, something about an infected nose ring, and then my cashier came down with the flu. In May! Can you beat that? Don't these people understand that June weddings are nearly upon us? No one, absolutely no one, is allowed to get sick during bridal season!"

I'm dashing to my car, my heels clacking against pavement. "Gaby, it's not a problem."

Her sigh sounds like wind rushing through the phone line. "Oh, are you sure? I owe you, I really do. Remember, I'll be bringing the salad, and it'll be *fabulous*! So you're really doing okay? You don't need my help? Because if you do, I'll shut down right now, brides or no brides!"

"Yeah, right."

"Oh, *gracias Dios*—thank God you didn't take me up on that." She giggles. "You're the best, you know that."

"Oh yeah, sister. You got that right. Now leave me alone. I've got to pick up my kid and his friends, and I can't be late."

"Ty called me today."

I flip a look upward, offering the good Lord a *Why me?* Gaby's got a one-track mind, and my schedule? *Fugeddaboutit.* "So," I say, "things going better for you two?" *Shall I cancel Saturday night's dinner and curl up on my new sofa with Douglas instead?*

"I think. We haven't seen each other all week—well, you *know* it's been a terribly busy week at the shop, but he sounded so upbeat when he called, like he could talk all morning. Of all the days to be shorthanded." I can hear the pout in her voice. "We talked while I arranged my Spring Fiesta bouquet for the Rutherfords. He's such a dream. Kept chatting on about my business, asking lots of questions."

"Yeah? Like what?" I start up the VeeDub and plug in my headset.

"Lots of things. What I thought about the new gift-shop idea, what kinds of things to offer in there—he says you're going to be their spokesmodel—that's sweet! He also wanted to know what kind of flowers you like—oops. Don't think I was supposed to mention that."

"What kind of flowers *I* like?"

"Act surprised, okay? He just thought I should get a hostess gift ready. I tried to talk him out of it." She giggles. "I told him that if it wasn't some kind of native scrub flower growing on sand, forget it. He insisted, though, so be nice!"

I snap my tongue. "I'm always nice. What's wrong with you?"

"Nothing a nice dinner with friends won't cure!" I hear a bell jangle on her end of the line. "Oh, Bri-Bri, I've got to go. Customers just walked in. See you Saturday. You're the best, chica!"

I pull into the parking lot of Nathan's school, thinking about my pal and her latest romance, and for the first time actually try to picture all of us under our one, high-pitched roof. I'm also wondering how I'm staying so calm. I am having a dinner party, at my house, this Saturday night. Let me repeat that. I'm cooking for people at my home *this* weekend. Big breath in. It's not like I've never thrown a bash at the beach pad before. I mean, c'mon, *everybody* loves the beach, do they not? Okay, Mona doesn't. But just about everyone else I know does. And I've always liked flinging open my doors and inviting them over to relax at our place.

But it's always been about the place, not the food. Location, location, location, people! The best shindigs we've ever thrown consisted of rigatoni from Meridians and a few pizza pies eaten around the fire pit on our front patio, just a pebble's kick from the sand. Call me crass, but never have fancy duds *and* a homemade meal figured into the deal.

Except for my gooey, finger-licking, handcrafted brownies, that is. My aunt Dot cooked and baked all the time when I stayed with her while growing up, but for some reason, only the brownie experience stuck. I slept in her second-story loft and would leap from her nubby 1950s-style couch at the first squeak of her pantry door. I'd slide down her narrow banister—okay, I now see where Nathan gets *that*—and swoop into the kitchen like a hungry seagull onto a bag of fries. By the time I turned ten, I was a brownie snob, making them all by myself without giving the recipe even a second glance.

Well. Other than when baking brownies, fussbudgeting is *so* not my thing. And I'm not about to add that personality disorder to all my others just now. I switch off the engine and wait for Nathan's class to line up.

———

My head hurts. It was supposed to be an easy thing. Just drive a few boys to see a water-garden exhibit and then back again. I knew these kids going in. They're top students, GPAs ranging in the high threes, every one of them. And they have servants' hearts too. "Let me get the door for you, Mrs. Stone." "May I carry that latte for you,

Mrs. Stone?" "After you, Mrs. Stone."

But these boys, these skinny, long-haired, testosterone-infused teenagers, they're imposters. *Who are you, and what have you done with my kid and his friends!* I'm thinking about the ride back from the exhibit, the twenty-minute drive that felt more like an hour in snarling traffic. Oh, the jostling, the wolf calls, the plastered skin against the car window!

I tried all of my tricks, but these *good* boys wouldn't budge.

Okay, so maybe I'm exaggerating. A little. But in the good ol' days, maybe just a couple of years ago, my lively spirit would have sent even these smarty-pants boys into peels of giggles. My VeeDub used to *rock* on field trips, making us the envy of all the SUVs filled with children made to stay quiet and sane . . . or else! Mine was the coveted vehicle. Kids simply begged to win a seat in Bri Stone's field trip car o' fun. But this time? This time all my expended energy, all my cool-mom attitude got was silence and red-faced stares. Who knew that acne and facial hair could make such an impact on those usually so immature?

Nathan and I return home, neither saying a word. I'm thinking I'd better not say anything, that my comments just might be returned with an icy-cold stare. The house seems quiet. No cars out front, meaning that either Trinka couldn't get past the negative energy in our home, or that she actually completed her masterpiece and we're about to embark on its unveiling.

I peek through the garage window and see no sign of Douglas and his sports car, and my stomach does a somersault. I'm not sure why. Is it because I long to hold him and he's not here? Or because I'm afraid of what he would say if he actually stayed put for several waking hours at a time?

I unlock the front door and push it open. Wordlessly, Nathan enters, his sullen outlook just a little too overdone, if you ask me. It's been a tough few weeks, and I thought I'd have some fun, but *no*. It's not like I mooned anyone, for crying out loud.

"Douglas, you home?" I call out, knowing that unless his car broke down and he hitched a ride, finding him is doubtful.

Nathan moves on ahead of me but stops at the base of the stairs. He's still mute, but something's got his attention. His chin moves upward and down like a pogo stick, and his mouth has fallen open. I follow his line of vision, and the first thing I feel when my eyes rest on my massive and newly unveiled living room wall . . . is dizziness.

"Whoa. Is this what you ordered?" Nathan's still staring at the vaulted living room wall.

I step closer. My heart's pounding, and blood? What blood? The blood that usually courses through a sane person's brain has drained from mine, leaving me slack jawed and suddenly very, very tired.

And then, for the first time all afternoon, Nathan laughs. Hard. The kid with the scowl and disapproving glare is howling at Trinka's creation and pointing at me. "You are in so much trouble! That's the dumbest thing I've ever seen." He wraps an arm around my neck and cinches me close against him, his BO overwhelming. The stench makes me want to vomit, or at least pull away, but I'm stuck in place, dumbfounded.

My eyes are fixed ahead. The curtain has been pulled away, and Trinka's masterpiece lives on my wall. It's not some type of faux wall treatment, no sponges or rags were used in its design. She didn't knock off a Hildi design from *Trading Spaces* and glue flowers or hay anywhere. (Although at the moment, I'm thinking that might have been preferable.) Instead, she's created a giant, golden bronzed portrait of *The Thinker*.

I learned about this sculpture, Rodin's most famous, in my Art History class in college. It's of a pensive man, head in hand, deep in thought, his sinewy muscles and veins exposed and taut, as if at attention, ready to pounce at any moment. I also remember that Rodin created this piece as part of a grouping called *Gates of Hell*.

Well. Now isn't that a coincidence? Because truthfully, it's getting awfully hot in here.

"What're you going to do now? Aren't you having a bunch of people over here tomorrow?"

"Saturday! They're coming Saturday." I walk around the living room, eyeing the painting and resting my forefinger and thumb on my cheek and chin, like I'm an art critic. All I need now is a pair of round eyeglasses and a shiny black suit. A glow from the setting sun slips in through the rake windows near the top of an adjacent wall and cascades down the thinking man, highlights spilling over his sculpted body.

Nathan's still laughing. "I *think* I'm gonna go call Gib. I *think* he's gonna flip. Have I mentioned that I *think* Dad's gonna be mad? I *think* you've got some 'splaining to do, Mom." He takes the stairs two at a time, in search of the phone, chortling the entire way.

I run my hand along the bubble-wrapped furniture placed haphazardly around the room, trying to imagine the entire *space* in its fully adorned and completed state. Okay, so the new artwork has thrown a wrench into my imagination, but then again, you gotta admit: It is original. Or at least an original copy.

Things have been moving so fast around here lately that I'm just trying to mentally keep up. Truth is, I'm not sure how I feel about Trinka's surprise wall finish. I'm numb. I'm confused. I'm intrigued. I'm also on the search for wisdom amidst a whole jumble of thoughts that spin around like a whirlwind inside my mind. A Dot-ism keeps jumping out of the vortex, her continual admonition about wisdom during my teenage years: *"Don't go pickin' any green peaches, dearie!"*

I'm just wondering. Was my decision to reinvent my world ripe for the plucking . . . or just plain premature?

Chapter thirty-four

I lay in bed last night with more tension in my shoulders than a jib line at full extension. Douglas had called once around eleven with a confession. He'd fallen asleep at his desk and awakened only when the cleaning crew had arrived at the office. He said he'd be home soon. I guess soon is a relative term. Because by the time he roused himself from his pile of work, drove home, and stepped softly up the stairs, midnight had come and gone.

By then I'd finally drifted off to a light sleep, only to be awakened myself by the familiar sound of his footsteps. My sleepy eyes stuck out from atop the sheets as I watched him enter our bedroom and strip down to his tee and boxers. With barely a sound he slipped in beside me, his body warm and comforting after so many days apart—including those that wracked him with illness. He snuggled against me and we lay there cozy like two spoons.

I let out the breath I'd been holding and relaxed against him. He's here. Life is good. Now if only I could get him to stick around awhile.

In addition to wondering when he'd make it home, I'd been struggling all night over the drama sweeping through our living room, the changes that seem to be moving at lightning speed. From what I've

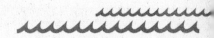

heard, makeovers don't usually get it together so fast, not unless you're on reality TV, that is. And just try to get a plumber or electrician in at a moment's notice! That's a trick. For some reason, though, my remodel has been anything but slow. I've had more strangers traipsing through this place at all hours than a beachfront open house.

Truthfully, though, I kinda like it that way. In and out. Get it done. Patience is a virtue, just not one of mine. Of course, all along I have had high hopes that this redo would show Douglas that our home's not just my dream—*it's not about me!*—but that it's really and truly his castle. I just hope that he not only doesn't hate it but that he *loves* it!

I never got a chance to learn what Douglas thought about the thinker man on our wall, though, that mysterious portrait that grows on me minute by sober minute. Douglas sniffled and groaned throughout the night, his head cold showing signs of lingering. His grumbling awoke me often, and I'd pull the covers up around him, only to slip back into a fitful slumber of my own. I figured he'd spend all day in bed, resting up for the weekend.

By daylight, though, Douglas had again slipped out of bed early. I half expected to hear a startled yelp when he reached the bottom of the stairs and found what Trinka left. Only I never did.

Nathan's dressed in black jeans and a button-down shirt, ready to go, while I stand in the kitchen still groggy and wearing my robe and flip-flops. "You driving me to school today?" he asks.

I take a sip of coffee and set the mug down at an abrupt thought. "Did you see your dad this morning, Nathan?"

He looks toward the door, as if for support, and fidgets with the straps of his backpack. He swings his gaze back to me but doesn't make contact with my eyes. "Not really."

"What's that mean? Either you did or you didn't. He got home so late last night and sounded pretty sick again. I'm surprised that he's gone again so early, that's all."

Nathan shrugs. "He's just got . . . I mean, he's probably going to work. That's all."

"Of course he's at work. I mean, where else would he be at this hour?"

Nathan's quiet. He's moving his head around, focusing everywhere but on me.

I rest my palm over my cup. A cold trickle runs through my heart. "You know something. I can tell. Don't try to fool me, kiddo. What's up with your dad?"

He drops his head back and gasps. "Nuthin'! C'mon, Mom, we're gonna be late. We gotta get Gib." He's staring at the front door now.

I move toward him and take his chin between my finger and thumb. I turn his face toward mine. "I need you to tell me, son."

His eyes are big. What is that I'm seeing in them? Fear, anger . . . laughter? He looks away and I'm stumped. "Can't," he says. "I don't know nuthin'." He pulls away from my grasp and bounds out the door.

I give my head a shake at my teenager's behavior. Sigh. Maybe he doesn't know a thing about Douglas's whereabouts. Maybe there's nothing to know. Traveling and a bad cold put my already "very important" husband way behind schedule, so I guess he's just paddling like a drowning duck to stay afloat. Or whatever.

The rest of the day blew through like a haze. As promised, Patrice's crew showed up and began cutting and tearing away at the plastic that held my new furniture hostage. A carpenter also showed up with a couple of cabinets to frame the fireplace, and two picture-hanging sisters came by with hammers and screws.

I stuck around only long enough to catch a glimpse of the chocolate leather sofas and plaid pillows in rich reds and browns, the same fabrics Patrice had bandied about during our consultation, being unwrapped and set and reset by professional home-stagers. Then it was off to the store to shop for the ingredients of our four-course Saturday night meal: Satiny chocolate soup, Gaby's salad, mushroom risotto, and Chef Kelly's yummy chocolate cherry fondue.

I'm zipping down the aisle, making a mental note to scrounge around the house for our never-used fondue set, the one we received as a wedding gift from who-knows-who, when Mario calls out to me. "Well, hello there, Mizz Stone. Come here. You gotta see this."

Ugh. Don't you ever get a day off? I smile sweetly and turn my cart toward the deli counter. "Hello, Mario. I'm in a hurry, but what you got cookin' today?"

"You are never in too big a hurry for Mario's homemade jambalaya, eh? Come here. Have a taste." He spoons some into a Styrofoam cup and hands it over the counter. I swig it down.

"You do have a way with shellfish, my friend. Okay, give me a pint."

"A pint! You need a gallon o' this, my specialty, Mizz Stone. You'll want to serve it to all your friends."

I laugh. "Then what would *all* my friends say? You want them to think I don't cook!"

He raises both eyebrows and tries unsuccessfully to hide a smirk.

I give him a wry smile. "Okay, give me more—but not a gallon! I'll take two quarts. Does it freeze well?"

"Of course it does!" With gusto he begins ladling up his soup. "But I promise you. You won't need to freeze it, Mizz Stone. Your friends get a bite of this, they're gonna think they've landed in paradise."

Back at home I load up the fridge with more food than it's seen in a decade, including Mario's jambalaya. I'm thinking that after a day's worth of cooking for six, these quarts will come in handy on Sunday afternoon when I'm laid out like a sea star on damp sand. There's still a jumble of commotion happening just around the corner, but I ignore it to grab the ringing phone.

"Brianna, it's me."

Douglas! I smile at the ground. "Hi 'me.' You sound chipper. Where've you been all my life?"

My husband chuckles. "I am 'chipper,' as you say. I think this cold has finally gone dormant . . . or is in the process of doing so. Sorry I missed you last night. I think I scared the janitor half to death."

"Lawyers have that effect on people."

He guffaws. "Funny girl. What am I going to do with you?"

I snicker and blush. *I've got a few ideas . . .*

Douglas clears his throat. "There is another reason for my call."

"Oh?"

He sighs, and I picture him hanging his head and raking his fingers through his handsome hair. "I hate to do this to you, but I've got a load of work here, and, well, what time are all of our guests arriving tomorrow?"

"Aunt Dot's coming sometime in the evening. Gaby and Ty should be here around six-thirty."

"Good. Good. I made an appointment for the morning, and hopefully it won't take all day. You didn't need me to do anything, did you? Maybe I can pick up the food—did you place an order with Meridians, or somewhere else?"

"Nope. I'm cooking."

Silence. Maybe Darla just walked in with a stack of docs to sign. Or maybe Douglas just gazed out his office window and caught sight of a pod of dolphins swimming in the waters just beyond the shore.

"You still there, Douglas?" I ask.

Then like a train careening through a tunnel and roaring into earshot, Douglas lets out a boisterous tumble of laughter. I roll my eyes. "You are *what?*" he asks.

"You heard me. I'm cooking. Stop laughing or you'll be eating at the kids' table in the kitchen!"

"All right." He stifles himself. "Wow. I don't know what to say. To what do we owe the pleasure of seeing you in an apron? You are making something other than brownies, right?"

"You're not winning any points here. First you disappear from my life for days on end, now you insult my cooking abilities. It's not like I've never cooked for you boys. You are going to be very pleased, I can assure you."

"Good. I can't wait to see what you have planned for us." He pauses. "Bri? Are you sure you can handle all this?"

"I am."

"Okay, then. Let's talk about the other reason for my call, shall we?" He's slipping into lawyer-speak. I hate that.

"Let's!" I say sarcastically.

"I'd like to schedule some time for us to discuss some things. Do you have your calendar handy?"

What am I that you have to pencil me in? Is this what I signed up for?

"Um, no, I don't. What is it that you want to talk about?"

He sighs wearily. "Bri, it's no secret that things have been rather . . . tense lately. I think it's important that we clear the air. I would like to discuss a recent development with you, and I'd like it to happen soon."

Recent development? Like selling our house? Like hanging out with the Erin Brockovich look-alike? Like never being home? I'm doing some emotional sleeve rolling here. *Where shall we start?*

"Brianna, please. Let's go to the evening service and then set aside some time on Sunday night to . . . talk. Is that good with you?"

"Yeah," I say, feeling more like I'm talking with a client than a husband. "That's good with me."

I hang up, acutely aware of the three decadent, foil-wrapped brownies waiting for me just inside those freezer doors. Leftovers from a past wallowing trip. The ocean sits just mere steps away, and although I'm tempted to fling myself onto its sandy shoreline with my basketful of richness, I sigh and realize that I'm just too busy to go.

Chapter thirty-five

It's Saturday. I'm alone in the kitchen, wearing the new apron I bought just for the occasion. The room bubbles and brims with aromatic meldings of chocolate, porcini mushrooms, and dry white wine. Not that these foods are actually combined into one oversized pot, mind you—just their scents. If Douglas, Nathan, Aunt Dot—*anyone*—were to breeze through the front door at this very moment and take one whiff of the air, they would think they'd just entered one of the more popular bistros on Paris's busiest street. Or at least downtown Ventura.

The look of the place, however, is another matter entirely. I feel like Jackson Pollock's wife. There are more splatters and spills on my counters and floors than one of the famed artist's action paintings—and not a rag in sight.

My feet ache too. But should I admit this? Who knew that standing in heels all day could bring on such pain? And I've got four-inchers planned for later tonight! *Sheesh*. In the print ad, the model actually danced in similar-style shoes. Me? I'm thinking they're just window dressing, and I should forget about wearing heels tonight and

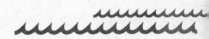

place them instead on one of the new shelves hanging on our living room walls.

Speaking of our new *space*, there's been a mysterious silence around here ever since the final unveiling last night. Instead of bright colors reflecting the many shades of the sea and contrasted with my penchant for crisp white, the living room now wears a more formal, dare I say *mature* look. Buttered Rum–colored walls, dark leather couches with plaid-covered pillows, cabinetry stained in black walnut, and of course, the thinking man, naked and bronzed, keeping watch over it all.

I expected more of a reaction from Douglas. I did notice surprise cross his face when he finally noticed *The Thinker* in all his glory up on our wall. Even thought he was about to say something. But then he coughed instead and drifted out the door.

Truthfully, he's been ghostlike the past few days, floating in and out of here with an almost vapor-like presence. Here for a while, then gone again, missing main meals, then found scrounging through the fridge late at night. Even when here in the physical, he's often mentally away, his thoughts fixated on a place where no map seems to exist.

Like this morning, when I asked him if he wanted a mocha-chip Balance Bar to take with him to snack on after his meeting, or if he'd be grabbing lunch out with his client.

"Lunch? No, no, there's plenty of stuff around." He grabbed a clean dish towel from the drawer—thank God there was one—and began wiping the lenses of his sunglasses.

"Plenty of food around the office?" I asked, painfully aware that my husband and I had lapsed into small talk. "Since when? You guys install a vending machine or something?"

He jerked his chin up, then lowered it slowly and focused on the shades in his hands. "No. I just mean I could drive somewhere. If I needed to."

"As in take your client to lunch. That's what I meant, you know."

Cleaning done, he put the sunglasses in their case and snapped it shut. "Oh, I probably won't be much hungry." He waved a hand at me and ventured a glance out the window. "Great day. Can't wait."

"Yeah, it is. Too bad you'll be stuck indoors all afternoon. Sure you can't cancel out and hang with me?" I smiled at him tentatively. "Then again, I won't be seeing outside these walls much today either." I tapped the stove. "Too busy playing Martha."

He turned away from the window, only to face me with unfocused eyes. Then like our patio solar lights when finally saturated with enough sunlight to work properly, I saw recognition flicker in his eyes. He glanced at the stove. "That's right. So . . . I'd better get going." He touched my hips briefly while kissing me on the nose before heading out. I followed behind him, tentatively, watching to see if he'd at least take another gander at the living room before leaving. He didn't.

With an exasperated shrug, I stepped back into the kitchen and have been schlepping around here ever since. The only interruption came when Nathan popped his head in. He wore a wet suit and a pretty-please grin. "Did Grandma call?"

"No," I answered, surprised.

He scrunched up his face and changed the subject. Actually, he started begging. "I don't really hafta be here tonight, do I?"

"Uh, yeah. You do."

He rolled his teenage eyes then and stomped off.

It's late afternoon now, and while I'm sure that Martha wanna-bees could lap me with their organizational genius, I'm still getting the hang of this dinner-party thing. It's more than the food. It's the dishes, the silverware, the tablecloth, even the flowers! Thankfully Gaby sent over a bundle of tall sunflowers in a clear glass vase. Their large, saucerlike faces greet me with a sort of cheery hello every time I pass by them just lounging there on our new glass and iron coffee table. *Luck-y.*

Which reminds me. I've still got five boxes of Douglas's childhood shot glass collection to set out and not a lot of time left. Granted, I've been putting this off. I mean, just what's our kid gonna think about Daddy's childhood toys? Enthralled? Delighted? Deprived? Maybe he'll ask to borrow them and then set up his own pub in the attic, just to get a head start on dorm life.

I shake my head. The short cabinets placed on either side of the fireplace were created just for Douglas's collection, Mona made sure of that. Right now they sit empty and boring, so I heave the boxes into the room, plunk cross-legged onto my newly polished wooden floors, and start digging through the collection.

There's a firm knock on the door. It's gotta be a stranger, because everyone else just blows on in. I kick off my too-tall heels and pad on over to answer the door, the knocking becoming firmer by the second.

"Brianna, you *are* here." It's Mona, and she's looking askance at my bare toes. "I was beginning to think you may have gone to the beach. Again."

"Mona. Hi." The glow of the sun against her right shoulder tells me it's late afternoon. *Do I really have time for a visit from my snobbish mother-in-law? Do I ever?*

She steps in, nearly knocking me over. "I've come to view your new space. Patrice told me she'd completed her design." She marches through the foyer and I shut the door behind her. She stops in front of the dark-stained shelves. "Oh my, those cabinets are lovely, aren't they?" She's wearing a Cheshire cat–sized grin. The same one she wears on all those billboards dotting the city.

"I guess."

She turns to me wide-eyed, and then sneaks a glance down at the glassware strewn about. "Oh, no, no, no. You must lay them out, Brianna, not just spill them all over the floor like they belong in some downtown thrift store."

Now, there's an idea . . .

She amazes me then. Despite her tailored suit in dusty apple, Mona kneels onto my floor. She takes her reading glasses from her purse and adjusts them onto the end of her nose. "I'm so pleased that I got here in time, Brianna. Here," she says, plucking a Disneyworld glass from the box. "I'll arrange these for you. You will want them in order and proudly displayed for your dinner guests, won't you?"

I gulp.

Her eyes bore into mine from atop her glasses. "You are having guests tonight, am I correct? Now what did I hear? Ah, that's right. You are hosting a little family gathering over here this evening. Is this . . . true?"

I'm suddenly glad for our cramped and square-shaped dining room. Mechanically, I take another shot glass from one of the boxes. "Just a mini dinner party. No biggie. Gaby's got a new beau and she wanted Douglas to meet him, that's all."

"I understand your aunt Dot will be here. That's a surprise, isn't it? And Nathan as well. Am I right?"

I stare at the left-hand side cabinet, like I'm pretending to plan out the barware display. Even though Auntie's been practically invisible over the years, Mona's always been rather curious about her. Like they're in competition or something. I gulp. "Yeah, they'll be here."

"Well. I believe that makes this a family dinner, then. You know, Nathan tells me he is rather busy tonight. That you're . . . twisting his arm, so to speak, about being here tonight."

Nathan!

She continues. "One thing I have learned from parenting a strong-willed young man, Brianna, is that you must never force your own ideas on him, no matter how much not doing so might frighten you." She stares at me again over the top of those specs. "In the end, they will do whatever they choose, despite your every warning."

Like on cue, Nathan comes skidding in through the front door. Sand sticks to his legs like sugar on a donut. He avoids my stare and looks at Mona. "You comin' for dinner tonight, Grandma?"

My glaring eyes could burn that sugar right off of his brown skin. I am Wonder Woman, with powers to amaze—and to fry. He ignores my attempt at the evil eye, the look that says, *Watch out, kid. You're in deep,* and just nods his head at me.

"Nathan, you are such a sweet boy, so much like your father. Thank you for the invitation, but I'm not sure your mother is up to setting another place at the table." She says this as if it's a question.

"You can just take my place," Nathan says. "Gib wants to show me the new board he and his dad are working on anyway. It's really long, and we're gonna take it out for a night surf. That all right with you, Mom? I promise to drop in and say 'hey' to Aunt Dot later on. That work for you?" He's grinning innocently.

Mona cuts in. "That would be lovely, Nathan. I'm sure your aunt will appreciate your attentiveness. And I thank you for offering to give up your seat to me. Oh, if you only knew the many times I have suggested to your parents that perhaps a move to a more formal home—one with a matching dining room—would be wise. I'm just so sorry that you have to leave so that I can stay."

She cocks her head to one side and lifts her gaze, eyeing me. "You are extending me an invitation, is that right, Brianna?"

I put on a sunny smile. *Why not?* "Okay, Mona. You're invited." I swing a daggered look at Nathan. "Be home by nine."

He forgets to shut the door on his way out.

"I'll be back in a flash," I tell her. The house has become stifling and I desperately want to go walk the shore. But duty calls. My satiny chocolate soup simmers, and it's time to stir the risotto. I take care of my chef-in-training duties, then cross back into the living room.

"Since you've got it all under control here, Mona, I think I'll just go on upstairs now and change." She waves me away and I jog to my room. Sweat dampens my face and arms, and I review all the possible reasons why. Only two come to mind: hot air rises and guess who's downstairs? I'm flinging clothes all over the place, stripping like it's a hundred and one degrees outside. Otherwise, things are going as smoothly as could be expected.

Except Douglas has been as scarce today as strawberries in winter.

Except Nathan ditched out on me, leaving Mona—*of all people!*—to take his place.

Except my long-lost aunt Dot chose *tonight* to fly in from who-knows-where.

I glance at the clock. Ugh—five o'clock already. Tonight I'm wearing a new outfit, one I found at Rudy's on Main Street, a little silk and cotton number that actually feels comfortable to move around in. I slip into my four-inch heels and survey my smartly dressed self in the mirror. Not bad. Even painted a light glossy pink on my nails.

Before heading down to stir the soup again and greet my guests, I think back on the past few weeks. Even I'm impressed. Okay, so that's not saying much. But it's true. Ever since realizing that Douglas had become increasingly bored with my laid-back style, I decided to make some changes, and I'm proud—no, relieved actually—to say that I have.

It's more than the hair, the clothes, even our new living *space*. I, Bri Stone, have changed inside. Years of hauling my clothes around in a duffle bag while my parents tried to make up their minds on where to settle (i.e., *nowhere*) drove me to set down my own roots, never to dig them up again. But changing myself for the sake of my marriage has taught me that I can make adjustments and not flip out. Maybe those changes are all Douglas and I need to recharge.

I head downstairs, hoping for a magical night, knowing that at least one miracle has already occurred—I am cooking from scratch tonight, am I not?

Chapter thirty-six

Could two men on this earth be any more different than my Douglas and Gaby's beau, Ty (and my boss, by the way)? Other than sharing that most attractive gift of height, these two could not be more at odds. Not that I've never noticed this. Douglas can blast away in the courtroom when duty calls, but in the everyday, his life is marked by compassion, by a softheartedness that I've always found irresistible.

Ty, on the other hand? Not so much. While he may be the only son of my beloved former boss, the warmth gene bypassed him by a long shot. I'm sitting in our square dining room—nearest the kitchen, *of course*—listening to Ty use more business buzzwords than a used-car salesman at his annual dealer convention. Skills set, organizational flexibility, gap analysis, and my personal favorite, the *multiphase strategic alliance* have all made it, by some twist of the linguistic tongue, into the conversation.

I stifle another yawn. Kinda helps me understand the definition of "coma factor," ya know?

Not that Ty alone stands out among our eclectic guest list. Oh no. Aunt Dot showed up dressed in her pixie-collared Sunday best,

looking sweetly demure yet cackling like a truck driver after too many caffeine-laden colas on the road. *Oh, how I've missed her!* Well-suited Mona sits next to Auntie, with an expression that alternates between bemusement and abhorrence. And Gaby? She's precious as ever, her tinkling laughter punctuating the air whenever Ty manages a decent joke.

It's Douglas, though, who shines among them all. He's drop-dead beautiful, his face tanned and lined in all the right places. My eyes linger on the dimple running down the center of his cheek, and I have to curl my fingers inward to keep from reaching over and stroking his face. He lifts his glass in my direction, offering me a wink and a silent *Cheers*. I want to cry happy tears.

Aunt Dot gazes at me. After humming along to the jazz tunes I've got playing softly in the background and nodding at me for the past half hour, she sets her elbows on the table and leans forward. "Well, Miss Bri, I'm seein' pink buds all over you!"

This is what my aunt says when she's pleased. Occasionally I heard those words while growing up. It's a reference to a tree of some sort in the springtime.

"Thank you, Auntie. More tea?"

She slides her teacup over. "But of course. Bring it on."

I glance at Mona, but she just shakes her head and turns her cup over. I move to serve Gaby, when Ty takes the teapot from my hands, saying, "Allow me." My heart lifts for Gaby over his small act of chivalry. A tiny thing, I know. But he's gotta start somewhere.

Mona's staring at me, her forehead bunching. Her nose is turned up—okay, that's normal—but she's sniffing the air. "Is that smoke? Brianna, do something. I think our dinner is burning!"

I leap up from the table. Douglas tries to follow me, but I motion for him to sit. *I'm the hostess. I can handle this. And what's Meridians' number again?* I notice my aunt Dot lean forward and press her hand over top of Douglas's. No doubt he'll be occupied for a while.

In the kitchen I see that I'd left the fancy-schmancy power burner on beneath our mushroom risotto. *Don't tell me.* While we were sipping satiny soup, the intense flame beneath our dinner was sucking the life out of it. I lift the lid, and for just a second think, *Phew—just in time!*

Only when I try to lift a heaping scoop out of the pot do I realize the damage done. The bottom half of our main dish has burned drier than sand after a hot wind has blown across a Southern California beach. I reach for the looped handle of the pot and yelp.

"Ye-ow! Ooh, ooh." *How dumb was that!* I shake my seared fingers repeatedly, thrust the faucet handle to cold, and submerge my hand into the quickly filling sink.

"Are you all right in here, Brianna?"

I roll my fingers under the running water and turn my head. "Ty? Ooh, yeah. I'm—fine." *I guess.*

He walks toward me carrying three soup bowls. I nod toward the dishwasher. "Could you just put those over there? Thanks." I'm fretting over the sting of burning fingers, yet curious. Call me old-fashioned, but aren't the womenfolk usually the ones to gather round the kitchen sink when the dinner is done? *Not like I really know.*

Not that dinner is over. It's only begun, really. I sneak a worried glance at the burned-up risotto, knowing I could probably scare up six small servings, yet wondering what to do if someone were to ask for seconds.

Ty follows my gaze. He smiles at me kindly. "Looks like you are having some trouble in here. I'm certain that if we try, we can salvage this." He takes a whack at the rice with a wooden spoon. At least half has hardened beyond edibility. The cool water streams over my fingers, and I shut my eyes, knowing that not only will a blister or two appear in my life tomorrow, but that my first-ever, homemade porcini mushroom risotto has moved on without me. *At least it's in a better place . . . grrr.*

Ty puts one hand on my shoulder. "Here, let me see," he says, pulling my hand from beneath the running water. He lays my hand on his open palm and examines my burns. *Uh, give me my fingers back, will ya?* With marked gentleness, Ty pushes my hand back toward the faucet, and I grimace. *Thanks.* I huff out a short breath, glad that he's gone.

Water gushes over my burns, and I'm wondering, *What would Martha do?* And then, just like that, I know. The heavens open, the angels sing their aria, and I draw in lungs full of joy. So I wrecked the risotto? What's a little rice between friends anyway? I shut off the faucet and move with resolve to Plan B. In my head I'm chanting, *I can do all things through Christ* . . . when I suddenly bump into Ty. He's standing way too close and holding chunks of ice in his wiry hands.

"Whaa. . . ? Ty, you scared me! I thought you left!"

He laughs good-naturedly. "I did leave, but only to get you some ice from the wet bar. Here," he says, placing them from his cupped hands to mine, "put them where it hurts."

I drop them into the sink. "I'm okay, but thanks. Um, I'm going to have to make a quick change here. Would you do me a favor?"

His face lights up. "Anything."

Well, it's not *that* big of a favor. "Um, would you stall everyone? Just ask Douglas to tell Aunt Dot about some of Nathan's surfing experiences, all right? Go relax. I just have to make a little change, and then I'll be out with the main course. I promise."

He nods before leaving.

Thank God for Mario! I'm thinking that my nosy neighborhood deli man just saved the day. Avoiding the raw spots on my fingers, I open up the fridge and pull out the two quarts of Mario's famous (yeah— in his mind!) jambalaya. I dump them into an empty pan and switch on the burner. With a lighter heart, I spin away from the stove, intending to retrieve more bowls. So what if we're having two kinds of soups? Is there any law that says we can't? Besides, this stuff's so thick, you could serve it up with forks.

I'm on my tiptoes, reaching toward the highest shelf, the place where all the lonely, unused bowls live, when a familiar voice breaks into my thoughts. *Again.*

"Allow me to get those for you, Brianna."

It's Ty. *Sheesh.* Something tells me he's like one of those famous male chefs, like Bobby Flay or Alton Brown, who feel more comfortable in the kitchen behind a big Viking stove than on a basketball court. *Great.* I'm serving dinner to a gourmet.

I step back to allow him to help me. He hands me a stack of bowls. I reach out to take them from him, but he doesn't let go. Instinctively, I tug again. It's almost an afterthought to squint up at him, a question forming in my head. Together we stand there, each holding one side of the stack of round bowls like we're at opposite sides of the wheel on Disney's teacup ride.

"You can let go now," I say with a tight laugh.

"I think we both understand what's happening here," he says to me, gripping the bowls tighter and staring at me with such intensity that I notice the fragmented color of his eyes.

An uncomfortable shiver runs through me, and I let go of the bowls. I motion toward the island. "Um, Ty. Go ahead and just set them there. I can take it from here. Thanks." *Now go!*

He doesn't go. Instead, he sets the bowls onto the island and slides closer to me in one easy step. He runs a finger along the silky sleeve of my blouse. I jerk my head up and leap backward. The four-inch heel of my right shoe slides out from under me then, and when I try to right myself, I twist my ankle and start to fall. As if moving on its own, my arm lurches forward, and I'm horrified when I latch on to Ty's sleeve.

Now, you'd think that a man of Ty's stature would be able to steady me in this ridiculously awkward moment. I flash on Danny Torres from my sixth-grade class. He had started lifting weights in his dad's garage and would always strut up to me holding his abs tight as an eleven-year-old body builder could. *"Hit me,"* he'd always say. *"Go on. Give my belly a good punch."* I always gave it my best, and he'd fold like a balloon after the prick of a pin.

Somehow, this moment is like that. My desperate attempt to avoid a painful crash onto my hardwood floors fails when Ty topples much like a matchstick in the wind. Seconds later, when Douglas finds us there, sprawled in a weird tangled heap on the kitchen floor, I'm red-faced from more than embarrassment, from more than acute annoyance directed at Ty. Quite frankly, my ankle hurts—and bad!

One look at Douglas, and Ty gets up in a hurry. *Where was that quick action a minute ago when I needed it, huh!*

"Bri! What in the . . . what's going on in here?" Douglas rushes toward me, and I relish the feel of my husband's strong arms as they slip around my waist and pull me up. I lean into him. "I got you. I got you," he whispers. "Bri, that sounded pretty bad. Can you stand?"

"Everything all right in there?" Aunt Dot strides into the kitchen, followed by Gaby. *But, Mona, Mona, where art thou?* My aunt's lively gaze lands on me. "Oh, Brianna, my dear. You're hurt!" She turns to Ty. "Well, what are you standing there for? Chop, chop—get her some ice, man!"

In a flash my sixty-eight-year-old auntie kneels on the floor and peers at my ankle through her pink spectacles. "There's quite a contusion forming there," she says, examining my foot closely before gazing up at me and winking. "That's some neat doctor-talk I learned on the mission field. Cheaper than four years of medical school, that's for sure. Plus, I got to work closely with a bunch of hotties."

I let out a resigned sigh. "Listen, all of you. I'll be fine." My ears perk at the sound of bubbling from the stove. "Please, please, go on back and relax. Have to make a quick menu change, so I need just a few extra minutes. Don't fuss anymore. I'll be fine."

Ty, Gaby and, reluctantly, Aunt Dot scuttle out of the kitchen. Douglas watches them go. When they're all out of view, he cocks his head toward the doorway. "What's up with that guy?"

I raise my eyebrows and shrug. "He's odd, but Gaby likes him. And he is my boss, you know." *Although I seriously don't understand what was happening there.*

Douglas's eyes penetrate mine. I attempt to walk the two steps to the stove.

"Ooooh . . ." I wince from the pain.

He sighs and rolls up his sleeves. "You're not fine, Bri. Tell me what to do here, all right? Let's get through this evening, and then I'm going to take a better look at that ankle."

I hesitate.

"Well?" Douglas stands in front of the stove, waiting for orders.

"I've never been a head chef before."

He lets loose confused laughter. "What?"

I huff. I barely know what to do myself, let alone give culinary directions to another. But Douglas isn't just some other person, he's my *man*, my *main squeeze*. I smile. Who better to order around?

"Okay. So here's what I'm thinking." I brace myself on the counter and lean near him. "Mmm," I say. "You smell delicious."

"Me?" he asks. "Or the soup?"

"Stop it. It's not exactly soup—it's jambalaya. Anyway, okay. Just scoop up a little of the risotto for each person, putting it into bowls, then top with some of that." I point toward Mario's creation simmering over the burner on medium.

Douglas lifts the lid and draws in a deep breath. He turns to me. "You make this?"

"Quit asking so many questions," I say and urge him on with a little scoot of my hand. "Could you hurry, Douglas? Everyone's waiting."

He heads out, carrying a tray full of steaming bowls of jambalaya.

Disaster averted. I glance at my fingers, noticing two thin pink marks forming. And it hurts to put my weight on both feet, so I hobble to the other side of the kitchen, where my fondue set waits. *What a mess.*

I've lost all sense of hunger, so while my guests start the main course, I ready the chocolate cherry fondue, starting with some very ooh-la-la dark chocolate, recommended by Chef Kelly himself. I strike a match and reach beneath the pot to light the fuel burner. The moment makes me giggle aloud, remembering the beefy chef and his fondue rules. Anybody who lost their cherry in the pot of melted chocolate had to throw back a shot of his "wee bit of Irish crème."

"Would you like to share your private joke with me?"

I gasp, surprised. My boss has, once again, entered the kitchen. "Ty. Um, ready for seconds already?"

He moves closer to me, those eyes so very intense. "I'd like to start with 'firsts,' Brianna."

I laugh nervously. "Oh? Sorry. Thought I sent out enough for everyone." I limp over to the pot of jambalaya and give it a distracted stir. "I'll get you some."

Ty takes the spoon out of my hand. "I'm not interested in dinner." He's still holding my hand in his, and I'm stiff as a statue, every nerve ending on alert yet too shocked to react. "I think we both know that it is *you* that I want."

I snap out of it and jerk my hand away. "What is up with you? You—you're Gaby's date, and you're my boss, and . . . I'm married, you idiot!"

He snickers. "Come off it, beautiful. You've been coming on to me for weeks. I knew it from our first . . . date. At Opa!"

"That wasn't a date, and you know it! You said you wanted to talk business."

"And you said you'd do whatever it takes to keep my mother's business alive. Isn't that right? Don't think I didn't notice the way you began dressing to impress me, Brianna." He takes in my clothes, my face, my new striped hair. "I especially love what you have done with your locks." He reaches up, as if to stroke my hair, and I swat his hand away.

Ew—gross! "Stop it, Ty. Just leave my best friend alone and get out of my house!"

He's inches from me, and I try to step back, but the movement lands me on my swelling ankle, and I wince. Ty loops both arms around me then, and I stiffen. My fingernails dig into his chest as I try to squirm and push away from him.

A loud, startling pop fills the air. I wrench my face away from his in time to see that the plastic ring at the top of our never-used, fifteen-year-old fondue pot has cracked. As if in slow motion, I watch the whole thing topple over onto the kitchen towel I'd left all wadded up on the counter. Flames engulf the towel.

Ty tightens his grip on me and moves his face in closer to mine. His breath strikes my face. "It'll burn out soon enough. But what we've got between us never will."

My eyes widen. I pull myself back and shout, "Fire!"

Chapter thirty-seven

It was Aunt Dot who had taught me to shout "Fire!" if I ever found myself in grave danger, flames or no flames. She always said that people may ignore other cries for help, but never the promise of a mesmerizing burn. So I guess it's appropriate then that she, along with the rest of my eclectic guest list, tear into the kitchen as I fight off my boss's unwanted advance.

Douglas breaks from the pack and grabs Ty by the collar, shoving my would-be attacker hard against the fridge. I've never seen my husband's face so red, nor heard his voice so snarling. Those strong hands that I love so much look ready to wrap themselves around Ty's bulging neck. *So who says chivalry is dead?*

Ty raises his splayed hands in a sign of surrender, his face twisted into a smirk. "Slow down, cowboy," he spits. The sight turns my stomach, and it's as if I'm seeing my boss for the very first time. He's been a liar from the start. A lunchtime quest for advice, a private breakfast in his office, even agreeing to a blind date with my best friend—poor Gaby!—he did it all to seduce me. *Yuck.*

Aunt Dot leaps past me and scoots the smoldering kitchen towel into the sink with her bare fingers. She turns and gives my face a

caress with a soft, wrinkled hand, but her eyes reveal something else. A question maybe?

I glance up to see Gaby standing across the room from me, stick straight. Like Aunt Dot, I can't read her either. She's got her arms crossed in front of her, and an indignant scowl marring her pretty face. She's not gaping at her erstwhile boyfriend, Ty, but at *me*.

Both hands behind my back, I'm leaning against the cold Formica countertop, reeling from the surreal image that is this moment. Vaguely, I notice the sting from the burns on my fingers and the throbbing of my ankle. Douglas drags Ty out of the kitchen with not much of struggle, while I reel from this dinner party gone wrong. I'm confused and shocked and more than a little aware of the lack of sympathy I'm getting.

Except from Mona. She glances back at Aunt Dot, then slides an arm around me. "No lady should ever have to endure something this terrible," she says simply and leads me into the living room. *Did I just see a pig fly by?*

Both Gaby and Aunt Dot find a seat. Everyone's in our newly remodeled space now, except for Douglas, who's apparently outside pummeling one of our dinner guests. I'm the last to lower myself into a plaid-lined chair, my eyes darting from person to person. Somehow the word *intervention* comes to mind, but the only thing I've OD'd on lately is chocolate. *And ignorance, I guess.*

Abruptly, Gaby stands. She starts pacing.

My wits come back with a fury. "Gaby, I'm so sorry!" I say.

She glares at me. "What happened to you?"

"You don't think I encouraged Ty to do *that*, do you?"

"I'm asking what has happened to *you*. What happened to the girl who told me that God loved her the way she was? The girl from the coffee place? You and I used to make fun of all the snoots who came in after church with their condescending tips and laughter. Remember that? But look around you, Bri." She gives the living room a sweep of her hand. "This place looks more like a museum than my carefree pal's beach shack. You've *changed*! You've become one of *them* now—a pretentious snob. And you tried to drag me along with you by setting me up with Tyler Minsk Holland, big man about town—and have I mentioned *loser*, by the way!"

"Tyler *Minsk*?" All heads turn. Douglas stands near the foyer, his jaw clenched. "*That's* who that guy was?"

"He's Rita Holland's son, Douglas," I chime in.

Gaby cuts in. "By her *first* marriage, Bri. I noticed his Visa card at dinner said 'Minsk.' When I asked him about it, he reminded me that his father was Rita's first husband. He said that he decided to take the name 'Holland' simply because he wanted his name to match his mother's, since he was taking over Coastal Tours."

"That's not the only reason for the name change, believe me, Gaby." Douglas crosses his arms. He's wearing his lawyer face, and I'm just thankful I'm not sitting on the witness stand right now. *Or maybe I am.*

"What other reason could there be?" I ask.

Douglas's eyes search mine. "That guy narrowly missed serving time for sexual harassment. Got his last company into a lot of hot water when they were sued. He won—on a technicality, of course—but the business and all its investors couldn't recover from the damage. They filed for bankruptcy and then folded. He may have told you that he was here to salvage Rita's business, Brianna, but isn't it obvious? He had no place left to go. Apparently hiring him was Rita's mission of mercy."

I blink. I'm thinking I could use some mercy right about now too. I glance at Gaby, who's crying into a napkin. "How do you know all this, Douglas?" I ask softly.

He rakes a hand through his hair. "From Kendall."

"Oh?" I say, sarcasm creeping into my voice.

He scoffs. "Kendall was Minsk's lawyer, Brianna. Worst client she ever had to deal with. She won the case, and in turn he made a pass at her. You're right about him being a loser, Gaby."

If I could peek into a mirror at this very moment, something tells me my skin would look as colorless as a limestone fossil, the kind found at the bottom of a littered reef. I'm serious. There's no blood left in this face of mine but plenty of egg on top of it. I mull it over again. Ty sued for sexual harassment, and Kendall his lawyer. *This* is the Mr. Perfect I dreamed up for Gaby? I squeeze shut my eyes and shake my head.

"Wait a second," I say. "What about Rita? She wouldn't do this to me. I can't believe that she would!"

"Maybe she didn't know," Gaby says, sniffling.

Douglas squints at us both. "Are you two serious? Of course she knew—this was big news in the Valley. That guy dragged the family name through the dirt. I'm sorry, ladies, but I have a hard time buying that Rita had no clue about this. Although why she'd turn over her business to a swine like that—"

"Because he's her son!"

All eyes turn to Mona. She's sitting with perfect posture in her tapered suit, knees together, her ankles crossed. Yet her eyes are like two black marbles and her hands have formed fists in her lap. "A mother will always do what's best for her son, no matter who might get hurt in the process," she continues, her voice both strong and shaking. "Don't *ever* forget that, Brianna."

Um, okay.

"Nonsense!" cries Aunt Dot. "That boy's mother should have let him loose to flop about on his own. Saving him from his own depravity just leads to more, by golly. And I think we all got a taste of what that looks like tonight!"

Mona's marble eyes narrow at Aunt Dot. "She's just showing her love to her son. There is nothing wrong with that."

Aunt Dot's tone softens, yet she's as bold as ever. "There is *never* anything wrong with showing true love to a child." She gazes at me. "But holding their hands too tightly once they've reached adulthood can do more harm than good. Maybe even keep 'em from being able to make good decisions on their own."

Is that why you left me, Auntie? So I could make it on my own? I cover my mouth with my hand, finally guessing at why Aunt Dot left once I was old enough to pay my own rent. For years I'd blamed her for abandoning me, like Mom and Dad did. Yet I'm looking into those soulful eyes and seeing a look of downright love, mixed in with a bit of something else. Pain, perhaps?

Douglas stands. "It's been a rocky night. I think we'd all agree with that." He huffs. "Who knows why Rita would hide this information from you, Brianna, and from you, Gaby. But she did." He glances around our living room, his eyes drooping. "There's a lot I don't understand these days."

"I, for one, would have to agree with you, Douglas." Mona stands up and reaches for her purse on the couch. "This has been an enlightening evening, I must say, but it is time for me to go." She strokes her eyes over me. Mona had nearly knocked me over a few minutes back with her out-of-the-blue kindness. Now? I'm seeing pity. *Oh brother.* "Stay away from bad apples, Brianna," she says.

I swallow and look away.

She steps toward the door and stops to speak with Douglas. I can just barely make out her words. "I don't suppose you would like to speak of this now, Douglas," she stage whispers, "but I really do need to have an answer on the matter I faxed you about."

"About that," I pipe up from where I'm still glued to the couch. "What about that mysterious fax? Are you planning a move, Douglas?"

More than one emotion flickers across my husband's face. "Not exactly. Sorry, Mother, but it seems that my secretary, Darla, is the one interested in the property."

She places a hand on her heart. "Darla?!"

A grin flickers on his face and then dies away. Reminds me of a boy who's just been caught with a pocketful of candy. "Yes, I stole the fax from her."

"Douglas! You stole it?"

"Just trying to teach her a lesson, Mother. Apparently Darla had been reading my email, unbeknownst to me. Anyway, when she saw your email to me about the listing you'd secured for a property up on Hilltop, *she* responded using *my* name. I figured it out when the fax came in, and I have to tell you, it just fried me to think she had been snooping like that. So I took the fax before she saw it come in."

"Douglas!"

Realization spreads through me like an uncontrollable oil slick. I'm hoping that no one notices the heat creeping across my cheeks. Douglas had no intention of moving us to Snob Hill!

Douglas swings his gaze over to me. "Brianna," he says, "how did you learn about the fax?"

I gulp. I've been blowing it ever since sneaking a secretive peek at Douglas's email. I'm seeing myself strung up over the fireplace, but I am *so* done with fibbing. "I read your email. And then I found the fax in your junk drawer."

The look of surprise on Douglas's face stabs at my heart. He opens his mouth to speak, but Mona cuts in.

"You are quite the storyteller, Brianna. Douglas would never have a junk drawer!"

I roll my eyes and sigh. Then I poke my finger at her. "And *you* showed up here unannounced with Patrice!" I gape at Douglas now, like I'm a six-year-old tattletale. "I found her measuring our living room and saying that we'd need to make some changes around here if we were going to get top dollar for this place! I put it all together . . . the email, the fax in your drawer, her showing up with a tape measure. I really thought you wanted out of here!"

As is his way, he runs a hand through his hair, and rocks his head from side to side. "Good night, Mother," he finally says and gives her a peck on the cheek. He stands at the foot of the stairs. "Good night, ladies," he calls to Aunt Dot and Gaby. And to me? No eye contact, no words . . . no nothing.

Chapter thirty-eight

If peace is like a river, then at the moment, I'm treading through a swamp. I'm thinking this as I sip coffee by the shore's edge, attempting to draw in deep, cleansing breaths of ocean air. The waves crest and drop, spraying me with their delicate mist, yet the continual motion doesn't do much for my mood today. Even the fussy strut of long-billed birds craning for sand crabs fails to thrill me as usual.

I glance at the two brown stripes scorching across my fingers, by-products of last night's fiasco. Not pretty. Thankfully my ankle's okay. A little raw, somewhat tender, but well enough to let me hobble over to my favorite spot on the beach.

It's my ego, though, that's taken the biggest bruising. You'd think that fending off a pass from a Fabio-wannabe would have the opposite effect, that I'd somehow feel flattered, even if somewhat grossed out. Instead, I feel more like a big dufus. My mind wanders back over the past few weeks, and I just don't know what I was thinking.

Maybe Gaby's right. I *have* changed. Sure, I've said I was doing it for Douglas, for our marriage, but maybe I wanted to become someone altogether different all along. I slip my fingers into the baggie on my lap and tear off another piece of brownie for breakfast,

contemplating my self-examination. I rub brownie bits between my fingers. Okay. So maybe some things never change.

"Not surprised to find you here, young lady."

It's Aunt Dot, insanely chipper at such an early hour. "Hi, Auntie."

She lowers herself into the sand, using my shoulder as a brace. "I always loved this spot. Missed it some too," she says, flicking a chip of driftwood across several mounds of sand.

"I've missed you, Auntie."

She gazes at me and flops an arm over my shoulder. "Now, now. I was off doing all kinds of things for the good Lord. You know that, right? I left you in good hands, did I not?"

"Well, you left before I married Douglas."

She gives my shoulders a hug. "I didn't mean his hands. I meant *yours*. And the good Lord's, of course." She draws in a whistling sigh. "Oh, Bri, I loved watching you grow up. You know, you reminded me of my little sister, your mama. What a feisty kid you were! You were such a bold one, and I did my best to point that will of yours to the Father's. Mmm-mmm. Those years are forever embedded in this old lady's brain. But then you grew up, and it was time for me to go."

"I don't really get that. Why did you go, really?"

"That was my calling."

I grimace. "Like Mom and Dad's."

She looks at me with kind eyes. "No, Brianna. I loved your parents very much, but they followed their own hearts. Even though I wanted to travel the world and do right by people, I never envied them."

"Really?"

"Oh no, because they missed out on seeing you grow up and come into your own! I wouldn't have missed that for all the orphanages in China, Brianna. And I didn't have to. The good Lord saw to it that after nearly raising you myself, I've stayed well and strong—strong enough to travel this world before I'm buried beneath it!"

I guffaw. "You'll probably outlive us all, you know."

"Eee, I hope not. When I'm tired, I hope God takes me home on a chariot like Elijah." She nuzzles me again. "Then I'll get to see your mama, and my own, and we'll have a big ol' party in the sky."

I'm laughing again from the deepest part of me. "So what brought you all the way back here, then?"

"Don't think it's a coincidence that my assignment was changed, giving me a short break at this very time. Oh, I know I've been scarce these past years, but I've never missed a day of praying for you. No never! So when I found myself with a week of quiet, I just knew what the good Lord would have me do with the time." She rests her palm on the back of my head.

"I'm glad you listened." I pause. "You know, Auntie, after what happened last night, I'm not sure you left me in the best hands after all."

She shrugs. "So you picked a few green peaches? So what. All lives are filled with flub-ups. It says in the book of Isaiah that even our best efforts are grease-stained rags."

I wrinkle my nose.

"It's those who flop around and don't jump back on the path—the *right* path—who find themselves in deeper trouble. Somehow I think you're not one of them."

I take another swig of coffee, my eyes fixed on the sea. "I guess I'm just not sure what to do next," I say.

Aunt Dot looks toward the ocean, both her eyes and mouth smiling. "I'm seein' a Proverb in you, my Bri. Get yourself some wisdom. No matter the cost, you go and get yourself some understanding."

———

The Lord and I huddled on the sand together for some time after my talk with Aunt Dot. I poured it all out to Him, how I'd gotten worked up over the past few weeks, believing the things that people around me said about Douglas, all the while never talking to him about my worries. Then, of course, there were the things that were as obvious as sand in a peanut butter sandwich, the things that I hadn't detected, like Ty's odd behavior. Why hadn't I noticed? I had a blind spot as big as a kelp bed on that one. I believed things about Ty that were false, like that his character and faith would be solid simply because I knew and trusted his mother. Yet I never confronted his many obvious failings. *Like I'm doing with my own right now.*

As for not noticing his questionable advances toward me? That one's easy. I never caught on simply because I always have, and always will have, eyes for Douglas alone.

Sitting there on the sand, my sights locked on the medium swell of the waves, I also realized just how little I'd talked to God about all of these worries. Can't go anywhere in California without someone smiling and saying, "No worries!" The phrase has become as commonplace as waitresses delivering food with the celebratory, "Here ya go!" But worries happen, and I just let mine pile up into a mountain.

I made up for my prayerlessness today, though. Oh yeah, I did. Prayed until I had nothing left to say. Then I listened for a long while too. Some women get soft and quiet after devotion time. Me? Not so much. For some reason, I became fired up by the revelations stirring within me, and a kind of energy burst forth, sending me on a quest for truth.

So while still sitting cross-legged in the sand, I decide to dial up Rita on her cell. For all I know, she's heading south from Cancun, totally unaware that her beloved tour company has just lost one tour host *extraordinaire*. "Buon giorno!"

Okay, so she's not on her way to South America. "Rita! It's Bri."

"Oh, is—is everything . . . all right, Brianna? Does this have anything to do with Patrice's work?"

Okay, uh, no. But now I'm curious. "Um, maybe. Why don't you go ahead."

"Well, I told her to be very, very careful. I'm quite sure you know that. It's, well, it's only that she has had a tough couple of years, Brianna, and when her last client called and canceled such a big order, I ached for her. But then, as fate would have it, you came along with your very timely request for a designer."

As fate *would have it?* "And you just had the perfect person for me, didn't you?"

"Why, yes. Yes, I did. Oh, and I certainly hope you didn't mind that she employed her daughter, Trinka, for that very ingenious mural."

Her daughter! *I should have known. . . .* "Hmm, well. Thanks for that, Rita. But that's not why I called."

I sense alarm in her voice. "No?"

I offer up a prayer before trudging forward with all I have to say to her. "I just wanted you to know that your son nearly mauled me in my own kitchen last night, and that I know all about his little dance with the law down in the Valley." I pause. "Why didn't you tell me, Rita?"

"Oh my."

"Is that all you have to say to me? After all the time we spent together, Rita, this is how you treat a . . . a . . . friend? You knew that Ty was dating Gaby. You could have at least warned us."

"Yes. I knew they were seeing one another. I'd hoped . . . I'd hoped . . ."

"You hoped what? Rita, I've put you on a pedestal for *years*! How could you repay me this way?"

"Wait just a minute, Brianna. You should never put me, or anyone else for that matter, on a pedestal—because I ain't perfect, dear one."

Did she just say "ain't"?

"Tyler is my son, yes," she says. "And I want desperately for him to embrace all that is good in life. I thought . . . well, I thought that he could start over in Ventura, Brianna. To make a new name for himself."

You mean a fake *name for himself.*

She continues, stammering. "I . . . I am sorry. Truly I am. But I did what I thought was for the best. You have a son, Brianna. I'm sure that you understand."

"Sure," I say. "I get it, Rita. You left your loutish son to take over your business, knowing full well what he was capable of. Then you took off to parts unknown, as if being absent somehow absolved you from any responsibility." I reflect on my wacky aunt Dot and the way she hung around all those years, even while itching to hit the mission field. "That's just not a style of parenting I subscribe to, Rita."

She's still on the phone. I hear her labored breathing.

"I'm so disappointed, Rita," I continue.

"I am terribly sorry, Brianna. More than you know."

With a whispered good-bye, I hang up and dial Patrice.

"Blanc Slate Designs!"

"Hello, Patrice. It's Bri Stone."

"Well, hello, darling. Is everything all right?"

"Just have a question for you, that's all. Um, just how was it that you were able to complete my room redo so quickly again?"

"I . . . I don't understand."

"Really? Huh. Because Rita just told me something about a big cancellation you had."

"Well, yes. Perhaps that is true. But does it matter where your furnishings' journey began? The question I'd have to ask is, are you happy with it, darling?"

Um, let's see. Am I happy with a design that looks more like a men's cigar club than a warm and inviting home? Then again, I trusted her, mainly because of her relation to Rita. "I just wish you'd been honest with me, Patrice, that's all."

I'm taking responsibility here for the final product, simply because I made the mistake of putting my trust in someone before giving it careful thought. And so I say good-bye and hang up the phone. I'm on a roll now, so I dial up Kate, almost unable to recall her number.

"Pitchenhauzer residence." *Bingo. Hit it on the first try*.

"Hi, Kate. It's Bri."

Silence.

"You there, Kate?"

"I am. It's a busy day around here, Brianna. The kids are all doing their chores, and I'm getting ready for the white glove. What is this about?"

"I was just wondering . . . why do you hate me, Kate?"

"I don't hate you," she barks into the phone.

"Sure you do. You've made that very clear." I'm on a new honesty kick and can't get enough of it. "I was just wondering why. Just spit it out, Kate. Don't hold back. I may hate it, but I gotta know."

She blows a sigh, like an oncoming train, into the receiver. "Meet me at the beach in one hour." *Click*.

I never got into the whole suspense craze, but even I'm seeing the plot thicken. An hour later, I'm back at the beach when I see Kate's lone figure walking along the shoreline from Marina Park. It's a surreal thought that I've been invited here, to the place that makes my heart soar, so someone can chew me out.

She tosses a deck of cards onto the sand in front of me, then squats awkwardly in the softness. She's wearing another one of her loose-fitting dresses, this one in pale cream, with a black cardigan buttoned halfway up. Her keys dangle from a strap hung loosely around her neck.

"We playing Crazy Eights?" I ask, curious. Or . . . Old Maid? *Bad Bri-Bri, bad.*

"Tom's been gambling, Brianna. That deck of cards is about all we have left to our names." Kate's chin juts out toward the sea. It's trembling. "I'm sorry I've been taking it out on you."

The wind that's been driving my sails all day has suddenly dissipated. I've stalled in place. "Oh, Kate."

"Go ahead. Say it. Tell me you told me so."

I drop my head back hard, searching the sky for words to say to her. "I don't think so. Kate, I really had no clue of . . . of any of this. I don't know what to say."

She presses her lips together and nods, still unable to make eye contact.

"Kate?" I ask. "Is it pretty terrible?"

She glances at me sideways. "What do you think?"

"Um. Yes, I bet it's been, uh, tough. So. What're you going to do? Or, I guess, what have you been doing about it?"

"Just about everything I can think of, but nothing's really working. I've been picking up odd jobs everywhere I can and still trying to school the kids and . . ."

So that explains the mysterious Kate-sightings. "No, Kate! That's too much. . . ."

She swivels her face to me. "You're right."

I blink. Kate thinks *I'm* right.

She continues. "I finally figured out that all I've been doing is hiding Tom's problem, while still trying to be as perfect as usual at everything."

At least she hasn't lost that natural sense of humility.

"Brianna, I am so tired of trying to work this out on my own," she tells me. "So just yesterday I said to God, 'Here, you take this,' and I laid all the embarrassment and the worry into His sizable lap. Just giving it all to Him gave me such peace. Now I'm just waiting to see what He'll do about it all." She sighs. "I've always been envious of you, Brianna. Douglas is a rare breed, and he takes such good care of you and of Nathan. Right before that last Bunko game, Tom and I had just had an excruciating fight. I had steam inside my head from the moment I walked into Suzy's overly gorgeous house, and when you made one of your off-the-cuff remarks—you know, you do that quite often—I just blew it all out on you. It was wrong of me, and for that I am truly sorry."

Well. When I called Kate to meet me here, I had symbolically rolled up my sleeves and readied myself for a good old-fashioned brawl. Not a meow of a cat fight, but a sparring of words where we'd spew our differences into the air and hopefully watch them disappear into the wind. But I don't want to fight her now. I'm feeling down-right sisterly toward my one-time nemesis.

"Kate, it's all okay. Really." I lean toward her and give her shoulder a shove. "And you're right about Douglas," I say, shutting out the memory of the disappointment I saw on his face last night. "He's my shining knight. I'm sorry if I ever flaunted our life, though. I never meant to do that. For what it's worth, things aren't exactly rosy with us all the time. We're, um, actually in the midst of some murky waters right now."

"You and Douglas? Really?"

I nod. "I'm sure we'll work it out eventually. You and Tom'll work it out too. I know you will."

"Thanks," she whispers.

I'm surprised by what I blurt out next. "I've always been envious of your large family."

Kate examines my face from top to bottom but says nothing.

I swallow before continuing. "I'm serious when I say that I'm pulling for you and Tom to work through this tough time. Please let me know how we can help you."

We stare at the sea, no more words between us, nothing but the crash of waves to fill our ears. I realize now, more than ever, that I'm not all that much different from Kate. I lack discernment too. All that leaning on my own understanding has been clouding my already shaky judgment.

"Hey, Kate?" I finally ask.

"Yes?"

"Would you teach me to cook?"

She turns to me. A smile belonging to the Kate I once knew forms on her face. "Maybe," she answers back. "If you'll share your brownie recipe with me."

Chapter thirty-nine

I hear my husband's even footsteps moving through the foyer. He shuts the front door firmly behind him and walks into our softly lit living room. Like when we first married, I've graced every open spot in the room with a lit candle. I'm curled up with my breath held, noticing the smooth dance of light moving across the surface of the walls surrounding me, an effect that has softened the edges of our rather masculine-looking room. In silence, Douglas moves nearer to me.

"Where've you been, sailor?" I whisper from the corner of the couch, where I've been curled in the fetal position for over an hour.

He lets out a long sigh. "Oh, Brianna."

"Sit with me?"

He doesn't hesitate but sinks into the couch beside me as I prop myself up. Our hands bump and neither of us pulls away.

"Douglas, I'm sor—"

"Brianna, I've got something to—"

I suck in a breath. "You first."

He slides himself to the edge of the couch, then turns to face me. "I want to ask you something, Brianna." He's quiet a moment, as if unsure of exactly how to phrase it. "Just why do you always call me Douglas?"

"Let me see. Because it's your name?"

He swings his gaze to the fireplace, with its flickering candle-covered mantel. "What I mean is, when did you start calling me by my formal name, as opposed to all those, uh, variations?"

I laugh nervously. "That's a word for them, I guess. But I don't know, exactly. At some point I just realized that I should begin showing you more respect. Guys like that sort of thing, you know." I wink at him, then glance at the floor. "Seriously, I . . . I just thought you'd feel more honored if I called you what . . ."

"What my mother calls me?"

Oh, sheesh. "Never thought about it that way, but I guess if that works, then okay." I slide my other hand over his and caress his fingers. "Somewhere along the way I started thinking that you deserved more honor than I was giving you with all those cutesy names. So I made a change. Does that bother you?"

"Actually, Brianna? You've confused me more than ever before."

"What do you mean?"

"For starters, this room. I thought you loved this place, but suddenly you weren't happy anymore. Then I noticed other things were beginning to change—your clothes, your choice in music, even your hair." He reaches over and brushes a highlighted strand from my forehead.

"I did it all for . . . you," I tell him, my voice hushed.

"So that's why this place sounded like the Cotton Club the other night? Because you thought *I* wanted it that way? And that ridiculous wall painting! And those shot glasses . . ."

"Your mother sent them to me. She told me that you loved them as a child—which, by the way, cracked me up—but I put them out for you anyway."

Douglas shakes his head at me.

I give him a punch. "What?"

"You can't be serious. My mother used those to keep me quiet so she could work 24/7. I suppose they were fun when I was, say, eight years old. Not now, though. And what ever gave you the idea that I wanted any inch of *you* to change?"

I'm thinking that the reasons are too many to mention. Yet it all boils down to one, really. "You're never around much anymore, Douglas." I shrug. "I just figured you had gotten bored with everything— this house, the beach . . . me."

He moves in close until our noses nearly touch. I feel the heat from his breath on my lips. "*You* could never, ever bore me, Bri. Don't you think I knew what I was getting into with you?" He's smiling now, a wide, dashing smile. "When I first saw you in that coffee-house, you opened my eyes to a vivacious way of life. I wasn't used to that. My parents were always so, so . . ."

"Annoying?"

"Uptight."

Oh.

"I knew they loved me, and I appreciated them. They stayed together through a rotten marriage just to give me some semblance of stability. But, Bri, I love the way you adore that big ocean that God created, and the way you swoon over dolphins and that silly way you always clap for the pelicans. I like seeing your naked toes every day in your many outlandish pairs of flip-flops. God made you the way you are, Brianna, and I love *both* of you for that."

It's as if the past few weeks have just been fractured moments in a ridiculous dream. If I didn't know that Nathan would be tearing through that door at any second, I'd attack my dream man, right here, right now, on this very new and not-yet-broken-in couch. I'm flooded with love for Douglas, and then a jagged thought catches me. *Kendall.*

"I need to ask you something now, Douglas. You seem to be

spending a lot of your time with Kendall these days." I gulp. "What's that about?"

"Jealous?"

"That's not funny. Not after . . ."

Douglas squints at me, the way I imagine he might at a deposition. "Not after . . . what?"

I blow out a long breath.

He straightens. "So you think I would cheat?"

"I know you wouldn't."

"Do you?"

I square my eyes with his. "Well, I'm pretty sure."

He's still squinting at me. I watch as the light comes on in his eyes. "After all these years, you haven't let it go, have you?"

I want to tell him that of course I have, but it wouldn't be completely true. For some reason, and despite all the years that have followed, I haven't forgotten his moment of insanity—that's what I prefer to call it—prior to our marriage when he met Denise for a good-bye lunch.

"Oh, Brianna. That was long ago. I thought you had forgiven me. You said you had."

"I . . . I did."

"I need more than that."

"More?"

"I need grace, Brianna."

Don't we all.

"And I need your trust."

I nod.

"Why didn't you talk to me about this?"

That is the question now, isn't it? I feel my heart pulsating in my chest. "Maybe, in some weird and stupid way, I really didn't want to know the answer."

His eyes look moist. "I am not a perfect man, and I never claimed to be. But I will not dishonor you by breaking my vow to you, Brianna. Ever."

I squeeze my eyes shut, but the tears manage to force their way through anyway. Douglas tips up my chin, and I feel a single tear meander down the front of my neck.

"Okay?" he finally asks.

"It's done." I brush away at a wet spot on my cheek. "You've spent the past fourteen years treating me like a princess. I'm so sorry I never let it go, Douglas, and that I let my imagination run crazy. So sorry."

He kisses me lightly. "I love you. Be upfront with me."

We sit there in the silence together, each of us lost in our own thoughts, until my arm starts falling asleep. Instead of feeling the weight of my worries and missteps, I'm content. I'd let my deep-seated fears run me, and it was time to toss them out to sea for good. I give my arm a shake, and Douglas smiles at me, the corners of his eyes crinkled.

"You okay?" he says.

"Yeah. I do have a question, though." I hesitate before plunging ahead. "That day I saw you and Kendall flying down Harbor. You seemed cautious when I asked you about it. Where were you going?"

He raises an eyebrow. "If you'll stop calling me Douglas, then I will tell you."

I wag my head. "Okay, okay, *Dougie*." The old throwback makes me giggle, causing leftover tears to spew. "Where were you and that beauty queen associate of yours *really* headed when I saw you speeding along in your midlife crisis sports car?" I'm laughing now.

"To see your surprise."

I pause. "My surprise?"

"I've been working on it for weeks. For months, actually. I'd wanted to surprise you, but it seems that all I've done is scare you. I'm sorry, Bri." He sighs, though I still see a sparkle of a smile in his eyes. "My parents were *driven*, you know that. They had little time or affection for each other. After I left for college, they had no reason to stay together anymore, so they didn't. Nathan will be leaving for college in a few years, and . . ."

"He's only thirteen!"

"Five years, Bri. Just five years until he graduates from high school." Douglas stands and paces in front of me. He runs a hand through his hair. "He'll be gone before we know it, Bri. And my practice has heated up lately. Which is why I've turned over most of the Wills & Trusts division to Kendall."

"You *what*?"

"Listen, like I said the other night, Kendall fled the Valley after one-too-many nefarious clients."

Ugh. Like Ty.

"I hired her and have been spending a lot of time training her on how to handle these types of cases. It has taken a great load off of my back."

"But, wait. *That's* what's been keeping you so busy? And what did you mean, um, about a surprise?"

"What I'm saying is that I hired Kendall to take over matters that were pulling me away from you and Nathan. I've got plenty of other work to keep me busy, but if I kept going as I'd been, I could see a future not unlike my own parents', with more work than time for family." He stops pacing. With a contented sigh, Doug drops to his knees in front of me and blends my hands with his. "I'm exhausted, Bri. In addition to training another lawyer, I've been working like a dog on a surprise for you. For us, really."

"And?" For a man who's spent his professional life coming up with just the right answer, Doug, it seems to me, is at a loss. He's just gaping at me with this sweet, goofy grin.

"C'mon, Dougie-poo. Just spit it out!"

"I, I mean *we're* the proud of owners of a fully restored, thirty-foot sailboat."

 *Epilogue*

One week later

I settle into my roomy seat and lean back, allowing the sun to kiss my cheeks good morning. My eyes drop closed. For a channel laden with boats all snug in their slips, the quiet surprises me. Distinct but brief seagoing sounds—the call of a seagull, the plunge of a pelican, the occasional seal bark—punctuate the silence.

"Do you trust me?"

My eyes snap open. I squint up at my handsome captain. "You ask me such a thing after I let you have your way with me last night, right here, on this boat?"

He wiggles his eyebrows at me. "This, m' lady, is a yacht."

"Yeah, sure. I bet you've never taken her out of the harbor." I'm grinning at him, knowing better. He'd been taking sailing lessons for weeks.

"Hold your seat, then, Bri. I'm about to show you what this thing's got. Anacapa Island, here we come."

I laugh and pull myself up from the cockpit-style seat I'd buried myself in. "I'm outta here," I say and make my move toward the bow.

Doug laughs heartily. "Be careful of the boom vang, my love!"

"The *what*?"

"Boom vang—keeps the boom down."

"Right. I get it. That's some fancy legal term, and you're just having fun with me. Okay, I'll watch out for the boom vang *thang*." I giggle.

He grabs my hand and pulls me back down. "C'mere. I'm not letting you out of my sight."

"Promise?"

"I do."

I wrap my arms around him and kiss his chin, grateful for the grace that offers second (and third, and fourth . . .) chances. I've forgiven myself for rushing ahead, for jumping to make changes to our cozy little world. Not that I don't believe there's power in transformation. Oh, I do, I do! I think, though, that it should start with the mind and the heart, not rumors and fears.

By the time we return from this maiden voyage, our living room will be stripped of all hints of a private men's club, and the walls will wear a fresh coat of sea-mist blue. I'm also back to padding around in flip-flops and have already made an appointment with Tami to weave back in my *natural* sandy hair color, which at the moment is covered by a white cowgirl hat. As for the rest of my new duds and my quest for better cooking skills? Let's just say that, as I've said before, not all changes are bad.

"So," says Doug, breaking into my thoughts. "I'm serious this time. Are you ready to take a ride on the *Brianna Dorothea*?"

"What did I do to deserve the honor of having this boat—uh, *yacht*—named after *moi*?"

He holds me close and draws in a deep breath of sea air. He lets it out while gazing into the cloudless sky. He drops his gaze to my face. "I was originally going to name it *The Other Woman*—but thought better of it."

I gasp, then give him a good slap. "Naughty!" My cell phone rings.

He grimaces. "Tell them to get lost."

"Stone Cruises," I answer.

"Captain Stubing, please!"

"Gaby, hi!"

"So what's a night on a yacht like. . . ? Never mind, I don't really want to know." She clucks her tongue.

"My kid doing okay?"

"Of course! I got him up early and made him blueberry pancakes, which he doused with far too much syrup, and I also grilled him several slabs of ham, then watched as he practically inhaled the entire breakfast!"

"You're a regular Aunt Dot," I tell her.

She giggles. *"Gracias, mi amiga!"*

No, I want to tell her, thank *you*. I'm momentarily overcome with emotion for my friend of forever. A couple of days after the event that's now become known as the Ugly Ty Incident, she and I baked a double batch of Aunt Dot's gooey brownies and headed to the beach, where she forgave me for my matchmaking stupidity. Other than finding out that Doug's only affair was with a sleek cruising yacht, I've never been so relieved in my life.

"So you don't mind hanging with Nathan for a couple of days while we take this bad boy out for a cruise?" I wink at my husband as he prepares to set sail. He throws me a good-natured eye roll.

"Not at all, honey, not at all. Your son's a dream. Don't worry about him. From the way he tells it, he's tired of the whole sailing thing anyway. Keeping a secret from you nearly gave that boy gray hairs! All he really wants to do now is ride the waves with his board and his best friend."

"Oh, good! Gib's been around today, then?"

"All morning! He managed to scarf down the last puny pancake too."

All is right with the world.

"Gotta run, chica. Max is beeping me on the other line."

"Max?"

"Probably wants to check on Gibson. Enjoy the island!" *Click.*

I climb back into my chair, marveling at Doug as he throws down the rigging for our maiden voyage together. *Tote that barge, hoist that sail . . .*

He steps to the helm. "Everything okay with Nathan and Gaby?"

"Hmm? Yes, yes, it is. She had to hang up quickly, though." I can barely keep the smile from dancing across my face. "Max was on the line."

Doug fires up the diesel engine and eases us out of the slip before turning to me with both eyebrows raised to the heavens. "Don't even *think* about it, beautiful!"

Acknowledgments

Many thanks to the following:

Dan and our kids—Matt, Angela, and Emma—for filling our home with love and adventure, and for offering me fat doses of grace when long writing days trigger that faraway look in my eyes. Love you!

My parents, Dan and Elaine Navarro, for always telling me that my writing rocks!

The gals who read this book in its infancy and bravely offered their input—especially when the story *didn't* rock: Rebecca Blasing, Tracy Burchett, Tricia Goyer, Alison Lucic, Rebecca LuElla Miller, and Cara Putnam.

Designer Sherrill Waters for your cleverness, and Hunter Leary for sharing your ocean expertise with me.

Randy Ingermanson, mentor from the Mt. Hermon Writer's Conference, and my fellow mentees.

The Bethany House team: Kyle Duncan, for steering this manuscript away from the slush pile and into Charlene Patterson's hands; Charlene, for acquiring this project and cheering me on with especially thoughtful comments; and Sarah Long, who edited this book—and laughed in all the right places.

My agent, Steve Laube, for inspiring me to keep writing long before our work together began.

My Blessed Hope friends for your faithful prayers and friendship.

My readers—we may never meet, but I'm grateful for you just the same. I hope you are entertained!

Most especially, my Lord and Savior, Jesus Christ. How could I ever really *live* without you?

JULIE CAROBINI is an award-winning writer whose stories often spotlight her family, the sea, and God's timely work in the lives of those around her. *Chocolate Beach* is her first novel. She lives in Southern California, with her husband, Dan, and their three children.